Don Bloch, born in New York C
novels, *Arising*, *Little Friends*, *Dou*
Wind. His last book, *Passing Th*
stories, was published in 1986.
Oxford, the author has travelled
Indonesia, as well as in Africa. He now makes his home in Amsterdam.

DON BLOCH

Face Value

PALADIN
GRAFTON BOOKS
A Division of the Collins Publishing Group

LONDON GLASGOW
TORONTO SYDNEY AUCKLAND

Paladin
Grafton Books
A Division of the Collins Publishing Group
8 Grafton Street, London W1X 3LA

Published in Paladin Books 1989

First published in Great Britain by
William Heinemann Ltd 1987

ISBN 0-586-08753-2

Printed and bound in Great Britain by
Collins, Glasgow

Set in Baskerville

R.W., a 40-year-old Californian whose legs were blown off on a Vietnam battlefield 17 years ago, recorded what race officials said was the slowest time in New York City Marathon history: 4 days, 2hrs., 45 mins., 17 sec. 'The first step was the most difficult,' W. said when he finished. 'The joy has been the journey.'

Some people mistook him for a beggar. 'I'm in the marathon,' he told them. 'I don't need your money.'

'Last in the Marathon, First in Courage', *International Herald Tribune*, 8–9 November 1986

For Maryanne Radner

Prologue

The neglected houses of Charter Street are among the few authentic slums-in-the-making to survive still in Boston's North End. At the top of steep Henchman's Row, neither tall nor wide, huddled together overlooking the confluence of the sluggish Charles and Mystic Rivers, they have not yet succumbed to the hot and heavy breath of speculators. All are fronted in red brick, but like slabs of meat in a butcher's window, the reds vary.

Copps Hill Burial Ground, dense now with crumbling tombstones, the final resting place of the victims of the Boston Massacre, straddles the narrow summit of Charter Street. Out across the brackish harbor waters below, swirling green and black, looms Bunker Hill, at whose graceless concrete foot the USS *Constitution* floats at anchor. Old Ironsides, the world's oldest commissioned battleship, relic of obsolete methods of war. And inland, right smack around the corner, gleams the Old North Church, white as false teeth. Here, under the graceful spire, every third Tuesday of the month, the Fellowship of the Lantern Light convenes.

In short, few places in this Land of the Free and Home of the Brave can boast of so much major history within arm's reach. And yet, it should be noted at the outset of this story, there are people living on Charter Street today, people for whom, let it be said, the past is as much of a blank as the future.

And the present? What about the present then? Oh, they manage to fill it all right, after their distracted fashion. A trip to the Freedom Trail Laundromat. A fire drill out in front of Michelangelo High School. Bad jokes about virgins and nuns, but not both. A garbage can sent rolling, crashing down the hill.

Part I

RECONNOITERING

1

Late one fine afternoon when Jasper Whiting entered the cramped vestibule of 39 Charter Street, tired to the roots of his eyes, he found a woman huddled over the row of battered metal mailboxes, talking to herself. Just as Jasper, intent on retreat to the solitary security of his dingy room above, tried to squeeze past, she began to punch one of the boxes with a fist.

'Oof.' Her elbow caught him in the midriff. The clang, the runny light, the stale smells – not a pretty scene. Then Jasper heard *ping!*

'Don't just stand there, Red.' The woman had dropped her key. 'Help me.'

She was even shorter than Jasper himself. Her clothes were ill assorted. She was wearing baggy blue cord trousers tied with a length of clothesline. Her bulky-knit brown roll-neck sweater had alternate rows of green reindeer and white wreaths stitched across chest and back. Her head was wrapped in a flesh-colored crêpe scarf knotted at the nape. This scarf couldn't contain waves of black hair streaked with gray that gushed out wildly on all sides of her sweet, round face.

'Thank you. The last gentleman on Charter Street. Or the first?' She accepted the key Jasper retrieved from the tile floor. 'My, your hands are cold. What's your name?'

'Whiting, Jasper.'

'Pleased to meet you, Whiting Jasper. I'm Rhoda.' Rhoda's

lips were small, perfectly symmetrical and moist. Her eyes, dark, shone with a sanity that contradicted everything else about her. 'Are you a new boy here?'

How slow he was on the uptake!

'You're not going to tell me you actually, pardon the expression, *live* here?'

'I'm doing my best.'

'Which must be very good indeed. Look, Whiting. . . .'

'You're going to break the key, twisting it like that.'

'Could you maybe do me another big favor and open this *goddam thing*!' Rhoda rammed her knee up against the mailboxes.

Jasper looked down at the scrap of metal Rhoda laid back in his palm. 'This key is the wrong size. Besides which the locks don't work.' With a flick of one finely manicured fingernail, he lifted the lid to Rhoda's mailbox. It was crammed with envelopes.

'I'll be fucked! So, come to mama, all you little messages of comfort and joy.'

The shop tag was stapled still to one corner of Rhoda's scarf.

'This calls for a celebration. Oh, come on, Jasper, don't be shy. It's not as if we didn't know each other.' Rhoda started up the stairs. 'Are you afraid I'll bite, is that it? Well, I do. I bite. But only friends.'

A few days had taught Jasper not to put his hand on the sticky banister rail. Now, however, he felt a need to steady himself on the way up. In the world outside it was mid-afternoon. Here, lit only overhead by a skylight streaked with dead insects, the day seemed exhausted, at its wit's end.

'Not today, thanks. So sue me. I dunno, some people live on credit, why can't I?' As Rhoda climbed ahead, one by one she tore open the letters Jasper had liberated from her mailbox. A glance was enough, a curse under her breath, a whistle, and then with a snort Rhoda crumpled them up and threw them over her shoulder. 'Hope not, want not. If I had the money, I could make a lot of people happy.'

Rhoda did not move like a heavy woman. She was sturdy,

hips broad, back full. Her calves were strong and muscular, her feet small. Purple veins snaked around the ankles.

On the landing of the second floor Rhoda stepped over a man pitched headlong, mouth open, trickles of drying vomit running from the corner of his lips. 'Lucky Murray,' Rhoda sighed. 'Heart of gold.'

Outside Rhoda's door, Jasper nodded and made a gesture to move on. 'Where's the fire, Jasper?' Rhoda tugged her sweater down and at once the reindeer which had been up on their hind feet nibbling at the wreaths overhead were brought to earth. 'Or don't you think Rhoda knows how to show her appreciation?'

Jasper laughed. What made her voice crackle so?

'Why if you hadn't galloped to the rescue, I'd still be down there making like a cretin and cursing the God who made me – made all of us, depressing thought.' Rhoda had small hands, too. Plump and damp. She passed the tips of her fingers quickly across Jasper's cheek, under his chin. 'Hmm, two o'clock shadow. Red hair. They say redheads like it a lot.'

Jasper was forever smoothing his hair down, but no sooner did he lift his hands than it rose again like smoke, or fine threads charged with electricity. Helen said he had mischievous hair.

Rhoda fished up a key hanging on a string knotted around her neck and opened the door to her apartment. 'A drink is highly in order, don't you think? To wash away the taste of life.'

To his own surprise, Jasper followed obediently inside. He turned the lock and fastened the chain. Rhoda approved, 'Atta boy.'

'Be it ever so humble, shit!' Rhoda flung herself down hard on the bed. Jasper lingered with his face to the door, like a child chosen to be *it*, waiting for a game of hide and seek to begin, counting to a hundred as fast as he can. Behind him he heard the bed springs creak. When he turned he saw a room in shape and size not unlike his own on the floor above. Rhoda had little furniture, too. A makeshift trestle table over by the two high windows was heaped with papers and objects. Exactly what

Jasper couldn't quite tell. Something like conch shells and starfish and a lot of old typewriter ribbons. Oiled shades were pulled low across the windows. The light they let through had the glow of a sick child's complexion.

What brought the dim interior to life, however, was the profusion of Rhoda's plants. On the window sills, the table, the floor. Few bore flowers, but many were unfurling new leaves, or putting forth shoots that shimmered an iridescent green. And from her bed Rhoda was talking to her plants.

'Sorry I'm late, dears. Did you miss me? You mus'n't be jealous. Must not. This is an old, old friend. He's only passing through.'

'I'm Jasper.' Jasper bowed politely to the plants. 'Pleased to meet you.' When he dared look over at the bed, he found Rhoda staring at him intently. The gray sheets, the swirling blankets and battered pillows had lost all semblance of the haphazard. The bed had become a setting, a grotto. There was nothing foolish about Rhoda any more. She looked at him with a mixture of amusement, need and fear.

Jasper knelt on the bed, almost losing his balance, and kissed her. Not on the mouth yet, but the side of the neck.

'Why not?' she smiled. 'We're consenting adults.' Rhoda raised one hand to knead her neck where Jasper had kissed it. 'Oh God, I'm tired, I'm so fucking *tired.*' She practically shouted the last word. 'See what you can find us to drink, Jazz. There should be something over there.' Rhoda waved with one arm in the general direction of the windows, both open a few inches so that puffs of wind off the harbor water ruffled papers and leaves on the trestle table. A large number of cardboard boxes were underfoot. Tangled clothing, too.

'Coming right up,' Jasper pressed. He was about as worldly as an onion. Certainly there was no shortage of empty bottles in the room. Soft drinks, mineral water, beer, wine, whiskey. Ashtrays, too, heaped with butts, and other cigarettes floating in the residue of stale coffee and tea in dirty glasses and chipped cups. He bent to explore under the trestle table, poking about with an extended arm between a stack of canvas tote bags and the cold silver ribs of the radiator. Straightening up, he banged his hearing aid.

'Careful,' Rhoda cried. 'Nothing? Then try the kitchen – the hole out there. If my memory serves me, and there's no reason why it should,' Rhoda laughed again – her voice might bolt in any direction at any time – 'when I realized what those little sneaks were up to, I stashed something in the breadbox.'

No, in the breadbox were only some warped slices of old rye toast smeared with jam, and a sack of granola someone had ripped open with his teeth.

'Come and get it! Rhoda's found the pain-killer. Bring us a glass, Jasper. Make yourself useful.'

The kitchen sink, slow distinct drops leaking from the tip of the faucet, catching the light, was heaped with greasy, mostly broken dishes. Someone had thought of cleaning up, but with too much haste or anger. Jasper inched a glass free from the tangle, relieved when the whole jagged pyramid did not shift and collapse with a crash.

'There's not much left. You better hurry.'

Jasper found Rhoda with her hair spreading out on all sides, electric shrubbery. She had wrestled off her heavy sweater and now sat with her house keys dangling between the purple eyes of her naked breasts. She sniffed under one arm and made a face. Then she raised one leg fully extended, pointing the toes. The muscles of her stomach contracted and started to quiver. 'While you're at it, do us another of your priceless acts of mercy, Jasbo.' Jasper eased off her scuffed pumps. 'Oh, that's lovely. That's a good boy, yes.' Jasper had taken her feet in his hands and was rubbing them. Rhoda purred. Helen purred when he massaged her feet, too.

'If you don't breathe, it's not half bad.' For a split second Jasper misunderstood. It was the whiskey Rhoda meant, sloshing around in the bottom of the pint bottle which she reached out to him. The gesture made her breasts jiggle.

Jasper Whiting, fifty by recent celebration – true to family tradition he had baked the cake himself – had never seen a woman sit on a bed like that, so matter-of-factly, half-naked, arm outstretched, head cocked to one side, licking her lips. He took the bottle and raised it to drink, triumphing over his instinct to wipe the mouth of the bottle first. He dropped his gaze and swallowed.

'Those kids will kill me one of these days.' There were black and blue marks near Rhoda's shoulder and above one hip. She was picking dandruff from her scalp, letting it accumulate under her nails and then flicking it out into space. 'Oh, honey, not so hard. A little bit at a time. Make it last.'

Only a few swallows of cheap whiskey but they burned like a fuse all the way down to Jasper's stomach.

'I used to have a cassette recorder,' Rhoda was saying. 'None of your walkman shit, either. A real instrument. Only some son-of-a-bitch ripped it off. Actually, certain things are a bit hazy. I might've sold it myself. What I meant to say was if I still had that recorder, I could put on some music.

'I bought the thing for my plants. They've done studies, scientific ones, to prove plants do better if you talk to them.' By now Rhoda had begun to undress Jasper Whiting, slowly and expertly. He lay back and let her get on with it. 'I'm out a lot of the time so I thought maybe I could tape a few hours of me talking and leave it playing when I have to go to work. They claim the human voice beats fertilizer.' Each article of clothing that Rhoda stripped from Jasper's body she held up and described for the benefit of the plants. 'After all, just because they can hear, no one has proved yet they can see. And I don't want them to miss anything.'

During lovemaking Helen kept silent. At times the pace of her breathing quickened, she even panted, but for the rest, no sound. Sometimes when it was all over she still had cold feet. Jasper did not want to make comparisons, but he couldn't help himself. Rhoda was a well of sounds. Much of what she said ran blurred together but Jasper thought he caught key obscenities in the flow. She called on Christ and God to witness, again and again. She addressed them familiarly, with respect, but not as distant or unapproachable, as if, should they ever find themselves in similar circumstances, they should feel free to call on her.

Whereas Helen, despite all the years of their marriage, still hesitated before she laid a hand on Jasper's body, as if she didn't want a caress to embarrass him by making him too aware of skin and flesh, Rhoda explored at once with confidence. Even more surprising, when Jasper broke, he shouted. The climax in his throat was prolonged and gratifying. With Helen he had wanted to scream, and never had.

Afterwards Rhoda did not turn coy and affectionate. Helen was always so determined to keep Jasper from becoming sad that in order not to disappoint her he gave reassurances he did not feel. His body would hardly stop quivering before Helen would turn playful, as if her responsibilities were over, discharged. Rhoda, she merely lay back with one arm thrown across her eyes for a minute or two, lips motionless, and then she turned over to sleep.

So abruptly abandoned, Jasper flooded with happiness. Funny, sex was everything he always imagined it should be. He felt like he had finally kicked off the wrong size shoes he'd been wearing all his life. Nothing had prepared Jasper for this meeting. No girlfriend, no partner in bed, no films, no heroine in fiction. No patient, no dream. He saw where his body glistened with sweat. His sex was still sticky, stirring again. Delighted with himself, he ran a hand through his hair, smoothing it down even though he knew it would spring up by itself again.

The world must be full, Jasper imagined, of people who met Rhoda and never stopped talking about her, like some whistling comet that dropped at their feet, then stood up and walked away. He wouldn't know how to begin to explain to Helen, but the idea of keeping Rhoda secret was absurd. He would have to be careful not to sound like he was boasting.

Rhoda shifted in her sleep, heaved up and came to rest again on her back. Jasper began absent-mindedly to stroke the length of her nose. Not too long, a bit flattish, the left nostril more developed than the right, the hint of a bump, enough to cast a slanting shadow just below the bridge. Jasper stroked on. At last it took conscious effort, willpower to lift, to remove his hand. He was sweating nervously. It would be all too easy to reach out, snap his fingers, crack that nose. Rhoda and the dangers of life would disappear. There would only be safety again, another of Helen's noses in place.

Some hours later when Jasper woke, despite the blanket tossed over him, he was chilly. It took a moment to remember where he was. The shades were up, the night sky enormous, studded with a few pin-prick stars. Rhoda was off by one window, humming, drinking scotch. She wore a duster, pink, torn under one arm and down the back. The knobs of her vertebrae gleamed. As Jasper watched she shook the last few drops from the bottle into her glass, then tossed the bottle out into the street. The sound of shattering was delayed longer than he expected. It was slow, almost musical when it came. It set dogs to barking.

'This,' Rhoda kneeled over him, reeking of sweat, 'is a bottle in, bottle out kind of building. Do you know Little Mrs Whosis on the second floor? The one with Moira, that hideous baby. She came back from the shops last week and what do you think she found? Four-month-old Moira asleep near the window, curled up in her crib with an empty fifth of vodka. A prize-winning photo. Lucky thing we live up high.'

Jasper's stomach growled.

'That's what I like about you, Jasper, you're subtle. There should be something in the oven.'

'I'll go.' Usually Jasper felt vulnerable naked, at least awkward, at a disadvantage. Not now. 'When do they sleep?' he pointed at the plants.

'Oh right now they're having a party.'

When Jasper flicked on the kitchen light, the glare made him blink. He had a sense of startling life, of moving shadows where there shouldn't be. In the oven all he found was a half-gnawed carcass of roast beef nestled in aluminum foil, leaking gravy.

'Don't go getting any wrong ideas,' Rhoda said from the doorway. 'I happen to be a great cook. And no one is a better housekeeper' – a cockroach, several, skated out from under the fridge and stood vibrating near Jasper's bare toes – 'when I try.'

'What happens when you don't try?'

'It's never happened.'

In the bathroom wet towels lay in twists on the small hexagonal floor tiles, once upon a time white, now the colour of neglected teeth. Rhoda dumped the remains of the withered roast into the toilet and flushed. In protest the pipes made loud, choking sounds.

'There was a lot of good meat left on those ribs,' Rhoda said, licking her fingers as she stared into Jasper's eyes, 'but if there's anything else around here that makes you unhappy, anything at all, you just say the word.'

'I'll bet when you try you're one helluva cook and housekeeper.'

'You learn fast.'

'No, no I don't. I used to think so.'

'But?'

'I was wrong.'

'Well, I'm afraid there's not much else in the house by way of eats. I wasn't expecting company.'

'It wouldn't hurt me to skip a meal.'

'We could always go out.'

'Whatever you want.'

'You haven't lost your appetite?'

They made love again, half-on, half-off the bed. Rhoda seemed impatient this time. She scolded Jasper for being clumsy. 'You're worse than a teenager. Take it easy, you'll live longer.' She gave lessons. He was, frankly, in awe.

'Wake up, we're there.'

Jasper slept like a stone until a hand on his shoulder shook him. The sun was up, barely. Ribbons of cloud were strung out over the Mystic River Bridge. Gulls wheeled, wings wide, now white, now black as they banked, hovering above water, then plunged, screaming. 'No, no, no, no – keep those eyes open. Here, drink this.'

Jasper half-sat, resting on his elbows. Rhoda pushed a tumbler of whiskey at him. Before he could find his voice to say no, he found the glass was hot. The drink was tea, hot and sweet, with a leaf of mint floating on top.

'I hate to rush you, but I'm sure you must have a lot to do.' Rhoda held out Jasper's hearing aid and crumpled socks. 'It was my pleasure. I've got to run. Late for school. Pull the door shut behind you when you leave.'

2

When a quick search didn't turn up the pumps Jasper had removed, Rhoda settled for sturdy sandals. That was a mistake. As soon as she stepped outside, her toes nearly froze.

At Haymarket Square where Rhoda boarded the MTA, the drivers all knew her and refused her fare. Whenever possible Rhoda sat near the back doors on one of the several slatted seats reserved for the handicapped. Who ever saw anyone disabled ride a public car in Boston? Ride where? To work? No one wanted them. Travel on an excursion? A day out? A visit to one of Boston's many museums or monuments, the park, the zoo? Why? To be stared at, aped, degraded.

Rhoda's last lover – each, now, she feared would be the last – his name was Malcolm Something. A song writer, guitar player, young enough to be one of her sons. Before leaving he had said, 'Don't you know anyone normal?'

'No, do you?' she answered.

Since meeting Rhoda, Malcolm complained, he hadn't been able to write a single healthy lyric. He stopped leaving Charter Street by day. She found him one sunny afternoon with the shades drawn, towels along the sills, bumbling around in the dark wearing sunglasses. 'The great ones,' he said, 'were all blind.'

She was not surprised, even a bit relieved, when he left. January was for kidneys. February cancer. Malcolm hung on until March. Heart month. 'I'll sing about whatever I damn please, hear?'

'You do that, Malcolm,' she said, meaning it sincerely. People were forever attributing resentment when she felt none. And missing it when it was there.

Rhoda sat in the trolley munching sesame wafers. A whole pack had spilled in her army surplus canvas shoulder bag. Chewing, her chin rubbed against the collar of her navy pea jacket. Men. They came and they went. Often they came back, checked in with her again, thanked her for all they had learned, so much more than they had any idea of at the time, confessed their selfishness, paraded their egos, praised her in bed and then, tickled pink with themselves for having behaved so handsomely, left once more.

And now, alicazam, there was this new one. Friendly, a bit slow, endearingly baffled by it all. That carrot-coloured hair, dry fire. The chins. The gray-green fish eyes. Wanting to please, wanting to so badly.

At Dudley Street Rhoda let herself be jostled off the tram. Here some of the streets were still cobblestoned, drainage was poor. The buildings, many at a tilt, stood closer together than elsewhere in the city. The New England School for Special Children was housed in an old brewery with solid yellow brick walls oozing salt, massive worm-eaten rafters, vast volumes of space. The corners were dark and cold but Rhoda kept the children out of the corners.

As Rhoda started up Mount Pleasant Street, facing into a sharp wind, children from the front steps of the school waved to her. They waved with careless extravagance. To see them there gave Rhoda a real kick. How long it had taken to get them to loiter out front before school began, to gossip, smoke, make a general nuisance of themselves – like schoolchildren anywhere. And some of the girls were even skilled now with their make-up, no longer too inhibited to flirt with the boys, or hurl suggestive remarks at passing men. A hundred times rather arrogance than cringe!

'Good morning, Rhoda,' piped a frail child bent by polio into the shape of a Greek letter. His collar was turned up, a cigarette hung from his lips like some master spy.

'Oh yeah, what's so good about it?' Rhoda put one hand on her hip and leered at him. 'Race you upstairs.'

On her way to the classroom, Rhoda Massler lost track of everything but the day's work ahead.

3

To finish his day's caseload early Jasper worked with his old concentration. He had to fight down the urge to take his patients on two at a time. He had decided to clean Rhoda's apartment. Decided? He was obsessed by the idea. By mid-afternoon he was back at Charter Street, time breathing down his neck. At the first switchback of the staircase, where the window was so streaked with filth it looked like a child's finger painting, Jasper nearly bumped into a sofa shoved up against the landing wall.

'She loves me,' said the man hurrying towards him down the stairs, 'she loves me not.' Thick-set, balding, with a bristling black moustache and a muscleman T-shirt tight over a flabby torso, the stranger wore a wide grin. In the half-light of the hallway his face gleamed like wax. 'Hello, friend.'

It was the collapsed drunk of last night. With a hand on Jasper's shoulder, the man pointed to the sofa and told him, with obvious delight, about the mad slasher loose in the building. After every attack, the super, who was worthless for the rest, wouldn't lift a finger to repair a leak or fix a faulty wire, nursed the cracked hide of the sofa lovingly. He mended the damage with broad strips of adhesive tape. As soon as the patchwork was complete, the slasher would strike again.

By now the rhythm of silent fury and dogged determination was second nature to the residents of 39 Charter Street. 'You see – she loves me, she loves me not.' The man bowed slightly, winked, slapped Jasper on the back and started down the stairs. The hand in his pocket was clearly cradling his sex. 'Oh,' he turned back. 'I'm Murray Cutler. I live upstairs. Next to you. With Madge.' He outlined a woman larger than life, all curves. 'Welcome aboard.'

'It's only me,' Jasper assured the plants after he let himself in with the keys Rhoda had left in his pocket. Briskly he stripped the bed. He bundled the sheets and towels and scattered clothes in need of washing down to the Freedom Trail Laundromat. While Jasper puzzled over the washing machine, he hummed, sex on his brain.

'Wife take a walk?' The woman who drifted over to help wore bright plastic barrettes, bluebirds and ladybugs and bouquets in her straggly, rope-coloured hair. White ribbed socks had plunged down to hug her badly scratched ankles. 'Happens to the best of 'em.

'Me, my husband was too good for me. Not that the big dummy would've ever figured it out for himself. Me and my big mouth.' Jasper listened to himself laugh from a great distance. 'See that window there?' She pointed up through the backwards lettering on the laundromat window. 'That's the one, with the cat sleeping. I didn't fucking find out for two fucking days. No ID on him. No note. Bounced off the roof of a Buick and broke just about everything you can think of.' The woman let her hand fall on Jasper's while she talked. 'Terrible waste of life, terrible.'

Jasper's eyes kept flying back to the wall clock. He was afraid he would run out of time. It took a while to sink in that the clock was standing still.

'Don't think about it' – while Jasper cleaned, he talked non-stop to the plants – 'just do it.' Funny, clinging pink rubber gloves! He threw the windows wide, rubbed at all the glass he could reach with wads of newsprint doused in vinegar. 'No half-work,' he egged himself on. He made the bed with hospital corners and turned back the top sheet invitingly.

And all the time at the back of Jasper's mind, Helen was watching, her mouth round with surprise, nodding praise. He tried to squeeze his mind shut, concentrate on the dirt at hand. Some spots and stains were too stubborn to come out. Still and all, the aches and pains in his back came from honest effort.

Daylight was waning when Jasper lost his nerve about cooking something special. The frozen capon he'd picked up on the way home had only just begun to thaw. The vegetables, inspected one by one before he bought them, had already gone limp and sorry. Besides which here he had none of the gleaming arsenal of accessories he took for granted back in the kitchen at Spy Pond Lane.

Guiltily Jasper made a dash to the Chicken Delight on Battery Street. A trifle sadistic that, the name, seeing as how the dismembered parts of hundreds of poor birds were kept spinning on chrome spits, dripping fat. At the counter Jasper held his breath and ordered through his nose. He was deliberately not extravagant in his choice of wine. A couple of bottles of reasonable Valpolicella. On the way back he bought flowers, too, refusing his change from a lady muffled in blankets on Paul Revere Mall.

Upstairs, with everything in readiness, candles melted into holders, matches in the pocket over his heart, Jasper couldn't sit still. When he heard footsteps rising on the stairs, keys jingling, he flapped. He rushed to the kitchen and clawed the capon out of the freezing compartment. Then he buried it in the laundry hamper among Rhoda's underwear. (He hadn't taken her underwear to the laundromat because he thought that was an invasion of privacy.)

The footsteps kept coming, but they were too slow and heavy for Rhoda. When whoever it was knocked, coughed, spat, Jasper didn't move a muscle. The plants all seemed to vibrate, sharing his terror. After a pause, the caller departed, in no more of a hurry than when he came.

Later there would be times when fists would rattle the door on its chain in the middle of the night and Jasper would sit bolt upright while Rhoda slept on peacefully at his side. Or notes would come whispering in under the door. When Rhoda picked them up to read in the morning, she tore them into small pieces afterwards, often shaking her head. She never spoke to Jasper about any of them.

To sit and wait inside Rhoda's apartment now felt wrong somehow. 'I'll meet her downstairs, how's that?' If he recreated yesterday's meeting down to a tee, then everything would work out all right. Maybe cleaning had been a mistake, a bad one. To wash a child's favorite doll drains the magic. 'This is ridiculous. You don't have to tell me that,' Jasper said to the plants. 'Helen would have a cow. See you later – I hope.'

In front of Michelangelo High, the janitor was hauling in the flag. It was a task he took seriously, careful not to let the cloth touch the ground. More superstition, Jasper thought, and smiled, his spirits reviving. Down at the water's edge the Coast Guard offices were emptying out, employees spilling from the gloomy building like bats from a cave. The sky, tinged with pink, droned with heavy air traffic circling before receiving permission to land at Logan. Planes with blinking lights sliced through ragged clouds. On Commercial Avenue buses snorted along the cobblestones, stopping short to spit out passengers.

What made Jasper think Rhoda would come straight back from work? Why shouldn't she have other plans? No – the thought filled him with panic. Please, let her come. Life seemed to depend on fucking her again, as soon as possible. All right then, good, he knew that. He accepted it, and refused to pretend otherwise. Jasper stretched and his mind filled with Rhoda's twisting body.

Color leaked from the sky. Cars streaming across the Mystic River Bridge turned on their lights. Still no Rhoda. There was less and less life on the streets. Three children ran by swearing like bandits, slashing savagely with sticks at the base of iron lamp-posts. Jasper took his first good look at the blind side wall of 39 Charter Street, painted in the best tradition of ghetto realism. Giant sunflowers – but their stalks were a totem of green rats' skulls and the crowns of petals were of flame. Hovering low there were bands of angels with bleeding smiles whose sweating bodies were coiled from waist to neck by bandoliers of ammunition and stick grenades. Their wings were studded with hundreds of staring eyes.

Wanting to look his best, Jasper had tried on three shirts, changed his belt. The kind of vanity Helen mocked in the children. Now his clothes were sweated through. And although it was warm for an early spring evening and the wind was slack, Jasper felt cold. Hunger, he tried to tell himself. Only he didn't feel hungry, just old and foolish. When he sniffed his hands, despite the baby oil he'd rubbed in, they smelled of cleanser.

'What's got into you?' Jasper badgered himself. 'Just think of that crêpe scarf with the price tag. The bottle out the window. Thank you, no.' Still, he knew for certain that Rhoda had the weight of the world on her side. And he was disposable.

All right, he'd go back upstairs then. Open some wine, sit by the window in Rhoda's apartment and watch the lights of the ships moving parallel to the shore. To do so, to kick off his shoes, to conspire with the waiting bed – but he didn't dare. One step, two up the front stoop and his heart balked. Patience, he didn't want to jinx things. Helen, God bless her, was never late for an appointment in her life. How much, Jasper wondered, did she miss him?

Then Rhoda arrived. Matter-of-factly, she was there, the straps of one sandal flapping. It thrilled Jasper to see her. He felt happy right down to his toes, then shattered. Rhoda showed him no recognition. None. Her arms were clasped around a large bag of groceries. In the confectionery lamplight her round face looked old, hard. She had misbuttoned her pea jacket, which made her still more lumpish. Even her wonderful, wild hair hung limp and lifeless. What would Helen think?

'Here, let me help you with that,' Jasper said softly when Rhoda walked past him into the vestibule and began to fumble at her mailbox.

'Hey, don't I know you from somewhere?' Rhoda closed one eye and cocked her head at him. 'You look awfully familiar. Then again a lot of people have been looking familiar lately.' She lifted a hand to her head. 'Something must be the matter with me. Not enough protein.'

'Protein?'

'Yeah, if I ate more fish and cheese probably I wouldn't have this feeling I'd seen you before.'

'I'm Jasper.' He nearly choked getting the words out. 'From last night.'

'The truth is I hate fish and cheese but how many eggs can you eat?' Jasper laughed a fraction of a second too late, and a bit too long. Rhoda pressed up against him, and kissed him hard, tickling his tongue with hers. 'How're you doin', Red?'

'Here, give me that. I'll carry it.'

'So tell me, how long have you been out there?' Rhoda asked, moving on ahead of him.

'Not long.'

'I'll bet.'

At the mad slasher's sofa, Rhoda paused, searching for new wounds.

'Yes, I know,' Jasper said, his elation making him feel reckless. 'Murray told me.'

'You get around, Jasper, you surely do.' Rhoda, Jasper noted happily, didn't ask for her keys back when he opened the door. 'Jesus, how did *they* get in here?' The first thing Rhoda did inside was throw away the flowers Jasper had arranged in a pitcher. 'I *hate* flowers. They make the plants nervous.'

'Sorry.'

'Don't be sorry, use your brains.'

In the kitchen where he carried Rhoda's shopping, Jasper stood straining to hear any comment she might make about how different the place looked.

'Did you miss me, darlings?' Rhoda asked the plants. 'I missed you. Thought about you the whole day.'

When Rhoda came out to the kitchen, by rights its sparkle should have blinded her. She was oblivious. 'What're you grinning at?' she growled at Jasper. Then she took a roast chicken out of her shopping bag. Shoestring potatoes, too, in saturated wax paper. Jasper produced his roast chicken and french fries from the oven. He fetched the Valpolicella from the window sill. Rhoda matched it, exactly, from the bag on the counter.

They ate in a charged silence. Rhoda attacked her food, lowering her face to the plate. She gulped down her wine. 'Remind me to show you my manners some time,' she said with her mouth full. Her lips slithered and shone with grease. Jasper tried to ignore his erection. The kiss he wanted to give was turning him inside out.

'How were the kids today?' he asked.

'Don't be nosey. Eat. You're going to need it.'

''Scuse me' – Rhoda pushed back her chair with the back of her thighs. Cheeks, chin and fingers were all streaked with grease. She disappeared into the bathroom sucking on her fingers, one by one. Jasper heard water rush into the tub. Tidying up the kitchen, he felt feverish.

'Want me to do your back?' No answer. Jasper lit the

strategic candles, opened the bed. The sheets were white, not gray. He half-unbuttoned his shirt, took off his shoes and socks. Such scheming!

Rhoda came out of her bath, body rosy, glowing. 'Look at this, will you.' There were new bruises. 'Here, here, here. Christ.' Rhoda stared at the bed, then at Jasper. 'Fuck me, Jasper, now. But no hands.'

'Why?'

Rhoda's rules. Jasper's heart was stiff. He felt connected and obeyed. And after they made love, naturally awkward under the set conditions but perhaps for that reason, because for once no excuse was needed for being awkward, Jasper's pleasure all but tore him apart. Maybe he would never use his hands to make love again. Rhoda says.

'Oh, no, don't tell me. Ah.' Rhoda rummaged at the bedside for her cigarettes. She lit one, inhaled deeply with her eyes closed, head tilted back. As she exhaled, she shook her hair and looked around the room. 'You know something' – Rhoda's lip curled in disgust – 'one of these days I'm gonna have to clean this place up.'

4

When Jasper woke, the blanket was on the floor, the top sheet more off the bed than on. Asleep, he had been far away and had to fight his way back every inch of the way, pushing out with his arms, churning his legs. Now, as the storm in his heart subsided, he realized he wasn't alone. Rhoda slept on soundly next to him; the skin of her neck, her shoulder, had the cool radiance of pearl. She looked ghastly in her faint fluorescence.

With a blend of surgeon's care and the giddy concentration of someone building a house of cards, Jasper unscissored Rhoda's legs and slowly raised one of her outflung arms so that he could slip free. His feet touched the floor and he shivered. To cover his bare chest he went groping for the sweater he'd last seen tossed on top of the trestle table. The wool was scratchy and straining to push the crown of his skull through the sweater's narrow neck, both arms flailing in the dark, Jasper felt lost. Fear of death stabbed him in the pit of his stomach.

But flash moments of despair were hardly anything new to Jasper Whiting, and so he didn't linger over them. A breath down the wrong pipe. Sand in his heart. Now eyes first, then nose, mouth and chin scraped their way through the neck opening into the free air. A fine how-do-you-do when pulling on a sweater almost turns into drowning!

In the bathroom Jasper dug the frozen capon out of its nest of lace panties. The plastic wrapping was cold and wet but still only the outer surface had thawed. Just as Jasper passed back through the bedroom, up on his toes, Rhoda rolled onto her back, arms wide, breasts sliding apart. The thick hair under her arms, twisted into tongues, seemed to lie in ambush. From her smiles Jasper made out that for once she was listening to the chatter of her plants.

With the chicken under his sweater, Jasper padded quickly along the corridor and up the stairs. Safe in his own apartment, he flicked on the garish overhead fixture, like an upside down pudding, and sighed with relief. Laughing half out loud he tossed the chicken onto the armchair at the foot of the bed. The photograph of Helen and the children had fallen out of the mirror frame onto the floor and just in time Jasper avoided stepping on their faces. He kissed them all, and felt less of a hypocrite than he thought he should.

'Hmmm, very touching.'

Jasper jumped nearly out of his skin. Sitting up in bed, covers to his waist, a young man stared archly at him. The youth's broad, powerful shoulders were draped in Jasper's own candy-stripe pajama top.

'Who are you? How did you get in here?'

'So many questions.'

'What . . . ?'

'Now, now – anyone who sneaks around Charter Street in the dead of night with a frozen chicken clutched to his bosom, shouldn't throw stones.'

'Get out!' Jasper blushed. 'I mean it.'

'Of course you do. They all do.'

'I'll give you exactly ten seconds to . . .'

'You must be Jasper. How do you do, Jasper.' The boy in the bed reached down to pick up a slim cigarette case from the floor. He took out a thin joint, lit it and then offered it with a nod and extended arm to Jasper. Shrugging when Jasper refused, he inhaled deeply before blowing out an expanding plume of sweet smoke.

'Who are you?'

'That's better. Why that's almost sociable.'

Jasper sank into the armchair, half-rising with a squeal when he landed on the frozen chicken. He fumbled it out from under him and chucked it onto the bed.

'A peace offering, aren't you sweet. You're just right for the part, you really are. That hair, it's perfect. Rhoda . . .'

'You know Rhoda?'

'We're like this.' Two palms rose together in a gesture of prayer. 'Pity to let a good bed go to waste – Rhoda's very words. And the keys' – the youth was extraordinarily handsome, Jasper had to admit, his face rapid in changes of mood and expression, strong, open, impressive – 'the keys' – he dug them out of his shoe – 'she wouldn't take no for an answer.'

Jasper had recovered from his shock by now and started to enjoy the situation himself. An entrance to remember! 'Sorry I woke you,' Jasper laughed.

'I'm Luigi.'

'Pleased to meet you.'

'Don't forget the light on your way out, Jasper, will you? I need my beauty rest, I really do. Oh, first get that *thing* out of here. I'm sure there's a perfectly good explanation, but I don't want to hear it. Self-defense, no doubt. Nightie-night, Jasper, pleasant dreams.'

By the time Jasper eased himself into bed again beside Rhoda, he was aroused. Her mouth was open slightly. She was obviously enjoying her dreams. He caressed her belly, nibbled at her neck, was pushed away and fell asleep.

'Want to know why I wasn't angry with you last night?'

It wasn't the voice that woke Jasper but the rattle of dishes and strong aroma of coffee.

'Poor baby, no one looks his best first thing in the morning, but you overdo it, don't you?'

As Jasper blinked his eyes open, a fragmented rainbow zoomed in on him.

'Your girlfriend's left for work. She said not to wake you. One or two?' Luigi held a spoon piled with sugar over a steaming mug of coffee.

'One.'

'Try two,' Luigi said, 'it's sweeter.'

Jasper laughed and entered the new day.

'Good. Score one for me.' Luigi sat on the edge of the bed. He was wearing a yellow T-shirt imprinted with a blue self-portrait in the telltale stipple style of computer art. His chest was crisscrossed with the straps of cameras. At Jasper's first bleary glance a severed ear appeared to dangle from a thong around Luigi's neck. False alarm. On focus this proved to be a small suede pouch.

'Better sit up, sweetheart' – the boy was also marinated in scent – 'or you'll spill.'

Luigi rose from the bed and made for the windows. 'Let's shed a little light on the subject, shall we.' As he snapped up the shades, one, two, sunshine burst into the room.

Before Jasper's eyes adjusted to the light, he actually *heard* something was wrong. Luigi had only one leg. He hopped with the aid of a twisted lucite cane, steering with swimming gestures of his free arm.

'Missing something?' Around the stump of his thigh Luigi

wore his trouser leg knotted and garlanded with plastic flowers, bright ribbons and small bells. 'That takes us back to where I wanted to begin. Drink up, don't let it get cold. Know why I wasn't angry with you last night?'

Jasper shook his head no.

'You're so clearly new to this kind of thing. Life, I mean.' Luigi went on to shovel so much sugar into his own coffee that Jasper could only stare in horror. 'I'm not putting you down, or anything. Perish the thought. True, some of the things Rhoda drags in off the streets are *amazing*, but' – here Luigi tilted his head – 'I can see how you could be called cute, in your own way.'

'So.'

'What I would like to do, dear Jasper, is invite you out to lunch. As my guest, of course. Last night I'm afraid I failed to be properly appreciative. Then it was a little late, you will admit, and the main course was a trifle underdone.'

Jasper laughed again. 'I think I've seen you before.'

'Not enough protein?' Luigi sipped his coffee by lowering his head to his cup, staring up with evident good humour at Jasper. 'My name is Luigi Sasakawa and it's the one thing I'm a bit sensitive about. At the moment I take photographs. These are my cameras. Nothing serious, nothing artistic, thank God. I hustle tourists. Hit and run.'

'I'm sure I've seen you.'

'You wouldn't be the first to find me unforgettable.' Luigi gave his stump a shake so the ribbons fluttered and the bells jingled. 'About lunch – we'll meet at the MFA?'

'Sorry?'

'Museum of Fine Arts. I'll be there working. Out front. Do try to look presentable. Rhoda says the things you wear are pretty godawful, but who is she to talk? One-thirty, please. I don't like to wait.'

Luigi had leaned forward, stroked Jasper's crown, and kissed him gently on the lips before, faster than Jasper would have thought possible, he was gone.

5

Dr Jasper Whiting stepped out of Mass General and stood on the sidewalk, blinking at the day. Leaving the special world of the hospital, even after so many years, it still took him a minute or two to get his bearings.

'Fa, Fa, Fa, Fa.' Carole Whiting waggled one long arm out of the window of the family Mazda. 'Surprise! Here, let me move those things.' Carole tossed some loose pages of sheet music, her bulky purse and a yellow sweater onto the back seat. As Jasper settled in, the springs creaked. 'So, stranger, how's life?'

Carole's attention was flattering. Right now, however, Jasper would just as soon forget his family. Unfair, ungrateful – but there it was.

'You didn't tell me you were coming, did you? I didn't forget?'

'Not this time, no. This was an ambush.'

'Is anything wrong?'

'I had a break between classes, that's all.' Carole was in her finishing year at the Boston Academy of Music. 'I mean, you still are my father.'

Even perfect strangers couldn't help being struck by Carole Whiting's vulnerability, but she liked to think of herself as a tough customer.

'Hungry, Fa? I know a place on the hill that does great pepperoni subs.'

'Sorry, honey.' Jasper checked his watch. 'I've got a lunch date.'

'Okay,' – Carole started the car – 'tell me where you're going and I'll drop you.'

'Museum of Fine Arts, please. Didn't expect that from your old father, did you?'

'Fa, there isn't anything I wouldn't put past you any more.'

Carole overcame the complicated traffic pattern surrounding Massachusetts General Hospital the same way she overcame most of the problems she encountered – by ignoring all the signs that didn't suit her.

'The recital's next week, isn't it?'

'The answer is no, Fa, you can't.' Whenever Jasper came to hear Carole play, she froze completely. Always had, ever since her first schoolgirl concert when she'd actually toppled from the piano bench in a full-fledged faint, taffeta and all. 'It's not going to be worth hearing, anyway.'

On Storrow Drive Carole accelerated, tapping the white-bone steering wheel near the top with both hands, goosing the gas pedal, too, ever so lightly. There were thousands of small waves on the river, encrusted with light. A few sailboats tacked against the wind, taking advantage of the fine day.

'Oh, guess what?' Carole smiled at her father. 'I'm giving it up.' Jasper felt a twinge at heart. 'No, don't worry,' Carole laughed, 'not music! This is not another sudden announcement of my professional retirement.' The last time Carole's reason – not, as she herself was the first to point out, that she needed one – was that she wanted to let her nails grow so she wouldn't look like a conservatory freak. Fortunately she soon had to come to terms with the fact that she was a compulsive nail-biter. Still and all Carole Whiting had a worrying, not to say – as her mother did – perverse pattern of likes and dislikes, taking pleasure in things she did badly, like driving, and displaying indifference where she excelled, as at music. The one sure way to put her off something was to encourage her.

'I decided this morning.'

'I'm sure you're doing the right thing,' Jasper nodded. 'You're dropping what?'

'You know, Fa, it's all well and good if you prefer not to take yourself seriously, that's your business – but it really would make me happy if once, just once, you took me seriously.'

Jasper stiff-armed the dashboard. Carole was tail-gating the truck ahead. 'Tell me, what are you dropping?'

'Ab psych.'

'So.' Jasper's eyes widened. He had approved of Carole's classes in abnormal psychology more than her other random schemes for self-improvement, even after Helen began to complain about Carole's using the family in her case studies.

'You know, Fa, you have a very irritating way of saying that word – *so*. Has anybody ever told you that before?'

'Next exit.'

'Sooo. You should try to break the habit, for your own good. With me you won't get in trouble. I'm not going to let myself get worked up by any silly little habit of speech. But say it like that one day to the wrong person, and I'd hate to have to pick up the pieces.'

Much of the Fenway looked trampled, but then green was returning slowly to all of New England that year. Jasper was fond of this wide, unruly breathing space lodged in Boston's heart.

'I thought ab psych was the best course you'd ever had?'

'The course is fine. Nothing wrong with the course – it's just the instructor.'

'Boring?'

'Not exactly – the problem is, he's fallen in love with me. Sooo,' Carole beat Jasper to it, just, threw back her head and laughed again. She was most likeable, he found, and the least like himself or her mother, when she made fun of herself.

'I had to see him during office hours. He called me in – to talk about my work. Ha! The poor guy was so nervous his lips went dry. I could smell the pass coming. "Carole, you have a very exceptional mind" – now let's face it, Fa, that's just about the last thing I have. "Of course," I said, looking him right in the eye, "it could be that you're only interested in my body." That floored him – out for the count.'

'Yes' – this, Jasper thought, was a story for Rhoda! – 'I can imagine.'

'What really gets me,' – Carole shook her head – 'is he didn't even know I was joking.'

When Carole was a baby and she cried, Jasper suddenly recalled, the only way to get her to stop was to cry with her.

'How's your mother these days?'

'Mom? Patient.' Carole waited for her father to go on. In the face of his silence, she added, 'So patient it's getting on our nerves.'

'And Daniel?'

'Impossible – like always. Fa, you're not still upset about all those things he said? He didn't mean half of it.'

'Oh?' At Jasper's eye level a furry fly buzzed madly, battling to escape through the hard transparency of the windshield. 'Which half did he mean?'

'He was angry you were leaving, Fa, that's all.' Jasper used his cupped hand to cuff the fly sideways towards the open window and freedom. 'He did like the running shoes you sent him. They were only a size and half too small.'

Jasper grimaced, but he could hardly blame Nurse Morrison. After all he'd forgotten his son's birthday completely.

On Huntington Avenue traffic was brisk. In front of the MFA Carole braked sharply. Behind her a gypsy cab had to swerve onto the tram tracks to avoid a collision.

'Meeting someone, Fa?' For the first time since entering the car, Jasper took a good sidelong glance at his daughter. She looked more scattered than ever, a shotgun blast of panic barely concealed behind the laughter in her eyes. 'Not that I'm trying to pry.'

At the base of the museum steps Jasper had already caught sight of Luigi setting up a small group photo, two women and a bunch of children – black, brown and white.

'Thanks for the lift, Carole,' Jasper said and pushed down on the door handle.

'Wait a sec, Fa.' Carole removed a large envelope from the glove compartment. 'First there's this.' She drew out some papers. New insurance forms for Jasper's hands – raising the coverage. It was Helen's idea – he owed it to his patients, they'd expect it of him. 'Your hands and Pele's feet, Fa,' Daniel had said. And then went ahead and made a party game out of it: The Most Heavily Insured Composite Anatomy in the World. 'Whose nose, Fa? Whose, um —'

Jasper smiled, and slipped the papers into the vest pocket of his jacket. Now that he'd discovered a new use for his hands – with Rhoda – let Helen insure them as heavily as she wanted.

'Then there's this.' Carole handed him a series of painters' colour strip samples. Helen's reminder he 'had to do something' about his office.

'And last but not least. . . .' Carole took out a wheel of quartz batteries for Jasper's hearing aid. 'So, Fa, who're you meeting?' Carole followed her father's eyes. 'Who does *he* think he's kidding?' she said. 'No one can be that good-looking.'

With great animation, Luigi was speaking and gesturing, maneuvering his subjects into position.

'Know what they call a paraplegic in a swimming pool, Fa?'

'What?'

'Bob.'

Despite himself, Jasper laughed. On the sidewalk he ducked his head back through the car window to say goodbye.

'Hey, Fa, what about coming home for supper? Mom could. . . .'

'Don't, Carole, please.'

'Okay, sorry – just asking.'

Carole reached out a hand which Jasper squeezed.

6

As Luigi's customers trailed away down Huntington Avenue, the two children who brought up the rear did exaggerated limps, casting looks, guilty and sly, back over one shoulder.

'How's business?'

'Hello, Jasper. I just finished photographing the United Nations.' Luigi rolled his earnings tight and tucked them into the pouch around his neck. Then he went into a fit. He threw out his arms, palms up, and tilted back his head. Jasper caught on: Luigi was imitating the lifesize Indian on horseback in front of the museum entrance. A feathered headdress, iron, trailed all the way down the chief's back.

'The Appeal to the Great Spirit by Cyrus Dallin, can you believe it?'

'My kind of art,' Jasper said. 'I can recognize what it's supposed to be.' Veins in the horse's flanks stood out in relief.

'It doesn't improve on acquaintance. Even the Great Spirit must've had enough of it by now.' Luigi knew the guards at the door. 'I can't tell you what a good job these fellows do, Jasper. Madmen are attacking art all over the country, but not in Boston. We're just going in to eat, boys, if that's all right with you. See this,' – Luigi tapped the leather holster on one guard's hip – 'in Boston we don't mess around.'

Luigi whisked Jasper through an exhibit of Japanese crafts. 'Kimonos. A Jap friend of mine with some silkworms says they've started on one for me. He has to stand over them with a whip, otherwise he says they'll lay down on the job.'

Leaving the stolid main building behind them, with startling agility Luigi swiveled into a glaring modern hall. Jasper, agape, followed.

'Impressive,' Jasper said, drinking in the gloss of his surroundings.

'Bunker architecture,' Luigi shot back. 'The aesthetics of scrimp.'

They passed slim ash trees set out in granite pots along the front of an elegant, glass-enclosed café. Every surface held such a high polish that Jasper began to feel dowdy.

'This is where we get off, Jasper.' Luigi ducked down a staircase of pale pink stone that doubled back on itself. 'How're you doing, Blanche?' A gray-haired black woman in uniform dragged her nose up out of the Bible open on her lap. 'Upstairs we shoot 'em, down here we save them.' Luigi patted Blanche's cheek, her face split with a smile. 'Don't tell me, sugar, I know. I'm too free with my hands.'

Their destination, the basement cafeteria, had a low ceiling, many square tables turned at hazardous angles to each other, awkward contour chairs, plastic, on thin chrome legs. The far wall, entirely of glass, gave onto an interior display courtyard now in chaos between exhibitions. White birches grew there in spindly profusion. A few rather squalid willows, the worse for winter, kept them company.

Jasper stepped to the end of the line that wound its way along the serving counter. Luigi nudged him and with one arm half-hugging Jasper steered him to a cluttered table near the window.

'No,' Jasper said, 'never. This is the first time.'

'It's my favorite place, bar none.' Luigi sat. 'Some of the coffee shops and lounges in the big hotels are not bad, but this cafeteria here rates a full four stars. First of all the portions they serve are big and second of all the clientele, most of them, have enough class to leave something over. Like look at that,' Luigi pointed to the shallow oval dish in front of Jasper. 'That ragout has hardly been touched. The self-help aspect's a big plus, too, of course. The staff here have none of that disgusting loyalty you can run into in private places.'

Luigi initiated Jasper into the rules of their meal together by example rather than instruction. First he selected leftovers which tempted him. Then they moved tables.

'All right, I admit it, I like to have a look at the people whose meal I'm finishing. I feel safer that way. The main thing is not to make any sudden moves. That's right, Jasper, take your time. Relax, sit back, enjoy the view. And when you eat, eat slow. Wine?' Luigi emptied the remains of three glasses into one. 'Cheers.'

Jasper found the waste hard to believe. Platters of fancy salad, roasts, rich desserts, nibbled and pecked, pushed around the plate and abandoned. Up for grabs, theirs for the taking.

'Uh-huh, here, in all the excitement I nearly forgot.' From one of his camera bags Luigi handed Jasper a silver knife, fork and spoon wrapped in a white damask napkin. 'I prefer to bring my own.'

'Do you do this often?'

'Not every day, no. I like to bring special guests here.'

It was, of course, absurd, Luigi's issuing instructions to act unobtrusively, for as the cripple swivel-hipped his way among the tables, dressed in such startling, bright colors, studded with pins and buttons, bells tinkling, draped with his criss-crossed cameras and stunningly vital and handsome, he drew every eye in the place.

'So what's your game, anyway? Rhoda swears she never laid eyes on you before you forced your way into her room and took her panting, like a beast. You're married?'

'I am.'

'Salt, please. So many unhappy marriages, a sign of the times.'

'Not unhappy, really.'

'Bored? A pleasure seeker? If you're looking for thrills, baby, what're you doing on Charter Street?'

'Long story.'

'I like long stories. No, that's not the whole truth. I like them when I tell them. Go on, who are you?'

'I'm a doctor, only not a doctor. . . .'

'An impostor?'

'A plastic surgeon.'

'Oh my,' – Luigi blushed – 'the company I keep.'

'The company *I* keep!' Jasper smiled.

Luigi snapped his fingers. 'Jasper Whiting, the Nose King of New England. How many in circulation? A thousand? More?' Jasper blushed. 'What does it feel like, your signature on all those faces? A celebrity luncheon! In that case let's head for the butterfly shrimp, there, near the corner. Don't bumble, Jasper, glide.' When they had resettled themselves, Luigi fixed Jasper with a shrewd stare.

'Does Rhoda know? I mean have you told her who you are?'

Jasper shook his head no. 'I'm one of the things we haven't talked about yet.'

'So you're Jasper Whiting. My, my, I really am impressed. The first man in history to do a black nose job. And Viet Nam. What was it they called you guys?'

'The Web of Life.'

'That's it. Why?'

'It has to do with a skin graft technique.' Jasper swallowed down his shrimp, took a fork and began to make cross-hatches on the table top to illustrate.

'Uh-uh, spare me the details. You must have a lot of guts.'

Helen had written every day. Jasper hadn't answered. They only spoke once, briefly, about his time in Nam. The day the Presidential Medal arrived, Helen stood at his elbow, beaming, while he unpacked and opened the box. 'It would have been so much easier' – Jasper weighed the small medal in his palm – 'not to maim them in the first place.'

'Maybe I'm naive,' Luigi said, 'but aren't doctors supposed to instill confidence by the way they look? Dessert?'

Again they changed tables. Reseated, Luigi reached over and took Jasper's hand. 'Run away, have you? I might as well tell you, I've got a weakness for people who admit that they're sick of themselves.'

'Didn't hear you,' Jasper touched his hearing aid, so convenient for covering lapses of attention.

'Let me ask you a serious question,' Luigi laughed. 'Listen to me!'

'What question?'

'Which side are you on?'

Jasper gave him a blank look.

'I see, Rhoda hasn't started in on you yet. That could be a good sign, or a bad sign, Or no sign at all. Jazz, do us a favor and do something every once in a while to show you're still alive. Wiggle those pretty ears or something. It's exciting actually, talking to you, like reading under the covers with a flashlight.'

Jasper Whiting felt nauseous. How it complicated things, to be ashamed when people assumed you must be proud.

Luigi had taken out a mirror and was renewing his blue eye shadow. 'You know, I hate to say this so soon in a budding friendship, but I'm not at all sure Charter Street's the right place for you. In fact, Jasper, I have my doubts.' Luigi's voice turned hard. 'Maybe you should go back where you came from – fast. That's not a warning, mind you. Just friendly advice. I'm not one of those who get a kick from watching other people come apart, that's all. Surprised? Don't be fooled by appearances, Jasper. Really, trapped inside this beautiful body there's a sweet and simple little boy, the kind who keeps both feet on the ground. Yeah,' – Luigi rolled more than shrugged his shoulders – 'but try to tell that to the world when all they can see is THIS!'

'Suppose,' Jasper spoke quietly, 'you tell me something about Rhoda.'

'Okay.' Luigi nodded and put away his eye shadow. 'Rhoda doesn't like her friends talking about her behind her back.'

With a squeal an elegant young man rushed up from behind Luigi and began to shower his face with noisy kisses. When his friend had gone, Luigi laughed and wiped his mouth with his damask napkin. 'I really love the vulgar, I do,' he told Jasper. 'It's so trustworthy. It only pretends to be what it is.'

Outside the museum, at the bottom of the front steps, Luigi slapped the rump of the Appeal to the Great Spirit, metal weathered to rich blue-green. 'It's so bad even the birds refuse to shit on it. We should do this more often, Jasper. I enjoyed it.'

'Correct me if I'm wrong, but behind our pleasant lunch there was a purpose.'

'You're a good cover, Doc.'

'No, something more than that.' Jasper spoke with a burst of force. 'You wanted to make sure I had everything straight.'

'Unfortunate word.'

'You fancy yourself quite an expert on Rhoda, don't you?'

Luigi smiled. 'I do, yes.'

'Thank you for the lunch. I enjoyed it, too. I'm afraid though I can't promise not to make my own mistakes.'

'With Rhoda it's sink or swim.' Luigi grasped Jasper's arm. 'She may be the only real human being you ever meet, so be careful.'

7

'Wha, wha. . . .'

Jasper woke with a start. Rhoda lay sobbing, fighting against it. Jasper saw a new face, one rearranged by pain.

'Shhh!' Rhoda let Jasper hold her close and stroke her hair. Several times she started to speak, but couldn't get the words out.

'Bad for the plants? Crying is bad for the plants, is that it?' Jasper rocked Rhoda in his arms. 'Water?'

There were still hours to go before first daylight would dilute the dark. In the kitchen Jasper let the cold water run. He filled a glass, drank half himself, spilled out the rest. He filled the glass again, too full, and returned with it, splashing his chest, to the bed. He was groggy with sleep.

'You're sweet.' The bedside lamp was on. Rhoda sat with her knees drawn up, smoking. 'Sorry.'

'For what?' Rhoda drank the water at a single go. 'More?'

'No, that's fine. Thank you.'

'If you want more, just say. It's no trouble.'

'Sorry, Jasper.'

'Don't be silly.'

'It doesn't happen often.' She went through the gesture of lighting another cigarette before she realized she already had one lit in her mouth. 'Oh Christ.' By mistake it was the burning cigarette she threw across the room. Jasper retrieved it.

'So.' Jasper put the cigarette out, came and sat back on the bed. 'Want to talk about it?'

Rhoda stared at him hard, arms wrapped around her knees.

'I had a letter from Alex.'

'Alex?'

'Haven't I told you about Alex?'

'No.'

'The ex-priest?'

'No.'

'The one who runs a school for the deaf and dumb outside Beirut.'

Jasper went out to the bathroom and returned with a damp washcloth. He lifted Rhoda's hair where it hung against her neck and rubbed the skin. She took the washcloth from him and wiped her face. She clenched it in her hands and started to cry again.

'Tell me,' Jasper coaxed. 'Try.'

'Alex's school is right smack on the edge of the desert. Literally – the wall to the school starts where the desert ends. I was out there not so long ago – two years now, no, what am I saying, three. Christ. What he'd done with that place was a miracle. When he gets them, the children are frightened. So frightened many of them tremble all over. They just sit all day and shake. Their parents bring them to the gates at night and leave them there. Nice parents. To be deaf in the desert, Jasper, maybe it seems funny, but you couldn't pick a worse place.'

Rhoda reached out and pushed the bedside lamp away so the light wouldn't shine in her eyes. 'When I first met Alex, and that's a long time ago – more than twenty years – Alex changed my life. Me, I was as dumb as they come. I knew nothing. The questions kept multiplying by the day and I didn't have a clue to any of the answers. How I kept going I can't tell you.'

Rhoda made Jasper stop stroking her hair. 'I sound like an idiot, don't I?'

'Not at all.'

'Think what you like. The thing about Alex was that he was so fucking alive. He was giving, all the time. Yet it never slowed him down or wore him out. And he wasn't keeping score.' Rhoda reached her fingers up and traced the curve of Jasper's lips. 'Alex taught me to read lips. He has beautiful lips, really. Yours aren't bad, Jasper, not half bad, but Alex's are a cut apart.'

'How did you meet this Alex?'

'He was a friend of Phil's – my second husband.'

'And?'

'I had just started giving one evening a week to teaching the deaf – a movement class. I used to be a dancer, Jasper – in another life. This was right here, in West Somerville. Phil had left me by then. This friend of his, Alex, Alexander Thane, was always hanging around. I really didn't know who he was, what he did, nothing. I don't ask people a whole lot of questions, maybe you've noticed. One night he showed up to watch me teach my class. Afterwards he came up and told me what I was doing wasn't helping anybody. Not them, not me. You can't stick your big toe in the water and pretend you're getting wet. It grew from there.'

'You were a number, you and Alex?' Jasper felt his jaw go rigid. 'Is that the way it was?' According to Helen, he didn't have a jealous bone in his body. 'What was in this letter then?'

Rhoda leaned across Jasper to rummage in the drawer of the night table. She pulled out a sheet of thin pink paper covered with tiny racing script. 'As long as you don't get any wrong ideas. The last thing Alex is is soft.'

Rhoda knelt on the mattress and sat back on her heels. She wiped at her eyes with the back of the hand holding the letter, threw the washcloth across the room with the other. '"Dear Rho",' she began to read, running a finger down the page, lips moving as she skipped a few lines. 'Okay – here it starts. "As if we didn't have our hands full already, they've been hammering the road to Damascus from both sides all afternoon. The noise is deafening. In such circumstances, I can almost envy the children."' Jasper frowned. Active fighting around Beirut? There hadn't been anything in the paper for weeks. '"As usual no one really knows who started the shooting, or why. No one cares any more, at least no one seems to. It's been going on too long."'

Rhoda read slowly. At times she had trouble deciphering the words. She would dive towards the paper for a closer look, correct herself if need be, then continue on in the same deep, unhurried voice.

'"From the school windows we *see* explosions. We look out together. Together we watch it happen but I'm the only one who hears the explosions as well as feels them. First something falls, something dark, like a bird. Then matter goes crazy. The air splashes like water, there are clouds of sand, trees float up, blow away. Walls crumble, flames fan out. There is rubble everywhere, thick smoke, debris, craters in the ground.

'"Then their eyes turn from the sight of devastation to my mouth. They hang on my lips – poor climbers, their last fingerhold slipping. Even for me to wet my lips with my tongue sends fear knifing through them. So I stand there trying to turn to stone, somehow to control my face, not to let the horror show.

'"Our staff is, has been, small for some time now. But can I really blame anyone for leaving? School of what? What lessons are there to be learned here? Rhoda, try to understand: I am numb. To write this to you costs no pain, and *that* I find painful, the discovery of my insensitivity. Remember how we began here? The optimism?"'

Rhoda looked up, her breathing uneven. 'Now it comes,' she smiled sadly, rubbed her cheek against Jasper's arm and went on.

'"Rhoda, what does God think he's doing? Forgive me, but I cannot continue talking to myself like some madman who thinks he has to keep silent to protect God's reputation. Rhoda, the school – those poor buildings huddled at the edge of so much sand, the bricks that deaf hands argued into place, one by one. Those crazy bastards, they fired on the school. Shells came tumbling out of the sky, end over end, and they hit by the well in the compound. Were we an intentional target? No, I won't believe that. I refuse to consider it. Does it matter, really? The bomb struck and the windows all blew in. Remember the time I had raising money for that glass? Right in front of my eyes the children turned into animals. Even the older ones went berserk. They flapped their arms, they ran in small circles. With bleeding hands they started trying to tell me things I couldn't understand. It was a pure slang of despair.

'"They saw the soldiers before I did. Not running, no, they entered our yard walking. Who can tell the sides apart? No one – war is insane, all war. This war is no exception. Always the same stupidity masquerading as bravery. Sumir came out of the kitchen with a large pan of beans cooked with tomatoes. He toppled dead in the yard. The top of his body spouted a fountain of blood. The old man was just carrying supper as usual, from the kitchen to the dining hall. Bullets scarred the walls, kicked up dust. And God forgive me, I put a hand over my mouth.

'"Rhoda, the children ran. They had no idea where to run, but when they saw the hand over my mouth, that was the signal for them that the world was coming to an end. They scattered screaming. I didn't move. I pressed my hand over my mouth so my lips would not betray me – us, Rhoda.

'"The soldiers, they were children really, too, most of them, dressed up in uniform, carrying weapons much too big for them. You could see they were frightened by so many people running every which way, screaming. The mules in our stables, too, were braying in terror. They came rushing out into the courtyard, slipping in Sumir's blood. The soldiers called to the children to stop. 'Stop, stop,' they shouted. 'Stop, or we'll shoot.'"'

Rhoda waved the letter through the air and closed her eyes. '"Peace, Alex."'

In no time at all it was morning. The first sound to reach Jasper's ears was Rhoda's singing in the shower, ever so happily. He shut his eyes and tried to grope back to find the wrong turn he'd taken somewhere along the way to consciousness. The blood-spattered soldiers shouting themselves hoarse, the children fleeing, their inhuman cries, feet slipping in the sand and broken glass, bodies birdlike in panic, the carnage – had Rhoda forgotten?

Narrow shreds of daylight dazzled around the edges of the drawn oil shades. Jasper lay back and clutched a pillow to his chest. 'Everything all right?' he was tempted to call out, as if Rhoda were showering the whole time in silence. Her singing was operatic, powerful. He let its promise of renewed strength flow over him.

But how would she feel when suddenly she remembered? Any moment now surely something would remind her, anything. A word in her song, a screech of brakes outside, an unpredictable change in the temperature of the hot water. In a flash it would all come back to her.

What should Jasper do? Put on a face appropriate to the bright morning, to all bright mornings? The face of a secret drinker who has quickly wiped his lips? Now Helen – as soon as her golden head hit the pillow, plunk, she was out and she woke, aaaah, as if in mid-sentence, mood intact, ready to carry on right where she'd left off, the absent hours no more than the turning of a page, just time enough to clear her throat.

Jasper smiled, ran a hand down his chest. After their talk late last night, Rhoda had given him a back rub to help him sleep again. The turn-up of his lips as he remembered where the back rub led he experienced as a betrayal – but of what? Come now, did he honestly think because of Alex's letter he had smiled for the last time?

Yet, such singing! Jasper sat on the edge of the bed, hunched forward. His stomach sagged like an anchor. He yawned without the energy to do it right. The shades across the windows looked like skin grafts. In fact the whole place looked odd. What was it? Familiar landmarks were gone: the ashtrays heaped with butts, glasses with smears and stale odors, shoes, belts, gone. From wet spots on the floor under the window sill it was clear, too, that Rhoda had already watered the plants. So. Today was to be a new beginning, was that it? Day one. Rhoda's chosen way to measure up and carry on, a fresh start, stepping over the bodies as if they weren't there.

The hiss of the shower ended, and Rhoda stopped singing. Jasper heard her yank back the shower curtain and climb out of the tub. She pulled a towel from the loose, rattling rack and with a gasp buried her face in the fleecy warmth. He held his breath, scratching his scalp, at ease only once her song began again, muffled as she dried her hair. Without the spray of falling water to shield her voice, she sang a bit self-consciously now. Her voice was rich, with warm tones. Who was he to bring her down?

Jasper was more disturbed now himself by Alex's letter than he had been last night. Listening to Rhoda read, he'd been too busy offering comfort for the bare facts to sink in. Well, now that he, too, knew the story, what was he supposed to do with it? Wasn't it exactly the kind of thing that every sensible person would agree it was best to forget? Helen strenuously objected to the way some people were always making anecdotes out of disaster. At a dinner party, by way of illustration, she herself might launch into just the kind of horror story better left unspoken.

'You all right in there?'

Jasper's eyes fell on the night table. Alex's letter was gone. He was certain the last thing before the light went out, Rhoda had tucked it under the base of the lamp. Aha, there it was, the familiar pink paper – on the floor, half-way between the foot of the rumpled bed and the bathroom. A draught must have caught the letter when Rhoda went to shower, sucked it from the table. Both windows were open a few inches at the bottom.

There was no time to lose. By now Rhoda would be in the last stages of brushing her teeth, soft bristles rotating, her belly pressed flush against the cold edge of the sink, tendrils of wet hair curling behind her ears and trailing down her nape. Oomph, Jasper heaved himself up from the bed and crossed the room, legs unsteady, to snatch up Alex's letter, to remove it from Rhoda's line of sight. As long as she *could* forget, he would help her. His chest swelled: Jasper Whiting, protector of rare moods.

Down on one knee Jasper picked up the thin pink paper. What? The page was covered with typeface, not handwriting. He held a reminder of an overdue electricity bill in his hand.

'So, Sleeping Beauty's up.'

Rhoda had wrapped her hair in a pale blue towel. Body glowing red, she stood in the bathroom doorway. Behind her the air steamed, a damp cave.

Jasper stood with the pink paper, holding it low, in front of his sex. 'The electricity bill,' he said lamely, 'fell on the floor.'

Rhoda shivered, slammed the windows shut, tracking wet footprints across the floor. Jasper tried to put the paper back quietly under the lamp. When Rhoda didn't face him, he spoke to her back. 'What was that you were singing?' His voice rang false to his own ears.

'You didn't believe it, did you?' Rhoda turned, trailing her fingers across the leaves of a plant. 'I could tell. The whole time I was reading I had a feeling you didn't *want* to believe. Suit yourself. I couldn't fucking care less. Who the hell do you think you are, anyway? Jasper Whiting, the Nose King. Pathetic.

'You know what I think? I think maybe you're just another one of those poor little shits who refuse to believe horrible things happen. They don't want to soil their minds. The kind that keeps calling for proof. Shit! Gimme that paper. What're you grinning at, goddamn it!' Rhoda's towel turban had tilted forward over one eye. She pushed it back and stood challenging him, hands on her hips. Water gleamed, trickling down from her navel.

Jasper put a finger to his lips. 'Think of the plants, watch your language.' He knew where he was again. He could breathe, think, feel pain – and love. Rhoda, flesh quivering, crossed to the night table and yanked the top drawer open so hard that it came all the way out. It dangled by the knob in her hand, contents spilling over the floor. Pins, pills, coins, matchbooks, photos, pencils and pens. *Ping*, crash. From the litter of odds and ends, Rhoda lifted a pink sheet of paper and shook it in Jasper's face.

'Here, you bastard.' Jasper took a step back. 'Well, now are you satisfied?'

'Hold still a sec, or how do I know it isn't just another unpaid bill?'

8

'Nobody's forcing you, but if you want to come, you'd better get a move on.'

The overhead light flashed on, pulsing slightly. Rhoda was across the room tossing things into a duffle bag.

'Sorry, guys,' she apologized briefly to the plants for disturbing them. 'Swim time.'

'I haven't got a suit.'

'They have them there. And don't sweat it, Jasper – it's no beauty contest.'

At quarter to seven when they called for the keys to the police wagon, the precinct was dead as a morgue. Times were bad for fund-raising with hypocrites crying poor and turning half their pockets inside out to prove it. But Rhoda's hustle paid off. The police wagon, for example: a relic really, open wire mesh sides and back, unstable on its wheel base, yet it was a vehicle and it moved.

'How you doing back there?' Rhoda called.

'Fine,' Jasper tried to say but a sudden jolt sent him several inches into the air and clamped his jaws shut with a snick.

In the entrance to the New England School for Special Children, the archway above the wedge-shaped front stairs, a number of adults stood waiting. Milling about, far freer than the grown-ups, were the children. Youngsters. In woollen caps, quilted jackets, breaths fogging the air, they might pass, at a glance, most of them, for healthy kids. Except for a few with blank faces. And some parents held their children too tightly by the hand, were too intent in their manner of fussing, too practiced at making light of things.

A ragged cheer welcomed the old police wagon as it bounced to a halt slightly skew to the curb. Without killing the motor, Rhoda jumped down to the pavement and bounded to the stairway.

'C'mon, kids, shake a leg.'

Jasper peeled off his gloves and stuffed them into the pockets of Rhoda's pea jacket – full of crumbs.

Huddled in place, he watched the bustle on the sidewalk, blowing on his bare hands, clenched now in a single interlaced fist in front of his face. The inside of the police wagon was a scandal, really – it hadn't been cleaned since God knew when. From dumps and jumble sales, wheedling and cajoling, Rhoda had collected cushions and pillows and blankets so that her passengers might ride in elegance. Some of the cushions stank, the blankets were foul rags. Jasper smiled contritely. How he carried on in Helen's terms! Or was that dishonest? Once hers, now, after sharing lives, his own as well?

Rhoda was everywhere, greeting, scolding, laughing, herding parents and children up onto the wooden benches in the rear of the wagon. She had her reindeer sweater on, her arms around everyone at once.

'That's Jasper, everybody,' she called out, to no one's apparent interest. 'He's an Olympic champion.' A few children had begun to cry. One even kicked violently.

'Carrie's doing her best imitation of a tantrum for you,' an admirably composed young mother told Jasper when she noticed him staring.

'Very convincing,' Jasper said.

'Yes, isn't she.' The mother smiled a warm, brave smile. 'Even knowing better, I'm inclined to believe her myself.' Wisps of frizzy wheat-colored hair kept getting in the woman's way when she wanted to talk. She would jerk her head rapidly to one side and say what she had to say quickly while her lips were clear. Both hands were busy controlling Carrie. Jasper wondered if he should tuck her hair back up under her wool cap for her. 'The only time Carrie stops kicking is when we throw her in the water. Wait'n see. Kids are perverse, I guess that's it.'

The wagon lurched through the early morning streets. For no reason he could think of, it surprised Jasper that Rhoda could drive.

'What's yours got?' – a father tried Jasper conversationally. A friendly face, owlish, crusts of sleep in the corners of his eyes. 'Mine's spastic. Like in the jokes.'

'Bah,' said the woman whose hair trailed into her mouth, glaring at the speaker with disapproval.

'I hope to God they've got that locker room heated.' The man inched closer to Jasper. 'Nearly froze my nuts off last week.'

Carrie's mother tried to ignite a song with her lilting voice. 'We could do it as a round,' she said. Jasper was willing to sing along, but the suggestion didn't catch on.

The Spinedale Pool is in South Boston where Story Street runs into Telegraph Hill. From the vantage of Rhoda's chosen approach, the pool building below looked like a sunken cathedral. Redbrick Gothic, complete with buttresses and spires and high narrow windows that tapered to a point. The illusion of sinking had to do with how the building nestled into a stone hillside where a few trees, most of their old roots visible, grew out over the pool roof at crazy angles. There was a low stone wall around the building as well, set along its top with shards of jagged green glass and rusty loops of barbed wire.

To Jasper the place looked like it would be guarded by alcoholic janitors who kept tripping over their own mops. He pictured dwarfish women posted outside the lavs, rhinestone clips flashing in their wild hair, eyeing every passing male with distrust and flirting without shame.

'Last one in is a rotten. . . .'

'Rhoda!'

Parents and children tumbled from the police wagon into a daylight thinner than any Jasper could remember. Together they surged as a mass through twin-entrance doors of milky glass.

Inside everything was bright, clean, efficient. The staff was young and cheerful, exuding health. No mean achievement, given the hour and their tasks.

Girls and boys, mothers and fathers separated at the squeaking chrome turnstiles that led to the changing rooms.

'Make yourself useful,' Rhoda found time to call out to Jasper.

'How?'

'How? See someone who has too many clothes on, take them off. Too few, help them dress. Play it,' – she grinned and at once the reindeer across her chest appeared to kick their heels – 'by ear.'

The changing room had runners of pitted rubber on a speckled granite floor. Separate booths with curtains hanging from shoulder-to-knee height provided skimpy privacy for stripping to suit up. There were low benches the colour of driftwood. Clothes hangers with wire baskets attached at the bottom for storing shoes and other belongings could be checked at a counter in exchange for a metal tag with an elastic strap to be worn around wrist or ankle. In addition to swim briefs and towels, there were goggles, nose clips and bathing caps for sale or hire. Small sounds echoed. There was the steady hiss of showers. Until Jasper detached his hearing aid, every time the door joining the changing area to the pool proper swung open, he could hear someone at the tip of the diving board practicing to gain height, springing in place over and over again.

Jasper's rental suit, a baggy gray wool antique, made him itch at first sight. Military surplus. There was a buckle in front with an eagle on it which baffled his fingers.

'Stand still, for Christ's sake! Okay, this is the last time then. Is that what you want?'

The locker room, a bit chilly, was hardly the arctic waste Jasper had been prepared against. It was the quality of light, he decided, more than the air temperature.

'I like salt water myself,' a young man who headed towards the pool was saying, 'and waves. Otherwise it's like being in a giant bathtub.'

In his trunks Jasper felt revealed, white, heavy, the bulge of his belly, the tight pouch of his sex pitiful, really, compared to what a body could be. He looked for someone he could help. Everywhere the curtains of the changing booths were swinging, jostled, the ground beneath littered with trousers and fallen T-shirts turned inside-out. At the checking counter, Jasper slowly drew his breath in. The children, ready to swim, were also revealed: their wasted limbs or swollen, misformed backs, their heads wildly out of proportion, bodies that appeared to move in several directions at once, the lips too moist. How clothes helped to muffle differences.

Among the parents, a new grimness and determination prevailed. Some actually, Jasper learned later, were uncles or older brothers and sisters. Yet the children, bare, were in a holiday mood, shrieking now, some holding inflatable toys, ordinarily a violation of pool rules, others enjoying brief freedom from heavy corrective metal braces. Children with slack bodies, incomplete, symmetry awry, each movement jerky. Self-protectively, Jasper found himself picking out noses to admire, extracting solace from perfect detail. He was wondering, too, when he appeared at the poolside, what half-joking remark Rhoda would make at his expense. It would help, oh yes, if he, too, could clutch a plastic shark or an inner tube with ruffles.

'Didn't I tell you? God, have you ever been so cold in your life?' Jasper received the good-natured slap on his shoulder with a start. The man's hand was like ice.

'Please,' a small man appealed to Jasper, 'could you give me a hand with Armand?' The man himself appeared to be losing a battle to balance his eyeglasses on the bridge of his nose. He had one arm around the flaccid waist of what Jasper assumed was Armand, a child, a boy. Armand's head lolled to one side, the forehead massive, bulbous, swollen with fluid that didn't circulate as it should through the spine, up and around the lining of the brain. Armand wore a nylon racing suit, dark green with white stars. His father was perspiring heavily. To all appearances he might have just dredged his boy, drowned, from the sea.

Jasper did not remember the boy from the police wagon but when Armand 'spoke' to his father, a series of slavering sounds too liquid to make sense to a stranger, a voice perfectly in keeping with the mistake that Armand had recently swallowed half the Atlantic, Jasper realized he had heard the voice earlier that morning somewhere in the background.

'Sometimes he goes all heavy on me like this. He just wants to be. . . .' – Jasper seized one of Armand's arms while the boy's head swung in half-circles, side to side, ending each time with a snap, then spinning back again – '. . . babied a little.'

Jasper felt himself shiver as he and Armand's father, whose eyeglasses dangled now by one earpiece from between compressed lips, maneuvered Armand out through the shallow disinfectant footbath and into the main swim hall.

'He says you're hurting him,' the boy's father managed to tell Jasper in tight-lipped precision without letting his glasses drop.

'Sorry.' Jasper had gripped Armand's arm harder than intended, his fingers sinking into the putty-like flesh. As he relaxed his hold, Armand's tongue appeared, flicking towards him, lips glistening. This time Jasper thought he understood the boy's words, 'That's much better.'

The pool was in a vast hall, the ceiling of which was peaked, a huge skylight really, panes of glass reinforced with fine wire, the whole supported by fluted iron girders with ornate capitals. The girders were painted a pale green, flaking in places to reveal a coat of silver beneath. Overhead the sky was neither gray nor blue. The pool water was a rich emerald, reflecting the paint of the pool lining. The border of the pool, rectangular in shape, was a sharp blue and the surface of glossy tiles which rose to the height of a man on all sides of the hall was a tint of off-white with pale mauve tones at the edges. Potted dwarf palms and lush Venus ferns were placed in clusters near the bases of the support pillars. The whole was beautiful, elegant, uplifting and took Jasper by surprise.

'Thank you, I can manage now. He's seen the water. That always excites him. And when he gets excited, well, he calms down.'

Jasper burned with fever. A fever of fear. He knew he was being perfectly ridiculous. No, worse. To the marrow of his bones he was ashamed, but he was afraid, too. What was he doing, pretending to do, taking these poor freaks for a swim? Was this a good deed? In whose eyes? Was this meant to be rewarding? How beautiful the swim hall was only made his panic worse. He heard the mixed sounds of the disabled immersing in the heavily dosed water, watched the calm surface churn, choppy now with their glad, uncontrolled flailings. His breath was on fire. Clouds above must have lifted for suddenly a flood of gold light struck the pool water, and the voices of children and adults rose in appreciation at the same time. A gasp of pleasure. The water was veined with light. Then Jasper heard Rhoda's voice and it steadied him.

'Time to get wet, champ.' She smiled up at him from the water, reached out a dripping hand. 'God, you look *awful.*'

'I'm afraid,' he whispered.

'Good – good for you. Now come over here and help me. This is Jeanne. This is Uncle Jasper, Jeanne.' Rhoda swam away, leaving Jasper to cope with Jeanne on his own. Fear crowded out fear, fear the child, recognizably that, for all, would drown.

While Jasper played, did his best with a succession of children, from time to time he saw his own body through the water, distorted by the play of light. Bloated the stomach, wavy the legs. His feet seemed miles away. How the children struggled and clutched. Their belief in buoyancy had to be earned. His kids – how had they learned to swim? Diving for pennies in the mud near the shoreline of New Hampshire's crystal lakes. Rhoda was constantly moving, a benign octopus, arms, hands everywhere. Her old-fashioned suit, with a frilly skirt, bones in the bodice, straps tied in a bow behind her neck. White cap with a chin strap. The eyes of the disabled blazed towards Rhoda.

'All right, all right, all right. That's enough.' Jasper had to break up a fight between two children over a flutter board. Their anger, their hate filled him with strength. Soon they were all blowing bubbles together, laughing.

Jasper Whiting had been influenced by the religion of his childhood to such an extent that, without being fully aware of it, he assumed creation had a point. It was no idle exercise of omnipotence. No slapdash time filler with here and there some rough edges, loose threads. Wasn't it, in point of fact, far more difficult to make an Armand, a Carrie, a Jeanne than a child like any other? One of a kind instead of a mass product. Why assume something had gone wrong? Something special had happened – with the clay, with the glaze. The challenge was puzzling out why.

Carrie weighed a ton. In Jasper's arms, on her back, arms spread, like her mother said, she refused to move a muscle. Impossible to say really who was deadly earnest, who was having fun. The maimed and spastic thrashing about, screaming their heads off, having the time of their lives. Not drowning, no, not for the present.

Parents and children. Could he pair them up? There have been regimes, of course, that advocated the methodical elimination of such creatures. Squash them, rub them out. Neighbors on the *qui vive* informing security police of a limp here, a stammer there. Round-ups, disappearances. Regimes, too, which made no bones about using cripples for experiments, testing medicines, poisons, tampering with genes. Yet was it perhaps not a consolation that such governments never sustained power long? Their failure, however, did not necessarily have anything to do with maltreatment of the disabled. No. It was just that the other dreams they sold, these, too, as soon as they were unwrapped, tasted of ashes. How many places were there in the world like Spinedale Pool on Saturday mornings? Wasn't one more than enough?

'Wha. . . .' Jasper spread his legs and looked down, Carrie flung an arm around his neck. Between Jasper's knees a body forced its way, rising, slippery and seal-like. A melon-shaped head surfaced, water streaming from eyes, nose, lips. There was Armand, reaching for him, surfacing behind his grasp, exultant.

The shower room, long and narrow, was dank and rather dark. It had small windows high up and a splotched cement floor. Some shower heads gave out a fine spray, others a lumpish twisted stream of water. The valves were too high overhead to reach up and adjust. Jasper waited for a father with a skeletal child in his arms to finish rinsing off. Then he stepped under the spray and turned. Years ago, light years it seemed, in Kenya, during scarce thundershowers, when he and Helen would race outside the hospital to stand under the broken drainpipe, the water fell with similar force. That water had tasted so fresh, however. Little Carole had danced about naked, head back, mouth wide, drinking the rain.

'Could you soap my back?'

'Luigi!'

'Right the first time.'

'What're you doing here?'

'Trying to find somebody to soap my back. It can get pretty slippery.'

Luigi handed Jasper a creamy, fragrant cake of soap. Then he pivoted on his leg, presenting his back.

'Harder. Come on, Jasper, like you mean it.' Luigi held onto the pipes of the shower, bent his chin forward against his chest. 'That's good.' His back was strong and rippled with muscles, one side more developed than the other. 'Mmmmm.' Jasper's eyes brushed Luigi's stump. He didn't let himself stare.

The children were tired now. Echoes in the shower room held a trace of sadness and temper.

'Now you.' Luigi spun Jasper around and began to rub his back, making large, sweeping circles with his hands, pressing into the soft flesh with his fingertips. Jasper, usually so defensive about being touched, accepted with pleasure.

How, he kept wondering while Luigi's hands worked up a lather, could he have been a doctor for twenty-five years and done so little except tinker?

'Ow!'

'Witch's hair. See. You didn't do half bad out there, Jasper, really. Getting in's always the hardest part.'

Jasper spat a soap ball from his lips, turned to face Luigi. 'Where were you?'

'You could have stuck out your hand and touched me half a dozen times, but you were too busy.'

'You were in the pool?'

'Don't let the water get to your brains, Jasper. Me. In the pool. Yes. Wouldn't miss it for the world, although it's death on the skin. Rhoda says I set a good example. Otherwise these poor kids might think grown-ups were all normal.'

'Here, I'll help you with that.'

'Huh-uh, don't overdo it, Jasper. When I need help, I'll ask, okay?'

Jasper hated wet hair. He began immediately to dry his head vigorously with his towel. Eyes shut, he felt young and happy.

'What. . . .' Luigi was talking to him. Jasper lowered his towel, hopped on one foot to clear a drop of water from his good ear. 'What do you suppose these kids find beautiful?'

'I haven't given it much thought.'

'Oh, you should. You definitely should.' Luigi's eyes held Jasper's. 'It more than repays the effort.'

As Jasper dressed, he was able to cluck at himself for his earlier fears. Peeling wet suits from misshapen bodies, he had slapped their cold, perfect backsides. Luigi came and plonked himself down on the bench just as Jasper was bent double drying between his toes. Armand's father paused in the aisle, water dripping from his beard.

'He had a super time.' Armand was meek now, skin pale to a point of translucence. 'The best yet.'

'Quite a swimmer.'

'Next week they're going to put a drain in. A pump and a drain. Him – not the pool. Armand? Oh, he knows, don't worry. He's agreed.' The man smoothed his child's forehead and kissed it. 'It's worth a try.'

'Yes,' Jasper said. How far away Armand seemed, behind his eyes.

'These days they can do' – the man's voice failed him – 'miracles. In a few weeks he'll be back though, my boy, swimming. Won't you, Armand? Rhoda's promised.'

'What are you doing now?' Luigi asked. Out of his shirt pocket Jasper had taken a small tube from which he was squeezing a tiny ribbon of white cream.

'It's for fungus – athlete's foot.'

'Not very sexy. Here, I'll do it for you.' Jasper shook his head. 'Let me do it, come on.' Luigi took the tube out of Jasper's hands. He sniffed the ointment, made a face. 'To each his own,' he said and pretended to dab a little behind his ears.

'You only need to use a very little.'

'Still damp down here, doctor. Towel, please.' Luigi shifted onto his satchel. Sitting at Jasper's feet, first he dried the toes carefully one by one, giving each a tug, then he smeared on the protective unguent. There was a crash. Jasper and Luigi looked across to the door. On the way out Armand, too stunned to cry, had upset a barrel full of towels, falling heavily. His father was helping him up.

'Didn't watch where he was going,' the father grimaced at Luigi and Jasper. Armand limped out, leg brace clanging, holding onto his father's coat with both hands.

'It was his fault, of course,' Luigi said, 'the father's. He took his eyes off the boy – for just a second.'

'No one got hurt.'

'Not this time, no. A split second, paf, that's all it takes. Loss of concentration, it happens.' Luigi shook his head to dispel unlovely thoughts. 'A relief, Jasper, isn't it, someone else in a cast or a brace?'

'A relief?' Luigi's hair, still wet, made him look younger. He wasn't much more than Dan's age. Jasper missed his son.

'Sure, admit it,' – Luigi cocked his head back and glared at Jasper. 'I don't mean it makes us happy exactly.' Luigi capped Jasper's fungicide and tossed it back to him. 'Deep down though we feel relief.' Uncoiling, he stood. 'These children, we feel sorry for them, of course. After all, we've learned that we should.' Underneath the skat, behind the razzle-dazzle, Luigi was in earnest. 'Also, I grant you, the spectacle of suffering, or helplessness, *can* be sad. But let's be honest. Pity's only part of it, spread pretty wide and thin. At the same time who doesn't hear an inner voice, one that whispers, "Serves you right"?'

'Now. . . .'

But Luigi continued over Jasper's protest. 'We deserve pain, you see, Jasper. Each of us knows that. Shake your head all you want, we do. Take my word for it.'

Luigi removed a straight razor from the pouch around his neck. Exploring his face with his fingers, without benefit of a mirror, he tidied up the shave he'd given himself on waking. 'I've thought a lot about this stuff, Jasper. Sin and retribution, right – otherwise the world falls apart. Each of us knows what he deserves, and it's only a matter of time until we're found out.'

Jasper connected his hearing aid. Was Luigi issuing another warning?

'Don't you see, Jasper, what a hypocritical position it puts us in, the witnessing of another man's pain? After all, in his heart every man is a victim-in-waiting. Every rotten break for the other guy is a stay of execution for us. Another close call – thank God it didn't happen to me. Like musical chairs – for high stakes.'

Luigi inspected the edge of his razor, then clicked it shut.

'Tell me,' Jasper was sorting his socks, 'who are you trying to convince?'

'If someone says, "Give me your pain. Let me share it," watch out. He's lying. "Thank you, sweetheart" - that's more like it. "Thanks for doing my suffering for me."'

'You're serious, aren't you?'

Luigi responded with a dazzling smile.

'You really mean it?'

'Christ, at birth what mother starts to breathe easy again until the inventory's complete? Eyes, two, ears, two, hands, two, feet . . . two. But just let Mary Jane there in the next bed lie cradling some little monster in her arms, what does the new mother of a healthy baby feel? I'm asking you, Jasper.'

'Pity.'

'If you insist. What else?'

'Profound relief,' Jasper kept his voice flat.

'Because . . . ?'

'The monster isn't hers.'

'Good. And what else?'

'Mary Jane has got what Mary Jane deserves.'

'Right on. But here comes the hard part. Here you're going to need all the help I can give. Who or what is a monster?' Luigi smiled. 'Where to draw the line? Different strokes for different folks.' Luigi was in form. He glowed with animation. Pride, too. 'There is a private line for each of us, we put the monsters on one side, the – what shall we call them – the beauties? Why not? We put the beauties on the other. The world is split up into two camps: the beauties and the beasts. But who's who, Jasper, who is who – that's a tricky one, because – ' Luigi did a little pirouette ' – tastes differ.'

'Almost every monster' – Jasper removed his keys from inside one shoe; he checked his wallet by reflex: nothing missing – 'will be a beauty to someone.'

'True,' Luigi said, 'very true. And every beauty? While we're into fairy tales, don't forget the poor beauties, Nose King of the big, mushy heart. Do you think the beauties of this earth have it so easy? Every beauty needs to believe he's somebody's monster. You see that much, don't you?'

'No. Why?'

'Otherwise, he's next. A sitting duck. Otherwise God will put out a contract on him.'

'And people in the middle,' Jasper asked, speaking softly, 'what about them?'

'People in the middle? Not the obvious beauties or beasts, you mean?' Luigi wound his towel, snapped it at a changing booth curtain, as adolescent as you please. 'Folks in the middle, they're the most screwed up of all. They can never be sure. Always in doubt. Lick above, kick below. Mirror, mirror, on the wall.' Jasper, who had been combing his hair, turned, blushed and slipped his comb into his pocket. 'They can be vicious, I tell you, people in the middle. If they think for an instant a lover has seen the tiny birthmark burning high on the inside of one thigh, the little curly hairs on the small of their back, if a casual glance lingers too long on a mole, a blemish, a weak chin – beg your pardon. And don't forget the ultimate weapon of people in the middle, the partial compliment and all it implies – "She has such nice eyes"!'

Jasper, in a hurry to tie his shoes, yanked on the lace which snapped in his hands.

'Make a wish,' Luigi laughed.

'I wish I had a new shoelace.'

Jasper and Luigi came outside together. The air had lost its chill. Spinedale Pool looked smaller, shabbier than before. The public had begun to turn up for Saturday swim, trickling in one by one.

'Get the lead out,' Rhoda called from the police wagon and banged on the horn. She had turned the vehicle around to face uphill.

'My, my,' – Luigi blew Rhoda a kiss – 'it looks like we're the last ones, Jasper.'

In the back of the wagon some children were asleep, heads on the shoulders of their guardians. One child – Carrie – was crying, but not with true heartache.

'Shh, shh, shh, shh,' her mother crooned. 'Of course you can, next week.'

Luigi leaned across to Jasper. 'You know what the one thing the beauties can't do is?' Jasper shook his head, hands in his pockets caressing the fur lining of his gloves. 'I'll give you a clue. It's the one thing the beasts really want more than anything. The beauties can't leave the beasts alone. They can't ignore them, that's what. Us. They can't afford to take their eyes off us, for a second. Or else.'

Luigi settled back in place. Armand half-tumbled onto his lap.

'I've got something that could settle the whole business very nicely,' Jasper said, turning his torn shoelace around and around his finger.

'What's that?'

'Tranquillizers.'

'Now when they go out to their dinner parties tonight at least the sons-of-bitches will have something to talk about.' Rhoda sat cross-legged in the middle of the unmade bed back at Charter Street, combing her hair out. '"Took the kid swimming today." Everyone thinks he's a hero.'

'They're great kids.'

'You think so?' Rhoda looked at Jasper with surprise. He lay on one side next to her. For the first time a small birthmark high on the inside of her thigh caught his attention. And fine down low along her spine. 'If you ask me, most of them are pretty hard to take. They think they're entitled.'

'To what?'

'Oh, all kinds of shit, to make up for their bad luck. Jeanne's okay. Jeanne's about the only one there who really has a good time. She's brave without trading on it.'

'Which one was Jeanne again?'

'The one whose mother's such a piece. You didn't notice? You must *really* have been out of it. There was only one bikini in the pool.'

They made love gently, abstractedly. Rhoda was childlike, almost shy.

'I don't know how much longer we can go on,' Rhoda said.

Jasper's heart stopped.

'Oh,' she laughed, 'no, I mean the Saturday swim.' She put her tongue in his navel. 'The manager's worried the news will leak out and nobody else will want to use the pool. People might think if they swim in the same water they'll catch something. Turn into monsters.'

'Aren't you?' Jasper asked. 'I am.'

'What?'

'Afraid. Superstitiously.'

'The manager has a brother though, messed up pretty bad in Nam. Lives alone in a dark room. So I think we're safe for a little while yet.'

Jasper's eyes still stung from the chlorine in the pool water. Rhoda's, too, looked bloodshot.

'What do you suppose it would be like,' Rhoda asked, 'to be the one whole person in a world of the deformed?'

'Oh, they might make you into a god.'

'How, by killing me? No, Jazz, not a god. Just a common freak. People would come to stare at you. Wheel themselves up, limp along to take a good look.'

'Or, if they were blind, to have a feel.'

'Ladies and gentlemen, step right up, see the one, the only Whole Human Being, nothing missing, nothing less than perfect. 100 per cent in all departments. There you go, do a slow turn for the folks, honey, let them see what they're paying for. I'm asking you, good people, isn't she something. Flawless. A sight for sore eyes. One of a kind.

'Know what, Jasper,' – Rhoda kissed him, eyes open – 'I bet you'd be real lonely real soon.'

9

'Jasper? Jasper, I don't suppose you could come out here and help me – *for once*?' From the sound of it, Rhoda had counted past ten.

'Coming.' Jasper tossed the crossword puzzle onto the floor. It was past rescue anyway from Rhoda's assault in ink. He heaved himself up from the bed, smoothed down his hair and shuffled out to the kitchen in his socks.

'Whatever idiot designed this *thing*,' Rhoda held up a can-opener, regarding it with undisguised hatred, 'should be shot.' Rhoda thrust the loathed object and a can of peas at Jasper. 'Here, doctor. Watch out for your precious hands.'

Three of the four top burners on the stove were blazing without anything on them. Asters in wax paper lay with white and yellow petals so close to the flames that any instant Jasper expected the bouquet to turn into a torch. The icebox door gaped, its interior shed a cold light. Odds and ends on the chrome racks smelled bad.

'You hungry?'

Jasper turned the can-opener this way and that. 'I could eat.' It took him some time to identify the cutting tooth, 'You're sure it's all there?'

'Are you sure *you're* all there? Christ, what kind of a man can't open a can of peas? Little peas at that.'

'Ah,' Jasper exulted as the can-opener took hold. A pop of compressed air marked the beginning of his circular voyage.

'Why don't we go out?' Rhoda held up some nondescript, shrivelled cutlets and sniffed at them.

'If you like,' Jasper said, twirling the can-opener key with pressure from his thumb. 'There!' The jagged top of the can of peas snapped free.

'Who the fuck does Luigi think he is, turning down a meal?' Rhoda poured a mound of salt onto her palm, licked it. 'Smartass cripple. To teach him a lesson, I oughta cook you something he really likes.'

Luigi had only been gone a matter of minutes. He'd burst into the room bristling with excitement at a new treasure. Gloves that glowed when you exposed them to cold. White at room temperature, put them for a few seconds on top of ice and hundreds of tiny red hearts came out like stars. 'I have until next week to figure out what to do with them.'

'Why next week?'

'The week after that at the very outside.'

'What happens then?'

'Some hotshot doctor's bound to come out and say they cause cancer.'

Luigi turned down Rhoda's invitation to stay for dinner. 'It's my night for real food,' he joked. 'Thanks just the same.'

Jasper had not been sorry to see Luigi go. He turned off the gas burners. As they went out, they seemed to hiccough. 'One thing I'd like to know. . . .' Jasper swung a hip against the icebox door to close it. He rummaged among the dishes in the sink for a glass which he filled with water for the flowers. Then, fingers fumbling in haste, he unknotted Rhoda's halter apron. 'How did Luigi lose that leg?'

'How should I know?'

Rhoda drained the liquid from the can of peas into a cup and drank it off without pausing for breath.

'You've never asked?'

'Oh sure. Actually when I met Luigi the first thing I did was ask, Hey kid, what the fuck happened to you?'

'And?'

Rhoda shook her head back and forth. 'You know you are out of this world.' She pushed past Jasper into the bedroom and began slapping the exposed surface of things. 'Jasper, since when did I stop smoking again?'

Jasper came in with the asters. He set them down on the trestle table.

'Didn't I tell you how much I hated flowers?'

Jasper was taken aback. 'Don't look at me. I didn't buy them.'

'No.' Rhoda came to his side. 'One of the kids brought me those today. Susan. You know why?' Jasper was afraid, by reflex, he'd forgotten Rhoda's birthday or some other flower-bearing occasion. 'Susan's parents want to put her away in an institution. One of the best, naturally. Acres of rolling lawns and swans. After a lot of soul-searching, of course. And sleepless nights.'

'The flowers?'

'To break the news gently. Not that they've had the guts yet to level with me. Stuck in with the flowers was a little note on scented paper to say they were removing Susan from school next week for an extended vacation. Susan didn't know either, but she was scared. The whole time I was reading the note she kept looking at me.'

Rhoda wrapped a pudgy fist around the stems of the asters and jerked them out of the water.

'What're you so angry about all of a sudden?'

'All of a sudden, nothing.' Rhoda tilted her head to one side, birdlike. 'You know, I hate to say this, but there are times when even sincerity sucks.' Rhoda pushed her face close to Jasper's. 'Tell me, Jasper, all those noses you *fix*. Some doll who thinks her face is a mess walks into your office and sits down. I'll just bet you anything the first thing you don't ask is, Christ, lady, what happened to you?'

'Not always, but a lot of the time, yes.'

'Bullshit.'

'My patients want to talk about the way they look. How they hate the way they look. Maybe not to anybody else, but I'm their doctor.'

'For your information, Luigi loves to talk about his leg, too. The missing one. The kid loves to talk, period, but about his leg there's no stopping him.'

'How'd he lose it?'

'He's got a lot of stories. One for every occasion.'

'So.'

'That bothers you?'

'Yes.'

'My favorite's how he stepped on a land mine in a dream. Look, if we're going out to eat, don't you think you should put on some clothes?'

Jasper hung his robe on the back of the bathroom door. Goose pimples rippled across his body. 'You know what the first thing many of them do, my patients, after they sit down?' While dressing, Jasper talked aloud to Rhoda. Out in the kitchen she didn't answer. 'They take out a little mirror. They look at themselves and ask me if I have any idea what it's like to have to live with a face like that. Most of the time they want me to come look in their mirror with them, over their shoulder. As if my mirror, any other mirror, wouldn't tell the truth.'

Buttoning his shirt Jasper smelled something burning. He rushed to the kitchen to find Rhoda had set fire to the flowers. Large black flakes floated up to the ceiling.

'Feel better?' he asked. 'That was stupid.'

Rhoda held the incinerated bouquet under the tap, and it hissed.

On the way downstairs, Rhoda turned suddenly to face Jasper, almost losing her footing. She caught herself on the handrail. 'How do you want Luigi to have lost his leg? That's what it comes down to, isn't it? Well? Suit yourself. Make up any story you like, he won't mind.'

Jasper caught up with her in the vest-pocket park below Copps Hill Burial Ground. Rhoda was studying the checkerboard carved into a stone table top. Bottle caps had been left in the middle of an unfinished game.

'Rhoda. Rhoda, don't you think it matters?'

'To me? To him? Why?' She swept the board clean. 'The leg is gone, the truth won't bring it back.'

'But. . . .'

'Look, do us both a big favor, drop it.' Rhoda was losing a battle with herself to stay calm. 'Don't tell me you swallow all the crap your patients tell you?'

'Why don't we just eat at home,' Jasper said. 'I can fix us something.'

'If you're so damn curious about Luigi's leg, ask him yourself. You can't embarrass him, so don't let that stop you. It's too bad you can't, but like so many things in life that are too bad, it's a solid fact.' Rhoda came into Jasper's arms. She had a way of doing so that seemed to open a door in his chest. Her breath warmed his heart directly. 'I've spent a lot of time on Susan. We were starting to get somewhere. Shit.'

They sat side by side on the stone checkerboard and watched freighters tow their shadows through the water below.

'Yes, I suppose I do believe what my patients say. They expect me to.'

'Come clean, Jasper. Hasn't there ever been a time you felt yourself slipping over the edge?'

'Meaning?'

'Meaning when you looked down and saw your patient lying there, nose up in the air, that was one patient too many. Meaning that you made a fist and had the urge to smash that waiting face past all recognition.'

'Never,' Jasper blurted out louder than intended.

'Well then,' – Rhoda smiled – 'maybe you still have something to look forward to.'

Back in the apartment Rhoda watered the plants. Jasper was cracking eggs on the side of a deep bowl, splitting them cleanly with one hand, when he felt Rhoda's lips on the back of his neck. 'Next time you see Luigi, tell him what a feast I made for you, okay?' She retrieved the charred flowers from the sink and crammed them into a vase. 'They almost look nice like that, don't they?' Ash smudged her fingers and came off on her cheek when she scratched an itch.

'What's wrong with Susan?' Jasper asked.

'Don't you ever run out of questions?' Rhoda's cheerfulness was gone. Had he been retaliating, Jasper wondered? 'I mean, really, who do they think they're kidding with that cock-and-bull story about a long vacation? Susan likes school and that's why they want her out of there. At first she didn't, but lately she's been getting into it. She can't wait to come and hates to go home. That's the real reason they're yanking her.'

That night, atypically, Jasper had trouble falling asleep. Rhoda, with her taunting question about latent aggression towards his patients, had planted an idea he could happily have lived without. Nor could he put the image of Rhoda out of his mind with her yellow and white asters on fire, the wax paper curling back, singed, her wild hair reflecting flames, her sad eyes concentrating on the destruction she indulged in to ease her heart. How she had made a fist and held it pressed against her own nose and raised her eyebrows at him, speaking with venom as she laughed and spoke the word, 'Smash!'

Never?

10

Did syphilis erode the vomer *before* the final stages? Jasper wanted to consult Speens. He stepped on the foot ladder and stretched his hand towards the familiar, dog-eared volume. Of itself, his hand came back down.

The way Jasper Whiting's eyes wandered through his office he might have been a prisoner measuring his cell. For more than fifteen years now he had maintained his practice in the same rooms. Here, in the familiar surroundings – high ceilings, most of the original, eighteenth-century oak panels and moulding still intact – he felt safe, in control. He didn't have to pretend to be anything more than he was – a gifted technician, skills conferring rather expensive mercy.

Back again at his desk, Jasper let his head sink onto his arms. His trapped breath was warm. On whose authority did he dare act? He felt himself surrounded by textbooks. Their illustrations, the matter-of-fact descriptive language dismayed, no, disgusted him. Sex, Jasper smiled into the dark, could be exhausting.

Through the years Jasper Whiting had developed something of an eccentric medical philosophy. One he kept largely to himself. Adam and Eve, when they ate of the apple, lost, he believed, their health as well as their innocence. Before temptation and fall, neither had ever sneezed, suffered indigestion or diarrhoea. Oh, like everything else there were viruses loose in Eden, part of God's strenuous six-day war with the void, but these had been free squiggles at swim in the air, harmless as butterflies and orchids. Until Eve felt a trickle of apple juice down her chin and Adam started poking in his stools for apple seeds and ridges, even cancers had only the innocuous effulgence of the rainbow.

Ever since, the history of medical science had been one long struggle to restore health to humankind while remaining powerless, utterly and totally, to do anything about lost innocence. Maybe they were just going about it, as Rhoda would say, ass backwards?

In his twenties Jasper Whiting had believed that Medicine was dedicated to nothing less than the alleviation of human suffering. To achieve that end he was prepared to put up with every sort of personal deprivation. He worked, studied, went without sleep. He drove himself relentlessly, high on altruism. The courage of his convictions kept him going, disposing of wormy doubts and noxious reservations along the way. One day he would be equipped to do fine and noble things. Yes, doctor. No, doctor. Thank you, doctor.

For one thing – Jasper shifted the position of his head, nestling it more comfortably against his elbow – even granted that the medical profession had been hell-bent on relieving human misery, they just hadn't been able to keep pace with those creating new forms of torment and anguish, had they? The physicist, the chemist, industrialists, generals, politicians.

Jasper Whiting, virtuoso giver of noses. Year in year out, patients kept coming. More than a steady trickle. It confused Jasper, even appalled him more than a little at times, how with so much going on in the world that cried out for attention and remedy, so many people made a problem out of the shape of their nose. And he was right there to help them. Set in motion, he didn't swerve. Prestige and success came like some lottery prize slipped through the mail slot in the door, one almost thrown away unopened because of the vulgar appearance and the bulge of the envelope.

'If you didn't do it,' Helen assured him, 'somebody else would. Only not so good.'

The world might be at flashpoint, men, women and children kept beating a path to his practice. They brought clippings of dream faces from magazines, they brought long, convoluted stories of their breathing problems or marriages on the verge of collapse. Jasper could never say no. Even when a woman he knew to be in the last weeks of an aggressive cancer of the liver came for a new nose, he was compliance itself.

To be fair, Jasper always counseled caution. He assured each and every one of his would-be patients that she – the women far outnumbered the men – had a 'perfectly nice nose' already. In point of fact he really only rarely felt that he was shamming. More and more patients came prepared to submit to Jasper's prattle as a necessary if tedious hurdle to clear on their way to redemptive surgery. They sat on the edge of the chair, half-hiding their noses behind their hands, or a handkerchief or veil, crossing their eyes now and then and looking down directly at the offending organ. They heard Jasper's pitch, rejected his attempt to dissuade them, flashed their mirrors of truth, paid a fortune for an operation.

First he made sketches. These were discussed, sifted, re-drawn. Then he made putty models. The patient tried on different noses. Took a nose home to live with. 'What do you think,' Jasper would ask, wondering how many patients thought something was comic about *his* appearance. The patient's face was photographed from all angles, Jasper manipulating the head gently from pose to pose. It was a kind of map-making. Every case the same, careful preparatory steps. Families were consulted. And in the end, after weeks of suspense, the unveiling invariably revealed to the gifted surgeon what he had known all along. Helen's nose again. Once more. Far from perfect, not a great nose, but friendly, human. Whiting's Nose as it was known in the trade.

Before the ink was dry on his medical school diploma, Jasper had packed up for the tropics. He devoted three years to running a bush hospital in western Kenya. An isolated place near Mumias Town on Lake Victoria. And with him went his wife, Helen, a lovely girl who, despite intimate and profound knowledge of Jasper's faults, idolized him. Yes, doctor. Certainly, doctor. Right away, doctor.

Years of round-the-clock dedication. And exhilaration. Never mind the administrative headaches, corruption, jagged supply lines. At such a post a young doctor did everything. Had to. Cookbook surgery was the least of it. The locals believed Jasper was a miracle worker. No amount of failure disillusioned them. Their adulation had been intoxicating. Helen was splendid, too. In the wards, in outlying compounds, charming the natives, often with their own proverbs, collecting and categorizing samples of traditional medicines, roots and leaves, restoring babies to their mother's breast, hurling plastic feeding bottles into the fire.

Upon return to New England, lean and confident, Jasper had wished to specialize in pediatrics or dermatology. As will happen, there were no openings, at any event not at any first-rate institutions. For a time Jasper had given thought to 're-enlisting', disappearing back to the deserts and swamps of the Equator for good, the servant of those unable to help themselves, and their idol.

But Helen craved another setting, different action. Her arguments centred on the children, Carole, born in Kenya, and Daniel, on the way when they came back home. She quoted the Children's Bill of Rights at him. Friends and holiday suppers, courses in flute and jazz ballet. 'Not exactly wasted,' was how Helen came to refer to the African years which had meant so much to Jasper. 'Come, do you really think we did that much good? They're still sticking each other with their spears, aren't they? And drinking scummy water out of ditches. They still won't give a drop of blood.'

Through Helen's well-connected family Jasper did secure a place to train as a plastic surgeon. The victims of burns, industrial accidents, car-crash survivors, post-operative cancer patients, all needed a smoothing touch. When his patients turned up for control during the passing years, it relieved Jasper to learn how their faces and bodies aged. On them, too, drink and worry left their marks. He had begun to fear his patchwork might stand out, like flowers in a desert.

In the late 1960s the national government, recognizing Jasper Whiting's professional eminence, called on him to perform cosmetic surgery on the Iron Maidens of Hiroshima. So misformed, so demure. Acclaim for public service had boosted his morale. Issues of mercy and salvation had pressed into his consciousness, left a thumbprint in his brain.

Some years and many noses later it had taken him off balance as a mild, haphazard critic of American involvement in Viet Nam to be invited to participate in the Web of Life. He'd accepted with alacrity, trusting the adventure would do him a world of good. Maybe he could even re-establish contact with medicine as a calling rooted in beneficence.

The flight to Saigon was long and cramped. His being so keyed up, restless, didn't help. His life, his career, all had been preparation for this mission. From Saigon helicopters had lifted them to the field hospital. To Jasper it felt like the rotary blade was growing straight out of his skull. He lodged in a reed bungalow with a direct view of the sea. At times he went out to wade until colliding once with the bloated corpse of a dog leaking intestines. Sounds of war reached them intermittently from inland, floating out of the teeming jungle.

At any one time there were usually a dozen plastic surgeons operating in tandem. They pushed their physical stamina past reasonable limits. Vast tents were pegged for them to work in. Crates of supplies lay heavily guarded in a shallow ditch near the clearing where the lifeline of helicopters landed. There were never enough bandages. The bustle of the premises rivalled a small city.

By far the majority of operations were performed on peasants scorched by napalm, many beyond recognition. The surgeons rearranged skins for these people. The Whiting graft was used, even as the Whiting scissors. Scraps of whole skin were made to stretch. Spirited technical discussions enlivened excellent meals. The liquor supply never ran low. Day by day, precision began to matter less. Sleep was brief, hallucinatory. It was not possible to prepare adequately for most of the surgery undertaken. Improvisation predictably led to disaster. Without any sense of the person on whose body he was to exercise his skill, Jasper felt clumsy, lost. Under the best of circumstances skin grafts required supreme patience. The climate was against them, too. Nothing healed easily.

At first Jasper had suspicions that the native nursing staff was hostile. Their intense, silent concentration was intimidating. Yet their efficiency, the speed with which they acquired technique, proved their dedication. Still, among themselves the doctors never tired of joking about Cong infiltration of their hospital. Cong as the sea breeze, as mosquitoes. It was about the only safe subject among them, certain to win a laugh. What remained unspoken was their bitter, mutual dislike. Rivalries flourished.

Awaiting operation, large numbers died. Their diminutive bodies were stacked, carted off to be incinerated on the sand along the sea. Three days a week an American army chaplain conducted mass funeral services. At times families came to steal back their dead. As for the successes at the hospital, no one raised the subject of what kind of future awaited those they managed to save.

Dreams of Boston patients, noses bright, found murdered in their beds, chopped and bleeding, issued fair warning to Jasper that the way back to his old life might be difficult to find.

On the flight home the stewardesses were among the most stunning orientals Jasper had ever laid eyes on.

'Doctor?'

Jasper sat up as Morrison entered.

'Two cancellations.' Morrison reclaimed a pair of files from Jasper's desk. 'Coffee, doctor?'

'Fine, Morrison. Thank you.'

One of the patients who wasn't coming wanted her nose back. Even though building up a small nose was harder than whittling down a large, Jasper had done a good, professional job. On her last visit, the woman had raged, practically accusing Jasper of operating under the influence. It wasn't his fault if she hated her new face, hated its dead, foreign center. He had let her scribble on the photos like the others – and then torn them up for safety's sake. 'I want my nose back,' just like that. As if Jasper might still have it in one of his pockets. As if she could search him and find it. Jasper was waiting for the right moment to tell Rhoda the story. Funny it didn't happen more often.

The second cancellation was a teenager, blissfully happy with her new nose. She was already worried, however, about whether she had to tell the man she might marry some day about her operation.

'You'll see,' Jasper told her when she asked his advice, 'when the time comes.'

11

'All right already!'

'Open up in there, Jasper.'

Even before fists began to pound the door, Jasper could make out two sets of footsteps on the stairs: Luigi moving fast, Rhoda hardly bothering to lift her feet. He slid back the safety chain.

'What's the. . . .'

Luigi's gale-force entrance swept Jasper back onto the bed.

'Party time!'

Luigi jigged about the room, pivoting on his cane. He hooted and hollered, hurling flowers every which way. Jasper was smothered in affectionate hugs. Bottles of booze sprouted from the pockets of Luigi's baggy trousers and limp burlap jacket. Under her arm, Rhoda carried a large portfolio, its cardboard covers decorated with green and yellow marbling.

'This little piggie's going to market!'

Rhoda translated for Jasper. 'Luigi's trying to tell you he's going to be famous.'

'Rich *and* famous.' Luigi showered kisses on Rhoda's plants.

'How?'

'He was down in the Gold Mine last night and struck paydirt. Matasapi was there and the man, I use the word loosely, took to our friend here like a boa constrictor to water.'

'Oh when I am good, I am very, very good.'

'Amen,' Rhoda said.

'Drink up, Jazz, this time it's for real.' Jasper found a bottle between his lips and his head thrust back. 'Matasapi has eyes in his head. He *sees*.'

Jasper gasped for breath, whiskey sloshing down his chin. 'Who's Matasapi?'

'He takes photographs.'

'Listen to her. Who is Matasapi? He takes photographs. What are the Pyramids? A pile of old bricks.' Luigi made a display of being indignant. 'As far as New England is concerned, Matasapi *is* photography. Fashion, my dear. He calls all the shots.'

Rhoda nodded. She played the cynic the better to set off Luigi's whirlwind excitement. His zest splashed over them. 'Poor Jasper, you're no exception. Luigi's had to educate us all.'

'At least I can leave the public to Matasapi.'

'Our Mr Sasakawa is ambitious.'

'What else is there to be – for a one-legged freak who also happens to be breathtakingly bee-yu-ti-ful?' Luigi poured whiskey over his head.

'And, honestly, I couldn't have done it' – Luigi ceremoniously bowed and kissed the back of his hand – 'without you!'

'But what's happened?'

'This has been building, Jasper baby, building a long, long time – like those Pyramids we were just talking about, brick by brick. One of life's itsy-bitsy ironies: me, I'm out there hustling my butt off, cameras twisted around my neck, sweet-talking moms and granddads and silly mooning couples into letting me document them for posterity, snap, and the whole time Matasapi's never let me out of his lens.

'Last night he made his move. Sidled up to me like some crab, his big bulging eyes pushed to their corners. He sat down, coughed, sucked on his teeth, sighed – God knows we'd probably still be sitting there if I hadn't put him out of his misery with one of my warmest shit-eating grins.'

'And you never knew he'd been following you?' Rhoda asked.

'Following? Stalking.'

'All this took place in the gold mine. Sorry to be so dense, but what's the gold mine?'

'A gay bar. You understand *gay bar*? A particularly nasty one at that, full of screaming tots who only play for pay.'

'What was Luigi doing there?'

'Remind me,' Luigi said, 'the next time I see the Pyramids to ask them what they're doing in the desert. What is the eye doing in the needle? Jazz, boy, haven't you ever heard of being in the right place at the right time?'

'The short and long of it is,' – Rhoda looked at Luigi proudly – 'our little Luigi's going to be a cover boy.'

'And this Matasapi character, how do you know you can trust him?'

Luigi patted Jasper's crown, breathed fire in his face. The boy's shirt front dripped with scotch. 'We sealed the bargain. A contract for sex weeks – what am I saying? Six weeks, with rights to exclusive renewal.'

Luigi kipped onto his back, kicked at the leaves of one of Rhoda's king ferns.

'Congratulations.'

'You hurt one of those plants and I'll ruin your pretty face.'

'Now, now. Make no mistake, you two. I've worked for this. I made it happen.' Luigi was sober, talking to be heard. 'The only question was where and when. Wait and see, a lot of people are going to grow addicted to the sight of me.'

'Do us all a big favor,' Rhoda said, 'and keep it fun, Luigi.'

'Can I have a look?' Jasper pointed at the portfolio.

'He shot them pretty much in a hurry,' Luigi answered, undoing the ribbons. 'Still, they're not bad.'

Indeed Matasapi's photographs were of an extraordinary, compelling beauty. The pace at which Jasper Whiting began to sift through the prints slowed. All were black and white, not glossy, stark and simple. There were no tricks of lighting or focus, at least none immediately apparent to the untrained eye. Luigi Sasakawa naked, or as good as, alternately sitting, reclining, posing against a zig-zag parquet, shot largely from above, or rather from the subject's own eye level. Small differences in angle seemed to matter vitally.

Without knowing it, Jasper began to shake his head slightly, his most common response to mystery.

'To him I'm "the Lost Explorer".'

Several pictures gave the impression that Luigi was enjoying himself immensely.

'Dizzy chatterbox. Runs at the mouth the whole time he works. Can't stand silence. Puts him off, he says. And would you believe it, the old fag is afraid to touch me? He can bring his hands only so close, then they flutter away. *Almost* not quite. Horrible hands he has, too.'

'Bet' – Rhoda moved one of Jasper's arms so she could see the pictures better – 'you felt a little stupid after a while?'

'Wrong. It was all very friendly and wonderful. Drugs'll do that for you.'

As for Luigi's deformity – for Jasper typically deferred consideration of the essence of any problem, even an aesthetic one, until last – while Matasapi's honesty was apparent, it was not insistent. One of the model's legs happened to end above the knee. This had implications for volume, for line, for composition. There was no coyness. Luigi was seen whole. The asymmetry of Luigi's body, strong, graceful even, but out of balance, skew through years of compensation, this asymmetry had powerful visual poignance – especially when played off subtly against various formal symmetries of composition.

'The Lost Explorer,' Rhoda repeated, 'meaning?'

'Just gassing away like a silly schoolgirl and all the time under cover of that babble there's a genius at work, watching and waiting. He didn't let me get away with a thing.'

'But,' Jasper finally ventured. He had spread the photos out next to each other on the floor so his eyes could travel from one to the other. That was the way he worked with his patients as well. 'I don't see how these are going to help your career. I mean you're not modeling anything – not as far as I can make out.'

With a laugh, Rhoda came to hug him, throwing her forearms around his face.

'The rest, friend, will be child's play,' Luigi said. 'The cars, the cigarettes, the silks and satins, the underpants, the soaps, the diamonds, they're on their way. A hard rain is gonna fall. This, baby, was the killer.'

'Are you wearing make-up?'

'Now?'

'No – in those.'

'Here, look.' When Jasper lowered his face close to the paper he could see long hairs from Luigi's nostrils, a shadow high on one shoulder where a scratched mosquito bite had healed. In one photo beneath the converging cords of Luigi's neck, perspiration streaked his torso.

'Models have nicknames, you know, in the trade. At least the ones at the top. The Face, the Thigh. Some get stuck with a part for the whole. Some have unfortunate habits. The Giggle. The Runs. Matasapi's christened me the Lost Explorer.' Luigi laughed. 'How am I going to live up to that?'

Rhoda had set to work watering her plants with a new white plastic spray gun. Luigi himself began scooping up the photos Jasper had spread out. One by one he smiled at them.

'What a relief to find out something you've always believed in is true.'

'He means himself,' Rhoda told Jasper. 'Don't forget your friends, Luigi. Keep in touch. Like what happens to the Lost Explorer if no one cares enough to go looking for him?'

With a style of magical thinking new since his meeting Rhoda, Jasper Whiting didn't want Luigi to shut the marbled covers of his portfolio. With the images rubbing up against each other like that, hard feelings could kindle.

12

Jasper dumped his briefcase next to the bed. Letters of recommendation to write – if only he could keep the residents apart in his mind! He poked about in the fridge for a clue to what might be for supper. Then he gave water to some of the plants which he was secretly sure Rhoda, for reasons best known to herself, was short-changing. Next he lay down, just for a minute.

'It's open,' Jasper sputtered, roused by persistent knocking.

'Rho?' The woman who entered was paper-thin. Although she stood no more than a few feet from the bed, Jasper couldn't focus on her clearly. She was so much in motion. Her mousey hair billowed above her pale face, she had protruding teeth, a clothespin nose. The gray-green dress she wore needed ironing. She advanced towards Jasper behind a shield of cheap perfume. Yet the woman's voice, sweet and self-possessed, was instantly likeable.

'That bitch! What's the time? Don't bother, I know, it's five. It was already when I started down.'

'You're looking for Rhoda?' The woman was snapping her fingers compulsively, fingers brittle, nails sharp. Her flat eyes flashed with an anger and resentment which she kept out of her voice. She apparently was used to exasperation, and self-control.

'Look, how about you? Are you busy at the moment? I mean, just looking at you, I can see that you're not.'

'No, no. I was just getting up.'

'Think you could give us a hand? I know I'm imposing but I can't keep Sloan waiting any longer. What the fuck's keeping her this time? It'll only take a few minutes. Eight minutes, no more.'

As the stick woman climbed the dim flight of stairs, Jasper had to hurry to keep up with her. Each time she picked up a foot, a loose slipper flapped. She had Bandaids taped across both heels. Once she threw a glance back down over an extruding shoulder blade, trailing a hand through the darkness in his direction.

'I'm Gayle Glintz, how do you do. I want you to know how much Sloan and I appreciate your doing this.'

The door to 4C stood wide. The apartment had two more rooms than either Rhoda's place or his own. The largest was the living room dominated by a long, narrow plank table with high legs. On the table was an oatmeal-coloured blanket with a pair of dark gray stripes running parallel to the edges that hung down over the sides. Both the man and the woman on the far side of the table looked up when Gayle and Jasper entered.

The man was short and swarthy, with a bushy moustache, dark, friendly eyes. He slouched with his weight to one side, his fingers drumming on the table through the blanket. Large hands, immaculately groomed, hairy, fingers so thick they seemed to miss the last joint. His white shirt had a starched collar, the sleeves were rolled back above the elbow.

'Hello, man,' the fellow called at the sight of Jasper. 'It's me, Murray.'

The woman was young, distracted. Jasper recalled passing her, too, on the stairs. She was always talking to herself, applying make-up from a compact, pivoting her head to examine herself in the compact mirror as she rushed downstairs. Before she reached bottom she usually turned around and went back up for repairs. Jasper saw now she really was quite pretty in a patched-up undernourished way. The smile she gave was brief, almost secretive. She needed sleep. She wore a striped apron.

'This is. . . ,' Gayle Glintz introduced Jasper to the others.

'Jasper Whiting.'

'Rhoda's stuck. One of her emergencies, no doubt. He'll have to do, won't he?' Gayle Glintz reached into a sack hanging by a strap from one corner of the table, and pulled out an apron. 'Here, put this on. I'll get Sloan.' The apron was decorated with cartoon seafood, shellfish grinning broadly as they cascaded into a steaming pot.

'Don't worry,' the young woman reassured Jasper. Her voice was surprisingly energetic, even happy. 'You'll get the hang of it quick enough. Pace yourself, that's all. And for God's sake, think of something else.'

When Gayle Glintz reappeared, there was a body draped around her neck, or rather cradled in her arms or climbing up, slipping, clawing to maintain a hold on the front of her skinny body. Too much was simply happening too fast for Jasper to take in all the details. This then was Sloan. From appearances the boy might be anywhere between eleven and nineteen.

Murray responded quickly to Gayle Glintz's signal for help. Together they pushed and rolled Sloan onto the table top. The young woman made a great fuss about rearranging the blanket so its edges hung even with the floor.

'All right, Murray. You're on the left foot as usual. Merriweather, how about an arm this time? Think you can handle it? Of course you can. I'll take the head and the other arm and. . . .'

'Jasper.'

'Sorry, I'm not wrapped very tight at the moment. We're late, and sticking to schedule is very important. Jasper here will hang on to the other foot. Watch what Murray does' – the man with the moustache smiled and bowed – 'and try to do the same thing, only you synchronize with the opposite arm. Is that clear?'

Then Gayle Glintz struck a glancing blow at an instrument hanging on the wall behind her and it began to emit a loud, regular *click*.

'All right, team. Eight minutes. Go.'

Murray and Merriweather initiated the action. They seemed intent on forcing Sloan's limbs to make running motions in place. Murry had to take a large stride forward to raise the boy's foot and knee high and then he retreated as he lowered the limb back and extended it to full length again. At the command 'Go', Merriweather grasped Sloan's wrist with both her hands and tugged until her arm flailed out straight, then with a slight rotary gesture she accordioned the limb back again, passing so close to Sloan's upturned face that her knuckles appeared to graze his nose. She and Murray plied together.

'Now us.' Jasper grasped Sloan's other leg with one hand low near the ankle and the other underneath a flaccid calf. It was heavier, harder to lift than he had supposed. He shifted the top hand up into the hollow behind Sloan's knee. Once the leg began to rise, however, it became obvious that to keep it from pumping too hard, to brake the initial movement in time to lead the leg back down smoothly and under control, would be even more taxing.

'Don't worry about hurting him. He likes it.'

Sounds came streaming from Sloan's lips steadily, noises Jasper had previously associated with pain, but he could also detect an undercurrent beneath the gasping and gurgling that held tones of celebration.

'Good . . . but do it . . . in time . . . to the . . . coun-ter.'

Jasper soon caught on. He began to set up a rhythm with his own body for the movements he was making. He was Gayle Glintz's partner. All four of them, five of them, were dancing together, enforcing symmetry upon the chaos of recalcitrant blood and bone.

This, then, was patterning. For legs to run, the brain must send out messages to the far parts of the body. Such messages, for a brain-damaged child, are beyond the brain's power to transmit. So the body languishes inert, in place. Take this elementary principle, stand it on its head, or perhaps more aptly, turn it inside out, and, as so often proves true, it emerges with a new vitality. To force the body of a brain-damaged child to move, as if the brain had, after all, delivered its running instructions all the way down to the distant toes, will, in effect, by triggering the relay of answering messages that the body is obeying and is now in full sprint, strengthen the brain, instill it with confidence, goad it to make new and ultimately successful attempts at communication. Grandiose and maniacal, really. Nothing if not elegant. Why must what we call thought originate always at the same fixed point along the circuit? Electricity was discovered when it set frog legs twitching. Well, why not twitch the legs mechanically and start electricity flowing?

If Jasper was not vigilant, if he let his thoughts stray, even fractionally, Sloan's entire body slid close to the edge of the table. Merriweather had advised Jasper to think of other things. Perhaps with experience that became possible. For now he needed to concentrate on the coordination involved, on keeping his balance, not letting his grip slide. Sloan's limbs were perspiring and seemed to be growing heavier. The instrument ticking off the passing time, Jasper could swear, was erratic. Intervals between what the instrument arbitrarily pronounced as the grid of reality (for what if Gayle Glintz had caught her breath before launching the metronome, then that which was now audible and thus positive would have instead been silent, an interval merely, negative, a split-second arbitrary accident of timing interchanging substance and absence) were of different length, unpredictably, like waves that appeared regular until you waded into them and found yourself struggling against a hidden undertow. Jasper also fancied that Sloan's voice was controlling time, distending it now, compressing it alternately. The quantity of pain expressed was not constant, there were long, dreadful stretches when no note of celebration mingled in the boy's agonizing cries. Were the others listening as intently, or trying not to listen? Jasper dared to glance across at Murray. Beneath his moustache the lips were moving. 'She loves me, she loves me not.' On the table Sloan's face pitched back and forth, side to side, features in a snarl, eyes racing.

'Hey, not bad,' Merriweather called across Sloan's thrashing body. 'Now's when the going gets rough. The last couple of minutes are a bitch.'

'Keep . . . time,' Gayle Glintz, slightly breathless, spoke curtly. 'Please!'

Jasper did not hear Rhoda enter. What with the clack of the metronome and the eddying sound of Sloan's pain and pleasure, with the muffled percussion of arms and legs returning from orbit to smack down on the flat surface of the table, her arrival was silent. He sensed her presence because the nature of the dance changed subtly. It became more precise.

Gayle Glintz drew one hand away from Sloan's chin and reached out a featherweight arm to stop the metronome. At the deathclick of the instrument, the rest of the team stopped work.

'Thank you.'

'You're sopping wet,' Rhoda said to Jasper.

On the table Sloan shivered like a glob of mercury, his cries and agitation continuing briefly. Merriweather, her face glowing, knelt to straighten the edges of the blanket.

'And you can let go,' Rhoda added, gently.

'I was volunteered,' Jasper told her. For the first time he now saw how his shirt stuck to his body with sweat. Salt stung his eyes.

'Something came up at school,' Rhoda apologized to Gayle Glintz. Jasper didn't see Gayle wink.

Rhoda crouched down and began combing the damp ends of Sloan's hair back from his forehead. Sloan's eyes were closed, he breathed heavily. With a pang Jasper thought of Daniel, his son, the grace with which he ran, how after a race he stood with hands on his hips, bent double, trying to catch his breath.

Gayle Glintz led Jasper to the kitchen. Coffee was set out in a Scotch-plaid thermos on a small, chipped enamel table. There were also platters of home-made cookies cut out in animal shapes with silver pearls and shavings of cherry and chocolate sprinkled on top. Pinned to a cork wallboard Jasper saw a complete patterning roster. It was more intricate than the New England Greyhound bus schedule hanging next to it. Dozens of names, an extraordinary feat of organization. Shift after shift to galvanize Sloan into his rehabilitary marionette frenzy. So many people chipping in to do their bit.

'That kid is beautiful.' Merriweather was primping in a small round mirror above the kitchen sink. 'I wish I had half his guts.'

'Here,' – Gayle Glintz tore off a sheet of paper towelling and handed it to Jasper. When he just stood there with it, she made a gesture to show he should wipe his face. 'You'll be stiff tomorrow,' she warned.

Jasper was grateful for the coffee. Gayle Glintz sat and told him a bit about herself. She was from California. She ran the beauty parlor across the street on the corner. She was also a medium, a graphologist and a sex counselor. 'Not in combination,' she added, 'not necessarily. Can do, though.'

In the other room Jasper could hear, indistinctly, Rhoda telling Sloan a story. Now and then the boy's own voice, indistinguishable phrases, ran together with hers. He pictured their faces close together.

'Are you new to brain-damaged children?' Gayle Glintz asked Jasper, tapping him on the wrist to recall his attention.

After a pause Jasper said, 'Yes.' It seemed the answer to spare him the most explanation. Besides, this had been new. Then Gayle told him she had recently read an article about a young man whose locomotion was impaired by brain damage but who could solve mathematical equations about the size of the universe and the phenomenon of black holes.

'That's all I'd need,' Gayle Glintz crowed, 'a boy genius in the house.'

Rhoda came looking for Jasper, took the last bite of the cookie in his hand, and led him to a small bedroom overlooking the steeple of the Old North Church. Sloan's bed was barred, like a cage. Overhead dangled gay constellations of paper birds and flowers. The mattress itself was wrapped in clear plastic. Folded at its foot, however, was a colorful quilt which Rhoda picked up and shook out to its full size. Jasper had seldom seen anything so instantly lovely. The quilt was made from thousands of postage-stamp-sized scraps of bright cloth stitched into symmetrical, geometrical patterns.

'It's amazing.'

'Luigi made it.'

When Jasper went to say goodbye, Gayle Glintz was already stationed at Sloan's head again, issuing instructions to the following crew that had arrived for Sloan's next patterning session. All the way downstairs, the sound of the metronome followed him.

13

'Tonight you get to strut your stuff, Whiting,' announced Rhoda as she came in from work. 'We're stepping out.'

'Where to?'

'The Gold Mine.'

'So.'

'Luigi wants us to meet his new friends. Or rather Matasapi wants to meet Luigi's friends and we're all he's got.'

'Just us?'

'Murray and Madge, too – desperate situation, desperate measures.'

'Madge?'

'Murray's policewoman. The big blonde who always comes down the stairs singing "Mockingbird Hill".' Rhoda did a stiff-legged, hip-rolling imitation of Madge's walk. 'She's on duty tonight though so Murray'll have to go it alone. Whoa, big fella, I walk in the door and you start tearing your clothes off?'

Jasper had indeed started to wrestle his jersey up over his head. 'That's not it at all.'

'More's the pity.'

'If we're going out, I thought I'd better get ready.'

'We're meeting at the Gold Mine at *one*.'

'Come again?'

'It's early, I know, but Luigi's making allowances for your habits.'

'What about Gayle Glintz?'

'What about her?'

'If Madge can't make it – '

'Okay by me. You ask her.'

'And if she wants to bring Sloan?'

'That's one it might be better to clear with Luigi first.'

'But he's always saying that kid is the only real friend he's got.'

'Yeah, well, Luigi says a lot of things. Sure, ask Sloan. The more the merrier.'

Jasper rang the bell at 4C. Through the peephole Gayle Glintz's wary eye stared him up and down. Then he heard the jangle of the chain lock being fumbled open. Hours later the same sequence would repeat when Luigi's friends were admitted to the Gold Mine – the bell, the stare, the wait, the door unlocked.

As Jasper had foreseen Gayle Glintz was flattered by the invitation to join the party, though when he thought to mention it was a gay bar they were going to, she frowned. What to wear?

'Anything will be fine, I'm sure.'

'Oh no,' Gayle fretted, 'you don't know *them*.'

'Well, Rhoda's promised to dream up something smart for Sloan.'

In the end Gayle Glintz outdid herself, appearing at the appointed hour in a fox stole, two furry pelts with beaded eyes chasing each other head to tail. Her printed silk dress, all eddying blues and emerald greens, fetched up above the knee. Her eyes were enormous, enlarged by shadow that picked up the tints of her dress. To complete her outfit she carried a small clutch bag covered in seed pearls and wore open-toed sandals with criss-cross blue straps and spike heels three inches high. The Bandaids across both heels were gone.

Rhoda circled Gayle admiringly, hugged her and told her she looked fantastic. Rhoda herself was 'dressed' in faded jeans and a black turtleneck jersey, not to forget her battered basketball sneakers with red laces.

To carry Sloan Glintz downstairs to the waiting taxi, Murray and Jasper made a seat by locking their hands. The boy looked like a ventriloquist's dummy. He was aswim in a secondhand tuxedo many sizes too large for him, one Rhoda managed to lay hands on at short notice and had taken in, hastily, with giant safety pins. Bow tie, starched dickie, cummerbund – nothing was missing. Either Sloan was feverish with excitement as well, or Gayle Glintz had daubed his usually sallow, sunken cheeks with rouge. Certainly she had taken great pains with his hair. It lay slicked back, rigid. Murray sported a tweed suit that screamed sale. Pinned to the lapel was a large IUD spiral of iridescent blue plastic. 'Luigi's' – Murray smiled when Jasper admired his ornament – 'New Wave.'

As for Jasper, long before midnight he had started to push the walls apart with yawns. Rhoda made him lie down. When she woke him later, he was mean and grumpy. But he accepted her offer of Dexadrine and then, to her amusement, elbows flying in all directions, he spit-polished his cordovan wing-tips.

To get anywhere close to the Gold Mine they had to circle Faneuil Hall and cut down Devonshire. 'My God,' Gayle Glintz had exclaimed en route after Murray paid her a compliment on her perfume, 'I smell of mothballs, don't I? Oh Jasper, just give Sloan a little push backwards, will you. Otherwise he might slobber down that nice driver's neck.' Finally their cab pulled up in the mouth of a dark alley. Cats' eyes flashed in the headlights.

'Here we go,' Rhoda said and led the others in. They had to pick their way among zinc pails and plastic bags spilling over with squeezed-out orange rinds. 'Watch your step.'

Although it was already past one-thirty, the Gold Mine was virtually deserted. A short stone flight of stairs led down to a checkroom. Beyond a tunnel opened into the club proper. Thick timbers were half-buried in the walls and all along the edges of the ceiling hung identical smudged-glass lanterns. Alcoves of darkness suggested greater depth. And there were many mirrors: the dance floor was surrounded and roofed by jagged, jig-saw mirrors; the long bar was backed by a mirror made up of square smoked panels. Out on the floor a solitary black man, roly-poly, one red ostrich feather skewered in his bleached-blond Afro, gyrated to the music of a weepy ballad. He drifted in and out of shafts of light from spots revolving overhead, red and yellow and blue.

The newcomers attracted as much attention as there was to give. From all corners waiters convened to hold inspection. It took some minutes to open and fix Sloan's wheelchair. There were too many helping hands and not enough light, really, even though someone came up with a high-powered flashlight. The disc jockey himself climbed down from his plexiglass booth to join in the fun.

'T-shirts,' Gayle Glintz whispered to Rhoda loud enough for the world to hear. 'Those poor boys. Look at them, so skinny, like whippets. They'll catch pneumonia.'

Rhoda dropped Matasapi's name and the party was escorted with every show of courtesy to a table right next to the dance floor. As Jasper's eyes grew accustomed to the dark, he began to pick out more and more solitary figures lining the walls on high stools. The music which filled the room pulsed so that the only possible way to listen to someone speak was with your ear an inch and no more from his lips.

Murray soon bounced up to ask Rhoda to dance. He bowed and pulled back her chair. For the first few minutes on the dance floor, Murray was disconsolate. Why was Rhoda teasing him, always retreating, refusing to be held? And worse still, why was she staring constantly at some point in space above his head, a tiny, unchanging smile on her lips. Only after two waiters, taking advantage of the early-morning lull, began to dance in a similar style, did Murray stop taking Rhoda's evasions personally.

Jasper didn't want Rhoda to catch him watching her, but he couldn't take his eyes off her. She was so light on her feet and graceful.

'Good evening, doctor. What a nice surprise.' A man crowded next to Jasper on the edge of his chair. 'Give us an inch. Thorndyke. Four years ago. Remember me?' Helen's nose in the Gold Mine! 'Who's your friend?' Jasper's ex-patient nodded towards Murray, waving his stubby arms above his head now, swiveling his hips in imitation of Rhoda. '*Bona.*' Then with a squeeze of Jasper's knee, Thorndyke was gone. 'Enjoy yourself.'

'Slowly, dear, slowly!' Gayle Glintz was coaxing Sloan to sip a Miner's Delight through a straw. With one hand she steadied a tall glass crowned with foam, pink and yellow. 'He likes to drink,' she told the waiter crouched at Sloan's side, a faun with silky hair and cornflower-blue eyes.

The waiter was holding one of Sloan's hands in his, stroking it with the other, purring at him. 'Oh, he's darling.'

Luigi made his grand entrance at a quarter to three. He was spectacularly dressed in a sheer white jump suit which, as he moved, billowed like a parachute in descent. Bright silk scarves trailed from every pocket. He wore earrings that looked like –

and were – tea bags. His eyes sparkled. In his wake half a dozen camp followers bobbed along.

'Sloan!'

'In seventh heaven,' Gayle Glintz said, prodding Luigi's midriff with a finger, 'thanks to you.'

Extra tables were pushed together to accommodate their party. More couples twitched on the dance floor now, and soloists. Veils of smoke drifted overhead. The laughter that rang out seemed to be of different colors.

'Oh God, I almost forgot. I am dreadful.' With this preface, Luigi introduced Matasapi.

'How do you do?' The much-vaunted Matasapi turned out to be whey-faced, fragile and shy like some small, jittery field animal. Nevertheless he wore a flamboyant crimson shirt of crêpe open in a deep vee across his smooth, sunken chest. The crown of his head, rather bumpy, was bald; the long hairs that grew starting at a latitude just above the top of his large ears rippled down to his shoulders. Almost jet where they sprouted from the skull, they turned white several inches before reaching the tip. Matasapi had thick kinky eyebrows, too, black and white. His lips were full and fleshy. Jasper could not fault the nose, although he found it a trifle bold and assertive in such a face. And when Matasapi shook hands, limply, Jasper was reminded of how Luigi had scorned them as horrors. They were merely rather small and shapeless. Moreover, Matasapi couldn't keep them still. They flew constantly to his neck, to his ears, passed and repassed in front of his face.

'I've heard so much about you,' Matasapi said in a high-pitched gasp, almost breathless. 'I can't thank you enough for coming to meet me.' What arrested anyone meeting Matasapi for the first time, however, were his eyes – their hypnotic no-color. 'Have they been taking good care of you?'

Gayle Glintz went clacking off to dance with Murray. By now he had ditched his jacket and rolled up his sleeves, white shirt sweated through in great circles under his arms. Luigi and Rhoda were also together out on the floor. Others gave them a respectful berth. Jasper found Matasapi at his side. In a sea of noise they sat riding an ever more embarrassing raft of silence. Jasper racked his brain for something to say, anything that wouldn't sound too inane. He stood at the door of his mind hammering with both fists, but it wouldn't open. The music, the din, made it impossible to think. Matasapi sat demurely, bit his cuticles, cracked his knuckles, sighed and sighed again.

'I believe you are a doctor, doctor. So the Lost Explorer's told me.' At last Matasapi began. 'What I'm doing now I realize is in extremely bad taste, unforgiveable really. But, well, frankly, I'm at the end of my rope.' Jasper had to strain to the utmost to hear Matasapi's voice. The walls, the floor, trembled with sound. Luigi, in fact, seemed to have warned Matasapi about Jasper's slight hearing problem, for the photographer enunciated with appalling clarity, lips precise, eyes unwavering. 'I need advice, doctor. You understand?'

Jasper nodded. Matasapi tugged nervously at the silver crucifix he wore on a chain around his neck. Christ, Jasper saw, was nailed to this cross upside down.

'Look, doctor, here. You see this. . . .' In tones of despair Matasapi pointed to a blemish, a tiny reddish mound beneath his lower lip. Voice, hand, eyelashes all fluttered. 'How can I make it go away?'

A shrill cry split the air close at hand – from the pretty waiter, Sloan's new friend. In petting and cooing with Sloan, the boy had leaned his cheek on Sloan's shoulder. Sloan had seized one of the boy's nipples through his T-shirt and given it a vicious wrench.

'He's so happy to be here' – Gayle Glintz rushed back to comfort the victim. Matasapi, forgetful of his own problem, laughed without control. First Sloan glowered at him. Then, he, too, broke out in a kind of glee. 'It shows he likes you,' Gayle Glintz said. The waiter rubbed his chest, smiling dreamily. Then he reached out his hand tentatively to pat Sloan's head.

'Sucking fingers,' Murray said, 'that's what he really likes.'

Murray was enjoying himself too much to sit down. He spoonfed Sloan the ice cubes from his drink, then went off on his own to invent more insect flights to the music.

'No, no, you go ahead. Don't mind about me,' Jasper said each time Rhoda tried to get him up out of his seat.

'Coward,' she teased.

'Coward yourself,' he grinned and leapt onto the floor. He didn't try to follow the music so much at first as splash around in it, loosening up. No one paid him any special attention, which put him at ease. Everywhere he turned smiles flashed, lights dazzled. He opened his mouth, ducked his head, closed his eyes and danced like an African. Rhoda was so close he felt her breath on his face.

As soon as Jasper lowered himself back into his chair, Matasapi turned to Luigi next to him and started whispering, eyes on Jasper, a frown like a crack across the photographer's eggshell forehead.

'Jazz,' Luigi came over to say, 'I hate to be a bother like this, but do you think maybe just this once you could help?' His voice was syrupy. What was he on? From across the table Matasapi sat looking at them expectantly, one curled pinkie pointing at his accursed spot. 'Be a pal.'

'Could it be something I've eaten, doctor, do you think?' Matasapi had leaned forward, his chin at the edge of a puddle of wine. 'Or an allergy to my scent?' To make himself heard, he was practically shouting. 'I mean that's what my skin specialist's trying to sell me. He's supposed to be the best. Everyone says so, but, honestly, the man's a complete and utter fraud.' Jasper attempted to take it all seriously. He lowered his chin to table level too, his reddish-blonde hair on end, unruly and skew, surrounding his features like copper wool. 'I don't get these things often,' Matasapi went on, 'or I'd kill myself. If you knew what it's cost me to find this scent.'

'I know, I know.'

'Not the money, Christ, but the *trouble*. The money *and* the trouble. Moon Madness. And now I'll go and turn out to be allergic.'

'We say' – Murray stood beside Jasper, mopping his face and neck with a handkerchief – 'that's what happens to someone who's greedy.'

'Oh?' Matasapi was all ears.

'A man who, when someone asks him for something, denies it.'

'We?'

'My family.' Murray stared into his handkerchief as if he could shake it and scenes from his childhood would tumble onto the floor.

'But, honestly, I never deny anybody anything. Not if I can help it.'

'I hear what you say,' – Murray put his finger on Matasapi's blemish and pushed it like an elevator button – 'but I also see the evidence.'

'Is there anything I can do?' Matasapi asked cheerfully. 'Or am I cursed with it for good?'

'The cure is simple. Give something without anybody's asking for it.'

Matasapi was delighted. His eyes seemed to flap wings. 'That's marvelous. That's just the kind of witchery that works.' He dumped the contents of his purse onto the table. Rings, a tweezer, pills and capsules, half-a-dozen colors and sizes, keys. 'Anything's better than monkeying around with more steroids. Maybe, oh, maybe I won't have to give up Moon Madness. Coke, anyone?' Luigi confiscated the twists of paper Matasapi held out on his palm, and slipped them into a pocket which he zipped closed. 'The thing is, it's so difficult to know what people really want.'

'In public it doesn't work,' Murray continued. He ran his damp handkerchief across Sloan's forehead. The boy rolled his eyes. 'The person receiving mustn't know who the giver is.'

Matasapi squealed and hugged Rhoda who happened at the time to be the person closest to him.

'And there's always plastic surgery to fall back on,' Matasapi said coyly and grew thoughtful. 'How lucky you are, doctor, to help so many suffering people.'

'It was the surprise. It didn't really hurt *that* much.' The injured waiter brought Sloan a new multi-colored concoction bristling with slices of orange and pineapple. 'So what if he's a little more brain-damaged than the rest of us? He has the future on his side.'

By four the club was packed. People of all descriptions, a mingling of costumes and accents. The music if anything grew more hectic and abrasive.

'Watch Sloan, doctor,' – Gayle Glintz tugged at Jasper's arm. 'See what he's doing? That's his imitation of you dancing.'

'Hello, excuse me.' The speaker was a waiter so frail his T-shirt hung from his rib cage like a flag on a breezeless day. 'I have a telegram for a Mr Luigi Sasakawa?' He bent forward stiffly at the waist and held out a silver tray with a yellow envelope.

'That's him there.'

'You want me?'

'Telegram, sir.'

'At this time of night?' Luigi looked worried. 'I haven't got anybody left who could die.' Uneasy laughter rose from the surrounding tables. Luigi took the envelope from the tray, held it up to a spot as the light changed color. Jasper was struck anew by the beauty of Luigi's hands and wrists, the speed and accuracy of his fingers. 'Here, you read it.' Luigi slit the telegram open with a fork and thrust it into Matasapi's protesting hands. 'I didn't bring my glasses.' Matasapi unfolded the telegram and began to read when Luigi interrupted him. 'We know the address, darling. Get to the message.'

When Matasapi read aloud, he formed each word with his lips before speaking it. ' "Congratulations Metropolitan cover. Stop. Can't wait for Interview. Stop".'

'How lovely.' Gayle Glintz leaned forward. The head of one of her foxes nearly flopped into a wine glass. 'Who sent it?'

' "Best wishes for continued success you so richly deserve," ' Matasapi concluded, accelerating. ' "Luigi Sasakawa." Oooooh,' the photographer gasped as he fell back in his chair. He fanned himself with the telegram. 'The Lost Explorer. Too divine.'

'Who sent it?' Gayle asked again.

'What an inspiration!' Matasapi found the prank delicious. 'Me, too. I want to send one now, to myself. All my life I have hated and feared telegrams. I can't begin to tell you how many I've disposed of unopened. But what can I say?' Matasapi wailed for help. The lanky waiter returned with pad and pen and Matasapi sat there looking down desperately at the blank page. 'Con-grat-u-lations,' he wrote in large letters and then pulled up short.

'Go on,' Rhoda coaxed, 'Think of something you've always wanted to do but never dared. It doesn't have to be real.'

'Ooooh.' Matasapi stared at Rhoda with true admiration. Under the table Jasper pressed his thigh against hers. Matasapi rinsed his mouth with wine and began pulling at his blemish, but nothing seemed to advance him further.

'Congratulations,' Rhoda said, 'on the success of your. . . .'

'No,' Matasapi interrupted vigorously. He crumpled the top sheet of the pad and sent it flying. 'I want to keep it simple and to the point. Hmmm. Best wishes for a happy love affair. How's that?'

'Make it a singing telegram,' Jasper suggested, 'more romantic.'

'Oh, yes, yes.' Matasapi clapped his hands.

Gayle Glintz, who had been feeling no pain now for some time, sent out a long arm and tugged Luigi's telegram from Jasper's fingers. Murray, asked to dance by a thick-set man in a red sequin gown, accepted with gallantry.

'I'm terribly sorry, sir' – the waiter was back in no time – 'a singing telegram won't be possible again until nine a.m.'

'I knew it was too good to be true.'

'You mean Luigi sent this *to himself*?' Gayle Glintz asked, persevering in her private time warp. She capsized with laughter. Sloan's eyes flew back and forth at her in alarm.

'Not bad.' Rhoda called Jasper's attention to the dance floor. Murray's partner, for all his bulk, danced very expressively, waving fans in both hands. His gown was split so far up the thigh that now and then a glimpse of lace garter appeared.

'Blood,' Matasapi gasped, holding up the finger he'd found guilty of picking at his face, 'my blood.' He rose and disappeared through the tables of the club without another word, reeling away as if ice floes were breaking up beneath his feet.

'Cancel.' Luigi tipped the waiter. He threw an arm around the boy's slim hips, snapped his finger at the tiny teddy bear hanging there from a chain.

'Cancel,' Jasper sang, 'cancel, cancel, cancel.'

Jasper's bladder had reached the bursting point. All night he'd noticed a trickle of men disappearing through an arch on the far side of the disc jockey's booth. A trifle wobbly, he made his way in that direction. Down two steps, ducking his head, he pushed past a heavy curtain and found himself in a small cavern. The air was rank with the stench of sweat and sex. The hole was dimly lit by a single bulb set in a niche behind red-stained glass. He tried to advance and collided with someone kneeling.

'Sorry,' Jasper said. His voice fell like a stone in water that sent out no ripples. He pivoted sideways and moved forward, one arm stretched in front of him feeling his way through the darkness, still expecting to find the facilities he needed. As his eyes adjusted, however, he found himself surrounded by naked and half-naked couples clutching each other, gasping. From one corner there came a steady, low moan of contentment. Behind him he heard a loud smack, like meat on a butcher's slab. Fingers grabbed Jasper's ass, cupped his crotch. He backed away and found himself in a group collected around one of the club's young waiters, clothes down at his ankles, hands above his head shackled to the wall. Different men were kissing, biting the body.

Somewhere else in the shadows a man was crying quietly. 'Shh, shh, shh,' Jasper heard a gruff voice offer comfort but the tears continued.

A small bottle was thrust under Jasper's nose and he breathed in without wanting to. Suddenly his head was detached and spinning away, his heart raced and the space inside him doubled and tripled. His body grew hot, enormous – he had to push someone from his lips and lurch free from a pair of hips grinding backwards into his groin.

'There's Jasper,' Luigi said as Jasper returned to the table. 'Now all we have to do is find Matasapi. Rhoda had us believing the two of you had slipped off together. Not true, I told her. Where have you been? Oh, don't tell me – I can see it from your face.' Luigi kissed Jasper's cheek.

'I didn't see Matasapi,' Jasper said.

'In the back room? Are you kidding? He faints at the mention of herpes. AIDS on the other hand has helped him save face.'

'How?'

'Everyone's swearing off sex.'

The contents of the photographer's purse still lay spilled on the table. No one could remember seeing him since he barged off with blood on his finger.

'It's just like him,' Luigi began to sound frantic. He had been ignoring Matasapi and flirting with everyone. Now he suffered a twinge of conscience. 'I'll have to listen for days about how I was so rude and inattentive. Days? Weeks. He's worse than a baby when it comes. . . .'

All at once the music died. Extra lights flashed on, rapid-fire strobes. The bobbing and grinding on the dance floor ceased. From out back, among the swinging kitchen doors, a candle-light procession of waiters entered. Single file they wove their flickering way through the congested tables. Last man in line carried a gleaming cake high in the air, frosted white and studded with a galaxy of sputtering small candles. Closer and closer they came. The hush in the Gold Mine filled gradually with chatter and whistles and hoots and applause and laughter, until finally the cake was set down in front of Sloan Glintz. Inarticulate with joy, he left no one in doubt about his transport. Sloan's tuxedo was already wet from drinks, his bow tie coming undone, his hair in funny peaks. He was radiant with wonder. Gayle Glintz laid her cheek against his, interlaced her fingers with his straining hands. Together – one, two three – they did their best to blow out all the candles in one breath.

'Guess who sent it?' Matasapi's smooth head and matchless eyes poked up between Luigi, Rhoda and Jasper where they sat stupefied. A neat circle of moleskin capped his blemish.

14

'Any bum can go to bed late,' Rhoda Massler told her first class, 'but it takes a real man to get up in the morning.' Only a short while ago she'd whispered the same thing to Jasper. 'Right,' he said, before turning over and going back to sleep.

'And once he's up' – Rhoda smiled, leaning on her desk for support – 'God help him.' Fun at the Gold Mine had dragged on past dawn. She would, she knew, have to pay all day for the late night.

Rhoda was in fact searching in her bag for a little help when there was a knock at the door and in walked Marcus Featherstone, the director. 'Morning, Mrs Massler.' There were guests – one, two, three – on his heels, women, white-haired sisters in style and preoccupation. 'I hope we're not intruding.'

'Not at all.' Rhoda turned flustered and cowlike. 'Come in, come in.' She began to thumb backwards and forwards in her teacher's plan book. 'Oh dear.' Featherstone was trying not to scowl. The guests edged closer to each other and smiled weakly. 'Yes, yes, I knew you'd be coming,' Rhoda fretted. 'I've known about it for weeks, yes, weeks and weeks. How. . .' It really was sickening how she carried on! Like that first time with Jasper and the mailboxes! 'We've been looking forward to your visit, but, well, somehow' – Rhoda blushed – 'you've caught us unprepared.'

Such visits used to mean something. There was a time when the survival of the school might depend on how much the Ladies' Auxiliary of God-Fuck-It could be persuaded to cough up. Now hardly a day went by without Featherstone's traipsing in with a prime collection of his blue-blood cronies. Getting the kids to concentrate, some of them, was hard enough as it was without his constant interruptions. And it wasn't as if anyone was about to give them anything any more. The school was supposed to be totally self-supporting. Ha! So now when the ladies came, they came out of prurience and curiosity – like sneaking into a sideshow or zoo. Okay, fair enough. A lot of people didn't know what to do with themselves. Maybe there were worse things to be into than chronic good deeds.

'Hole in the bucket' – Rhoda tapped her skull – 'sorry. Well, you're here now, aren't you. Yes, yes, you certainly are. Kids – kids, these kind people have come all the way downtown this morning to visit us. Let's make them welcome.' Rhoda spoke with her hands while she talked. Most in this class were deaf mutes.

'You'd like to get some idea what goes on in our classroom, right? That's why you've come, I take it?' The ladies nodded as one. 'What if we just carry on then – as if you weren't here? As if you were' – Rhoda paused for effect – 'invisible.

'How does that sound to you? Good?' Four of the older children carried chairs up to the front of the room. 'Oh careful – don't lean back. That one's a bit rickety, I'm afraid.'

Rhoda kept up her breathless and baffled number to perfection. She didn't dare look the kids in the eye. Any form of deceit, as long as they were in on it, the little fuckers ate it up.

She, too. 'When you came in, we were just about to make a little music together.'

'Ah, indeed, music? How interesting. With *these* children?'

'Go ahead, go right ahead.'

'Do, please.'

Rhoda clapped and pointed to the supply cabinet and a couple of the kids took out and rigged up a battered old film projector. They did so with a lot of well-oiled confusion. The school had a much better one, true, but Rhoda didn't waste it on visitors. This relic came from an auction. She'd paid $1.50 for it and Luigi had made the necessary repairs.

At another signal someone killed the lights and suddenly, hey, there was Toscanini himself with his back up against the brick wall. Toscanini, none other, conducting some crack symphony orchestra.

'Philadelphia,' one of the guests whispered.

The picture crackled and flickered. There was no sound track. Just old Toscanini, Il Maestro, gyrating away – the wild cloud of hair, the arms, the mouth. The noble ladies watched the wall, puzzled. The kids watched the ladies. Rhoda swallowed a pill. Featherstone's staying made her nervous. How far should she let things go?

When the film ended with a great synchronized sawing of bows and close-ups of kettle drums and tympani, Rhoda snapped the lights on. Two of the kids began passing out musical instruments. The school had boxes and boxes of all kinds of junk Rhoda had collected down through the years. Cast-offs and hand-me-downs. Trumpets without valves, torn drums, triangles, sand blocks, you name it. Washboards and thimbles and castanets. Old rubber bike horns. Then the class pushed their chairs into half-circular rows, like an orchestra.

Angel, a rather sour-faced boy with an insolent walk and soft blond curls, came to offer the visitors their choice of instruments, too. Things that made really obscene noises.

'No, thank you, dear,' was the usual response. Every once in a while though there was a live one. A good sport who was going to participate if it killed her.

'Oh, a kazoo.' The lady with her Phi Beta Kappa key in prominent view was one of the dangerous ones. 'I don't know if I still can.' You had to watch them. They wrote reports.

The class made short work of selecting a Toscanini. Anselmo got the nod, St Anselmo, named after a saint of the twelfth century who prayed to God to strike him deaf because there was so much profanity in the world. Anselmo showed symptoms of the Weerenberg syndrome. One out of every thousand deaf and dumb has a pug nose and a streak of white hair running straight back from the middle of the forehead. And above average intelligence. Anselmo, smart as a whip, was tall and graceful. He had star quality.

Rhoda took a baton off her desk and handed it to Anselmo. He mussed his hair, practiced a few highly sensitive facial expressions and stepped up onto a box in front of the class right where Toscanini would have stood. Surreptitiously Rhoda dug a pair of dirty, flesh-colored balls of wax out of her pocket and sealed her ears. Then the fun started.

Anselmo tapped his baton, a one, a two, a three, and all hell broke loose. Anything that made noise, the kids loved it. The more the better. As an orchestra they produced the next best thing to white sound. The poor ladies, bless them, didn't know where to look, what to do. They were dying to stick their fingers in their ears, but that wasn't very ladylike. They might so easily offend somebody's feelings that way. What a performance the orchestra put on! Anselmo conducting like one of the all-time greats. Now you, now you – ah, shhh! shh! *Fortissimo!* The visitor slavering over her tin kazoo played right along with the rest of them.

Rhoda waited for the climax, one eye on Featherstone. He just stood there back against the door the whole time, a look of high moronic serenity plastered all over his face. Smug as a —. Of course he knew what was going to happen. Of course by now someone had let him in on the secret of Rhoda's little orchestra. She wouldn't put it past him to have paid informers in her classes.

The ladies were at the breaking point. What was Anselmo waiting for? Had he let himself be carried away by the music? Ah, there it was, the arabesque with his baton, the signal. In the back row of the orchestra, the kids started screaming, 'Rat. R-a-t.' More and more dropped their instruments and knocked over their chairs – some to get away, some to chase the rat. A rat which didn't exist. Never had. They did it beautifully though – so convincingly. 'Rat! Rat!' Lovely.

Rhoda was screaming, too. Did it show, how much she was enjoying herself? Maybe she should have played safe? There were alternative numbers to do. An hour of Zen guaranteed to paralyse any visitor with boredom. And they were working up a history lesson where the kids acted out charades, weird, obscene things. No one in his right mind could possibly guess what they were supposed to be. Oh when they ironed out a few kinks, Charades was going to be sensational. Anselmo was devastating as a comic.

Yet today Rhoda had gone with Orchestra. Her eyes narrowed, her lips drew in slightly with determination. 'Rat, rat.' There had been a lot of aggression building lately. Too much. Something in the air. Hostility, fear. And the kids felt it. Featherstone or not, she figured they had a little release coming to them.

'Then something brushed my leg. Christ,' Rhoda giggled when she told Jasper the story that evening, 'there *were* rats. Fucking hell, three of them. Right on cue, too. Horrible, furry monsters, big, black mothers. You should have seen the Ladies' Auxiliary. Horror isn't the word. Those women were too scared to faint. If you ask me, Toscanini, Anselmo, smuggled them in. He'd be up to it. Then one of the kids, Angel, maybe, let them loose in the back row. And then they chased them – and how.' They chased them until they had them cornered and then using the chairs and the instruments they clobbered the rats to death. 'Blood all over the place.'

'How did Featherstone take it?' Jasper asked.

'He was not amused,' Rhoda snorted and turned worried.

'He's out to get me. Does that sound crazy to you? I built that school out of nothing. And now, I could see it on his face today, in his eyes, he's made up his mind. He wants me out.'

15

When the next week Rhoda received a substantial hike in salary, this fact did nothing to allay her anxieties. It only confirmed her in the certainty that Marcus Featherstone was the enemy.

'He *caught* – need I say the word is his – two of the kids feeling each other up in the john. Good, right? Just what we've been working for. What does the clown go and do? He has locks put on the doors to the loo. Now to take a crap the kids have to ask for a key and carry a signed pass. I'm telling you, it's science fiction.'

Soon afterwards Jasper Whiting turned up at the New England School for Special Children near the end of the school day. For a long time Rhoda had been urging him to come. She especially wanted him to meet Anselmo. Rhoda met Jasper down in the entrance hallway and led him at once all the way up to the attic of the former brewery. Extra-curricular training in martial arts was offered here. Various techniques of self-defence. Padded mats covered the floor, wall to wall. An assortment of odd-shaped mirrors stood leaning against white-washed brick walls. Rhoda had recently introduced these sessions, an idea in one of Alex Thane's letters. Overnight they had become enormously popular.

Near the windows fronting on Mount Pleasant Street, an instructor dressed in a loose-fitting quilted white jacket and trousers stood in a pose that reminded Jasper of the Appeal to the Great Spirit. Disabled children were scattered on the mats in bright odds and ends of training suits. The air was electric with their concentration. Over and over again they repeated the instructor's moves. They did their best.

A slow backward motion of the extended arm ended in a lightning-fast reversal and snap of the wrist. The instructor's easy animal grace impressed Jasper; his ironic wisp of a smile unsettled him. These weren't innocent small children, abashed, retiring. Not the Saturday swim crowd. No, they were large and they were angry, with bunched muscles and long hair. Face to face with an enemy, they wouldn't flinch to inflict damage. *And* these were creatures bursting with sexuality.

'What's going on here?' All eyes turned to the head of the attic stairs. The man who stood there, the distinguished grey hair, could only be Marcus Featherstone. Jasper liked him at once. 'I thought we had *agreed*' – Featherstone, slightly breathless, addressed himself primarily to the instructor – 'there were more useful ways to keep busy.'

However Jasper tried to turn away from the scene, he saw it repeated in the salvaged mirrors. 'That at least was my understanding.' The instructor, bowing and scraping, was the first to leave the room.

'No more after today. And I mean it,' Featherstone said to Rhoda and walked out, shaking his head. The man's habit of authority was apparent. Still Jasper could see what Rhoda meant, that the face was perfect for play money.

Rhoda smiled gamely at the kids while they packed their gear. Jasper stared down out of one of the open windows. The drop made him dizzy.

'That prick,' Rhoda said after everyone had gone, 'who does he think he is?'

Jasper had mixed feelings. Foolishly, he said so.

'What, you, too?'

'If you want to know the truth, from the little I saw, I found it horrifying.'

'Jesus.'

'I wanted to stop it myself.'

'But it's very important,' Rhoda tried to explain, wearily. 'How else can we make those kids believe that they're not helpless? All of us, we're so, what's the word, lazy about looking after ourselves. Just look at your body.'

Rhoda had a point.

'Complacent, not just lazy. We're all so fucking complacent. Well, you'd be surprised how much it means to these kids to hit back. Hit, kick, scratch, bite – it makes such a big difference for them to know they can hurt someone.'

'Great.'

'Why not? They like that.'

'They do,' Jasper said. 'I don't.'

'Goodnight, Rhoda,' Featherstone left the building just as they did. Jasper admired how graciously he defused an awkward situation.

'Dr Whiting, Mr Featherstone, our esteemed director.'

The men shook hands.

'Rhoda's been giving you a look around, has she?'

'It's quite a place.'

'We're coming along. Can I give you a lift somewhere?'

While they stood waiting for the tram, Jasper broke the silence. 'Featherstone surprised me, pleasantly.'

'Oh, really? He thinks they're *ungrateful*. Can you beat that?'

'I've heard you say the same thing.'

Instead of bristling, Rhoda gave way to amusement. 'That Anselmo though, he's sharp. He's sharp as tacks. He's got Featherstone eating out of his hand. You have to see it to believe it. He's *so* thankful, *so* appreciative, *so* humble. The two of them together, it's priceless.'

'Which one was Anselmo?'

Rhoda chuckled, 'You *are* blind. He was the instructor.'

16

'Oh, Rhoda, there you are.'

With the door to his office open, Featherstone had been watching the corridor.

'If you have a minute.'

Rhoda followed him into his office. She was very late. On the way to work she had stopped in Haymarket Square to recruit a new student. A spina bifida. The child's mother, startled at first, had agreed to bring her son around soon. Featherstone, Rhoda knew, wished to put a stop to such practices.

'I know you'll want to start class as soon as possible.'

Rhoda expected a reprimand, dressed up as a friendly reminder. Or perhaps this time curt and cutting. Wrong as she was, it still wasn't going to be easy to get the word *sorry* past her lips. Yet today Marcus Featherstone had other aces up his pin-striped sleeve. From behind his magnificent, out-of-place rosewood desk, he gestured grandly for Rhoda to make herself comfortable in one of the antique armchairs he had also brought with him. And then he introduced her to the elegant woman seated in the other one. 'Mrs Massler, Mrs Benedict-Vincent.'

At the sound of her name, the woman leaned forward. Until then Rhoda hadn't in all honesty noticed her.

'How do you do?' The angular woman in expensive clothes

flashed an overkill smile. Her out-of-size eyeglasses were humorless. 'I'm Susan's mother.' Legs crossed, one pointed pump dangling from arched toes, Mrs Benedict-Vincent projected total self-control, and nearly as much self-satisfaction. 'I've heard so much about you, and your work.'

'We've met before,' Rhoda said to Featherstone. 'Once. The day Mrs Benedict-Vincent *dropped* Susan at school. I was there to pick her up.'

'That was a traumatic moment, I dare say, but. . . .' Mrs Benedict-Vincent lifted her glasses and squinted at Rhoda. 'Yes, I remember now, I think. You were so warm, so reassuring.'

'Must've been something I ate.'

Marcus Featherstone laughed good-naturedly. He offered cigarettes, which were refused. He offered mints next. Both women accepted.

'Rather like a choice of weapons, isn't it,' Mrs Benedict-Vincent observed.

Featherstone cleared his throat, a signal the preliminaries were over. 'You certainly don't need me to tell you, Mrs Massler, that Mrs Benedict-Vincent here is one of New England's nationally celebrated authors.'

'Well I'll be. . . .' said Rhoda with a straight face. There was no protest, no false modesty forthcoming from the tawny Mrs Benedict-Vincent. In fact, her toes wiggled.

'Historical romances,' Featherstone went on, 'authentic sources. Correct me if I'm wrong.'

'My kind of thing is an acquired taste,' Mrs Benedict-Vincent said self-deprecatingly, 'so I've been told.'

'And now, fortunately for us all, Mrs Benedict-Vincent is planning to do a book about Susan.'

So that explained Susan's last-minute reprieve from her 'extended vacation'!

'It will be something of a departure for me.'

'Oh?' Rhoda said. 'No authentic sources this time?'

'In connection with her project, Mrs Benedict-Vincent would like to interview you.'

'Interview?' Mrs Benedict-Vincent demonstrated the extreme care she took with language. 'Interview is such a loaded term, isn't it? What I would like, very much, is for us to have a chance to chat.'

'And she is hoping, unless, of course, you should have any objection, to sit in on your classes.'

'Just a fly on the wall,' Mrs Benedict-Vincent whispered.

They made quite a team, Rhoda couldn't help thinking, the self-winding director and his hot-chicken-shit lady friend.

'This book, the one you want to *do* – what's it for?' Rhoda was walking into a trap, she was dead sure of it, but there seemed no honorable way out. Even as slightly as Featherstone knew her, he must have known better. To bring Rhoda and Mrs Benedict-Vincent together, however briefly, was like striking a match in a room full of ether. 'You're famous already, so it must be to add to your fame, is that it?'

'You see' – for an apologetic instant Mrs Benedict-Vincent looked at Marcus Featherstone before turning the full force of her attention on Rhoda. Presumably Featherstone himself had just sat through the same story, word for word. Munching a mint, he smiled. 'You see, Mrs Massler, we feel we owe Susan a great deal, my husband and I. She has taught us such a lot – about ourselves. Most people only know about the dark side of living with a special child – I'm sure you'd be the first to agree.' Mrs Benedict-Vincent paused. She looked down at her dangling shoe, she tugged the hem of her dress over her knee and caressed the knee cap. She waited until it was clear to all that Rhoda chose to pass up the golden opportunity to agree. 'Well, there's a bright side as well, a brighter side than people suspect.'

'I see, you're out to open people's minds.' Rhoda took the plunge. 'You're a very exceptional woman, Mrs Benedict-Vincent.'

'Cinder – please, call me Cinder.'

'Exceptional and brave, really.'

'Oh, no, I wouldn't say that – not exactly.' Even Featherstone, the seasoned ex-politician, blanched at that.

'No, no, really. With all praise where praise is due, other people with your problems would have thrown in the sponge a long time ago. But you, instead of giving up, instead of feeling sorry for yourself, you – you want to cash in on it.'

At this point Marcus Featherstone waded in, delaying the inevitable. 'Suppose you tell Mrs Massler a bit more about the book. I'm sure anything you can tell us will help . . . clear the air.'

'Yes, of course. This book, I should tell you, has been on my mind for some time now. I've discussed it with my publishers on a number of separate occasions. Well, as you are well aware, we're living in the International Year of the Disabled,' Mrs Benedict-Vincent's voice ran rapid now, a voice that licked itself off, 'what better time to realize this long-standing ambition of mine?' The tip of her tongue flicked across her frosted lips.

'Susan isn't our only child, Mrs Massler. She is simply the only *special* child we have. Perhaps the story of what we have all lived through together as a family can be of help to others.'

Rhoda made no effort to conceal her doubts.

'Susan thinks it's a terrific idea.' Mrs Benedict-Vincent, Cinder, brought this claim forward as a trump.

'Mrs Benedict-Vincent would like to sit in on classes for. . . .'

'Oh, just a few days. That should be more than sufficient. All I want' – voice meek, a conspirator's whisper, nose wrinkling – 'is a *taste* of what it's like.'

'When were you thinking of beginning?' the director asked.

'No,' Rhoda said and stood up. 'Out of the question.'

'But it's going to be a good book.' Mrs Benedict-Vincent sat forward, brought to new life by the pleasure of open confrontation. 'It was, you see, thanks to Susan that my husband and I first realized there was something wrong with *our* lives. Rhoda. . . .' When Rhoda did not object to the use of her first name, Mrs Benedict-Vincent's confidence increased. 'Will you find it strange when I tell you that I can still remember everything – where the car was parked, what I was wearing, how the light was shining through the trees – every last detail of the instant when I realized that Susan's death wouldn't solve all our problems?'

What Rhoda shouted on the spot remained hazy to her afterwards. Something about the kind of people that make calls on the handicapped baby hotline. She had little doubt, however, that her behavior, the scene she threw, would cost her her job.

'Tell me, do you still threaten her with matches to get her to do what you want? Do you force alcohol down her throat so she'll go to sleep and not be such a bother? Is there going to be a special chapter in your book about how you humiliated her, how you intimidated her in front of company, how you cursed God the day she was born?' Marcus Featherstone looked like he was going to protest. Mrs Benedict-Vincent raised her hand to silence him.

'Perhaps,' she said, levelly, to Rhoda.

'You know it's taken me the better part of a year, a whole fucking year to convince Susan her mother isn't a monster. If only we'd had this *chat* sooner, I could have saved a lot of trouble.'

'I'm sorry you feel that way.' Mrs Benedict-Vincent reached down and slipped her shoe firmly onto her foot. Her diction, her admirable restraint, convinced Rhoda that a chapter in the book – and Rhoda had no illusions about her being able to prevent the book's being written, nor about its runaway success – would 'deal' with the present encounter.

'This book of yours will be an obscenity,' Rhoda had called from the door, 'and I'll not be a party to it.'

Jasper was a victim of Rhoda's mood when he came home that night.

'Work?' he asked.

Rhoda nodded.

'Something wrong?'

'I'm not going back there ever.' Her face showed an intensity of loathing that made Jasper's heart contract. She glared at him, daring him to contradict her. 'I'm through. There *are* limits.' He put one arm around her and she leaned against him heavily. 'Why do I make it so easy for them?'

Jasper slipped off Rhoda's shoes and massaged her feet. He wanted to take things nice and slow. Lately their sex had turned into something of a spending spree on stolen credit cards. He was running his hands further up Rhoda's legs, when Luigi walked in.

'Rhoda, I'd like you to meet *Benjamin Ficus*.' He had a new plant for Rhoda.

'Thank you.'

'Thank you. Is that all I get?' Luigi pulled a long face. 'That's the last time I procure for you. Hey, Jasper, what do you call a paraplegic in a swimming pool?'

'Robert.' Jasper put his hands over his face. 'Bob.'

'Why am I always the last to know? Jesus, Rhoda, what's with you?'

'Rhoda's through with her job,' Jasper tried to explain.

'I never said that!' she flared up. 'Never!'

Luigi's eyebrows rose. 'Well, are congratulations in order or aren't they?'

'If only I could learn to take a little distance,' Rhoda whined.

'Hmm, I think I know this number.' Luigi did a hip-wagging Latin American dance step that set them off laughing. 'Yes, and no. Yes and no. Yes, no, exactly.'

Rhoda was pleased with her new plant. To make room for it, she pushed some others aside on the sill. Getting acquainted, she tamped the earth down with her fingers, blew at the leaves. 'Featherstone knows just how to get at me, I shouldn't let him.'

Luigi gave them an account of his first skirmishes in the inner sanctum of New England high fashion. 'The long and the short of it is I may need someone soon for crowd control. The competition will be brutal, but who's to say, Rhoda, the right word in the right place and. . . .'

'Goddamn, I need those kids,' Rhoda burst out. 'That's

right, you heard me. Just don't sit there like idiots with your mouths hanging open. *I* need them.'

'Talking of idiots,' said Luigi behind one hand to the plants.

'The only time I feel alive is when I'm with those kids. Who knows why? But it's the one thing I can do – without getting sick of myself.'

'What happened exactly?' Jasper ventured. 'How did it end? Did you quit?'

'I don't know.'

'How can you not know a thing like that?'

Rhoda shook her head, raised her hands in a gesture of confusion.

'Did he fire you?'

'I'd like to see him try!'

'What are you worried about then?'

'Come on, even I've got some self-respect.'

'Drop out now' – Luigi made a sign, thumbs down – 'and see what happens to that place.'

'No one will notice. The kids'll get along fine.' Rhoda put a hand to her head. 'Only me, I'm the one who'll come apart.'

17

By leaning forward and moving his forearms like windshield wipers, Luigi cleared a small area on Rhoda's trestle table. He set up a standing mirror, round, with magnifying properties. 'Hey, Jasper, push that thing so it won't shine right in the mirror. More. More, that's it.'

Saturday brought drizzle. The sky looked smudged. Rhoda

was off at Spinedale Pool. Jasper kept trying to talk about her. Luigi wanted to talk about himself instead.

'This face and body,' Luigi said, 'you do realize, are about to become household words.'

Stripped to the waist, Luigi was luminous with youth. In front of him he arranged an assortment of make-up kits. They looked like so many children's watercolor sets, buttons of color. Mixing bases and blushers, he tried on face after face.

'What I mind most of all,' Jasper said, 'is that Rhoda's not objective.'

'Objective?'

Jasper had begun to notice how people looked at the disabled. Hostile, contemptuous glances. How in conversations with the handicapped their voices changed. It wasn't easy, a strain in fact, to undo a lifetime of learning not to notice. To look and not see. And yet Jasper challenged the accuracy of his new discoveries. He trapped himself more and more often looking at the world through Rhoda's eyes.

'What's up, doc? Why all the concern? You know you're no good at it.'

'I'm not really that *concerned*.'

'Stick to smuggling chickens in the dead of night.'

Jasper smiled. He lay on his stomach at the foot of Rhoda's bed, chin on a pillow. He held another pillow between his ankles, kicking himself with it in the rear end. For Rhoda, he knew, people were split into two embattled camps. Under the surface, concealed beneath the petty give-and-take of daily life, hatred, real and palpable, divided the Whole from the Impaired. When he tried to voice his misgivings and doubts, he met with hostility.

'People are people,' Jasper would say.

'Whether they can walk or crawl or feed themselves? There are differences, for God's sake,' was Rhoda's reply. 'Surely even you can see that.'

'Why force a group identification on them they don't feel?'

'Force *schmorce*. It's there. If you'd only open your eyes and ears for a change, you'd know that's the way the world works.'

'If that's the kind of thing you're teaching those kids, you'll only end up making things harder for them, believe me.'

'Believe you, shit.'

'And harder for yourself.'

'What do you propose to do about hate then? Ignore it, and expect it to go away by itself?'

'Us and Them – that's the way it is?'

'That's the way.'

'All right then, suppose you tell me this. We don't all just drop dead, do we? We're not all so lucky. Most of us, we come apart slowly. We decay. And along the way we cross one boundary right after another. We go downhill. What about aging then? What's that – No Man's Land? With some the teeth go first, or the legs, with others it's the eyes. . . .'

'Or,' Rhoda snapped, 'the will.'

'I just think maybe under pressure Rhoda's lost her ability to keep things in proper perspective.' It was a relief for Jasper to be airing his thoughts. 'She expects too much of those kids – it's all very fine for her to carry them high up in the air, but what happens once she lets go?'

'Objectivity – what is it?' Luigi turned to face Jasper, rubbing at his face with Kleenex. 'I mean, really, what's it worth? Shit, right?'

'Still. . . .'

'Look, Jasper, I like you. Believe me, I do. I'm happy we met. I'm ready to put up with a lot of things in someone I like, but, please, don't expect me to take you seriously when you say, "What Rhoda doesn't see is *sus*, what Rhoda doesn't see is *so*." '

'But it's so one-sided – what's missing is any idea how quickly if you don't watch out the victim becomes the victimizer.'

'Come on, Jasper.' Luigi slapped the trestle table so hard that everything on it jumped. 'That's like the First Commandment you're talking about. Don't you realize by now that Rhoda sees more, feels more, hears more than you, me and any ten of us put together?'

'So.'

'Face it, you're never going to meet anyone who's remotely in her league.'

'I keep forgetting you're the world's leading authority on Rhoda.'

'As proof of my friendship, I'll choose to ignore that goosish remark. Victim become the victimizer, my ass. The unique thing about Rhoda is she doesn't get off on other people's suffering. You'd be surprised – no, come to think of it, maybe *you* wouldn't – let's say I was surprised, for a long time I was naive and so it surprised the hell out of me how many people I met who expected me to embrace my crutches. Fade, boy, that was their advice. My parents, everybody. I was supposed to be grateful if people didn't notice me. Think about that for a minute, Jasper. Call that living? Fuck it, man. I was supposed to do everything in my power not to bother anyone by making him aware of my existence. Like if I could learn to climb on a bus without embarrassing the diddlyshit behind me, or holding him up, I was really accomplishing something. Jesus.

'No one even mentioned bed. No one dared. Bed's a great equalizer, Jasper, take it from me. Between the sheets there aren't many places to hide. Ever kiss anyone *objectively*?'

Luigi flung himself over to the bed. 'Want to know what makes Rhoda so special? She's got this fantastic ability. . . .' But here, typically, Luigi broke off in mid-sentence. So much of his meaning he conveyed by leaving things unsaid. He went out to the bathroom to douse his face and neck with a few quick handfuls of cold water.

'Look.' Luigi came back and sat next to Jasper with a hand on Jasper's shoulder. 'There's every chance in the world I'm just wasting my breath, but still I'm going to try. There's no such thing as peace, Jasper. If you can accept that, maybe we can still talk to each other. At least, if there is peace, it never lasts longer than that.' Luigi snapped his fingers. 'You can't build on it. You can't count on it. Often you can't even recognize it until after it's gone.

'Blacks and whites hate each other. Christians and Jews and Moslems – they hate each other. Who can blame them?

Husbands and wives? Parents and children? Brothers and sisters? Colleagues? You want to tell me about peace? These are the things we tend to forget: the facts of life. We let ourselves be misled. We get carried away by scare stories about atomic missiles and submarines and the enemy who lurks across the waters.

'Man, Jasper, there is enough hatred right here at home. I mean hatred is *everywhere.* Whenever you want to, you can breathe it in. A lot of people do, all the time, and get high on it. To hate, to get yourself hated, you don't have to travel one step from your bed.

'When Rhoda tells you that aggression is the natural state of things, she knows. Believe me, *she knows*. She lives on the front lines. Cripples – we're an army, man. The walking wounded. Whether we like it or not, and I happen not to like it, not one lousy little bit, we're in action every crazy minute of the livelong day. There is no peace, none.'

Jasper reached up and pressed the hand on his shoulder.

'One of the reasons Rhoda is Rhoda, take it from me, is that deep down she hates like a champion – and doesn't pretend it's anything else. Hate makes her clean, keeps her young and strong. Rhoda – you really want her to be objective? That's as silly as wanting, what. . . .'

Jasper's breath lodged like a fist in his throat. 'When *I* climb on a bus,' Jasper said, 'I embarrass the person behind me.'

Luigi slapped Jasper's backside. 'You know all it takes to cure a cripple of being a cripple? A few minutes of intimacy. Now that's not much, is it – in a lifetime?'

'The beauties and the beasts, Luigi, you're the one who said it – they don't only hate each other,' – Jasper looked up – 'they need each other.'

18

There were magicians, Jasper knew, who could pull the cloth right off a crowded table without budging a dish. Well, with the same steady sleight-of-hand, Helen had wrenched his soul away. He'd been walking for a long time now, putting his one foot down in front of the other. Walking and waiting for an emotion, something recognizable to swim up out of the void inside. His mind was empty, but solid and smooth. Had Helen intended to lead him by the hand with her into the fire? Wasn't it about time he, too, stopped playing?

When at last Jasper stood shivering outside 39 Charter Street, staring up at Rhoda's windows, it had been dark already for several hours. Hand over hand he hauled himself up the sticky staircase banister. At Rhoda's door he wiped his face with his overcoat sleeve, rubbed hard, trying to erase recent history.

Jasper slumped forward and the door opened under his weight. Rhoda, off by the window, looked back at him over her shoulder.

'I'm late,' Jasper said. 'Sorry.'

Rhoda, in her torn pink robe, was trimming her plants by hand, scrunching up dead leaves and dry tendrils. It took Jasper almost forever to shake off his coat. When he went to kiss Rhoda, moving unsteadily, she turned away. Then, letting out a long sigh, she turned back and hands raised behind his neck, leaves in her fingers, she kissed him – gently. Once, twice. She knew.

'You're freezing.' Rhoda chafed his hands between hers.

'Don't exaggerate – that's a very bad trait.'

'You're ice-cold.'

Out in the kitchen Luigi was perched on the counter by the sink, next to his stump a nearly full bottle of whiskey. On Luigi's lap the *Boston Globe* lay open to the centerfold. Upside down Jasper stared at scenes from the fire.

After Carole had broken the news to him at his office – O, my God the news! – he'd set out for Roxbury. At the smouldering ruins, there were kids poking through the hot bricks and ashes. Glass fragments had been swept up into a neat mound. Somewhere here – Jasper moved slowly – Helen had collapsed on the pavement, hair singed, a gash in her leg, smoke clogging her lungs. Witnesses quoted in the paper agreed that when she staggered out of Thomas Alvah Edison Junior High she'd looked like a human torch. Still, by removing her jacket and wrapping it around her face – Helen was never at a loss in an emergency – she had saved herself from worse injury.

'"Heroic Effort in Vain",' Luigi read aloud. Of all the pictures on the page, the one exhumed from Helen's college yearbook stabbed the deepest. Smith '54. Like yesterday. Radiant. Teeth, pearls, eyes, hair, skin, smile. The first time Jasper had brushed her neck with his lips – on the downstairs porch of her dorm, just out of the lamplight, dozens of couples whispering, giggling, saying goodnight – how coarse his lips had felt!

'She's all right' – Jasper lowered his voice so Rhoda wouldn't hear – 'except here – the face – one side. Doesn't want to take advantage.' Luigi poured Jasper a drink into a chipped white cup with no handle. 'That's what she said. Won't see me. Doesn't want to take advantage.' Jasper looked up into Luigi's eyes and laughed. 'Jesus, my wife must be about the only woman in the world who could be in shock and still say shit like that.'

'What a nice surprise,' Jasper had said when Carole came bursting into the Pinckney Street office.

'No,' – Carole shook her head – 'listen.'

Morrison shooed the waiting patients home.

'She'll be all right, except part of her face, the side, here, see.'

'It was arson.' Luigi rapped the paper with his knuckles. 'The school was closed down more than a year. Bunch of dumb kids.'

'Didn't think twice.' Jasper swallowed. 'Thinks twice about everything her whole life. Always. Twice? Three times. Now – not. Just stops the car, gets out and runs into the fire. My wife, the hero.' Jasper made a little circle in the air with his cup, scotch sloshing over the rim. 'Oh, Jesus. Burning flesh, it – the smell is unforgettable. To fix it – takes delicate work. Oh, Jesus fucking Christ.'

'What're you saying?' Luigi took Jasper's cup away and put it down.

'She doesn't want to see me.'

Then Luigi pulled Jasper's hands from his face. 'What are you saying, Jasper, I can't understand you.'

'He says' – Rhoda stood in the kitchen doorway, biting her lip – 'crying is bad for the plants.'

Later Jasper Whiting and Rhoda Massler lay in bed, the two of them alone in the imperfect dark. Streetlamps cast rippling plant shadows onto the ceiling. 'Helen'll be all right,' Jasper said. Their bodies didn't touch. Their fingers rested on the sheet an inch, no more, from each other.

'I have to get right back.' All in all Carole had stayed only a matter of minutes. 'Mother wants help with some letters.'

Jasper went to get his coat. It was his intention to go with her. Face to face, Carole towering over him, their whispers had turned to shouts.

'Humor her,' Carole said. 'It's nothing personal.'

'I'll stop by tonight.'

'No – do it her way.'

'Not *no*, yes.'

'Oh, Fa – you can't have it your way all the time.'

Jasper had followed Carole out into the empty waiting room. Its dinginess struck him now as a further accusation.

'Don't worry, Fa.' Carole was wearing a yellow sweater that belonged to her mother. 'Try not.'

And when Carole left, Morrison was right there holding Jasper's hands. He sat hunched forward on a chair that wobbled under his weight. Dear Morrison, who had no life of her own. No! That was Helen's pernicious idea. Everyone had a life of his own, her own, precious and gemlike, however small and secret, and however forbidden. Even Jasper himself.

Before Jasper knew it, he was blaming himself.

'Don't be so hard on yourself, doctor.'

'What good have I ever done? I mean really, Morrison, for whom?'

'You've helped a lot of people.' And all the muscles of Morrison's face had been dancing, only the eyes, bottomless, sad, held steady. Reliable Morrison in her starched uniform. Morrison for whom Jasper could do no wrong. The world needed such people, didn't it? Well, didn't it? Ten times more than it needed useless and indulgent Jasper Whiting. Did Helen – hadn't Helen realized it was real fire, not play fire? Christ, didn't she know by now that life was made up of two kinds of actions, with consequences and without?

Walking out on a marriage, that just wasn't the same as walking into flames.

'You'll help her, too,' Morrison said. 'I know you will.'

How was it possible that while Jasper sat in his waiting room, Morrison's large, capable, sexless hands folded over his, he could only think and feel sorry for himself! And want the impossible – to run to Rhoda. To burrow in the stale wool of her sweater, the full softness of her breasts, to find comfort in a gentle rocking that would grow hard.

'What about those poor women from Japan, doctor?' Morrison was just talking to keep him talking, Jasper knew. How often did she wash her sheets? 'Remarkable work, everyone said so.'

The Iron Maidens of Hiroshima again – how they haunted him. Before their operation, Helen had them out to the house for a barbecue. Chunks of meat, marinated. Marbled chops, sausages crammed into skins to the bursting point. The sunset was the perfect setting for Helen's blonde beauty. Helen, complexion flawless, squirting starter fluid onto the pyre of briquettes, then dropping a lit match and stepping back, face turned away as – *whoosh* – the flames flared up. Those tiny twisted women with their dark eyes cast down, black hair arranged with precision, led by the nose half-way around the world by two guilt-ridden governments. Victims again, this time of publicity. Their guests had eaten next to nothing, said less. When the meat began to crackle and smoke, they had lifted white handkerchiefs to their faces.

'And don't forget Viet Nam, doctor. What you did. Few people in the world could have – or would have.'

'I had no choice.'

'Not everyone went, did they? Some they asked wouldn't go.'

'Was she crazy?'

'What, doctor?'

'Helen must have been crazy. No one in his right mind would do what she did.'

'I'm sure she thought there were people in there who needed help.'

'Morrison. . . .' It wasn't fair but Jasper was going to do it anyway. 'I hope it never happens to you.'

'No, doctor. What, doctor?'

'I hope you never wake up and discover how much you regret your life, everything you've ever done.' In his pain Jasper needed to hurt someone close to him. 'You're too good a person for that to happen to, Morrison. Too generous, too kind.'

Morrison gritted her teeth.

'We only live once, Morrison. Dead is dead.' Jasper freed his hands. They were sweating. He wiped them on his thighs, ran them over his hair. 'Everything I have done in my life has been wrong – that's what it comes down to. Or weak, or false. Or both.'

'You can't mean that.' Something in Morrison's voice made Jasper look up. 'You *can't*.'

'But Morrison, it's all my fault.'

'Oh why' – Morrison tossed her head back, suddenly angry, eyes glaring, a handsome woman, her plain features kindled by her conviction – 'why does it always have to be somebody's *fault*.'

Jasper reached out for Rhoda's hand.

'I. . . .'

'Shh,' Rhoda said. 'Not now. Anything you say will be wrong.'

19

Saturday Rhoda slipped out of bed early without a word. Jasper, pretending to be asleep, felt her stare at him through the dark.

'How about it, Jasper?' she whispered. 'Think you're up to it?'

He heard the door close, firmly, but not harder than usual. Since Helen's accident – what else was there to call it? – Carole had visited him every day, at least once. At his office, the hospital, or Charter Street. Bulletins. Helen was doing 'nicely.' She remained adamant, however, about not seeing him. Not speaking to him on the phone either.

Long after the sky was light Jasper lay tossing in bed, a self-wrapping mummy. Finally Madge passed by on her way downstairs, singing 'Thumbelina'. Then two people came clambering upstairs, no doubt to pattern Sloan. Jasper sat up. His eyes ran around the room. Amazing, how a man could get used to practically anything. He wasn't like Rhoda, though. Every bit of her heart she cut away grew back.

How often Rhoda had needled him, 'Go back to where you belong, Jasper, back to your wife and family.' In jest, but never, he felt, completely. Since Helen's accident, by mutual consent, tacit, the joke had been dropped between them.

'My, look at the early bird.' At the Freedom Trail Laundromat Jasper's friend with the rope-colored hair and fallen socks had a way of flapping her arms in greeting that made her look like a disheveled angel. She had clearly taken a liking to him. He suspected she took likings easily. 'Use no. 4, that's a good one. The others are pumping dirty water.' The place stank of wet clothes and bleach. Her breath reeked of rum. 'You know what today is? Eleven years ago to the day' – dutifully Jasper turned to look up at the fatal window ledge across the street, the site of her late husband's final leap – 'I stopped drinking. That *fool*' – she pulled herself erect – 'said I never could do it.'

Soon the laundromat was packed. Mostly women, half-dressed in housecoats and slippers, no make-up, more asleep, some, than awake. The older ones brought thermoses with coffee. Pets curled at their feet and chased things through dreams. When all the machines were running, the sudsing and rinsing, the click of changing cycles, made a soothing racket. Jasper sat face to face with no. 4. Pretending to do a crossword, he nervously sketched noses. When the machine switched onto rinse, he stood and went to the pay phone. He plunked in some coins and dialled his home. No answer. He let it ring thirty times. Normally on a Saturday morning at least he would be home to answer the damn phone.

'God, God, oh God, don't stop.'

From a dim area in the back of the laundromat, a dwarf scuttled past. He couldn't move faster because both hands were tugging at the fly of his trousers. The dwarf's enormous face, dappled with birthmarks and moles and warts so that it resembled nothing so much as a sprouting potato, was split from ear to flapping ear with a grin. And he was chuckling to himself, a high self-satisfied chuckle, eyes glazed with lewdness.

'Oh,' the unseen moaning continued, 'oh,oh, oh. Oh!' Was everyone else deaf? It was Jasper's angel, down on the floor next to the fuse boxes and mop closet, her voice. 'Oh, oh, oh,' the breathless erotic whimpering, the gasps of pleasure joined the music of the churning, rumbling washing machines.

'That dirty little man.' The woman came stumbling forward. The buttons down the front of her dress were open. She held a thin white plastic belt in her hands. 'If that *freak* sets foot in here again, he'll be sorry.' She rubbed herself as she spoke, low, between her legs. 'See,' she came to Jasper and challenged him, 'see what happens when you try to be friendly? Christ, I wouldn't marry him if he was the last man on earth.' Then she started to laugh, holding her hands with the belt across her mouth, but with the fingers spread.

'We're all adults,' she said, looking around her. Then in a flash she began to strip. Still, no one except Jasper paid the least attention. She took off everything. Slip, socks, flimsy bra, the cups padded, frilly with lace. Everything but the colorful barrettes in her hair. She wasn't putting on a show, it was all extremely matter-of-fact. The way prisoners of war strip, about to be deprived of their belongings and then their lives. No, there was something else familiar about her manner. She undressed herself the way a mother undresses her child at the doctor's. At last she sat her narrow, unloved body down in the chair next to Jasper, clothes bunched on her lap. 'When you're finished with no. 4,' she said, 'I'm next.'

They sat side by side, not speaking. Jasper didn't dare move his pencil. What would she make of the pages of noses he sketched? Then she began to rock with pleasure, backwards and forwards, laughing again. 'It's *not* the first time,' she whispered to Jasper. He could feel all eyes turn to them. 'When

I catch him, when I get my hands on him, I'll throw him into no. 4.' Her laugh rose in pitch. 'He'll fucking shrink.'

Clean and folded, Jasper's wash seemed to weigh more than when he'd brought it in dirty. His phone call to the house was a dumb stunt. If Helen had answered, what then?

On the way back to the apartment, Jasper had a feeling he was being followed. He turned casually, just in time, he thought, to see the dwarf rapist nip behind a parked station wagon. A second later a fat dog wandered out from behind the car, yawned at Jasper, and trotted away.

Back at Charter Street there was a surprise waiting for Jasper Whiting. His son, Daniel, sat on the stoop, chin tilted to the sun, eyes closed. Under one of Daniel's earlobes, a trace of shaving cream had dried and crusted. Jasper's hand was half-way there to wipe it away when Daniel's eyelids lifted.

'Hi, Fa,' Daniel said slowly, dreamily. 'Doing the laundry?' Jasper hugged his package instead of his son. 'Croissants, from the market.' Daniel held up a brown paper bag. He stood and all at once Jasper remembered something he had forgotten. Daniel was inches taller than he was.

'Well, for once Carole wasn't exaggerating. It is a dump.' Daniel took the stairs two by two. 'What floor is your girlfriend on?'

Jasper pretended not to hear. At the landing they had to make way for Murray who came barreling downstairs with a shopping cart on his head. Although Jasper was worried about the state he would find his apartment in, Luigi, to his relief, had left it neat as a pin.

'Not much room to maneuver in, is there? TV bust?'

'I never watch it.'

'Yeah, but still. I know, I know, I know' – Daniel threw his arms up and imitated his father's voice – 'it could be a lot worse.' Then he leapt on to the armchair and swept a long arm up over the curtain rods to peel away festoons of smoky cobweb.

'Is that supposed to be us?' Daniel crouched in front of the formica dresser to look at the family photo tucked into the mirror frame. 'I was an ugly little monster, wasn't I?'

'You still are.'

'Mom looks great though.' Jasper saw Daniel stiffen at the sound of his own words.

'Don't you have a meet today?'

'I just got here, Fa.'

From the kitchen where he went to make coffee and spill the flaky croissants onto two plates, Jasper could see Daniel's back as the boy stood staring out the window. 'Is she there?' he called.

'Who?'

'My punk neighbour. She's a real home movie.'

'Fa' – to see Daniel trying to get up his courage, helped Jasper with his – 'I thought maybe we could talk.' Daniel didn't look well. His face was drawn. He was, in ways, prettier than his sister.

'Okay, talk.'

'Man to man, all right?'

Rhoda was always saying the Saturday swim was therapy for parents who didn't dare touch their children on dry land. Now Jasper knew what she was talking about.

'Well, to make a long story short, Mom wants to know if you could recommend a plastic surgeon.'

'What?'

'A good one, of course.'

'Did she send you?'

Daniel delivered his lines as if he had rehearsed them. 'Under the circumstances, we can see that you're not likely to want to take on the job yourself.'

'Answer my question, Daniel. Did your mother send you, or didn't she?'

Daniel drew in his breath. 'Not exactly.'

'This is all your own idea?' Jasper's heart expanded with love.

'No!'

'What then?'

'We talked it over – Carole and me.'

'I see.'

'We're not backwards, you know.'

'So the two of you talked things over – and this is what you came up with?'

The kettle began to shriek in the kitchen. Jasper went and poured out two mugs of instant coffee. He carried them on a tray together with the croissants back to the bedroom. Daniel was inspecting Luigi's make-up on the dresser, his assortment of scents and lotions.

'You'll have to drink it without sugar.'

'Yuk.' Daniel dunked his croissant. 'You'll do it, Fa, won't you?'

'Daniel, there's one thing you've got to understand.' Helen would never come right out and ask his help, that much Jasper knew for certain. She'd bite her tongue off first. 'Your mother has a mind of her own.'

'I suppose I'd better tell you how things really stand. She plans to keep it.'

'Keep what?'

'The scar.'

'So.'

'If her face makes other people uncomfortable, she says too bad for them. She can live with it. Fa, you can't leave her looking like that, you can't.

'Jesus.' Daniel pointed out across the air shaft. In the apartment opposite Jasper's neighbour with spiky blonde hair, naked to the waist, in tight black leather shorts, was exercising with a chest-expander. Her face strained grotesquely, legs spread wide, thighs quivering, large pink nipples in imminent danger of being caught in the springs. 'Ow.' At that very instant the girl glanced up and caught them looking. She nodded slightly and gave them an unexpectedly sweet smile, still holding her hands as far apart as possible. Father and son stepped back out of view.

'All right, Fa, why don't you tell me. Why'd you go?'

When Jasper failed to come up with an answer, Daniel began

to pass his hand back and forth along the railings of the bed. 'Maybe it just runs in the family. Like I used to run away, remember?'

'You?'

Daniel held up three fingers.

'Why?'

'Now we're getting somewhere.' Daniel laughed. 'That's more like the Fa I know – answer a question with a question. Why I ran away is simple. I hated you all.'

What passed for hate, Jasper wondered, in little boys?

'The first time I was nine. I wanted you to come looking for me. But you cheated and sent the dog.'

'Steel?' A beautiful Doberman, black, brown, gray.

'He led you right to me. Under the big rock out by Fresh Pond.'

'You're trying to tell me you had run away and we were *finding* you?'

'Then the second time I thought I really had you. I took Steel along – but he was too damn strong. He got hungry and dragged me home.'

'You could've let go of the leash.'

'Sure, and lose my self-respect.' Around Daniel's chin, pimples swarmed. There were crumbs sticking to his lips as he talked.

'And the third time?'

'Come on, Fa, you must remember the third time.'

'Must but don't.'

'When I hid in the bushes under the kitchen window? First I made this big production out of leaving for good, then I snuck back where I could hear you people moving around inside. By the time I came in my lips were blue. It was freezing cold outside. Nobody had even missed me.

'Okay, Fa, your turn. Why'd you go?'

With Daniel's eyes on him, Jasper felt he was standing in the rain soaked to the skin without the power to move. At Spinedale Pool – he shivered – would anyone ask for him?

'Fa?'

'What does your mother say?'

'About what?'

'Why I left.'

'She says — '

'She says — ?'

'You bought her a nightgown for your anniversary.'

'So far, so true.'

'It was too small.'

'Maybe, maybe not.'

'She exchanged it for a more expensive one – and you left.'

Jasper started to put laundry away in the dresser drawers. A pair of Rhoda's pants was mixed in with his boxer shorts.

'It's still in the box, Fa, for crying out loud. She hasn't worn it. What if I make her take it back and get the one you gave her?' Daniel was so much more animal than Jasper remembered his being. 'How about that?'

Jasper had seen the nightgown of Helen's choice hanging in the shop. And he knew right away she would like it more than the one he settled on. It wasn't the price though that had stopped him. That other nightgown, the more expensive one, was for a younger, or sexier woman.

'Run the film backwards?' If that was possible, Jasper asked himself, at what point would he cry out, 'Stop!' 'You ran away because you hated me. Now *I* run away, and you hate me again.'

'But I'm older, Fa. And you're older.' Daniel chewed the irritated skin of his chin with his upper teeth. 'You know something, on the whole track team – I only figured this out yesterday – there isn't one person with the same father and mother he started out with!'

'We're all on the relay team, is that it?' They both laughed. 'Dan' – Jasper sat on the bed – 'you don't always know why you do things, do you?'

'No, but I'm seventeen.'

One day in the hall next to Jasper's office at the hospital a notice had gone up on the bulletin board about a furnished room for rent. '*Not luxurious*', it had said and someone had circled the two words and written in: '*the understatement of the year!!!*' The second time Jasper had walked by the notice he tore off one of the phone numbers hanging there on fringes of paper. Later the same week he called and took the place unseen. When he told Helen, she rubbed her eyes and smiled without parting her lips. 'What surprises me,' she finally said, calmly enough, 'is how long we managed not to talk about this.'

'What I can't figure out, Fa, is how someone like you can just turn his life upside-down without having a good *reason*?'

That morning in the laundromat, briefly, Jasper had felt part of the world, in it instead of outside looking in. A woman took her wash out of the machine and found everything covered in lint. She had missed a Kleenex in some pocket. When she burst into tears, the others had laughed, but they had comforted her, too. 'It happens to the best of us.'

'Listen.' Jasper's mind raced. Did he want Daniel to know how far off course he felt? Could he really tell his son how the opinion he had of himself, small to begin with, had been shrinking steadily until there was almost nothing left? 'People used to believe – people? – scientists, I mean, philosophers. Minds at any rate much better than mine. They used to think they could *prove* that because the sun rose yesterday, and the day before, and the day before that, it would, like clockwork, rise tomorrow.'

'Induction.'

'Exactly, induction.' Jasper paused. 'But then this century, the second half at least, has gone sour on induction.' Daniel nodded. 'We look at the sunrise, at the break of day, differently. Completely. We say – they say – the smart ones, that it isn't good enough for something to have happened so often in the past to be sure it will still happen like that again in the future. Let me finish – they've stood the whole thing on its head, really, and now they say that the closest we can ever come to proving that the sun will rise tomorrow is to fail to find evidence that it won't. Unless there is a way to be convincing that the sun is likely to be off somewhere else at the usual time, then you can safely expect to see it back in the morning. Something like that.'

In his hands Jasper seemed to cradle the sun, as if he had the power either to lift it and hang it high in the heavens or else to let it drop and plunge beyond oblivion. 'If we do our best and we still can't find a way to prove the sun won't come up, then it will.' Jasper shrugged and smoothed back his hair. 'By leaving your mother maybe I wasn't trying to prove anything. Maybe instead it was some kind of negative test to help me predict tomorrow.'

'And this Rhoda,' Daniel asked, 'she came later?'

'She came later.'

Downstairs Daniel's racing bicycle, gleaming silver, stood locked with a chain to the fire hydrant in front of Gayle Glintz's Beauty Shop. Daniel unlocked it and straddled the saddle up on his toes, lock and chain around his neck, one hand on Jasper's shoulder to steady himself.

'Run well,' Jasper said.

'Sure thing.'

'And thanks for the croissants.'

'Thank you for thanking.'

Jasper smiled, pleased by Daniel's use of the African formula. 'Hey, what're you grinning at? Nothing's been settled, you know.'

Daniel leaned over and hugged his father, then he pushed off against Jasper's chest. 'See you!'

20

'Yes, all right.' Helen had accepted Jasper's decision to return coolly. 'If you're sure that's what you want.' Enough effort to keep calm had showed through, however, for Jasper's heart to turn over. 'I can't promise you anything. I won't,' she went on to say, as if to herself. 'I can't.' She twisted a lock of hair low on her neck around and around her index finger. An aid to thinking, really, a physical tic familiar to Jasper, more precious than he had realized. 'Don't expect it to be easy.'

'It's what I want, yes, definitely.'

When he said it, Jasper, to his relief, discovered that he meant it.

'Any time,' Helen said, 'is fine by me.'

Jasper rinsed his cup in the stained, chipped sink. He shook the cup dry, stood it alone upside down in the plastic dish rack on the kitchen counter. Daniel had begged and pleaded to be allowed to move into the apartment on Charter Street for the remaining months of Jasper's sub-lease. In the end Morrison had come up with a girl from Hong Kong studying psychiatric nursing. Jasper looked at the chair where he had sat on the frozen chicken. The bed sagged, waiting for its next occupant. And since a few days ago his neighbour across the air shaft was no longer blonde. She had dyed her hair black. Or she had rinsed away the blonde.

Jasper hadn't told Rhoda. Not yet. In some ways, even with Carole downstairs waiting to drive him home, Jasper himself hadn't accepted yet that he was leaving. That he had made love to Rhoda for the last time was inconceivable. Her neck, breasts, soft belly – how she opened, hung, climbed, tightened, turned, the sounds, the smell, the greed and excitement, the closeness, the coming down, the peace. Bodies lighter than air, the floating. The tip of her tongue visible through her lips. How she arched, straining. Jasper shuddered slightly.

Had there ever been a moment when Jasper believed in a permanent, exclusive relationship with Rhoda? He wanted to please her, to measure up, to impress her – and, perhaps, most binding, to conceal nothing. No defenses. But from the first he had understood he would have to share her. With her past, for one thing. With her present strength of purpose, to call it that charitably, for another. Rhoda, for all her signals of need, direct and indirect, was alarmingly self-sufficient. She said it herself when she boasted of being a teacher.

With Helen Jasper had always been simply himself. When that self was embarrassing, Helen contrived to overlook it. With Rhoda, Jasper had constantly tried to be more than himself, better, keener. On tiptoe until his feet cramped. In constant erection. It wasn't that Rhoda made such demands on him, either. Not consciously or by design. He demanded it of himself. That was the effect Rhoda had on him. He had never felt so close to another human being before – released from the limits of identity. Yet these experiences, the breaking of barriers, were not without cost and intimations of danger. A persistent whisper in his blood told Jasper that a time would come, inevitably, when he would fail Rhoda. He would fall short, a disappointment to them both. And if he ever let it come that far, neither of them would be able to pretend it had never happened. Was it so cowardly then when failure was the only possible outcome, to skip out on the trial in advance?

'Yes, all right.' Helen trembled, fingers, mouth, voice. 'If you're sure that's what you want.'

Jasper wanted to protect Helen from that terrible fire, the burning ceiling that collapsed on her back, disembodied voices just beyond reach crying for help. He wanted to protect her from hearing her husband say, Yes, he was leaving her, while she sat pouring his coffee, one hand on the handle, the other on the top of the pot.

'It's what I want, yes, definitely.'

Now that it was too late, Jasper wanted to protect Helen from oh so many things. From affection diluted to habit, from a preference for memories over expectations. He reached a hand under Helen's rug and held her ankle. Her blood seemed to flow through his hand up his arm.

'Move forward, Helen, so I can see you better.'

'No, I'm not ready for that.'

All these deep new urges to protect his wife! What were they, really, if not self-defense?

'I'm a doctor, remember.'

'You're also my husband.'

There were tones in Helen's voice Jasper hadn't heard in years. The brittle girl he'd met as a virgin, full of resolution not to be scared to death of life. Rhoda he had never known young. Ultimately that made a difference now.

'There may be people who need fear and disgust on the faces around them, at least Carole tells me so,' – Helen smiled – 'but not me, Jasper, thank God.'

Jasper mechanically checked the closet and the dresser one last time. Mothballs rattled and jumped as he pulled the drawers loose. It wasn't as if Rhoda never showed her feelings. Not at any rate when it came to other things and people. Take the helpless children scattering under gunfire in the courtyard of the desert school. Or Sloan. Or Anselmo, slowly, steadily drawing his long arm back through space before releasing it lethally, face void of expression. Or the much maligned Marcus Featherstone. About Jasper, however, her feelings towards him, Rhoda was guarded. There had been no mention of love between them, none, never.

Jasper reached a hand out, fingers spread to cover his face in the mirror. The ears set high on his head, the rippling chins, the strawberry hair, thin and frizzy. 'What would you do if you were me?' More and more Jasper Whiting felt like a man in the power of his reflection. Only when his image in the mirror looked up could he look up. Only when the image in the glass closed its eyes could he close his. The lapse of time between the two sets of movements was short, infinitesimal. Anyone watching, not on the alert, would fail to notice anything unusual. Anyone with no reason to suspect otherwise would see what he expected to see, the familiar sequence, not its unholy reverse.

If Rhoda said, 'Stay,' he might. There was that distinct possibility. But Rhoda wouldn't.

'I have an idea,' Helen had started to say, 'no, maybe I'd better not say it.'

'Say what?'

Helen's eyes had held his a mere instant. 'Just make sure you know what you're doing. From everything you tell me, Rhoda isn't someone you can put out like a candle.'

Outside Gayle Glintz's apartment, Jasper paused. The metronome was on. Jasper's heart raced faster than the methodical tick-tock. He heard the coordinated one-two, one-two thwack of Sloan's limbs against the flimsy table top. He could visualize the team at work, the blanket squirming. He didn't disturb them to say goodbye but turned and went back downstairs again.

At Rhoda's, ear to the door, Jasper heard water running. He knocked. No answer. He knocked again.

'It's open.'

Suddenly the house on Charter Street had never been so still before. It was as if the building, torn from its foundations, was hurtling through space. Jasper himself felt light and insubstantial. God might snatch him up and wipe the heavens with him as a rag, points of unseen stars lodge their barbs in his silly smile. Was there anything remotely as futile as trying to say goodbye to Rhoda?

'It's open.'

How long would it be before Rhoda added him to the collection of stories she took such pleasure in telling at her own expense, accounts describing the treachery of men? 'Don't you know anybody normal?'

Jasper turned the doorknob and walked in. He was hollow and oh so powerful. He loved two women and wasn't whole enough for either. 'Hello.' He smoothed his hair. This time it felt like it stayed down.

'Oh Jasper,' Rhoda turned. She was spraying her plants. 'We were just talking about you.' She was in a good mood. As she fired her spray gun a fine mist fogged the windows, but quickly evaporated. Jasper tripped on the hose of a vacuum cleaner stalled at the foot of the bed. 'Finally made up your mind, have you?' She looked young, too. 'Back to the bosom of your family. That's good. I'm glad.' She sounded glad. 'For them. For you.'

Jasper was totally unprepared for her glib, good-natured behavior. He was afraid he would lose control. He didn't have anything to say. He wanted to touch her. He had never wanted to do anything more in his life than to run his fingers over her face and down her neck.

'Tcha, saw it coming from a mile off,' Rhoda went on merrily. 'I'm sure it's best for all concerned.'

'That makes one of us.'

'Glad you stopped in before going. I appreciate that.' She wasn't just keeping it up, either. Her smile was uninhibited, sexy, her eyes bright with a luster free from deceit. She wiped a hand on her corduroys and reached out to shake Jasper's hand. 'All the best, Red. Let's keep in touch.'

He must've looked a sight. Couldn't they lie down on the bed together? He wanted to erupt inside her. Confusion, anger, disappointment, relief, astonishment. Contradictory emotions, Jasper Whiting was late in learning, didn't necessarily cancel each other out.

'Guess what?' Rhoda asked. 'Wonderful news.' She aimed the spray gun at Jasper playfully and squeezed the trigger. He took a step back, closed his eyes and threw his arm up instinctively. Just water, a fine mist. 'Alex is coming home.'

'What?'

'Alex. He always said he would come back' – here Rhoda paused – 'when it might do some good.'

'I love you, Rhoda,' Jasper thought, frightened by the discovery.

'Ah, good old Jasper, baffled to the very end. The war, Jasper.' Rhoda winked. 'Alex is coming back for the Good Fight.'

Part II

SKIRMISHES

1

As Rhoda Massler cut under the dank elevated MTA station at Charles Street, hundreds of footsteps rumbled across the iron footbridge above her. Stepping up into sunlight on the far curb, she felt at once the pull of the crowd. There was a tidal surge towards Boston Common. The sidewalks overflowed. In the street people were walking four and five abreast, arms linked, waving. Cars struggled to escape; like flies caught in jam.

'So, you decided to come after all.'

'No, I only . . .' Rhoda, stung, whirled about ready to protest and defend herself. The remark wasn't aimed at her, however, but at a woman with crutches bobbing gaily on ahead.

Indeed Rhoda had quarreled with Alex about the rally on the Common, over its timing. Or she had come as close to a quarrel with him as anyone could. He was quite simply quarrelproof. 'You're rushing things,' she said. 'You've been away. You're out of touch.' One by one Alex conceded her points. Then he went right ahead and did exactly what he wanted.

In the end Rhoda had set her lips and told Alex, unequivocally, she wasn't coming. Now here she was, the lure irresistible. It was one of those rare New England April days warm with false promises of imminent summer. People had left home wearing too much clothing. Under way they began peeling off layers, knotting scarfs and sweaters around their waists or shoulders, slinging jackets over their backs as they moved along. In the Public Gardens for the first time of the season swan pedal boats, white wood gleaming under a thick coat of fresh paint, churned in circuits. The week before it was all cracked mud.

Between the Common and the Public Gardens red and white striped barricades blocked the normal flow of traffic. Squads of mounted police sat about in twos and threes beneath scattered trees in early leaf. The brass of their uniforms, the sheen of their horses' flanks suggested power. They pretended to have no eyes for the throngs converging from all sides in a holiday mood. Nervous rookies, Rhoda sized them up. Here and there, too, along the fence, police wagons, armour-plated, were pulled up in readiness. Even the old wagons with wire mesh sides had been called into service, full of agents in cramped waiting, jostling each other, telling jokes, eyes at prowl.

'Jesus, now I've seen everything!' Rhoda was not used to crowds, the way people spoke to be overheard. 'Can you believe that?' Left and right chartered buses loaded to capacity with handicapped from all over New England were creeping forward. Leave it to Alex – no hamlet unturned. During his years away Alex's gifts as an organizer, someone who inspired others to excel themselves, had grown. Oh, he had never been in such haste before, so impatient, so clearly driven – but his rare personal magic was intact.

A lanky teenager had jogged up out of the crowd and was running alongside the procession of buses now, back and forth, holding up a large, round mirror. In front of Rhoda's eyes the passengers began to writhe to life – to stand, to crowd the near windows, struggling to push them down, some balling their fists, faces twisted in rage.

'Hey, you. Hey, wise guy!'

The prankster turned, mirror still high, flashing over his head. In the middle of the glass, pasted on, was a death's head, a grinning skull. Then with a laugh the boy was gone, ducking away, weaving between vehicles. Passengers in the buses began to point at each other and laugh, too.

Rhoda's misgivings about the day returned with a rush. She

was willing to bet the grim looking-glass was going to have a long day's entertainment. As she entered the southwest gates to the park she told herself, 'I'm here for Anselmo. Angel, Carla and the rest.' They had enough to forgive her for already, she felt, without piling on new desertion. There was that – and the Mayor's surprise last-minute advice to the public on the morning news to stay away!

Boston's hawkers in any event were already out in force. Men, women and children arranging goods on display, dusting, buffing, smoothing down. They were on edge, expecting a big day. Everything imaginable was for sale. There were buttons spangling felt boards and bright pennants in profusion, beanies and corsages and inflatable vinyl cushions, miniature collapsible wheelchairs and iron lung puzzles attached to key rings and nail clippers and pocket flashlights. There were eye-catching balloons in vast molecular clusters, yellow and red mostly, and a chilling chartreuse. A fill with helium cost extra. Gas cylinders gleamed in a row like a giant cartridge belt, complex pressure gauges on top, the stalk eyes of so many crabs or lobsters. There were raffle tickets, too, for more good causes than you could shake a stick at. And personality posters of famous cripples, dead and alive: writers, athletes, film stars, painters, puppets and politicians.

'Hey, Rhoda. Y'r lookin' good.'

'How you doin', Terry?'

'Never better.' Terry was the anchor man of a promotional act to push trial memberships in a chain of health spas, Fitness for All Inc. He was a dark, musclebound weight-lifter with a comic-strip face. 'Time to waste, huh? Come to dig the freaks.'

'Wrong, Terry. I came to kick sand in your face.' Terry threw his head back and roared. 'How much you pressing these days?'

'Seeing is believing,' Terry replied. He rubbed his hands with resin and took his place on a low bench. As he spread his hands to grip the barbell in the rack above him, his torso bulged in special cutaways. Terry's club foot, the left one, was encased in what looked like a skiing boot.

'Hi, Rhoda.'

'Hi, Lilah.'

A svelte blonde poured into a clinging tank suit, fire-engine red, was working as Terry's back-up. She distributed spa leaflets to people who stopped to watch. Her hair slanted down sexily over one speckled green eye. Her upper arms both tapered abruptly into shrunken flippers. Accepting the leaflet, some people flinched at the last moment. Lilah's smile never deserted her.

'Terry still ticklish?' Rhoda asked. Terry was grunting now, straining, his massive arms almost fully extended under the chrome weight.

'Sure' – Lilah winked – 'if you know the right places.'

Darkness! From behind two hands pressed over Rhoda's eyes. Even before she pulled them away, she knew who it was. 'Anselmo!'

They hugged.

'Step back and let me look at you.' The boy beamed. Over a white shirt Anselmo was wearing a long gray cape lined with shiny blue. And he trembled with excitement.

'Nervous?' Rhoda signed. Anselmo started to shake his head, no, but changed midway to yes and laughed. 'What time are you on?' Anselmo shrugged. 'Two' – he held up fingers – 'maybe three.'

'Hey, you guys,' Lilah called, 'look up!' Rhoda tugged at Anselmo's elbow and pointed to the sky.

In a clear field of limitless blue, three small planes circled overhead, engines groaning. Nets with advertisements streamed in their wake: 'Handicap Holidays – vacations to treasure forever'.

Rhoda didn't say so but she suspected the planes were up there for security reasons, to film the crowd.

'So.' Rhoda stood squeezing Anselmo's hand. 'Big day.'

'How does it feel' – Anselmo tugged his hand free, eager to talk – 'to be part of the herd?' They laughed together. 'Seen Angel?'

'No,' Rhoda mouthed, 'just got here.'

A frown. 'You're staying for the show?'

'Wouldn't miss it for the world.'

Rhoda, recharged by Anselmo's energy, made her way through a thickening tangle of bodies up to the shallow buckling concrete oval known, for obscure historical reasons, as the Frog Pond. Here the blind sat about on the ground calling out insults at each other. No one wore dark glasses. Such a variety of unseeing eyes, some opalescent, others bruised and raw, all without center. Every once in a while one of the blind would pick up his long white stick to give his neighbor a love tap. Then they would fall in each other's arms and thrash about, wrestling, tumbling recklessly across the legs of one and all. They could be such a pain in the ass, Rhoda thought, the blind.

In the Frog Pond itself, behind ropes slung about the perimeter, seeing-eye dogs were leading blind masters through a maze of burning hoops and standing snares implanted with sharp, broad-bladed knives.

'Easy, for God's sake, *go easy*. Chuck, sirloin, you name it, porterhouse, rump, anything, prime ribs, only take – it – fucking – easy.'

Skeins of bells were stitched to the dogs' harnesses. Their thick coats shone. They advanced without hesitation, paws prancing forward. But there was little joy to their barking. The whole time they let out a piercing whine.

Then Rhoda saw Jasper Whiting – with a boy who just had to be his son. They didn't see her. Jasper looked diminished, older. That, she smiled, was what happened when your children outgrew you! Rhoda sidestepped behind a group of spectators, peering out from the cover of their backs and shoulders. Look at that wild carrot-colored hair! How intoxicated she had been at the first whiff of his conventionality. He had been a frozen vegetable, all right, and she had thawed him out. Mr Decency. What was Jasper doing here? Rhoda's thighs clenched. And way deep down she smiled again.

'What time are the speeches, Daniel?'

'Don't worry, Fa, they'll be late. Wonder where the Chariots and Spokes are?'

'Other side,' a boy wheezed through a slit in his throat, 'the tennis courts.'

'Right, thanks. C'mon, Fa.' Daniel set off. 'It's the fastest sport there is.'

Jasper had to hurry to keep up with his son. Boston hadn't seen a demonstration on such a scale in years. To be sure, Jasper himself had never made it down to any of the tumultuous anti-war protests. Either he had an operation or lecture scheduled or was away at some conference. Helen had marched though, with Daniel and Carole carrying placards.

'Mom,' Daniel had said at breakfast, 'why don't you come?'

'Thank you,' – Helen smiled – 'but it's the last place on earth I want to be.'

'Suit yourself, only it's not every day you get a chance to see history in the making.'

'You'll tell me about it, dear. You and your father. Blow by blow.'

Conscious of his bad behavior, Jasper studied the crowd. Withered arms, chloracne, neck halters. A good many limped, clanked along slowly and rigidly with shiny prosthetic devices. Predictably there were more men than women, but women were turning out, too, especially younger women. A clique of housewives, all spruce and immaculately coiffed, were cheerfully setting out home-baked goods for sale on a checkered table cloth. Jasper didn't have the heart to track down what was wrong with them. He also saw hare-lips, spastics, the near corpses of various dystrophies, hunchbacks, persons bent, gnarled, mutilated. So many it unnerved him.

Yet young people, radiantly healthy and alert, had come too. That was something.

'Hey!' Daniel had waited for Jasper to catch him up and from a knoll stood pointing down to a flurry of stop-and-go action on the green hard-tru tennis courts over towards Tremont Street. 'That's him, there at the back of the key. Swish. Did you see him float that hook shot!'

Daniel broke into a trot downhill, loose and easy. Jasper took his own good time descending, cutting back and forth. Most of the lawn space, slopes, level stretches and odd hummocks were hidden by growing numbers of demonstrators and the just plain curious. Jasper veered around a knot of veterans in uniform, soldiers and marines bristling with medals and decorations. They were taping enlarged photos of war atrocity victims to tree trunks. Often as not their sleeves or trouser legs hung empty. A small group of slim Vietnamese stood giggling at a Citizen Soldier display about Agent Orange, book bags slung over their narrow shoulders, pastry boxes held by a hooked finger under the string.

To pull off such an event took work and organization, and blind faith. Yet, if he were truthful, the pageantry around him only deepened Jasper Whiting's suspicion that too much attention was going into the surface of things.

At the bottom of the Common slope a growing collection of bike boys in black leather milled around their machines. Jasper could only guess at handicaps concealed by their riding suits, criss-crossed with zippers and snaps like so many scars. There was a swarm of limber blacks, too, on roller skates and wired into cassette headsets. Usually they had free run of the area, space to burn, but today they whirled and danced in a small radius, so many displaced persons, upstaged. Tourists with guidebooks, strays from the Freedom Trail, were taking things in agape. Photographers roamed at large, too. Their fear for the safety of their equipment was so sharp you could practically smell it.

When Jasper found him, Daniel's face was pressed to the wire mesh around the tennis courts. The nets had been taken down. Two basketball hoops had been set up at opposite ends of the courts, fixed to transparent backboards with padded posts. Ten men in flashy uniforms, strapped into wheelchairs, were locked in combat. Other players sat waiting on the sidelines, shouting even louder than the crowd.

'Not only do those guys have all the shots, same as any pro,'

– Daniel spoke into Jasper's good ear – 'but they handle those bikes of theirs like racing drivers.'

'Ever try one of those things?' A boy with thick eyeglasses in a motorized wheelchair asked Daniel. 'It's like the difference between a kayak and a rowboat.'

There she was, Rhoda! Reaching one hand back to scratch her scalp, chewing gum, she was watching the Spokes and Chariots screech after the ball. Rhoda – holding the hand of a skinny black girl with stringy garter-snake braids who was jumping up and down. No, it wasn't Rhoda. Didn't look like her at all, really, except for that very first instant. A trick of the light filtered through branches, plus the baggy sweater, the mane of hair – and wishful thinking. Now that his heart had begun beating again, Jasper laughed at himself.

'You'll see her, won't you?' Helen had asked Jasper on his way out the door. He hadn't looked back, pretending not to hear.

In the past months every time an incident involving the handicapped appeared in the news, a story about the cohesion of a movement on their behalf, at every photograph of Alex Thane, every quote, Jasper had felt amusement and annoyance – in that order. And in company he was highly critical, quick to ridicule the whole thing. Unless someone else started first. Then he found himself rising to the defense.

And when the first notices about the planned rally began to appear, early the next Saturday morning he had rolled a bathing suit in a towel and gone off to Spinedale Pool. He found a lot of healthy kids splashing around in the water. How lifeless it had seemed, how desolate. Even the building, the plants in their pots had looked drab. No one could tell him anything he wanted to know. Jasper had stood high in the visitors' gallery and watched a girl below, a sylph no more than ten, execute a dive of impossible twists and turns. At the perfect entry of her compact body, in the absence of splash, he had been flooded with sadness and had left. Her approach and spring had hardly set the diving plank in motion. Someone must have pulled the plug on Rhoda's program.

'Jesus!' From the far corner of the court a fat player with curls and a walrus moustache pumped a one-hander that sailed clear behind the backboard. 'Get that cripple out of there,' the boy in the wheelchair next to Daniel shouted, cupping his hands to his mouth. The crowd broke into roars of derision, hoots of mocking laughter. 'Why they're playing that clown beats me,' the boy confided. 'He must be getting it on with the coach.' The boy practically stood now, hauling himself upright with fingers curled in the iron mesh so the entire fence rattled and swayed. He shook one fist at the clown. 'Send that cripple to a home!' The crowd loved it, picking up the cold-blooded insult. 'Break his arms!'

Suddenly the action stopped. There was a hush.

'What is it?' Jasper asked. 'What's happened?'

A number of players slid from their shiny wheelchairs like water down a drain. They were crawling now, sliding across the playing surface, faces mere inches from the ground.

'Contacts.' The little woman right behind Jasper was the first to solve the riddle. 'One of them's lost a lens.'

From the corner of the Common nearest Charles Street came rapid bursts of hammering. Last-minute touches to the main stage – wood scaffolding, heavy curtains, iron pipes. Loudspeakers lashed to the trees crackled with static. Rapid announcements went winging overhead. Jasper couldn't make them out. Daniel, forehead wrinkled with concentration, interpreted.

'The official part of the program's about to begin.'

Jasper and Daniel dutifully headed for the stage. 'Dr Whiting, sir, nice to see you.' A distinguished man stepped forward, putting a hand on Jasper's shoulder.

'????'

'Marcus Featherstone, remember me?'

'Of course.'

Suddenly on all sides Jasper noticed students in cobalt blue sweatshirts printed with large white letters, N.E. School for Special Children. They were fanning out, stopping passers-by, collecting signatures on a petition.

'More state funds,' explained Featherstone. 'We're bursting our britches,' he laughed. 'The turn-out' – from the way Featherstone spread his arms, he seemed to claim credit for the thousands on view – 'is very gratifying, don't you think?'

Anselmo, Rhoda's favorite, was conspicuous. Half a head taller than the rest to begin with, he held himself so erect. His streak of white hair, the hardness of his flashing eyes, had something princely. And he wasn't chasing signatures.

'Going places, that one,' Featherstone said, following Jasper's gaze. 'Mark my words.' Then he lowered his voice, crept an inch closer. 'It is, I think, a great shame that Rhoda – Mrs Massler – had to leave us.'

'What?'

'Yes, quite a loss.'

Now as he shifted with Daniel to within convenient hearing distance of the stage, Jasper Whiting felt old, old and irritable. Rhoda had left the school? *The* school – *her* school. Jasper stumbled over a child who rushed up with candied apples for sale. Overhead scraps of cloud had begun to stick together and float south off the river. Jasper began to think of going home.

'Fa, ever stop to consider the sex life of a basketball star?' Daniel asked.

'The what of a what?'

'Skip it.'

The air swarmed with sounds, magnified whispers, tatters of static from electronic devices being tested. Through the din, despite a nagging wish to go, to be alone and bury his head in his arms, never to have touched the human body with his hands, not as a surgeon, not as a lover, Jasper Whiting, heartsick, registered a familiar gurgling voice, one that sounded like to understand it you had to put your own head under water. Again the gurgle, this time more frantic. Slowly Jasper turned and saw Sloan Glintz behind him.

Sloan had in fact seen Jasper first. Now the boy sat straining forward, wagging the upper part of his body in greeting, slavering.

'My friend!' From behind a firm hand grasped Jasper's elbow. 'Come.' Murray Cutler maneuvered Sloan's wheelchair through the crowd. Step by step Jasper and Daniel followed until they came to a woman seated bolt upright on a tablecloth weighted down at the four corners with smooth stones. They approached from behind. On the ground beside her rested a thermos flask and platters of cookies with sugar pearls and bright slivers of maraschino cherries.

Gayle Glintz, unmistakable even from the back, posture impeccable, was wearing her frayed fox-piece and fine silk dress. Today she also wore a small skull cap of blue and green feathers. Scanning the Common with large binoculars, little did she dream that she herself was under observation, not until Jasper circled around and crouched down inches in front of her lens.

'Oh!' Had Gayle Glintz aged so in the interim? Or had Jasper simply never seen her by the light of day before? Her wrinkles were caked with a faint pink powder. 'Jasper Whiting, you scared the living daylights out of me.' Gayle adjusted her hat, patted the cloth next to her and presented one gaunt cheek for a kiss.

'How 'bout a couple of burgers, Fa?' Daniel squatted at Jasper's side.

'Gayle, would you and . . .'

'Thank you, but no thank you. We brought our own provisions.'

Daniel crumpled up the few dollars Jasper gave him, nodded to the others and trotted off.

'Your boy?' Gayle Glintz cocked one eye shut. 'He's going to be a heartbreaker, all right. Those eyes!'

'So,' Jasper said for lack of anything better, 'a reunion.'

'Yes,' – Gayle smiled – 'we've wondered how you'd been keeping yourself.'

'Sloan's certainly looking very well,' Jasper said. 'Slow and steady' – Jasper raised his arms above his head and moved them about like he was drowning.

'Oh no, doctor. I put a stop to all that long ago.'

'So.'

'*She* didn't like it either, Rhoda. But after all, whose child is it?'

'I see. I thought . . .'

'People make such extravagant claims for patterning, doctor,' Gayle explained. 'That's the trouble. And with what result? Extravagant expectations, extravagant disappointment. And all that hard work!' Gayle idly laid a hand on Jasper's knee. 'No, I don't have to tell you about the sacrifices involved, do I? Coffee?'

The first time Gayle Glintz paused, while she hammered with the heel of her hand at the top of her thermos, releasing short, sharp jets of strong, fragrant coffee into plastic cups, Jasper risked the one question that was burning his tongue. 'Is Rhoda here?'

'Is the Pope Catholic?' Gayle retorted, a bit huffily. 'Of course she's here. Busy, busy, busy. I don't doubt she even cancelled her rehearsals.'

'Rehearsals?'

'Oh yes, Mrs Massler's very grand these days. Speak of the devil . . .' Gayle pointed with her chin to the far side of the stage in front of them. First Jasper only saw Anselmo. By leaning to one side he could see a woman talking up at him, Anselmo's eyes fixed on her lips. Anselmo wore a long gray cape. In one hand he held a wooden baton which he kept slapping flat against the side of his leg. The woman was a stranger to Jasper. Short hair, a waif cut, black laced with silver. An embroidered white draw-string peasant blouse, cheesecloth, plunging at the neck, too small, encasing heavy breasts. The face was round, distant, reserved, the flesh loose beneath her small chin. The only striking thing about the face was the woman's eyes. Set in sockets bruised from lack of sleep, they looked so illimitably sad, yet glittered with mischief.

'Rhoda*lin*da,' Gayle Glintz called out in a shrill, unnatural voice, waving one hand. 'Rhoda.' The stranger turned, smiling. For the merest fraction of a second her eyes locked with Jasper's. She waved offhandedly and went back to her conversation with Anselmo.

Jasper had argued in his heart against her. Over and over he had run her craziness down. A hundred times a day he found himself shaking his head at their irreconcilable differences. He had gone back to his old life with a vengeance, picked up where he'd left off seamlessly. And now his body nearly leapt out of its skin with longing towards her. His need, undiminished, made him dizzy.

'And there's another of your old friends.' Gayle gently turned Jasper's head with a fingertip against his nose. Not more than twenty-five yards away, seeming to tremble where he stood like some deer alone in a silent wood, Matasapi was surrounded by lean boys. They hung on his words as if at any moment he might spit coins. All looked vaguely familiar and effete, their gauntness cultivated and prized. Above their heads stretched a banner, green on yellow.

'The Fallout Shelter?' Jasper read aloud.

'New England's first and foremost cripple bar,' Gayle Glintz said snidely. 'Don't look at me, I'm not making it up.'

'Cripple bar?'

'I believe they have some other name for it themselves. Remember the Gold Mine? Of course you do, that club – the one we all went to.'

'Behind the Old State House?'

'Sloan's visit changed it forever – that and the fact Matasapi owns it now.' At the mention of his name, Sloan abruptly reached out in an ill-coordinated effort to grasp Jasper's hand. Murray guided Jasper's hand into Sloan's. The boy raised it to his lips, concentrating as hard as any alcoholic on a cup of coffee.

Without any warning the first notes of 'The Star-Spangled Banner' burst in mid-air. Many in the crowd simply went right on talking, moving about, but Gayle Glintz rose and stood at attention. She folded one hand over her heart and sang in a surprisingly husky, not unpleasant voice, while staring, it seemed, at some flag flapping majestically in her mind's eye. Sloan's fingers continued to play with Jasper's, making Jasper acutely aware of the skeleton packaged in his flesh.

A trio of Siamese twins led the singing. Jasper caught sight of the band: bright uniforms, blank faces. The drum bore the insignia of McCleans, New England's poshest bin. As the final stirring note of the national anthem rang out, a long cheer arose and crested like a wave.

'Isn't it a beautiful day?' On stage a small man in dark clothes stepped forward. Behind him a great deal of activity was still going on. People moving back and forth. His warm, confident voice floated out over the Common reassuringly. Down front someone below stage level pushed a standing microphone closer to the man's face. 'And I'm proud to say' – the added volume helped – 'a lot of beautiful people have come out to celebrate it!' Whistles, shouts, applause. 'But you didn't come to listen to me.'

'That's *him*,' Gayle whispered to Jasper, a trace of contempt, cautious contempt, in her voice. He had freed his fingers from Sloan's manipulations, and caressed them now with his other hand.

'Him?'

'Alex Thane.'

Jasper sat up to take notice, but too late. Rhoda's miracle worker was gone. To the accompaniment of rhythmic clapping and hoarse cheers, a young man in a bright purple satin jersey was spinning in circles in a wheelchair, rocking back on two wheels in a mothlike dance around the microphone.

'Swish,' Murray said to Jasper.

' – wish,' echoed Sloan.

'I'll tell you who's *not* here' – Gayle Glintz had reseated herself and sat nibbling at the edge of a sugar cookie – 'and that's our friend Luigi Glow Worm. They asked him, all right. You can make book on it. They wanted him for one of the main attractions, but oh no, not him, not Glamour Puss. Frankly' – here Gayle Glintz spoke so softly that Jasper had to lean close to hear her – 'I think that one's calling the shots.' Her elbow jutted unwaveringly in Matasapi's direction.

Swish's voice thundered on. 'Handicapped people are a wasted resource, a hidden population. Oh, I know what they say. We've given you Section 503 and 504, they say, what more do you want? First of all, no one's ever *given* us anything. We had to fight every inch of the way. Sections 503 and 504, big deal. You want to know what we have? We have less income, less education, less employment and more poverty!' The paraplegic basketball star was haranguing the crowd. And they loved it.

'Well then, that's what we have, but what do we want? What do we here today *want*? "Know what you want, boy," Daddy used to say to me, "and you walk tall." All right then. Are you listening out there, all you policy-makers too damn scared to come out here today and play the game of democracy according to your own rules? We want – work! Real work. Not just selling Bibles door to door or walk-ons in video nasties. Something better than risking our lives twelve hours a day at a corner newsstand.

' "What? Work, you say?" ' Here Swish turned his wheelchair first to one side then to the other, and masterfully switching voices, Bones and Interlocutor both, he treated the spectators to a comic dialogue.

' "There aren't *even* jobs for the able-bodied." ' Swish shook his head slightly and laughed out loud. ' "Shake your head any way you want, young man. Shake it left, shake it right, shake it center. It's not going to change things." ' The Governor's voice grew indignant. ' "Why, look at the unemployment figures," ' – Swish pointed to the sky – ' "and they're still going up."

' "I know," I told him. "I know, I know."

' "So what do you expect?"

' "Governor, *let us compete*." ' Here Swish tossed up an imaginary left hook and watched the ball arc and come down cleaving the net neat as you please.

' "You can't be serious." '

' "Oh, can't I? I've never been more serious in my life. We can't use our legs, then I tell you our hands do better work. Faster, more accurate, stronger. We can't use our eyes – put our ears to work, our sense of smell. It *can* be done, and you know why? You know why, Mr Governor? It's a question of motivation. We *want* to work. We're dying for a chance to work. Motivation, Governor, God love it, I've seen it win so many ball games. Oh, and",' – Swish winked – '" – we're honest."

'You know what the Governor said then? He said, "Swish, a man with a family, that man needs work."

'"I couldn't agree with you more" was my answer.' Here Swish pounded both forearms down on the sides of his wheelchair so hard the wheelchair left the ground. '"And now, Sir, suppose you tell me what makes you think that the disabled don't got families?"'

As the crowd cheered and whistled, Swish wheeled himself back into the shadows at the rear of the stage.

'They were all out, sorry.' Daniel handed crumpled money back to Jasper. He was breathing hard and holding a bunched handkerchief to his head, the cloth streaked with blood. 'It's nothing, really, don't worry.'

'What happened?' Gayle Glintz asked Jasper's question for him. She gathered in the tablecloth to protect it from bloodstains.

'Nothing.'

Jasper forced Daniel to let him look at the wound. Curls were matted with blood at one temple. It was merely a surface scratch. The scalp bleeds profusely at the slightest abrasion. Daniel helped himself to a heart-shaped cookie.

'*What happened*, Daniel?'

'Nothing.' The boy shrugged. 'A little accident. Some joker pulled the mustard jar off the wagon. People are such slobs, the outside was all sloppy and slippery. It was one of those big jobs, see, and all he had to hold on to it with were these two hooks. Me and another kid both bent down to pick up the pieces at the same time and bunked heads. Don't make such a big deal out of it. Everybody's looking.'

A wave of applause drew their attention back to the stage. 'Rita Kern,' Murray filled them in. 'Alex, he just gave her a medal to honor her father.'

Rita Kern, compact and composed, looked about twenty-five. Her wavy hair was in a helmet cut, she wore high snakeskin boots. Before she spoke she lowered the microphone, gripping it with one fist around its throat. With her other hand she held up the medal for everyone to see. Photographers snapped pictures with their cameras at arm's length above their heads, viewfinders inverted.

'My father . . .'

'Louder,' voices out back called.

'My father, I know, would have been very proud to receive this medal. The world loved him as a comic. He made millions laugh at things they never dared to find funny before. But he had a serious side as well.' Rita, aggressive and unsure, was not a natural speaker. 'He would have found it an honor to be here, to share this memorable day on the Common with you all.

'What do we want? That is the question we have been asked to address today. If you'll permit me, I think I can speak for my father. As kids, and later, as we were growing up, how often we heard him say, "Save us, oh Lord, from our loneliness." And, for once, he wasn't kidding. You have already heard one answer to the question what we want. Work. Yes, *work* is terribly important. What I want to add now, what my father would add if he were here, is touch. Touch, that's all. Nothing impossible about that, now is there? No employment statistics for any politician to get the wind up about and throw in my face. Yet, friends, if anything touch will be even harder to achieve than work.'

Alex Thane came forward with a glass of water. The girl smiled, gulped thirstily, the sound of her drinking magnified by the microphone. How much, Jasper wondered, would the crowd accept from her? Rita Kern was, after all, unlike her late father, whole. In time Sam Kern's most famous joke had lost little of its impact: a black man and a blind man jumped off the Washington Monument at the same time, who hit the ground first? Who cares.

'Accidental, casual touch.' She was back at the microphone, crowding it, speaking more rapidly now. Maybe Alex had told her to pick up the pace? 'The way other people are with each other when they don't stop to think. As a people, we Americans may not be particularly free or easy with our hands and bodies, no – but still it happens, we do, we will touch each other – a hand on the shoulder, brushing elbows, a friendly hug, a good-natured shove. But the disabled, they live *isolated from touch.*' The girl was crying now, silently. The tears, which by and large embarrassed her listeners, also fascinated them.

'Isn't it ironic that with all our so-called modern advances for the handicapped we're moving so fast in the wrong direction – away from touch. Have you ever stopped to consider that? I mean all our new technology, look at it, the results of engineering research to help the disabled. Mechanical, all of it. Machines to increase efficiency and reduce contact. Ramps, buses that kneel down, traffic lights that buzz on red, whistle on green, hoists, separate but equal drinking fountains, micro-computers with controls you only have to breathe on to make them work. What is it all about, really? These things cost a fortune – do we need them? The answer is yes, of course we do, if we'd rather not touch the disabled. No, if we wish to improve the quality of their lives.'

'Whacko.' Gayle Glintz's comment was a little too loud for Jasper's comfort.

'It may be more difficult to help a cripple into a car by grabbing hold of him around the waist from behind and lifting him. Don't tell me about it. Sam Kern was a big man. You may even need two people, someone for the legs – but no invention where you just push a button and step back to watch a bunch of chains and pulleys do the rest can ever replace the intimacy of that struggle, flesh on flesh – the commitment!

'Maybe you've heard cripples don't like to be touched? You have, haven't you?'

Sloan had leaned his head back and closed his eyes. His cheek rested against the back of one of Murray's hands. The boy kept licking his lips, over and over again.

'Well, it's a lie. In fact it's the kind of Big Lie at the heart of the whole problem. Why do cripples let other people think out loud for them? How long will they go on accepting the way people in power put their own words, their own fears, in cripples' mouths? To anyone who listened, my father's jokes taught us that. Here, today, let's agree not to carry the conspiracy any further. Let's not conceal the fact from anyone who wants to know that cripples love to be touched – and to touch.'

Kern's daughter stepped back from the mike, embraced Alex, and walked briskly to her chair upstage. She didn't acknowledge the clapping, hard and long, that followed her, but sat, still and small, clutching her father's medal in both hands. Gayle Glintz made a show of bending over to kiss Sloan's eyes which fluttered with surprise.

'What now?' Daniel said. 'Oral orgasm's a hard act to follow.'

Jasper was too preoccupied with trying to spot Rhoda in the crowd to bother about Daniel's banter. She had melted from sight. He felt stranded, utterly alone.

Up on the stage students from the School for Special Children, some thirty-odd, a real mob, all in blue sweatshirts, formed themselves into three semi-circular rows. They were carrying musical instruments, a strange array. Once the orchestra stood in place, Anselmo strode forward. First, with commanding presence, he bowed to the ever-growing crowd on the sweeping Common lawn. Next he unfastened his cape and flung it theatrically to one side. Then Anselmo turned his back on the public and stepped up onto a low platform. He tossed his mane of hair and stood with both arms raised, conductor's baton upright in his left hand. As Anselmo's straightfaced musicians lifted their motley instruments, Jasper blushed. He couldn't say what was coming, not exactly, but unless he missed his guess, the crowd was in for it.

For a long instant the eyes of all the other special children riveted on Anselmo's hidden features. Somehow the vast crowd fell silent, that included birds, babies, hawkers, motorcycle engines. Anselmo's poised baton worked as a lightning rod for silence. Jasper was not the only one whose heart detonated in his ears. When tension had been stretched to its limit, only then did Anselmo break his freeze. Down came his arm and he began conducting. A blast of music, scratchy and shrill, spewed from massive amplifiers flanking the stage. Sloan was in heaven. The cacophony of the deaf and dumb orchestra with its desperate dissonances sent shivers of delight through his body. Anselmo's arms snaked through space, baton flashing. He was stationary from the waist down but a mass of writhing energy across his back. Flocks of sparrows, until then unseen, began to scream, launching themselves from the trees in fearful dark compact clouds above the heads of the spectators. Many in the crowd craned their necks back, laughing. People cast about for 'instruments' to add their bit to the volume of noise, the cascade pouring from the stage.

'Look out!'

At first one small voice from the wings of the stage, low, almost inaudible, sounded the alarm. A thin voice, far away, all but drowned out by the harsh parodic concert in progress, the cry muffled, overwhelmed, too, by the sounds of the crowd, the snorting and jeering. So distant, so remote, the voice hardly had a tinge of urgency about it.

'Look out! Get back!'

The stage, assembled in haste, was buckling, about to collapse under the weight of too many people, too much equipment. As one huge amplifier tumbled forward off the apron of the stage and landed with a crash, panic began to do its dirty work. People went running, scattering, hobbling this way and that, struggling to put a safe distance between themselves and the whole teetering edifice of the makeshift platform. With perfect mistiming, police on horseback came charging into the edges of the crowd, some horses rearing back mightily, overexcited, others prancing in place, nostrils huge and moist. By now the orchestra, too, was in shambles. Curtains and banners which had decorated the performance area were flapping free.

Wisps of smoke, too, had begun to drift, to curl out above the heads of the crowd, like a fine haze at first, a floating cobweb, but then thicker, more involved, losing the quality of gauze and turning into bales, dense, dark and menacing. Trash barrels had been tipped over and sent rolling, their contents ablaze. Up by the Civil War Monument a tree on fire seemed to twist about trying to shake free of flames. Among the hunched figures scurrying for safety, some were bent double coughing. Balloons began to pop. Great swarms were released, swept up and away by hot gusts of air.

'Get those tanks out of there!'

'Helium's bad,' Daniel said. 'Come.'

'Tear gas!'

'Oh, good God.'

Although the stage was like a raft breaking up, going down, the microphones and audio system were still working. Screams and shouts, commingling cries of pain were picked up and broadcast. More and more voices were crying 'Help' and 'Oh God.' There were sounds of cloth ripping, thuds, metal clashing on all sides. Where people fell, no one stopped to help them up.

'Fa!'

Jasper, rooted to the spot, threw an arm around Daniel, and hugged him, doing his best to master the fear which rose now like smoke inside him. Where was Rhoda?

'Ladies and gentlemen. Ladies and gentlemen, *please*.' Alex Thane's voice seemed to break from the churning layer of clouds that had blotted out the sun. A series of sharp, short explosions made the ground tremble. 'Ladies and gentlemen, don't be afraid. Everything is under control.' As he spoke these words with the sound system at full volume, 'Stay where you are. As long as you stay where you are there is *no* danger,' the clouds parted. There was a crash of thunder and a sun shower broke.

For a few minutes it rained hard. The McCleans band, regrouped on the softball diamond, picked up a tune. They played 'This Land is Your Land, This Land is My Land', a bit too slow but liltingly. 'We Shall Overcome,' a voice shouted out. People began reaching out for each other's hands. Slowly, a few instruments at a time, the band changed tune. Here and there frightened children were turning in circles, crying in need of comfort. Jasper took a half-step backwards and tripped over one of the anchor stones on Gayle Glintz's tablecloth. All around their little group people were helping to remove each other's shirts now, to wring them dry, standing and shaking themselves, joking. More and more naked bodies signalled that the immediate danger had passed. Faces, washed by the downpour, shone. Up near Parkman's Bandstand a single police siren wailed, red eye whirling. Agents, many in plain clothes, were cramming people into the back of two special vans, nothing gentle about their herding tactics.

'The Common is closed. The Common is closed. Please leave by the nearest exit in an orderly fashion.' A police vehicle with a cluster of megaphones on the roof came inching along Common pathways. 'Clear the Common. The Common is closed.'

'Good thing Mom didn't come,' Daniel said.

Mounted police were dividing the crowd into sections now, prodding groups towards separate gates. Jasper couldn't reach Gayle Glintz, Murray and Sloan who were shunted off in another direction, the remains of their picnic, drenched, trampled underfoot. And above, the small twin-engine planes advertising vacations for the disabled were making ever wider circles.

2

'Lucky, weren't we?'

It was Featherstone, soaked to the skin, distinguished gray hair bedraggled over his ears and high cheekbones. His nose appeared enormous now, his eyes recessive, for all the world like a water rat. 'Things got a trifle out of hand,' he said, 'didn't they?'

'Could've been a lot worse.' Jasper regretted his words as soon as he spoke them. Daniel's wound had begun to bleed again, trickling down to the corner of one eye. By reflex the boy lifted his arm and brushed at it with his sleeve.

It was once more a brilliant afternoon. Clouds raced flashing with gold seams. The crowd seemed to sense it had been written into history and was reluctant to disband. Near the fence surrounding the Common and on the facing sidewalk people hovered in threes and fours and fives. Here and there across the park grounds, empty now and heavily littered, police stood in dark clusters, their horses riderless.

'Did you see Anselmo' – folded over one arm, Featherstone was carrying Anselmo's cape – 'how he got everybody safely off that stage? A born leader.' Then Featherstone sneezed and they parted.

Taxis were scarce, and in demand.

'Can you walk as far as Mass Ave?' Jasper asked Daniel.

'Because of this?' Daniel tapped his head. 'You must be kidding.' Daniel's legs were longer than his father's, he seemed constantly to be half a step ahead of Jasper, talking back over a half-turned shoulder. 'Which one was Rhoda, Fa? The cowgirl blouse?'

'What?'

'Come on. I know you heard me. I'm not Mom.' Daniel leapfrogged a fire hydrant. 'And I'm not blind either. Don't you think I know what's going on?'

But still Jasper didn't answer.

They didn't have to wait long for their bus across the bridge to Cambridge. When it came it was crowded, though, and they had to stand, wedged in among elbows, hips, backsides. None of the passengers seemed to know about the rally and its havoc. They chewed, they read, they stared in front of them with potato-white faces. How easy, Jasper mused, to re-enter the familiar world. Through the bus window he watched people going about their business as usual, moving in and out of stores, stopping to let their dogs lick tires, bending down to tie their shoes, no more urgency, or less, than any ordinary spring day.

At Harvard Square they had to transfer. A street string quartet under the clock in front of the Coop made their wait more pleasant. 'If they slaughtered us for consumption,' the woman in the queue in front of the Whitings told her companion, 'we'd be rejected.'

'Us, too, Fa.' It was the first time Daniel had spoken since leaving downtown. And all the way to Arlington he slouched in a window seat with the bruise along his hairline pressed against the glass.

Alex Thane had calmed the crowd, true enough. But he might just as easily have stirred them, roused them into action. At his bidding they might have split the sky with their Five Points, their Six or Seven Demands. Freaks, born and made, on the march. They might have spread out from the Common angry and rebellious. Set certain forces in motion and you could forget about calling them back. How hard Jasper had tried to make Rhoda see that. Yet, without his realizing it, the same held true for the heart.

'Fa, Fa.' Daniel tugged at Jasper's arm. 'I just remembered one of Kern's few good jokes. 'What do you call a man without arms or legs?'

'What do you call a man without arms or legs?' A telltale small smile on Daniel's face warned Jasper he probably wasn't going to like what followed. 'I give up.'

'Trustworthy.'

Swish had said there were at least 500,000 paraplegics in the United States alone. Half a million. And how many blind were there? A million? Probably more. If not blind a lot of people saw *very* badly. How many deaf? How many lame? Even allowing for duplication – the poor souls who suffer in spades – even so, the ranks of Rhoda's 'army' were not inconsiderable.

'Mrs Bacharach, with her mastectomy – I wonder if she counts?'

'What?' It was as if Daniel could read his thoughts.

'Then there are the new neighbors, the Millers.' As the Whitings, father and son, made their way up Spy Pond Lane from the bus stop, Daniel began to point from house to house. 'Her mother's been gaga for years.'

What had made Jasper think Rhoda had a monopoly on information about disabilities and handicaps? She was a walking mine of facts perhaps, but not the only one. The weaknesses of others, their suffering, was the meat and marrow of daily gossip.

'Who knows what the Coxes have got tucked away in their back bedroom?' Daniel grinned. 'You can't be sure of anyone any more, can you?'

'Stop talking nonsense, Daniel.'

'Nonsense?'

'Yes, and you know it.'

Yet Jasper himself could hardly shake a premonition that the gathering momentum of events begun that day on the Common might reach as far as even this familiar, safe street – the stately homes side by side, lit up early for a cozy family evening – and change it beyond recognition.

'Allegiances are a funny thing, Fa.'

True. And who may once have had a disabled mother or father, or child, or spouse – now dead – and have turned bitter, prepared to go to desperate lengths to guard the secret, or to revenge themselves, to hurt others as they themselves had been hurt?

'You'd better hope this holy war is all in your mind,' Jasper had argued with Rhoda, 'the sides are so uneven.'

'That's where you're wrong,' she'd fired back, 'and you've got a shitload of company.'

'And then of course,' Daniel sighed, 'there's home.'

Daniel's pace quickened up the slate front walk. As Jasper followed, the image of Anselmo rose genie-like behind his eyes, Anselmo the chosen one, Toscanini at the rally. The boy's deep, gracious bow to the crowd, eyes steely and mocking. The raised baton, motionless, and then, at last, the crisp downbeat, a signal – as Helen appeared in the open doorway, smiling, frowning, too, Jasper smoothed his hair – for war to begin.

3

The Monday after the rally on the Common began for Jasper Whiting as usual. He let himself into his office at 8.15 a.m. through the side door on Peirce Alley. He hung his light raincoat on the antler prongs of the rack in the far corner of the consulting room. With a yawn he moved to the windows where he twitched the blinds open so that slats of runny April daylight fell onto his wood desktop and rippled half-way across the thick dun carpet with its faded rose medallion, 'Dad's pool of blood,' as Daniel dubbed it.

Then Jasper fed the fish. He used a Whiting scissors to sprinkle a pinch of dried flies on the surface of the aquarium. He watched flashes of color rush to feed, rapt at the pulsations of their mouths. Fish had no arms or legs. He thought of Rhoda again, and the children at Spinedale Pool. She was no crank, or enthusiast. She had given herself to the handicapped. Why then had she left the school?

Plop! The *Globe* from the pocket of Jasper's raincoat spilled to the floor. He let it lie there.

Behind his desk Jasper rested a hand on each of the two stacks of files Morrison had put out for him. One, newcomers. The other, cases for whom he had already begun to draft noses or on whom he had actually operated. From the height of the piles, the waiting room must be full.

'Ready or not.' Jasper stepped down on the buzzer under the carpet next to his desk chair. When the door opened and the morning's first patient stood on the threshold, Jasper was searching in the top drawer of his desk for a pen that would write.

'Come in,' Jasper said, 'please.' The patient, male, slight of build, hesitated. Jasper gestured to the sturdy chair turned to face him at the side of the desk. The man closed the door gently and stood with his back against it, studying the room. 'Please, won't you sit down.'

The patient wore a hat with crown and brim, dark glasses and wide gauze wound loosely around much of his face. Through the years Jasper had grown blasé about disguises, masquerades, shyness. He reached out a hand and slapped the seat of the chair. Then, once the man had slowly eased himself down, Jasper pursed his lips and made a slight unwinding gesture, a spiral with his hand in front of his face.

'Let's have a look, shall we?' Jasper's voice sounded false in his own ears, his smile oversized and dry. 'That's what you're here for, I take it.' Was this going to be another case on the rebound? A runaway patient bitter with complaint about a colleague? True, Jasper had seen some godawful bungling. For some, after the first tinkering with their nose, there was simply no stopping. A lifetime of discontent.

Still the patient didn't make the slightest move to divest himself of any of his protective wrappings. Instead his two hands crept up to the glass plate on top of Jasper's desk and began to push it back and forth, an inch or so, not more. Fine hands, well cared for, not young. Through tinted lenses, the man was scrutinizing Jasper.

'I'm sorry,' Jasper joked, conscious as always it was something he didn't do well, 'but I don't have X-ray vision.'

'No, of course,' the man mumbled. Slowly, with two hands, he lifted his hat and laid it, cavity up, on the desk in front of him. With two hands again, up behind his ears, he removed his dark glasses. When the man began to unknot and tug at the gauze, by habit Jasper looked away. Recently these stripteases distressed him increasingly.

'That's better.' Stripes of sunlight and shadow barred the man's bare face, made him blink and duck his chin. There was nothing wrong with him. Nothing.

'You know who I am?' he said. It took Jasper a long moment to recognize the speaker.

'Yes. Yes, I do.' He was face to face with a man who never stared into space or at the edges of things, who always stared straight at whatever or whoever concerned him. Alex Thane. Alex Thane sat winding the long, loose skein of gauze around one index finger. It was he who finally broke the spell of charged silence. A quizzical look stole into Alex's eyes. He raised his free hand to the side of his head, running the fingertips lightly back and forth across small lines near the earlobe. By instinct Jasper's gaze had lingered on the faint ridges.

'Good work?' Alex asked.

Jasper nodded, and swallowed the compliment he was preparing to pay the surgeon who had done the face lift. Not good, that, Jasper felt – wide awake, blood racing. Definitely not a good beginning. Subtle communication without words. If once they chose that route, there could be no end to the misunderstandings in store.

'A remarkable place, your waiting room, Dr Whiting.'

'My wife wants . . .'

'Oh, no, no, no. I mean the people. The ones waiting. They're what make it remarkable. How they don't dare look at each other. Only the ones bandaged up like mummies, through their slits, they let their eyes go back and forth – like this – but they try not to get caught looking.' Jasper laughed. 'Poor things. So much fear of . . . ugliness.' Alex spoke the word with what amounted to affection. 'The relatives, of course, the escorts, they talk a blue streak. Pick a magazine up, put it down. Check their watches, brush the dandruff off their shoulders. Perpetual fidget. You know, by the way, someone's stealing your *Punch*? At least February and March are missing.'

Jasper laughed again – pure nerves – and sat forward. 'I think it's my nurse. My wife tries to convince me it can't be, Morrison's never laughed in her life.'

'Maybe she has friends who do.'

In standing Jasper bunked his hip against the corner of his desk. He crossed to the coat rack to pick the *Globe* off the floor. Smiling at Alex he furled the paper tightly and put it back into the pocket of his raincoat. The headline read COMMON COMMOTION. He, too, was sending wordless messages. At the sink in the alcove behind a curtain of brown velvet, Jasper splashed a few handfuls of cold water on his face. Then he rubbed himself dry vigorously, smoothed down his hair without a glance in the mirror and went back to his desk. Alex had reached across and pulled a leather-framed photograph of the Whiting family towards him.

'So, you were saying that you find my waiting room remarkable,' Jasper said.

'For openers.' Alex pushed the photo back to its original place. He pulled at the back flap so it would balance upright. 'I've been looking forward to our meeting.'

'Likewise, but . . .' Jasper swept a hand over the files stacked on the desk.

'A bad time, yes, I apologize. If things had turned out differently, we would have met before.' Alex began to push the glass top of Jasper's desk with his thumbs again. 'You were there, I know, at the rally. I had you pointed out to me.' Alex in fact had far finer, smaller features than Jasper had registered while Alex stood addressing the crowd. From a distance the face gave the impression of strength, from close up, of delicacy. It was – there was no escaping the word – a beautiful face. A silent film star's face, out of time, painstakingly preserved.

'In the paper' – Jasper's eyebrows came together – 'it says you're missing.'

Alex tossed his glasses and the roll of gauze into the hollow of his hat and spun the hat around. 'I am missing.'

'Was there – it also said you might be wounded. There was gunfire.'

Alex's eyes widened. 'The things one misses by not reading a good paper.'

When Jasper went to feed the fish, the sight of floating residue reminded him he'd just sprinkled their food on the water a few minutes before. 'Any news from your school?' But Jasper wasn't asking, really, he was telling.

'Sorry?'

Jasper wanted Alex to understand there was no point to Alex's trying to play The Great Imperturbable. However polished the act, his pose of nonchalance, Alex, Jasper knew, was susceptible to despair.

'Your school in Lebanon, is there news?'

'I see,' Alex said, 'that.' He spread his hands now an inch above the desk as if smoothing a cloth, magician style. 'Things are much as I left them.'

'It must be very terrible for you.' Jasper had told himself, and meant it, that if he ever met Alex Thane, the one thing he would never mention, *the one thing*, was the invasion of Alex's school.

So much for resolutions.

Another bad sign.

'Every pain, Whiting, every moment of shame has its time

and place. And function.' Alex wagged his head slightly. 'We are, I put it to you, alive in the here and now. Whatever happens, we must wake up each morning and greet God.'

'I, too, have been looking forward to meeting you.' Jasper knew he was talking louder than necessary, but couldn't help himself. Intent on proving cautious, he was little less than reckless. 'You know, of course, Rhoda is a great admirer of yours.' Alex frowned. 'And something else you don't need me to tell you, Rhoda isn't someone who admires easily.'

'Dr Whiting, dear doctor.' Alex gave a half-snort, half-laugh, exhaling a jet of air through his lips as if blowing out a match. 'Can a woman admire a man she's never gone to bed with?' Jasper gave no answer. 'Really, that kind of admiration is such a hair's breadth from pity.' Alex hurried on, easily. 'In some things, doctor, there are still a few, even a bungler is better than nothing.'

'To Rhoda, you, your work . . .'

'Look, let's get something straight from the start, you and I, doctor, let us at least try. Whatever you may have heard about me, whatever you may have read – forget it.' This then was the voice that Rhoda swore changed lives, a manner direct, audacious, and yet personal. 'I am not a hero. I never was. I never will be. This is all there is to me, look.' Alex held his arms out, shoulders rolled slightly forward. 'I am just what you see. A small, lonely man. Shirts, socks, shoes – I take a small in everything. A hero? Don't make me laugh, doctor. Not old, no, not yet, but that, too, is coming, rapidly.' Alex's fingertips again hovered under his earlobes. 'Small, lonely, frightened – well, *almost* frightened. And missing. That's the list.'

Alex produced a crumpled box of cigarettes from inside the dark jacket he wore. Black paper, gold tips. When he struck a match, he stared at the flame an instant, seeming to relish some private joke, and then he raised the match in a steady arc to the tip of his cigarette. Was the man balanced mentally? Alex tilted his head back and exhaled, watching the smoke distend and rise, musically, through the bars of light that came into the office through the open blinds.

'Rhoda told you about Beirut?'

'Yes. Some of it.'

Alex pursed his lips. He tapped the accumulated ash of his cigarette into one cupped hand.

'If you haven't seen a paper, perhaps you don't know what else happened at the rally?'

'So much happened.'

'A group from Rhoda's school, eleven in all, deaf and dumb . . .'

'Yes?'

'. . . they killed a policeman.'

'Are accused of killing, surely?'

'There are witnesses.'

Alex went on smoking, oddly distant and at peace. He spilled the ashes from his cupped hand into his jacket pocket. 'Tell me,' he asked at last, 'that boy, was he in on it? You know the one I mean. With the white in his hair.'

'No names have been released.'

'Anselmo. Poor thing.'

Outside clouds slid across the sun. The room plunged into semi-darkness. Here and there from the shelves that lined the office, gold letters on the spine of books gleamed dully. Jasper twisted the switch to light his goose-neck lamp.

Smudges, thumb prints, stood out on the plastic covering of the Whiting family portrait.

'We all play God in our own little ways, doctor, don't we? No matter what we try to tell ourselves, the temptation is too great.'

'I don't understand.'

'Of course you do.' Alex spoke sharply, with impatience. 'You understand even if it doesn't suit you to, doctor. If only I could be as sure of everything as I am about how much a man like yourself understands that he would rather not. What would life be like, doctor, have you ever considered, if every once in a while we didn't, couldn't put ourselves in God's shoes?'

'Whatever size He takes.'

'Yes, exactly. Dr Whiting,' – Alex stubbed his cigarette out in his palm and stood up so he could look down at Jasper across the shade of the desk lamp – 'I need a place to hide. Will you help me?'

4

Hurrying up the front steps of the Boston Opera, under the party-cake marquee, Jasper Whiting slipped on the wet stone but regained his balance without falling. Close, he thought, but no cigar. Workmen were scrubbing away at the graffiti which twined around twisted pillars. They used long-handled brushes dripping with suds to efface swastikas, Jewish stars, names, numbers and enlarged sexual organs.

Deep in the rococo lobby of the former movie palace, Jasper, watched by hundreds of his reflections, rattled the handles of door after locked door.

'Going somewhere?'

Over by the advance booking window, barred and shuttered, an old man in an ill-fitting pair of overalls sat on a three-legged stool.

'I'm looking for Rhoda Massler.'

'Are, are you?'

'Yes.' Was the man simple or playing with him?

'You're looking for Rhoda?'

'I was told she was having rehearsals.'

The man stood, turned his eyes up to Jasper. 'What's she got that I haven't got?'

First they went through a narrow side door edged in brass and down a winding wrought-iron staircase. The man walked like a bird fallen from its nest. At the bottom they entered a narrow sloping corridor both of whose walls were lined with runny yellow tiles. The drop in temperature gave Jasper a chill. And, short as he was, Jasper had to keep ducking to avoid the pipes of various diameters that came and went without rhyme or reason. Finally they boarded a freight elevator piled with painted flats and stage property, including a stuffed, spotted wildcat on wheels, baring its fangs.

As they rode the rickety cage back up to what Jasper guessed must be about street level, the guard scratched behind the wildcat's ears. It was a very unpleasant combination of sounds. Finally Jasper realized who the man reminded him of. A facial contortionist at a Republican fund-raising dinner he and Helen had attended years ago. As the climax to his act, the trickster had pulled his lower lip all the way up over his eyebrows.

When the elevator clanked to a halt, Jasper's guide pointed to a door half-way down the hallway.

'In there?' Jasper asked.

'Rhoda really makes her men shake,' the man observed with a loose grin, and slowly sank out of sight.

Rehearsal Studio B. Above the door the red lamp was on. Jasper slipped inside, heart pounding like a frog about to jump.

The room was deep and wedge-shaped, with only a few small windows high up along the textured concrete of the converging walls. Cold light streamed down from neon fixtures, frosted parallel bars eerily white above egg-carton aluminum grillwork.

Rhoda. Short hair made her look younger, less entangled in thoughts she couldn't quite control. She was wearing a free-flowing smock, purple, with deep pouch pockets in front. And she had on ankle-high boots with rolled tops, like a cat playing pirate. Jasper stuck close to the door, hands behind him, back to the wall.

At the far end of the studio, Rhoda was talking to a burly man who stooped to listen, one hand on Rhoda's back. He kept nodding. They stood, both with one foot higher than the other, on a segment of raked stage heaped with half-painted papier-mâché boulders and a quantity of rag vines straggling overhead. The only musical instruments Jasper saw were a white piano, an upright on wheels, and a harp. Some music stands, skeletal, stood in a clump nearby. A table so close that Jasper could cross to it in a few steps had a small closed-circuit video unit on top. Jasper could watch a three-inch Rhoda on screen, but that image, black and white, was decapitated.

Jasper stepped over several coils of cable and edged forward to a rack of folding wood chairs. Rhoda was making swift, windmill motions with one arm, holding her other hand cupped to her ear.

'Mickey, honey?' Rhoda called and all at once a man with blood vessels burst in the tip of his bulbous nose materialized at the white piano, hands scudding across the keys. And as for the nondescript fellow with the hanging paunch Rhoda had just been leading up and down, up and down a set of three steps among the rocks, when he opened his mouth, out came a voice pure and dazzling.

A hand on Jasper's cheek made him start.

'Easy, sugar.' Luigi straight-armed the seat next to Jasper down and lowered himself into place.

'So,' Jasper whispered, pleased, 'you're back.'

'And you.'

A row of diamonds glittered along the rim of Luigi's left ear. His T-shirt still bore his own computer print-out portrait, but now the material was silk and the quality of the image superb.

'How was New York?'

Luigi shrugged. 'Hard work.'

'You sound surprised.'

'We also did shows in DC and San Juan.'

'I saw – on the news. Some crowds.'

'How're you?' Luigi looked Jasper up and down.

'Can't complain.'

They fell silent, so did the singer and piano. Rhoda was

leading the man by one hand now, apparently coaching him how to climb down the rock steps as if frightened what might be lurking there at the bottom. 'It scares the shit out of you,' Rhoda was saying, 'but you've got no choice. What? *Can't*, my ass. Of course you can. Just try.'

Luigi brushed some loose red hairs off Jasper's shoulder. 'Good to see you.'

'I can't pick up a magazine or paper without . . .'

'If you gentlemen don't mind,' Rhoda called to them from across the room, feet wide, hands on her hips, 'this *is* a rehearsal.'

Jasper and Luigi retreated, first out into the cramped hall and then across the way into the opera canteen. The smell of coffee barely prevailed over disinfectant. It was almost impossible to take a step without half-sticking to the linoleum. 'Fly-paper floor,' Luigi said, shifting a good bit of his weight onto Jasper's arm.

They sat at a corner table and smiled at each other. Jasper thought Luigi, slightly drawn, had gained in beauty. The bracelets he was wearing turned out to be the separate halves of a pair of handcuffs.

'Tell me,' Jasper said, gesturing with his head back towards the studio, 'what do you know about all this?'

'*Amor Encore Sano.*'

'What?'

'*Love Comes to Its Senses.* Italian, early eighteenth century, anonymous. Hmm, it would never do, would it?'

Jasper was puzzled until he realized Luigi was eyeing the half-gnawed remains of a melted cheese and bacon sandwich.

'Just like old times, eh?'

'Luigi, what is Rhoda doing here?'

'Rehearsing.'

Jasper laughed despite himself.

'One for me. I like you.'

'Come on, be serious. What does Rhoda know about opera?'

'Looking down our noses time, is it, doc? Tut, tut, you of all people.'

'But . . .'

'Haven't you ever heard Rhoda in the shower?'

Luigi shrugged off his lightweight backpack and began to rummage around inside it. 'I brought you a little something from the Big Apple, Jasper. At least I thought I did. Ah, here it is.' Luigi handed Jasper a small, soft parcel wrapped in brown paper and tied with dirty string.

'Thank you,' Jasper blushed.

'I shouldn't have, I know,' Luigi laughed, 'but I couldn't resist.' He shook his head. 'You'd never believe some of the people I've been working with, Jasper. Come to think of it, maybe *you* would.'

'Like?'

'Like one designer who wanted to do a spread of me playing slot machines. Come on, boy, you see how bizarre that one is? Luigi and the One-armed Bandits. Another time I walked onto the set and there were all these naked mannequins with missing limbs. It was like Los Alamos.' The boy's eyes were frank, arrogant and playful. 'Nothing could quite compare, however, to the other models. *So* friendly, *so* helpful, *so* obliging. And there was one thing they were all dying to know.'

'How you lost it?'

'How I lost it – but a promise is a promise, Jazz.' Already Luigi was having the effect on Jasper he always had, making him happy with a thin edge of fear. 'If I ever tell, you'll be the first to know.'

'Funny, I haven't really thought about it in quite some time.' They laughed again, at ease.

'You look good,' Luigi said, 'relatively speaking. What brings you back to the fold?'

Before Jasper could reply, Rhoda came into the canteen with her assistants and some of the cast. They bustled about at the counter and slapped the cigarette machine around. Rhoda drifted loose and came to join Jasper and Luigi at their corner table. She sat and rubbed her eyes hard with her knuckles.

Luigi reached behind her neck and massaged the muscles there. Jasper sat on his hands.

'Nice,' Rhoda swivelled her head, eyes shut, lips compressed in a thin smile. 'Hmmm, just what I needed.'

Rhoda, too, had lost weight, a little. Her face was more lined. Thinner, she looked more childlike and sensitive. Up close, her hair, even cropped short, had lost none of its wildness. To cover his confusion Jasper pulled a paper napkin from the chrome container and pushed it around the table.

'God, it could only happen to me. I've got an opera to do about a princess who no can hear in love with a blind prince and I end up with a tenor who's tone deaf and a leading lady who needs a cornea transplant!'

Something was wrong. Jasper didn't know what, but something was definitely not right. Rhoda was 'on'.

'It's a cunning piece, really. The parents, his and hers, are country neighbors. The firstborn of each couple enters the world on the same day. Right then and there the prince and princess are promised to each other as man and wife once they reach the ripe old age of sixteen.

'Every year, on the common birthday, the daddies meet, the kings, to boast about their kids. You should see the one mine's got, right? As soon as the little ones start growing up, however, it becomes clear things aren't going to turn out so happily ever after. Vera's hearing isn't worth beans and Fidel, he's as good as blind.'

Under the table Rhoda grabbed one of Jasper's hands and squeezed. Her eyes avoided his. 'Kings being kings they keep on singing about their perfect children but meanwhile they hide them away from the world, the little boy with a tutor, the girl with an old nurse. Finally, on the eve of the promised marriage, tutor and nurse are sent off into the deep dark woods, the one with Vera, the other with Fidel. Both carry sealed orders only to be opened once they reach the lonely heart of the forest. As for the kids, they think they're off to a holy spring, one last scrub before the big night. Well, they get to the forest and there's a terrible storm.'

'There always is.' Luigi, Jasper remembered, didn't like to listen to long stories.

'Hey,' Rhoda snapped alert, freeing her hand. 'You guys want more coffee? Some cake? You're sure?'

'No. Go on, please,' Jasper urged.

'Excuse me.' Rhoda was called away by someone from the wardrobe staff.

'Look, let me take you to dinner tonight.' Luigi stood. His manner went crisp. 'I'm at the Ritz Carlton.'

'So.'

'Be there, out front, 7.30 *sharp*.' He swung away without looking back.

When Rhoda returned she was chewing on a pencil. 'That designer – now he wants a costume change *in the cave*. Caterpillars in, butterflies out. I tell him it's unlikely the prince and princess would happen to find something down there just their size, maybe one of them but not both, and he accuses me of being literal-minded. Where's Luigi?'

'He had to go.'

'Good.' For the first time Rhoda looked at Jasper. 'Now we can talk.' She wasn't too vivacious any more. 'Come.'

Rhoda led Jasper from the canteen, greeting people who flashed by with sheaves of music or props in their arms. Up a staircase and two flights later they entered a small office. Old opera programs behind glass, many autographed, lined the walls. There was a battered roll-top desk piled with papers and paperweights and a white ceramic vase of limp pink roses, petals large as moths.

'Sit down. What are you standing around for?' Rhoda removed a bottle of whiskey from one of the desk drawers. She found some tumblers, too, none too clean, and poured them both drinks.

'Luigi,' Rhoda said the name with nostalgia, 'the kid resents what's happening. As if it's just by accident he's burst on the scene when he has. There's nothing worse than an anti-Semite Semite. Cheers.'

'Cheers.'

'So then, Dr Whiting, to what do I owe this unexpected pleasure?'

'Alex.' At the name Rhoda started, but almost imperceptibly.

'Oh?'

'He came to my office.'

'And?'

'Look.' Jasper searched Rhoda's face. There was no sign she was willing to meet him even half-way. 'I don't want to be involved in your fun and games.'

'How was he?'

'Rhoda, did you hear me?'

'*My* hearing's fine, thank you. Where is Alex now?'

Jasper took a bigger swallow of scotch than he intended. 'Why isn't he where he belongs?'

'Which is where?'

'Back at the edge of the desert, rebuilding his school.'

'I don't know if you've noticed – but there's enough to keep him busy in Boston these days.' Rhoda smacked her lips and nodded in agreement with her own words. 'Careful, Jasper.'

'Careful about what?'

Rhoda smiled exorbitantly. 'Alex Thane changes people's lives. Don't say I didn't warn you.'

One step, two, and he could hold her. Taste her. 'Have you lost *all* touch with reality?'

'Ha, tell me about the reality you're in touch with, doctor.' Rhoda put a finger under her nose and pushed up the tip. ' "Actually, ma'am, I think we should keep the nose, bob the rest." Didn't that rally. . . .'

'Exactly!' The pulse throbbed at Jasper's temples. 'That rally . . . after what's happened, aren't you satisfied?'

'You mean that cop? He had a weak heart.'

'Rhoda, a man was murdered!'

'They should have given Lyons his pension years ago. What about Alex?'

'Rhoda?' In answer Rhoda simply raised her eyebrows and gave an innocent stare. Jasper's face turned an outraged red. 'A man was beaten to death – children used their bare hands as a weapon. And what makes it worse, frankly, is you and I both know it was only a matter of time until something like that had to happen. Train kids like that, teach them a skill and sooner or later they're going to use it.

'You mean well, Rhoda. Christ, I hope you mean well, but you don't know what you're doing.'

'I don't have to listen to this.' Rhoda tried to leave. Jasper blocked the door.

'Yes, you do. I hate to say this, but just because Anselmo . . .'

'You know something? You're a toy person, Mr Plastic Surgeon. You don't know fuck-all about shit. Why don't you go back to sticking cups and plates together – or whatever it is you do. Here.' Rhoda dug into the top desk drawer and came up with a manila folder. 'Here, take a look.'

The folder was full of photographs. Acts of violence on the Common during the rally. The victims were handicapped. Jasper saw chains, sticks strung with wire, brass knuckles.

'There – that's the dead man, Lyons. He and his buddies didn't exactly wear themselves out trying to stop it, did they? Take a good look.'

Bleeding faces, rage, pain. Police stood by, turning their backs. In one shot a crowd was kicking, stomping a fallen figure, one of whose arms ended in a metal hook.

'Tell me, Jasper. How sorry am I supposed to feel?'

Jasper Whiting felt sick to his stomach and weak in the knees.

'Funny thing – none of these made it into the papers though, did they? Why not, Jasper?' Rhoda's voice was harsh and full of mockery. 'Why do you fucking suppose not? And you, you stinking cunt, you walk in here and tell me you don't want any part of our fun and games.'

'This war of yours' – Jasper tossed the photos onto the desk and the roses came apart, petals dropping – 'is fantasy. Make-believe.'

Rhoda bit her lip, poured herself another drink.

Perhaps at that very instant downstairs the thick-set tenor was by himself, practicing how to creep down the rock steps, fear of the unknown in his eyes. Perhaps he was doing it brilliantly, with no one there to tell him so.

'Rhoda, it's a delusion.'

'Get out,' she said softly.

'What?'

'Get out.'

Jasper started to go. He opened the door to leave – then shut it again. 'You know what I think? You want to hear it? You and Alex, your preoccupation with the disabled, your *devotion* – Christ, it's become a kind of deformity in itself. That's right. This war of yours you're so fond of talking about – no, really, it's more than that, isn't it – it's gotten far beyond the talking stage – this war you're so dead set on starting – forget it! Forget it, Rhoda.' A note of pleading entered Jasper's voice. 'Let it drop and you'll be amazed, just amazed, how quickly it will all blow over.'

'It's just my hang-up, is that it?'

'All this hatred for the disabled, where's it supposed to come from?'

'Ask your wife.'

Jasper's head was spinning.

'It's nothing new, Jasper,' – Rhoda put the bottle of scotch, and the photographs, back in the desk – 'what's new is that we're taking care of our own. Because Carla couldn't scream did Lyons think he could just help himself?'

Rhoda reached out and touched Jasper. Both held their breath, eyes joined. Her fingers drained the animosity from his heart. What pleasure and happiness Jasper felt now, here, trapped as he knew he was in a vicious circle of crackling hatred.

'What's that?' Rhoda asked.

'This?' Jasper held up the package Luigi had given him. He was gripping it so hard his fingers went right through the paper. 'From Luigi. Something he brought back for me from New York.'

Rhoda clawed open the wrapping, bit through the string. Out flopped a large rubber nose. They shared a laugh uneasily. Jasper held the nose to his face.

'Where there's life,' Rhoda sighed, 'there's hope.'

'How're the plants?'

Downstairs a bell rang. A shrill sound. Rehearsal was about to start again.

'All right, tell me, Alex, where is he?'

'I have no idea.' Jasper's nausea returned.

'What do you mean?'

'I told him I couldn't help him. Rhoda, Rhoda, wait.'

At the door, Rhoda turned. 'You came here to tell me Alex came to you for help, and you turned him down?'

Then she was gone.

5

Although Murray Cutler and Sloan Glintz had become a common sight together in the neighborhood of Charter Street – 'Hey, here come Drip and Dry' – the harmony between them, their pleasure in each other's company, still made people stop and take notice. Murray's feelings for the boy were the first in his life that had ever connected him deeply to another human being. When Gayle Glintz put an end to Sloan's patterning sessions, inadvertently she had left Murray high and dry. He kept turning up for his shifts anyway. Gayle Glintz would let him in, pour coffee and wait stoically for him, like all the rest, to bore her to death with his problems. But, no, instead he drifted to the bedroom doorway to look in on Sloan and smile. Gayle wasn't the one Murray came to see.

'Does he ever go out?' Murray asked one day. And suddenly he remembered Sloan at the Gold Mine, the concentration of bliss. 'Wouldn't he like to?'

'Can't hurt' – Gayle had shrugged.

'You would like to,' Murray spoke to Sloan directly, 'wouldn't you?'

'Doesn't miss a thing, that boy,' Gayle Glintz was fond of reassuring people. She liked to ramble on to one and all about how Sloan heard and understood whatever was said to or around him. At such times her voice filled with such confidence she surprised even herself. Similarly she gave Sloan more credit for being able to make his desires and wishes known than, in her heart of hearts, made her comfortable.

To give credit where credit is due, Gayle was the first to see that Murray could genuinely converse with Sloan. And she did not rush in to interfere. She left them tranquil in their clearing, stepped back into the bushes, letting the branches swing into place as silently as possible, not to disturb them. She valued Murray and Sloan's friendship as evidence that she had appraised the boy's intelligence accurately after all, even if she had overestimated her own.

'Man's talk,' she referred to their communion lightly. Sloan began to eat more. She felt his eyes begin to follow her critically. 'He's got a marvelous sense of humor,' she bragged to Murray and was relieved when Murray didn't contradict her.

Even so circumstances might have hampered Murray and Sloan's maturing friendship if it hadn't been for Murray's ulcer, the fractional rip in the muscle wall of his stomach. One searing attack followed hard on another. He tried to laugh them off but then one day while shaving Murray slumped unconscious to the bathroom floor. When he came to, he lay stretched out in a bed in Peter Bent Brigham.

'Dead? My God, are you sure?'

Typically, Murray didn't want to disappoint anybody, but his eyes opened of their own accord. The nurses and doctor beside his bed were talking about a famous film star, a recent suicide.

Murray had hated it there in the hospital. Being bedridden meant separation from Sloan. Madge came three times a day. She fluffed pillows with a vengeance – not only for him but up and down the rows of beds. He found her tenderness touching but at the same time as soon as she entered the room it was full.

When the doctor told Murray the bad news – he was not fit to return to his job, for the rest of his life he would have to keep to a special diet, no alcohol, and not overdo things – Madge, listening intently, nudged Murray to pay closer attention. The whole time he was looking out the window, tasting his freedom.

'Any questions, Mr Cutler?' the doctor had asked.

'When can I go home?'

'When you're ready.'

'I'm ready.'

But here the doctors disagreed with him. Murray still had a fever. He tampered with the thermometer but they caught him at it. To calm his impatience Madge promised to look in on Sloan – if she could find the time.

In any event, after Murray's release Madge began to suspect profound changes were taking place in her husband's character when Murray proved not to need her reminders to swallow his medicine. 'One step ahead of you,' he'd grin. By then he was in fact sharing his medication with Sloan, biting pills in half. Sloan was very fond of pills.

With work for Murray out of the question, he revealed a new domestic streak. To keep the apartment looking clean and nice became a matter of pride. Ironing Madge's uniform, he whistled happily. He would ask about her day when she came home, polish her shoes for tomorrow. In bed he began to make little experiments, certain affectionate gestures and impulses of tenderness. Poor Madge responded in more ways than one – so much attention and effort gave her gooseflesh.

And all this time Murray was seeing more of Sloan. More and more. He bathed him, fed him, saw to his grooming. He didn't tell Madge about all their excursions together.

'What are you going to do today?'

'We'll see. What would you like to eat tonight?'

At first when he went out with Sloan, the responsibility almost paralyzed Murray. Had the world always been so full of danger? Nothing was as harmless as it seemed, from birds to planes, from screaming schoolchildren chasing each other, to cats and car doors, ladders, umbrellas and bicycles. He had other things to worry about, too. He couldn't always understand what Sloan was saying in the beginning. What if the boy had to repeat himself until his hoarse voice stuck like a siren? Or something might happen to Murray, an ulcer attack carry him off. That would be a fine how-d'ya-do, Sloan stranded in the middle of nowhere with a corpse at his feet.

When Murray insisted, Gayle Glintz made a wristband with Sloan's name and address. Rather than submit to a label, however, the boy chewed it clear through. Finally, while Sloan slept, Murray screwed a metal tag to the back of his wheelchair.

In the beginning it was Murray who made up his mind where the two of them would go. Gradually, however, Sloan's preferences bubbled to the surface and Murray honored them. The boy liked the sight of water and tall trees. To say he disliked playgrounds is putting it mildly.

'What did you do today?'

'Nothing special.'

'Like what?'

'How were things at the airport? Anybody ask for me?'

'Cora and Irving always ask.'

'Maybe I should visit one of these days. What do you think?'

'Honey, stop trying to change the subject.'

'I went for a walk.'

'I – do you really think you should be spending so much time alone?'

Murray was on to Madge's tricks. She said the opposite of what she meant, not out of calculated deviousness, but by reflex, the way some people never sort true left from right in a mirror. Still, after a full day with Sloan, Murray, peaceful inside, could cope with Madge. He cooked for her happily, slept with her effortlessly. There were times they lay in bed, Madge on her back, eyes closed, talking on and on about drifters or pickpockets while Murray, propped on one elbow, eyes wide, played with his hand between her legs. He would stare at his fingers as they moved in and out of his wife's body, growing wet, and wonder absent-mindedly whether Sloan had dreams – and desires.

For a time Murray had even tried to talk to Madge about his feelings for Sloan. This had not lasted long. She would listen with her lips set, chin lifted slightly, the way some drivers wait in silent fury at a red light.

'What do you think of his mother?' Madge asked.

'Nice woman.'

'Has she ever thanked you for taking the boy out?'

'Sometimes.'

'She should pay you, really. Something, a token. But,' Madge laughed, 'I admit, I have a thing against skinny people. Women especially.'

At the rally on Boston Common Murray's worst fears seemed to come true. Such a happy day – and then. Despite pandemonium on all sides, however, somehow he hadn't lost control. First of all he'd tied a wet cloth over Sloan's nose and mouth – while the boy's eyes followed a swarm of balloons as they receded so rapidly above. He had also wrapped a napkin bandit-style around the lower part of his own face. He'd swung Gayle Glintz's heavy binoculars around his neck and given her an arm. Then he had steered Sloan to safety, step by step, through a labyrinth of dangers. On the way Rhoda had come up to them and kissed Murray, calling him a hero. Gayle, too, couldn't praise highly enough the way he handled the situation. None of their kind words had mattered, however, compared to how Sloan had looked up at him with the utmost confidence, how – while the world seemed to be coming apart at the seams – Sloan's eyes were brim full of trust. That had given Murray strength and the saving conviction that nothing could harm them.

Again today as soon as the door clicked behind Madge, Murray stopped feigning sleep. He threw back the duvet and ran naked into the living room, forgetful how the neighbours below complained that his running on the wood floor sounded like thunder. Down on all fours he reached one arm behind the sofa Madge brought with her when she moved in. Slowly, carefully he drew out the fine Japanese paper and special dowels Rhoda had given him for Sloan's kite. Sloan's because it bore markings the boy had seen swimming in the air, squiggles and dots. With Murray's hand resting on Sloan's the way the arm of a phonograph may need the weight of a penny on top to keep the needle steady in the groove, Sloan had sketched his vision. Murray had, secretly, transferred it to the kite. He worked with utter concentration. Hair sprouted from Murray's body in lush symmetrical patches, shoulders and back and buttocks. For all the world, hunched over the toy he was making, absorbed in fitting the joints, he looked like a bear that had just crawled out of the rose bramble of the sofa fabric.

Last night's dinner remains stood on the kitchen table, a half bottle of wine as well, the corkscrew still jutting the tip of its twisted prong through the cork. Madge had scotch-taped a note to the coffee pot. Xs and hugs. After dinner Murray had loved Madge in ways that left her whimpering and girlish, curling her blunt toes, covering his face with swift, light kisses. He had launched her and played her out to pitch and dance in high unseen currents of wind – like a kite. With her large body suddenly weightless, fused to his by a column of heat, her thighs clasped around his hips, eyes closed, mouth open, he had stood and walked through the apartment, swerving, blowing her hair to keep it off her face. The folks downstairs had thought it was the end of the world coming. They banged on the ceiling with broom handles. Their thrusts had kept time with Murray's lovemaking and delayed the final upheaval.

Once the kite itself, a simple box affair, was assembled and shreds of rag had been knotted in place as a tail, Murray sat back on his haunches. Would it fly? In the kitchen he poured some of the leftover wine down his throat, splashing the rest in purple waves down the sink. Then he wrapped the bottle in a dishtowel and tapped it smartly against the edge of the kitchen counter. On and on he continued to break the glass, using a soup ladle and finally, the clothes iron. From time to time he opened the towel to inspect the fragments. At long last satisfied, he spread the towel with the pulverized bottle on the floor next to the kite. Then he immersed the cloth strips of the tail in a jar of paste and, using his fingertips, transferred lustrous green glass powder from the towel onto the impregnated strips of fabric. Weighting the tail was an old kite-fighter's trick. Sun would catch the kite sailing on high, and the fine glass would shimmer.

'Back to the Common,' Murray told Gayle Glintz. 'See what it looks like. All right?'

Gayle was in a rush to get to the beauty parlor – and she couldn't find either her keys or her clippings – cutouts of the latest hair styles which she'd put somewhere she'd be sure not to forget them. Since the end of patterning had freed Gayle Glintz's hands, the day always seemed to begin too soon for her.

'There's a lunch packed in the kitchen. The grape jelly's for him, don't let him get it all over his shirt. What time do you expect to be back?'

Sloan was washed and dressed. He had on an old army shirt and black harem trousers with an elasticized waist. His feet were stuffed into red tennis sneakers. First Murray brought the wheelchair down to the vestibule. He hung the kite, wrapped in plain brown paper, from the handles. Next he hurried back upstairs and, with Gayle's help, Sloan climbed onto his back, throwing one arm around Murray's neck, making breathing difficult, while with his other fist he held onto Murray's thick hair. In this way when Murray leaned forward Sloan's feet didn't drag along the floor.

'Don't give Murray any trouble.' Gayle patted Sloan's cheek and hurried down the stairs ahead of them. 'Enjoy yourselves,' she called up before leaving the building, 'it's gorgeous out.'

Murray had worked out the easiest method of descent, one where he went downstairs backwards, step by step. Sloan's cheek rested against his own. At Rhoda's landing, Murray paused. First he checked there was no one coming. Then he dug into a pocket of his trousers and came out with a small pen-knife. He flicked it open. Crouching slightly, shifting Sloan's weight forward, Murray went over to the battered, scarred sofa. He squinted for an instant, running his gaze across the cushions, and then lashed out twice, leaving two long, criss-cross incisions in the upholstery. He stuck his fingers into the slashes and wiggled them in the wadding. Sloan's lips were next to his ear. 'He loves me,' Sloan said. Murray could swear to it.

To reach the Common took them the better part of an hour, but no matter. They were in no hurry. It was a lustrously clear day, clouds seemed to polish the blue of the sky as they passed. Boston's morning shoppers were out in force. At every crack in the pavement Sloan's wheelchair jolted. He took the bumps as amusement, craning his neck back to look at Murray upside down and backwards, and laugh.

'Hold the fort,' Murray told Sloan when he fixed the brakes and left him under the awning of the supermarket. He only needed a carton of fruit drink and it was difficult to maneuver the wheelchair between the checkout counters. When he came back, two policemen were interrogating Sloan. What was he doing there and who did he belong to? Sloan had folded his arms across his chest, shut his eyes and screwed his lips together. At the sound of Murray's voice, a spasm shook Sloan's body. His eyes flashed wide and he waved an arm dismissively at the policemen.

'Take my advice,' the older cop told Murray, 'don't leave him alone. Not around here.'

When they came to the Common, Murray ran with Sloan downhill, knees crashing against the kite. Rubble marked where the stage had stood, workmen were unearthing the roots of a charred tree. For the rest, the rally last weekend might never have taken place. Bacon and Scrambled Eggs – another local nickname for Murray and Sloan – carried on to their favorite spot, the broad lawn behind the backstop of the softball diamond. Here Murray ripped away the brown paper wrapping and showed the kite to the boy.

Sloan's brush with the police appeared to have put him out of sorts, but now he brightened, recognizing the markings at once. Murray kicked off his shoes and rolled the bottoms of his trousers to midcalf. He kept his socks on. As he prepared the kite and string for flight he talked with Sloan. 'Don't be disappointed if it doesn't stay up right away. We can fix it. See what I did to the tail – strong.'

Murray walked away, keeping in Sloan's sightline. Then, short thick legs pumping hard, he pounded back across the grass field with the kite up over his shoulder. It took him several runs, pain building in his lungs, but at last the paper caught enough wind so that, languidly, reluctantly, it ascended. Sloan tried to shade his eyes with his hands, avidly following the pitch and toss of the airborne kite as it climbed.

'Okay?' Breathing audibly, Murray handed Sloan the kite string, knotting the very end for safety around one arm rest.

'A shame to keep him all covered up like that, don't you think?'

'Merriweather!'

Murray shook hands heartily with the young woman in a nurse's uniform who had come up behind them unnoticed. She, too, stared up at the kite, reduced now to a quivering speck in the sky.

'Can I try?'

'Ask him,' Murray said. 'It's Sloan's kite.'

Merriweather tossed her canvas bag with bamboo handles down on the grass and crouched beside Sloan.

'Can I try, honey? I've always wanted to.'

'Yes, please, he says,' Murray interpreted. He undid the knot and when he turned around again to hand the string to Merriweather he found her standing there in a pink bikini, her white uniform in a heap at her feet. She ran gracefully, her body strong and young. The pull of the kite on her extended arm seemed to tug the tension from her face as well. She tripped over her own long legs, fell, laughed, stood again and ran.

'What does it feel like, Sloan, to be a kite?' Merriweather said when she brought the flight string back. 'A kite has no arms, no legs, and still it flies. Help me with him,' she said to Murray. 'It's such a glorious day.' Together they wrestled Sloan's shirt off over his head. Merriweather decided the harem pants had to go, too. She pulled them down, peeling them with some trouble over the red sneakers. Sloan lay exposed at last to the eye of the sun, his spindly legs, his crumpled, misaligned chest. All he had left on were a pair of leopard-skin briefs.

'Do my back, please.' Merriweather handed Murray a tube of suntan lotion. She tucked her chin to her chest and braced herself on the arms of Sloan's wheelchair. In large circles Murray rubbed the lotion into her flesh. 'I'll smear Sloan in,' she said then. 'You can wipe your hands on me if you like.' Murray gave back the sun oil but he cleaned his hands on his face. He liked the sweet smell.

Merriweather shook the tube and then squeezed trickles of white goo onto Sloan's thighs, his stomach, and high up his chest. 'Rub a dub dub,' she laughed and slowly and thoroughly and professionally anointed the boy's body. 'It lets in something and shields out something, too. And besides it feels good. You're going to be' – Merriweather winked at Murray – 'irresistible with a tan, Sloan.'

Murray glowed with family pride. As Merriweather moved, the triangles of her flimsy bathing suit came loose like postage stamps that had been licked too quickly. The line that stretched to the kite overhead was taut as a harp string.

'My God, you are hairy,' Merriweather said when Murray took off his shirt. She fished in her bag and pulled out a pack of cigarettes and a lighter.

'No.' Murray shook his head, hand spread over his heart. 'Thank you.'

Seated on the grass with her hair trailing over one of Sloan's thighs, Merriweather took the first few puffs on her cigarette rapidly, her eyes shut, head back.

'I should run more often,' she said. Murray did not like to look at her that way. She was so vulnerable. As if she could read his thoughts, a shadow seemed to pass over her features. Suddenly her eyes opened and she scrambled to her feet.

'Rude of me, Sloan. Sorry. Here.' Merriweather took the cigarette from her lips and placed it between his. 'No, don't bite it.' She giggled. 'Don't nigger-lip it either. Keep it dry. Watch.' Merriweather demonstrated how to inhale. She blew out a cloud of smoke. Sloan was delighted. The lotion had melted into his body which glistened now. A breeze caught his hair. 'You're not cold? If you feel chilly, Sloan, say so.' Merriweather put the cigarette back in Sloan's mouth. His eyes grew enormously wide, his lips fluttered.

'Good.'

Alternating drags, the boy and girl smoked the cigarette down to a stump.

'When I was a girl riding my bike I once got hit by a car. It was after school and I was on my way home. I was starving. I had this roll I was eating, see. The whole thing was in my mouth. I never saw what hit me. I just went flying through the air and when I came down, miracle of miracles, I was all right. Nothing was wrong with me, not a scratch. The roll was still in my mouth, too. But you should have seen my bike. It was twisted and bent and smashed. Hopeless, hopeless.' Merriweather didn't need to say more.

'Smoking,' Murray said, 'isn't good for him.'

'Once in a while can't hurt,' Merriweather laughed. 'Do you think' – she looked so deep into Murray's eyes it took a tremendous effort of will for him to look away, like uprooting a weed that comes free with a clump of earth clinging to the roots – 'do you think he cares about us?'

Merriweather lifted a hand so Sloan's eyes were suddenly cast in shadow.

'Wouldn't that be nice.'

6

Rhoda Massler was dead tired. From the Boston Opera to Charter Street was an easy enough walk, but these days she always seemed to have too much to carry. Her music, her notes, her paraphernalia.

'A bag lady at last,' Rhoda joked with the driver of the Leechmere car before she climbed down at North Station. 'My lifelong ambition.' She crossed to crooked Haverhill Street and scuffed her weary way along the chipped and spattered sidewalk as far as Abel & Son. Her visits here, too few and far between, always revived her.

The ceiling of the shop was hung with every imaginable species of plant, a riot of greens, just the way Rhoda imagined a tropical rain forest must be. Abel, passionate about plants, had a connoisseur's eye and an inexhaustible fund of knowledge. It was Abel's son though, Billy, who had the green thumb. Good cheer incarnate, that was Billy, born with a mere stump of flesh for a tongue. Whatever he touched, grew.

'Rhoda! So you haven't forgotten us.' Abel hugged Rhoda. He was small and pear-shaped. His bald pate reflected the abundance of green overhead. 'How's that little climber doing, and the selaginella? Tell me, tell me. That was a sparkler!'

'Abel, ever heard of Vi-Gro?' Strapping Billy with his dark rock-candy eyes came to listen. 'My stage manager says it's so good you can hear the plants licking their lips.' Rhoda had a lot to make up to her plants. She was away such long hours. And more often than not when she came home these days, alone, she didn't feel like talking.

'Not too much,' Abel cautioned Rhoda as he rang up the Vi-Gro. 'You'll wind up killing them if you try to make them grow too fast.'

Rhoda made room in one of her bags for the fertilizer. Billy sprang to hold the door open for her. He followed her out to the street, wiping his large, soil-stained hands on his long rubber apron. Pretending to lift two heavy suitcases, he shrugged both shoulders up and tilted his head to one side.

'Thanks, Billy,' Rhoda said, 'but I can manage.'

Then the boy went into a crouch and viciously sliced the air with a series of lightning karate chops and kicks. Afterwards he made a shy thumbs-up gesture, winked at Rhoda and retreated back into Abel's leafy world.

'What do you think of them apples, Dr Whiting,' Rhoda said aloud as she headed home. 'You haven't had the last smirk yet.' But the boast didn't help much. It felt like she was carrying three heavy loads: two packages and a weight in the pit of her stomach.

'We'll miss you' – that had been the last thing Alex said to her when she told him she would skip the rally. Since then Rhoda had slept only a few hours a night, at most. The whole time she'd been waiting, as patiently as possible, for word of or from Alex. Jasper Whiting had been the last messenger in the world she'd expected. Rhoda's faith in Alex was, despite their differences of opinion, intact – but still it was hard at times to believe he knew what he was doing. Anselmo behind bars, with the rest. Prisoners. Rhoda shuddered at the memory of what she'd seen and lived through on the Common. Her foray into the front lines. For Rhoda had fought, too – kicked and punched and scratched – like a madwoman. Or more like a child. Eggs were broken all right, but what guarantee was that an omelette was in sight?

'The new Pied Piper,' Luigi gibed about Alex – calling

cripples forth, drawing them out to follow him proudly into the public eye. Rashes of disabled on the streets now, however high their humor, weren't likely to help the prisoners' cause. First, for God's sake, get Anselmo out.

Rhoda trudged on up Hull Street, land of headless parking meters, humming 'Murder, Murder, Dire and Foul'. Good that, not bad at all: how the old people unsealing the kings' instructions to kill Fidel and Vera were at a loss to grasp the motive, while the prince and princess weren't surprised at all, not in the least. Pity victims weren't always so quick to catch on.

At Charter Street Rhoda's postbox was empty. She searched twice. Nothing. No instructions, no reassurances. Not even another magazine with half a dozen glamor photos of Luigi junked out on success.

On her way upstairs Rhoda stopped at the first landing to refill a saucer with cream. There was a new litter of kittens under the mad slasher's sofa. Then just as she was about to straighten up she heard voices above, outside her door. Fear tightened like a vine around her heart. Slowly, eyes turned up, she kept climbing, lifting her feet on the stairs.

No, false alarm – the voices were familiar. Madge, and Gayle Glintz. Shit, those two were all she needed.

'It's Rhoda.'

''lo, Rhoda.'

Madge was in full rig, badge, nightstick, walkie-talkie, cap. Gayle was in uniform, too – curlers, a lime green beautician's apron, and her frayed mules.

'. . . to fly, sorry.' Before Rhoda even had time to greet her, Madge, looking sheepish, went caroming away down the hall. '. . . tomorrow.'

'Oh Madge,' Gayle called after her, 'the milk is boiling over.'

Madge bent a little stiffly and hoisted up the few inches of lace hanging below her skirt. Then she darted up the stairs, two, three at a time.

'You look bushed, kid.' Ever since putting a halt to Sloan's patterning, Gayle had been trying to repair the damage she felt the decision had done to her relations with Rhoda. 'How's it going?'

Rhoda didn't want to ask Gayle in. It was going to be a long enough night as it was. Gayle wasted no time, however, in telling Rhoda she was terribly busy. Business was almost more than she could handle. She'd just run up to check on Sloan. 'Not back yet. Expect them any minute. Murray took him to the park again today. *She*'s not going to like it, but tough darts.'

'Hmm.'

'Why do all the good men in the world end up with trash? Or does it only seem that way?'

Rhoda laughed. 'You're sounding more like Luigi every day.'

'If Madge would leave me alone, fine. I'm the last person in the world to start meddling in somebody else's honey pot – well, practically the last.' Gayle Glintz fussed with her curlers. 'I like to be helpful, I admit.'

'Madge needs help?'

'That woman keeps making the kind of insinuations I wish she wouldn't. It's bad enough such things come into her head, how she gets them over her lips without puking beats me. "They really spend a lot of time together, don't they, Murray and your boy. I wouldn't worry though, I'm sure it's all on the up and up.'"

'To which you answer?'

'Uh-huh, uh-huh. Maybe I should say more but I figure the less I say the sooner she'll catch on and get lost.'

'Uh-huh,' Rhoda said.

'He loves that kid, you know. Murray. And Sloan's not exactly your run-of-the-mill adorable armful either, is he? What does Wonder Woman want from my life? What does she think I'm going to do? Does she really expect me to stop Murray from taking Sloan out? It's just jealousy, plain and simple. I'll bet you anything she dots her "i"s with little round moons.'

Rhoda made a show of getting out her keys.

'I'd offer my services as sex counselor – but then Madge'd

probably start coming to you with stories about me and Sloan. Or me and Murray.'

She already has, Rhoda thought, but didn't say.

'Know what Madge told me just now – right before you came up the stairs? She can't look at Sloan without feeling sick. Nice words for a mother to hear. All right, fair enough. Some people have a thing about honesty – at all costs. And there are certain things a person can't help. All right. But does that give her the right to dish Murray because he can?'

'Can what?'

'Look at Sloan. Her latest stunt is a real killer. If I'm keeping you, just tell me.'

'I'm a little tired, that's all.'

'Just listen to this, then I'll let you go. Madge comes up to our place and starts talking to me like the two of us are alone – and Sloan's sitting right there in the room. "Look," she says, "I know a man isn't everything but don't you miss having one around?" I keep giving her these looks but do you think that stops her? Oh no, on she goes. "I mean it must get lonely for you sometimes *with just him*." That's what she says to me, honest to God, and the whole time Sloan's right fucking there!'

'Why tell me, Gayle? Tell Madge.'

'Her? You think she'd listen, that one? Don't get me wrong, Rhoda, I like Madge. Madge isn't so bad. We all have our little foibles, right? You, me, everybody. Hers just happen to be rather enormous, that's all. She . . .'

'Honey,' – Rhoda sniffed the air – 'I think I smell hair burning.'

'Long day, huh.' Gayle squeezed Rhoda's arm affectionately. 'Why not drop up later? Sloan would love a bedtime story.'

'Hello?'

Rhoda was disappointed to find no one waiting in her apartment. Who had she expected really? In one way or another she'd succeeded in driving off just about everybody who mattered to her. Oh boy – she'd have given anything to see the look on Alex's face when Jasper, that fucker, told him to get lost.

'Look what Rhoda's brought you,' she called to her plants, so much false cheer in her voice it almost made her wince. 'Strawberries with whipped cream.' When she bit open the plastic Vi-Gro bag, she used too much force, sending turquoise pellets in every direction.

7

Jasper Whiting showed up a few minutes early for his date with Luigi in front of the Ritz Carlton. Darkness was settling slowly, light as a feather. A few stray stars pulsed dully in the remote distance, nothing to pin hopes on. Motorists made do with their dims. Along the hotel marquee lights burned brightly and, glimpsed from Arlington Street, the plush lobby inside was dazzling, like the lining of a human chest, cut open and peeled back, one from which a gold chain or string of pearls, not removed in time, had tumbled into the gleaming cavity.

Jasper was no stranger to the Ritz Carlton. More often than he cared to remember he had been confined to one or another of the hotel conference rooms, or to the gaudy ballroom with its host of rosy peeling cherubs floating on the ceiling, and three-ton crystal chandelier. Here over the years for many a good cause Helen had bit her tongue while Jasper stepped on her feet.

Luigi had told Jasper to wait out front. The large revolving door was hectic with guests, coming and going. Potted box hedges on either side had been trimmed precisely. Against the evening chill Jasper turned up the collar of his jacket. He popped a pillow-shaped mint under his tongue and crumpled the empty packet, plunging both hands to the bottom of his pockets where they toyed with keys and loose change. Rhoda was right, of course. His turning Alex Thane away was nothing to be proud of.

Actually Jasper had told Alex he could stay until dark even though it meant that during the morning Jasper had to find excuses with a number of patients not to examine them in the alcove behind the curtain. He had smuggled Alex coffee and a sandwich. When he found Alex curled asleep on the examining table, he had covered him with his raincoat. He had lifted Alex's arm which hung heavy in space and laid it back down at his side. What message had he sent then through Alex's brain?

'Take it.' Jasper had given Alex a key to the door to Peirce Alley. When he returned from his rounds at Mass General in the early afternoon, the key lay on his desk. Alex was gone. It was then Jasper took a cab to the opera.

By the time he came back from seeing Rhoda, Morrison was getting ready to go. He chided her about the missing issues of *Punch*. 'I'll keep my eye out, doctor,' she said. Morrison had a way of wrapping a scarf around her neck which Jasper had never understood. 'Morrison,' – Jasper hadn't been able to check his annoyance – 'excuse me for saying so, but there are better ways to tie a hang-knot.'

'What, doctor?'

'Nothing, Morrison.'

'Is anything wrong, doctor?'

'No, Morrison.'

'See you in the morning, doctor. Goodnight.'

Jasper Whiting had stewed a good hour in the dark. He went over and over every word he and Rhoda had spoken. And shouted. He interpreted every look she gave him, every gesture, half a dozen different ways. He tried to be honest with himself about his feelings, but soon gave up the attempt as hopeless. What was honest one minute, two minutes later was patently absurd. At last he'd turned on his desk lamp. In the cone of light he'd changed the battery of his hearing aid.

'Don't hold what?'

'Dinner.' Phoning Helen had slipped Jasper's mind. When she called, for some reason he lied about his movements. 'I won't be home, sorry. I know. Sorry, no.' He kept his meeting with Luigi to himself. He didn't mention the events of the morning, or afternoon. Helen, sighing, told him not to make it too late. Now Jasper rolled the remaining sliver of mint onto his tongue so that he could feel its dwindling sharp edge.

'Enough noses' – that was what a voice inside Jasper kept repeating. The voice wasn't new, his inclination to listen was. Only he wasn't certain, somehow, it was his own voice. There was something young, naive and attractive about it, but at the same time something curiously flat. And the gesture of stopping now wouldn't be enough to satisfy Rhoda, not in itself. Should he take Luigi into his confidence at dinner? If Jasper started complaining again about Rhoda's obsession, would he still receive a loyal tongue-lashing in return? 'War,' Rhoda had said, 'doesn't wait for a show of hands.'

Odd, how people who hate never were lonely. There was always their relentless intimacy with the enemy to sustain them.

Jasper took up a position along the near curb where he had the full sweep of the front entrance to the Ritz Carlton in view. Just behind him a black limousine stood parked with its hood up, crocodile-style. A black driver in white uniform, whistling, bent peering into the entrails of the motor with a long silver flashlight. His aimless search was a time-honored tactic to beat No Standing regulations.

The revolving door of the hotel disgorged occupants in fancy fur-trimmed coats, hats, scarves. Staggered bursts of sound spilled into the early night. The shrill whistle of the doorman hailing cabs, music from a hand organ on Newbury Street added life to the scene. Now and then the hysterical twitter of thousands of sparrows drowned out other sounds, birds swooping, wheeling in a great cloud, darkness moving through darkness. Occasionally a few hard edges veered into the glow of streetlamps, wings casting swift, sharp shadows.

Growling. At the sound Jasper's heart skipped. He pivoted just in time to see a thick blur hurtle through the air towards someone on the point of emerging from the revolving door of the Ritz Carlton. As the man threw one arm up in front of his face, the lining of his overcoat flashed out, shiny red. The man tried to retreat, staggered back, lost his footing and went down under the weight of the dog, a German shepherd. The beast's snarling almost smothered the victim's shrill, breathless cries.

Inside the lobby people waiting to enter the revolving door, a group, found it jammed. Without investigating the root of the trouble, they applied force. Jasper waved at them, rapped his wedding ring against the glass of a side panel. 'Stop pushing,' he shouted. They were pinning one arm of the fallen man.

A crowd collected rapidly in the street. From a safe distance people called advice. One man set a book of matches on fire and threw it, screaming, at the dog. The doorman took off his jacket with braided shoulders and used it like a whip, snapping it through the air, but ineffectually. No one dared wrestle the animal off its victim. Its tail went on wagging violently.

'Water,' someone suggested. 'Get a fire extinguisher.'

'That's a seeing-eye dog, good Christ.'

'You see those shoes – any idea what shoes like that cost?'

Jasper scanned the area for a blind man. Two policemen ran up following an excited child. The hood of the limo behind Jasper banged shut. The long, sleek vehicle screeched away. A policeman went down on one knee and holding his revolver steady with two hands shot the dog. The sound made a woman shriek. Men on both sides of her laughed. The impact of the first bullet spun the animal around, sending its hindquarters slamming into the glass. Its muzzle dripped gore, its fur stood on end. As the wounded German shepherd turned to face its attacker, the policeman shut his eyes and fired again. Another shot, again. Snarling alternated with whimpering now. The policeman inched closer. At last he stood. His hat fell off. At close range he emptied his gun into the dog's pointed ear. The body heaved and twitched, paws paddling in the air.

In the vacuum created by gunfire, the savaged man lay moaning, writhing slightly from side to side, wriggling. Presumably he was a foreigner. His skin was dark. His coat, his evening clothes, were in shreds and tatters. Blood gushed from his face, chest, arms, thighs. With his hands he kept gripping at his stomach, trying to stuff his entrails back in place.

'What happened?'

The people trapped in the lobby had pushed through a side door to join the public out front. They must just have come from a dental convention: women in strapless gowns and capes or jackets carrying enormous papier-mâché teeth, molars, incisors and canines; a larger-than-life toothbrush, man-size, in the arms of two men, had flowers for bristles. The policeman who had done the shooting fumbled, reloading his weapon. His buddy was asking who had seen the dog's owner.

'Here.' The child who had fetched the police handed them a leather harness and muzzle. 'They were over there, like I told you,' – the child was careful not to step in blood – 'where the organ was playing.'

Jasper hung back, pain in his chest.

Veils of water were eddying from the steps across the sidewalk into the gutter. So quickly had the hotel staff begun to hose down the bloodied pavement. A taxi pulled up, wheels spraying the legs of the crowd at the curbside. The cabbie, a small man with cauliflower ears, helped his passenger out. An elegant, full-bodied woman, extraordinary dark eyes flashing, a high-domed forehead, like Helen's. 'Watch yer step, Madame.' Her every hair, billowing up and back, was in place, just as every hair of her full-length fur. Instinctively the crowd shifted to make room for her.

'Tell me' – the woman let one jeweled hand fall on the crook of Jasper's arm – 'what is going on?'

Heads turned at the sound of a siren. An ambulance rounded the corner, tilting onto two wheels. More and more teeth had collected on the sidewalk now. And a pink tongue, wavy, with red lips in segments. For the first time Jasper noticed a figure in sunglasses with long hair slicked back a few steps behind the woman. Clearly, wherever she went, it was this man's duty to plant both feet on her shadow.

'Tell me,' a bit imperiously, 'what has happened?'

The ambulance drove half onto the sidewalk. Some had to jump to get out of its way. The siren died. Two attendants in white raced to the fallen man. They kept shouting at each other and began to shift him cautiously onto a canvas stretcher. He appeared lifeless. There were more policemen now. How young they looked!

'Serves the asshole right,' Luigi whispered over Jasper's shoulder. 'No, don't turn around. You don't know me.'

'What happened?' A newcomer, arm around his girl, called from the edge of the crowd.

'Man shot his wife.'

'She isn't going to like that.'

Ambulance doors slammed open and shut. With some rough flat-palm shoving, police opened a corridor through the ranks of the spectators. While the stretcher was eased forward and loaded into the vehicle, the flashing light caught Jasper in the eye. The dog's victim revived and kept up a low-key wordless moan.

'Whoa.' Luigi restrained Jasper when he felt him start to move forward. 'No playing doctor tonight.'

'Ricardo!' The woman at Jasper's side threw up her arms, wide fur sleeves sliding back, wrists flashing with gold. 'Ricky!' Her voice broke piteously. 'Oh!' She slumped forward but before she hit the sidewalk her bodyguard caught her and scooped her up in his arms. A few bounds and he was through the hotel door and had disappeared into the glare of the lobby.

'Miz Scarlett, I do declare. Follow me, doc, *now*,' Luigi hissed, 'only don't make it obvious.'

Someone had covered the dog's body with a blanket except for the tail. The giant mouth-model parts were straggling off in the direction of the river, singing. The toothbrush bobbed up and down, leading them. The last thing Jasper saw before he turned his back on the Ritz Carlton was a police expert with a scissors cutting out a sheet of white paper to fit the chalk outline of the sprawled victim's body.

'Hey, what happened?' a latecomer asked as the crowd dispersed.

'Police shot a blind man.'

8

First Luigi headed for Park Square. Then he ducked behind the Continental Trailways bus terminal, wove his way through the lines of passengers waiting to board, and crossed to the far side of Kneeland. Stores were doing brisk business during late opening. He followed Kneeland up to where it cut across Washington Street. He walked on two legs.

Once they reached the heart of the downtown shopping area, brightly lit, crowded, Luigi let Jasper catch him up. Luigi's face had lost every trace of prettiness, and all color. 'Come on.' Jasper followed his friend into Jordan Marsh and up the escalator to the men's toilet at the back of the second floor.

'Guard the door. Don't let anybody in. Let somebody else shit in his pants for a change.' Luigi tore off his trench coat, and sat unceremoniously on the tile floor. Then he leaned forward like he was rowing and rolled back one trouser leg. With a few grunts and a little fumbling, he removed a complicated prosthetic device, a lower leg complete with foot encased in a shoe. This shoe matched, almost, not quite, the shoe on Luigi's own foot. With both hands he rubbed the stump of his leg, wincing slightly.

Out of the pouch around his neck Luigi pulled a small

blunt-nosed pair of pliers. He twisted a few nuts and the detached limb folded compactly. He dropped it into a nylon carrying bag which he removed from the pocket of his coat. A few telescoped pieces of aluminum tubing materialized from the other trench-coat pocket. Shaking these vigorously, and deftly joining them, he produced a cane.

'Alley oops.' Luigi hauled himself erect, grabbing hold of the edge of one sink. He splashed cold water on his face and winked at the dripping image in the mirror. 'Not bad, considering. Why, Jasper, fancy meeting you here. Going my way?'

They rode the escalator to ground level. At a perfume counter Luigi accepted free sample squirts on his wrists, wrinkling his nose disapprovingly. 'That's better,' he said. 'At least I don't feel quite so naked.' On their way out Luigi stopped dead in his tracks. Pointing ahead at the revolving door, he shook his head, no. 'Not on your life, I won't.' Out in the street Luigi put his chin on Jasper's shoulder and asked him, 'You know everything – who's the patron saint of revolving doors?'

Halfway down Essex Street Luigi turned into a small basement restaurant.

'But you *hate* Chinese food,' Jasper protested.

'I used to work here, in the kitchen.'

The place was popular with a college crowd. A lot of talk and laughter. Eyeglasses, sweaters, long hair. Only one or two narrow booths towards the back weren't taken. The interior was mostly red, heavily lacquered, carved wood, hanging paper lanterns, some torn, wading birds painted sketchily on cloth walls, storks poised on one thin leg.

'Well, doctor, how's life?' Luigi's game attempt at his familiar brio fell short. His voice was strained. A waiter came. With the side of one hand he knocked some crumbs and rice from the tablecloth and slapped down a pair of food-stained menus before disappearing. 'I like this place, none of the waiters ever smile. They get fired if they do. Order something, Jasper, anything,' Luigi urged. 'It all comes out of the same three pots anyway. The kitchen's the size of a food stamp.'

Jasper went through the motions of opening the menu. 'Your hands are trembling, doc.'

'I thought you might like company.'

'Yeah, but you guys, you're not supposed to be squeamish.'

The waiter returned, a toothpick jutting unappetizingly from the corner of his mouth. His head swiveled between Luigi and Jasper whose eyes had locked.

'The Red Purge Special, why not?' Luigi said. 'For two.'

The waiter stabbed his pad a couple of times rapidly with his pencil. 'Drink?'

'Brandy.'

'Two?'

'No, my dear, four.'

They sat silently, enclosed by an animated hum on all sides. Luigi took his right hand out of the hip pocket of his coat. It held his razor, open at a forty-five degree angle. He let the blade spring straight. 'No shit, Jasper, it's lovely to see you. At least you're someone who'll never let his ideas run away with him.' He snapped the razor shut and returned it to the pouch around his neck.

Jasper was a captive audience for a voice from a corner table. The speaker, a man, was hidden behind a coat rack swollen with jackets and hats. 'Afraid? Why? Should I be? If I have a stroke tomorrow, next week, next month, God forbid, I only hope you have the decency to finish me off – and be quick about it. The sight of them limping around, waving their claws in the air – I'm sorry, this isn't really the kind of thing to talk about while we're eating, is it? How's your egg roll?'

'Delicious. Keep your voice down.'

'Look, Chrissie, not long ago they'd have been left out to die, wouldn't they? And I'll bet they didn't mind either.'

'Jasper?'

'Like your mother said when she thought we'd called it quits.'

'What?'

'Good riddance to bad rubbish.'

'Jasper?'

Luigi had reached across the table and was shaking Jasper by the wrist. Jasper's brows knit, blood pounding in his ears. 'Sorry, I . . .'

'That dog was meant for me.' When their brandy came, Luigi dumped two heaping spoons of sugar into his, held his breath and drank it off. When he spoke again, wet grains glistened on his lower lip. 'Not to kill, I don't think so. But the result was not intended to be pretty.'

The beaded curtain to the kitchen flapped and suddenly there were many small birdlike Chinese waiters smelling of oyster sauce and sesame oil hovering over their table. All had round faces, straight black hair, eyes imprisoned in their sockets like coins stuck half-way in the pay slot of a telephone. Quick hands loaded the table with oval plates too hot to touch, heaped with enough sizzling, steaming food for dozens.

'Tea?' Luigi's irrepressible spirits were rising. What he poured from the squat pot, however, was virtually clear water. 'Give me a break, Jasper. I may be a rotten person, but the way I figure it, there are some around who make me look good.'

When the couple from behind the coat rack got up to go, their leaving was a relief, a headache that lifted.

Luigi raised a chopstick, tapped it on the table to command Jasper's attention. His gesture brought Anselmo to mind. In jail. 'About seven the desk rang up. My fans, a delegation, were downstairs. Would I see them?'

'What . . .?'

'I talk, you listen.' Jasper nodded assent. 'Down in the lobby that slimy Ricardo was waiting. He asked me to step outside to meet the others. My admirers. They didn't want to crowd the lobby. He played up to my well-known vanity and, I must say, he did it very well. Jasper,' – Luigi exhaled slowly – 'I don't think he knew what was in store for me. Not really. He had his brief, that's all. Or maybe I still have too high an opinion of my fellow man.'

'Maybe we can discuss that some other time?' said Jasper.

'Good. Back to Ricardo. Yes, yes, I assured him. I would be *thrilled* to show myself to my fans, more than. Half a minute to freshen up, to look my best, that's all I asked. Then I spun him around and sent him out to tell the others the good news – Luigi Sasakawa was on his way.

'I hobbled over to a phonebooth and screwed on that abominable leg. Then, burying myself in this hateful coat, I slipped out onto Boylston Street and circled around to meet you.' Luigi was shaking, sipping at his tea, struggling for self-control. 'When I found you, it was all over.'

'The dog attacked him by mistake?'

'Good boy, Jasper.' Luigi didn't speak much above a whisper. 'Rin-Tin-Tin did just what they taught him to do. Who knows, maybe he had a cold?'

'Are you all right?'

'Now that you ask, no.' Luigi held the hand Jasper reached across to him.

'Did you know something like this was going to happen?'

'There have been warnings, crank letters. The usual.' The brandy from Jasper's snifter flashed as Luigi poured it into his own. 'Ricardo was a real looker.'

'Oh, they'll fix him up.' Jasper didn't sound very convincing. 'Bites can do a lot of damage though.'

'Poor son-of-a-bitch. She was one of them, too, your lady friend who threw a faint. And the greaser. And the "blind man" too, the one who sprang the dog. Nice touch that.' Luigi swirled the brandy in his glass, staring into the vortex. 'I'll let you in on a little secret, Jasper. I can't stand pain. A splinter's enough to send me up the wall. And, you were right' – Luigi threw back his head, tossing off his drink like a sword-swallower – 'I hate Chinese food.'

'What's going on in this city is crazy,' Jasper said.

'What's new?'

'If it wasn't happening, you'd never believe it. I still don't.'

'You know, Jasper,' Luigi answered him, 'this is one of those things where it really doesn't seem to matter all that much whether you believe it or not.' Luigi picked up a shrimp with chopsticks, dipped the white flesh into the few remaining drops of his brandy, and sucked on it thoughtfully. 'Why me? Why me, why *now*? Just when I'm almost *there*!' Luigi held up a hand. 'Don't tell me that's the whole point, Jasper, I know that. But I never hurt anybody. All I ever wanted was to be rich and famous. And happy.'

'So.'

'*So*. I wish you'd stop saying that.'

'The rich and famous bit, I've heard that before. But not the happy.'

'The happy is new. And – I want to make other people happy. Sounds like a punchline, doesn't it, coming from me. The original Kid Ego. All right, *selfishly* then, I want to make other people happy – I never thought I had it in me, but I do.'

'Yes' – Jasper nodded, thinking, you do.

'What're you smirking at now?'

'Victims in waiting, Luigi, remember? The beauties and the beasts.'

'Surprise, you do listen.'

'Sometimes very carefully.'

'Then try this one on for size: *I just don't care*. Maybe I'm a bastard, but I don't feel it, Jasper, it's not my cause.' Luigi folded his hands against his heart. 'What's the use of pretending? Oh I could. I'm good at pretending, one of the best. Super Pretender – but first I have to see the point. Luigi Sasakawa, Public Cripple No. 1? Auntie Maim? Doc, that's one doll that would never sell!'

'Maybe you're looking at things differently,' Jasper said softly, 'since you want to be happy.'

This time from his neck pouch Luigi removed a small elegant black flask and, squinting slightly, read out the label: 'Moon Madness'. He sniffed at the open neck of the bottle, to all appearances lost in thought. If God had favorites, Jasper wondered, how did He show it?

'To think this dreck' – Luigi's lip curled back – 'may have saved my life.' Then he spilled Matasapi's priceless perfume out onto the tablecloth, watched it seep into the fabric and spread. Where there was grease already, the perfume made a detour.

'How'd it go at the opera after I left?' Luigi seemed pleased at Jasper's embarrassment. 'Dear Rhoda, she doesn't like me very much right now, does she?'

'I must be hearing things. Is the expert asking for help?'

'She has her hands full, so do I.' Luigi took out a pile of charge cards. 'Let that opera go over big,' Luigi smiled, 'and you'll see how fast we're friends again. Even Rhoda has an ego.'

'I couldn't believe what she said to me today.' Jasper looked hard at Luigi. ' "War doesn't wait . . ." '

'Look, Jasper, listen to Rhoda. Do what she asks.'

'What's this, a new tune?'

'How so?'

'You once told me, the first time we went out to eat together in fact, it would be wrong of me to trust her. And that was when she liked you very much.'

'If Rhoda's mad, Jasper, at least she's mad for the right reasons. At this point in history that's more than you can say for the rest of us.'

'How was the food?'

'How you doin', Mickey?' Luigi looked up. 'Superb, really.' Their dinner lay spread before them, hardly touched. 'Haute cuisine. Jasper, this Irishman owns the place.'

'Kid's all right,' the man told Jasper, jerking his thumb at Luigi. He had a very large red face that matched the décor and stood with his belly pressed against the edge of their table.

'Mickey here's still sore. He feels I was a little rough on some of his dishes. I wouldn't settle for half-clean.'

'Now's your chance to make things up to me.' From concealment in a menu, Mickey pulled out a color photograph of Luigi. Luigi accepted Mickey's fountain pen and with a flourish signed his name illegibly below his smile to end all smiles. 'Thanks. Feed's on me.' Mickey blew on his prize and disappeared.

'His lover's a rabbi,' Luigi said. 'Honest to God.'

'A rabbit?'

'Good old Jasper, no one's ever going to put anything over on you.'

Outside the cold air felt good. Arm in arm, Jasper and Luigi strolled along, each absorbed in his own welter of thoughts. In Copley Square, side by side, they stood staring at the reflection of the old John Hancock Building in the new.

'Why'd you go to see Rhoda today, Jasper?' Luigi ended their silence. 'I thought you broke it off?'

Jasper didn't answer at once.

'Just asking. You can tell me to mind my own business. I won't but you can tell me.'

Jasper responded by squeezing Luigi's arm. In fact Jasper had been puzzling over whom he could trust – and how far. And then suddenly it occurred to him that the others might be asking the same question about him.

'German shepherds aren't very smart, Jasper, are they?'

'What?'

'As dogs go. I mean you can't train them overnight, can you?'

'You think they'll try again?'

'Anyway one thing is sure. I'm not going to do any dog food commercials.' Luigi spread his arms, lifted his cane and balanced on his one leg. 'Coming with me?'

'Where to?'

'The Fallout Shelter.'

'Safety in numbers?'

Luigi laughed. 'Come on, for old times' sake.'

'Better not.' Helen was waiting. She'd be worried. But Jasper didn't say that. 'Late. Work tomorrow.'

Before Jasper climbed into his cab back to Arlington, Luigi hugged him tightly. 'I hope you have better luck than the last person I did that to.'

'Oh.' Jasper smiled. 'I almost forgot. Thanks for the nose.'

Once the driver reached the Charles, wider by night than day, he picked up speed. Jasper sat back and rubbed his eyes. Rhoda was probably sorry by now she'd ever had anything to do with him. Could he blame her? The simple truth of the matter was, Jasper was beginning to realize, he had never believed in anything enough himself to afford to judge someone who did.

With the fingers of one highly insured hand Jasper Whiting kneaded the rubber nose in his pocket all the way home.

9

He opened the front door of his house and walked into the dark. 'I'm home,' he called. Then he went from room to room downstairs turning on all the lights. The click of each switch, the swift flow of illumination, was reassuring. So was the sight of familiar objects in familiar places.

'Honey?' Helen's voice from upstairs. 'That you?'

'Coming.'

The clock from Helen's father, the desk, the curtain, tables, chairs – they seemed to press forward to greet him like old friends. But still, behind their smiles, they were leaving something unsaid.

'Jasper?'

At the first-floor landing, even though he warned himself to be careful, Jasper tripped on the loose runner. Daniel's Do Not Disturb sign hung from the handle of his door. Under Carole's door shone a thin bar of light. Jasper heard a series of high-pitched squeaks from within. At her yoga, no doubt. Down on the floor, one leg wrapped behind her neck, straining to do the Lion, the Cobra, the Frog on her special slick exercise mat.

'Hard day?' Helen was propped up in bed, reading. As Jasper entered the bedroom she looked up and smiled at him, folding her book closed with one finger marking her place. Her fine blonde hair was brushed straight back from her forehead. Her clear eyes were full of questions. The scent of Helen's cleansing cream, a few streaks of white on her chin and forehead, had an erotic effect on Jasper. It was so unlike her not to have rubbed it all in. 'You look beat.'

The good half of Helen's face was turned towards him, her burns, like the far side of a planet, were sunk in shadow. The rims of her eyes were red.

'I thought I felt like reading but ever since I got into bed I've been staring at the same page and I still have no idea what it says. Not the faintest.' Jasper's voice on the phone that afternoon telling her not to wait with dinner had unsettled Helen. The intervening hours had stretched out long enough to make her afraid. 'I'm sure it's me, not the book. They say it's very well written.' Now, the moment she saw Jasper coming towards her, she knew she was losing him again.

'I nearly just broke my neck on the carpet.' Jasper was shivering. A delayed reaction to the scene in front of the Ritz Carlton. The growling, the attack, the series of revolver shots. That and Rhoda's anger. His own weakness. It was all too much.

'I missed you.' Helen opened her arms. Jasper pulled back the satin quilt and buried his face against her stomach, clawing at the smooth material of her nightgown, the one he had bought her, running his two hands up her legs until he felt warm flesh under his cheek. The penetrating smell of Helen's sex meant safety. He forced his hands up under the spread of her buttocks. She lifted her body slightly to help him. Familiarity. Helen's fingers danced through his orange hair. She turned, raised her knees, cradled her husband, rocked him. He lay trying to kick off his shoes, pushing with the toe of one foot against the heel of the other. 'What is it, Jasper? What's happened?'

But Jasper just held on tight. Helen's body took him seriously, and smoothed enough edges from his fear that afterwards sleep came with surprising speed. Jasper's face relaxed into a sad, childish smile – confessing even more things perhaps than he knew he had on his conscience. He had come back from Rhoda a better lover. A depressing thought but, Helen sighed, it had its compensations. She swallowed half a Mogadon and swore an oath to protect him.

Only when Jasper absent-mindedly, not with any intention, had stroked Helen's scar, the coarse, uneven flesh, the rest of her had frozen, locked immobile, breath held, heart stock-still until his feathering fingers drifted down and away.

In the middle of the night, the morning really, both woke. They lay in the stillness some time without speaking, neither wanting to disturb the other, each hoping the small sounds and little movements from the far side of the bed might mean the other was awake, but not daring to risk doing or saying anything that might wake them if they weren't.

'Jasper, hungry?' Helen finally whispered, laying her fingers, which were cold, on Jasper's hip. Downstairs they both silently turned off all the lights except in the kitchen. While Helen made hot cocoa, dawn broke. Jasper sat huddled in his robe, bare feet one on top of the other. On the round kitchen table a crystal vase with full clusters of fragrant white lilac stood at the center of the pale blue oil cloth. Water had spilled at its base. Jasper leaned forward and blew gently across the surface of the drops.

'What is it?' Helen asked when she turned from the stove and saw Jasper sitting there, grinning.

'Something I just thought of,' he said. 'Nothing.' At the end of their Chinese meal, when he and Luigi had cracked open their fortune cookies, Luigi had accused him of switching the cookies in the dish. Jasper's future, according to the slip of paper that fell out, had promised riches and fame, Luigi's held a grand passion in store.

'How'd you get home?' Helen asked. 'I thought I heard a car drive away.'

'Oh Jesus, I took a cab. The car's still downtown.'

While Jasper waited for his cocoa to cool, Helen massaged his neck, thumbs soothing against the top of his spine.

'What's your friend Luigi like?' Helen asked, a shade too

casually. Did she know then about their meeting, Jasper wondered? Maybe Luigi had called the house that morning looking for him, and had talked with Helen?

'Luigi?'

Helen retrieved a magazine from the kitchen counter and went flicking through it, back and forth, until she found what she was searching for. 'Carole brought this home to show me.' Blood rushed into her cheeks, she half-bit her lower lip. 'Have a look.'

Luigi Sasakawa in a white fishnet vest, silver hot pants, one high white vinyl boot, reclining on a polar bear rug, his head back to back with the bear's. A glittering white helmet and barbed trident lay by his side. It was the given of the advertisement that Luigi had been wounded, in what devious battle of the sexes was left open to surmise. Now he was being revived by a transfusion – of vodka. Voluptuous nurses in starched white ermine-trimmed mini-uniforms surrounded Luigi. Some carried silver platters heaped with ice-shavings in their bare arms. Others sported pointed caps studded with lemon peel and olives. White doves and snow owls perched on their wrists. A German shepherd sat with one paw raised, tongue and teeth visible, a stethoscope around its neck.

'What do you want me to say?' The picture of the dog brought on a sudden rush of nausea. Jasper closed the magazine, but there was Luigi again waving at him from the cover.

'Jasper, Carole's in love with him.'

'So.' Was that what Luigi had been going on about tonight then, really, all that new talk about his wanting to make other people happy? Was that the purpose – undisclosed – behind their dinner together?

'Jasper?'

'Leave your face alone.' In his heart Jasper Whiting wished Luigi well with a force that spread through his body and even made him curl his toes.

'And for once' – Helen looked away, out the window to the lightening sky – 'she says it's mutual.'

Guiltily Jasper longed to be with Rhoda, to be starting something himself, full of risk.

'You know him, Jasper.' Helen poured out a second cup of cocoa. She caught the skin that had formed on top in a strainer. 'What's he like?'

'One thing he's not' – Jasper took Helen's hand, the one with the strainer, and kissed it, each of the knuckles in turn – 'is the boy next door.'

10

As departmental meetings went, this one was lively. Barsky read his new paper on micro-capillary techniques in reconstructive surgery. Barsky's work was always top shelf. The paper was a case study of the canning factory employee who had walked into Mass Gen Emergency with his severed hand wrapped in paper towels, casualty of the assembly line. The hand was now in place again, with, Barsky beamed, almost total mobility in all five digits right down to their tips. In an unexpected postscript, however, Barsky, removing his glasses, added that the patient, far from being grateful, had developed such a violent hatred of his restored hand that he was threatening suicide unless the surgeon consented to remove it.

Christianson, the hospital director, sat in on preliminary discussion of the Spitz Experiment, a new plastic-surgery program. Operations were to be performed on a sample of state convicts with protruding or, alternatively, receding jaws who were serving sentences for manslaughter or involuntary homicide. Spitz, a leading Harvard criminologist, had identified 'facial insecurity' as a decisive influence behind deviant behaviour. Spitz's hypothesis wasn't new, not by any means, but he was the first to use computers to analyze tens of thousands of prison records. He had also asked inmates to rate their own appearances on a scale from 1 to 10, attractive to grotesque, and, similarly, to rate a series of twenty additional photographs which he showed them. For his control group he had used prison staff. Criminals persisted in seeing themselves as more unsightly than others saw them. Generous federal funding had been made available for cosmetic engineering to test the degree to which surgery might reduce craving for violence.

The meeting went on longer than scheduled so that a point came when Jasper was obliged to excuse himself. To reach Pinckney Street in time for office hours he would have to hurry. Outside, as Jasper rounded the hospital corner next to Charles Street Jail his eyes rose to the small barred windows. Anselmo was still there, in custody. What a mockery the boy's beauty made of Spitz's lame-brained theory.

'Sorry.' Jasper, not watching where he was going, bumped into an old man who had one hand pressed to his face and was crying. Only once the figure passed did Jasper recognize him. Marcus Featherstone. Jasper turned but by then Featherstone had crossed the street and was almost out of sight. And that was how Jasper happened to notice a black limousine pulled up in the No Standing area by the hospital entrance, the hood thrown open, a liveried driver in white, whistling, crouched over pretending to inspect the engine.

Jasper retraced his steps and marched into the hospital lobby. At the admissions desk, the volunteers on duty, senior citizens, were nibbling doughnuts, drinking coffee, and chatting away a mile a minute.

'Anyone brought in last night for dog bites? Early – about half past seven, quarter to eight?'

The volunteers seemed to be playing Do Not Disturb. Jasper pounded a fist on the counter. 'Hello, anybody home?' When he repeated his questions, 'No, doctor,' was the peevish reply.

'Let me see the list, will you?' Jasper held out his hand. 'Now.'

Scanning the arrivals from the previous evening left Jasper little wiser. Two males had been admitted at roughly the right time, however. One with a ruptured appendix, the other 'for observation'. Jasper, still running on adrenalin, decided to check them out.

'Half an hour, maybe three-quarters at the outside,' he told Morrison. 'Weed out what you can.' Jasper hung up the phone, took a deep breath and set off to see what he could find.

Even after so many years Jasper Whiting was a stranger to much of Massachusetts General Hospital. The complex as a whole was a bewildering honeycomb of wards and wings. He was only at home in the little world of plastic surgery. The rest was alien territory – where the corridors seemed to echo with false hopes and fear.

As Jasper approached the first of the rooms he intended to visit, above the door the call light flashed on. He began to run in the cautious, lumbering way men do who have to think of their heart. The change in his pockets jingled in alternating rhythm with his stride.

The door was open. As Jasper went in he heard the patient moaning, 'God, God, oh God.' The man's face was bandaged heavily, muffling his voice. He was not alone. By the far window a nurse, largely in silhouette, held a syringe at eye level. At the head of the bed stood a plasma drip, the inverted bottle swaying. Jasper's eye automatically followed the tubing down and he saw it was leaking onto the sheets, the lower end free, no longer tamped into the patient's arm.

'Nurse, the drip's pulled.' Jasper's voice startled the nurse. Needle and ampoule fell, shattering on the floor. Jasper saw her face, the eyes with a look of guilt.

'Quick, then.' Jasper bent to retrieve the end of the pale rubber tubing which hung now free in the air. The last thing he remembered was a blow across the base of his neck and tumbling headlong under the bed.

'How do you feel, doctor?'

Jasper revived on the couch in Christianson's office. The

director was smoking a cigarette, practically blowing the smoke in Jasper's face. Christianson had a gray crew cut which he never let grow out more than a fraction of an inch.

'Nurse Shaw had the boys bring you here.' Jasper blinked at light. The parts of his body felt scattered. There was a dizziness lodged in his brain, holding on tight, not willing to let go. He reached up tc adjust his hearing aid. 'Don't worry, I have it here,' Christianson said. 'Can you hear me?'

'Yes.'

'Nurse Shaw found you.'

'Found me?'

'On the floor.'

Jasper sat up. His body responded much more rapidly than he expected. To keep from pitching forward he had to stick out an arm. 'What about the other one then?'

'Quite a mess you made, doctor.'

'Look, Shaw I know. There was another nurse in there when I came in. Small, dark.' Jasper put a hand to his head.

'Another nurse?' Christianson exhaled smoke through his mouth which he inhaled again through his nostrils. 'Nurse Shaw spoke to the patient. The patient rang when you collapsed, doctor. No one said anything about another nurse. Not as far as I know.'

'So.'

'As far as we can reconstruct what happened, when you bent over to look at the charts – you kept right on going. Pulled the whole damn drip down on top of you.'

'The call light was flashing *before* I entered the room.'

'Don't get excited, doctor. Easy does it. You gave yourself quite a nasty bang on the head.'

Christianson's secretary came in with cognac. Jasper, choking down his anger with difficulty, was grateful. The director poured himself a drink as well, chased his secretary away with a firm smile, and came and sat on the arm of the sofa.

'Here's to your health,' Christianson said and they drank. When Christianson spoke again, his voice was treacle. 'After a certain age, make rapid movements with your head and you can lose your balance I'm afraid.'

Jasper found his shoes on the carpet and began to put them back on. The whole time he tied the laces, clumsily, he felt Christianson's eyes on his hands.

'How's the patient?' Jasper asked, sitting back.

'Why do you ask?'

'For the simple reason that the drip had pulled.'

'The patient was concerned about you, doctor. Very. What took place was very upsetting for her.'

'Her?'

'This whole thing's been rather curious, doctor. I hope you won't mind my asking what you were doing in that room?'

'I . . . I was passing and the call light came on.'

'I see. Since when' – Christianson stood behind his desk consulting a ledger – 'have you had patients in E Wing?'

Jasper wanted more cognac. He wouldn't ask, however, and the bottle was just out of reach.

'You want to know the whole story? Yesterday evening, quite by chance, I was in front of a hotel downtown, the Ritz Carlton, when a dog attacked a man. Made a pretty bad mess out of him. Then today, just as I was leaving the hospital I noticed a car that shouldn't have been parked where it was. I'm sure it was the same car that drove away after the dog attack. The same one.' As he told it, Jasper's story sounded silly and thin to him. 'I came back to see if maybe the victim was here.'

'I see.'

'Do you think I could have another drink?'

'Certainly.' But Christianson made no move to pour. 'Why all this personal concern, doctor? Was the victim a friend?'

'I was there. I felt involved.'

'One thing I still don't understand. There were no admissions for dog bites, doctor. You knew that already. You asked.'

'Night admissions doesn't always get everything straight.'

'Oh I'd say they're pretty reliable.' Jasper got his cognac. 'Come, doctor, what were you doing in that room?'

'You sound like I must've been doing something wrong.'

'Why do you say that, doctor?'

Jasper was thankful he'd kept quiet about his being hit from behind.

'From the admissions desk downstairs I understand you were a trifle testy about wanting information, not your usual self.'

In answer Jasper smoothed down his hair.

'How're things at home, doctor? Better, I gather.' A buzz sounded from the telephone on Christianson's desk. He picked it up and listened, gesturing to Jasper to help himself to more cognac if he wished. 'No, definitely not,' Christianson said and replaced the receiver in its cradle. He turned back to Jasper. 'Although it is not altogether satisfactory, I propose we agree you went into the wrong room by mistake, doctor, and leave it at that.'

'If. . .'

'I suppose it *could* happen. Once.'

Jasper stood, but he was unsteady on his feet and had to sit back down again.

'What does your schedule look like for the coming days, doctor? Why not think about a rest?' Christianson took a third brandy on his own. 'I wish I could take one.'

11

This time Jasper took the stage entrance to the opera, at the end of an alley tangy with cat piss. Only shreds of daylight filtered through the dense scaffolding of old iron fire escapes above. In every last cell of his body Jasper raged. If Rhoda would have him, if *they* would – he was theirs.

'Do Not Enter Unless Necessary' was pinned to the door of Rehearsal Studio B. Jasper eased the door open no further than he was wide and squeezed in. Across the room a pair of technicians were immersed in their work, huddled over a lighting switchboard. Otherwise, except for a massive pile of swords and lances, the piece-of-pie-shaped room was deserted.

'How about this?' One of the lighting men let his hands glide here and there, throwing levers, and a series of flickering rainbows were discharged overhead.

'You're getting warmer.'

Upstairs Rhoda's office was locked. Jasper rattled the door for consolation. His head throbbed. Back at the bend in the corridor he found a secretary sitting in a cloud of cigarette smoke. Whatever he asked, the answer was always the same: 'She didn't say.'

'I'll leave a note.' But pencil in hand Jasper reconsidered. 'No, no, I'll come back.'

Jasper was on his way out when, without warning, children, half a dozen, came whooping, running up the stairs towards him, pushing and shoving. Nymphs and cupids, an early fitting. As they hurried past him, they split like water around a rock. Last of all came Death, a towhead in a skin-tight costume, white bones on black. Death was taking his time. He had pushed his mask, a grinning skull, back onto the top of his head. As he climbed he was eating, with unabashed pleasure, a cone of deep-fried clams. One by one he tugged each clam loose from the swarm and dangled it in front of his lips, stepping up to devour it whole.

'Go ahead' – when the boy reached Jasper he held out the cone – 'try one.'

When Jasper emerged from the rococo lobby onto Washington Street, the world seemed more itself again. He licked the grease from his fingers and decided against tracking Rhoda to Charter Street. He'd acted on enough impulses for one day.

At Spy Pond Lane Helen twisted ice cubes in a dish towel and pressed it against the goose egg on the back of Jasper's head.

What he told her about the scene at the hospital was the barest outline. It was a bit tricky, for he hadn't described the attack on Ricardo earlier. Helen, no doubt, understood he was keeping things from her, selecting. Still she had no comment. Nothing further, that is, than to say, 'Hold still. How long have I been after you to have your blood pressure checked?'

'My blood . . .'

'I don't care if it didn't have anything to do with it – *this time*. Honestly, when it comes to looking after themselves, men are worse than babies.'

'If you were to look at it through his eyes,' Jasper started to say.

'Through whose eyes?'

'Christianson's. It must seem odd.'

'Don't defend him. He has no excuse for not treating you with more respect. You're entitled.'

'How could I have made such a fool of myself?' Jasper was fishing. Helen didn't bite. Instead of saying maybe he hadn't made a mistake, she reapplied his compress.

'When you do something, darling, you don't do it by halves.'

'Fa, why not do what Christianson says?' Carole in love sparkled. 'Go away.'

'So I'll stop imagining nurses with hypodermic needles?'

'As far as I'm concerned you can imagine whatever you like. The more the better. But why not take a vacation? I'll make sure Daniel behaves.'

'You'll what?' Daniel shouted in from the porch.

'When was the last time?' Carole asked.

'I can't think,' Helen said. 'Not for years.'

Jasper thumbed through his pocket agenda. Part of his conscience nagged him. To leave Boston now would amount to desertion. But his conscience, possibly also suffering from the blow on his head, had begun to feel numb. After seeing Rhoda again, it would be better to give his feelings time to settle.

'Well, yes, ten days. I suppose it could be arranged, assuming Morrison has no objections. Two weeks actually – if we decide to stay over that last weekend.'

'Where will you go?' Daniel wanted to know. While everyone else made suggestions, Jasper sat quietly. He was on the verge of accepting that, after all, the vacation idea wasn't practical, when a thought came bubbling up from deep inside him.

'I know what I'd like to do,' he said.

'What, Fa?'

'Go back. To Mumias.'

'Sorry, dear. Daniel, you'll break that chair sitting in it like that. What did you say?'

'Kenya.'

They all grew silent.

'Yes,' said Helen, putting a hand on his knee. 'Let's. Good idea.'

Part III

A SHOW OF HANDS

1

'God, you look *great.*' Carole hugged her mother through the Gamba baskets, scrap-metal mousetraps and cluster of clay pots Helen was carrying. 'You, too, Fa. How was it?' Indeed, despite the long flight, Jasper and Helen looked rested. Tans hid their fatigue. Only Helen's scar hadn't changed color under the sun.

'What've you got in there,' – Daniel took charge of the suitcases – 'bricks?' When the Whitings were a few inches away, the glass exit doors slid back and the family stepped outside.

'Chilly, huh.'

'The weather's been good though, most of the time.'

'Has it?'

At curbside a beggar caught Jasper's travel-weary eye. A lean hunchback like some long-legged bird with one wing crushed and pinned behind his neck. Jasper reached into his pocket and pulled out a coin. The gesture had become reflex in Kenya. You gave without looking back, nodding as you walked on. A torrent of thanks followed you down the street. Jasper didn't pause to consider he was back in New England where beggars weren't a standard part of the scenery. He pressed the coin into the hunchback's outstretched hand. He must have pressed too hard. The hand turned over, the coin fell to the pavement, *ping*, and rolled a looping half-circle on its edge. The man's smile didn't waver.

'Sorry.' Jasper was a bit surprised that the man didn't even try to trap the coin with his foot. It lay glinting on the pavement. Jasper walked over to retrieve it. A Kenyan shilling. In embarrassment he added a second coin and dropped both into the beggar's upturned hand. The man's eyes brightened. Both coins fell. It was as if in addition to the disfiguring outcrop on his back, the hunchback couldn't coordinate his fingers. The coins rolled this time in opposite directions. For an instant Jasper thought the man had deliberately let the coins drop, like some child testing his power over the world by hurling toys from his crib. Yet, the man's hand was out once more, smile intact, eyes imploring. Jasper crouched, slowly, and picked up the coins. He really was much too tired for this sort of thing. He was about to give them again, a last time, when Daniel held his arm.

'That's enough.' Daniel actually shoved against the hunchback's chest. The man staggered back and collided with a concrete pile. His smile broadened into a wide rictus.

'Dan!'

People were stopping to stare.

'You don't know. You've been away. They've crawled out from all the cracks.'

'Daniel!'

'It's just to humiliate you. A stupid game.'

Carole and Helen, arms around each other's waist, had walked on ahead. They turned back to see what all the noise was about.

'Get away,' Daniel shouted at the hunchback, waving a fist at him. 'Go, get.'

'Daniel!'

Hand outstretched, the hunchback approached Jasper again.

'Come on, Fa.' Daniel pulled at Jasper. 'Get away, you.' Flecks of Daniel's saliva landed on one of the hunchback's eyes. He didn't lift a hand to clear the wet away, merely lowered the lid. Another passenger who didn't understand the situation hurried to scrunch a dollar bill in the beggar's hand. The beggar's fingers spread and a breeze caught the currency and carried it fluttering away.

The Whitings wended their way through a series of identical parking lots. So many cars, green, blue, white.

'Don't tell me you can't find where you parked?'

'Where *I* parked? Weren't you there?'

'Daniel,' – Jasper put a hand on his son's elbow – 'what was that about back there?'

'It started while you were away.'

'What started?'

'The begging. Only they won't accept anything. It's his bright idea. That Alex Thane. At least that's what the papers say.'

'They've found him then?'

'No, he's still vanished.'

'Here, you keep that one and give the brown bag to me.'

'I can manage, Fa.'

'Come on, boys,' Helen called from ahead, 'we've found it.'

'As long as they don't take anything,' Daniel told his father, 'the police can't touch them. Just acting like they're begging they're not breaking any law.'

Helen slid next to Jasper in the back seat of the Mazda and put her arm through his. 'Vacation's over,' she whispered and gave him an affectionate squeeze.

Little was said until they disappeared into Callahan Tunnel. Midway under Boston harbor, Carole spoke. 'The Deaf and Dumb Eleven's in one helluva mess.'

'Who?'

'That's what they're calling the gang who killed the policeman at the rally on the Common.'

'What kind of mess?' Helen asked.

'Their leader says he's proud of what they did.'

'Oh Jesus!' Helen looked at Jasper. He looked out the window. He disliked tunnels, always had, the way tires hummed. A camping wagon passed. Inside a row of small children had their faces pressed up against the back window and were waving, trying to get somebody, anybody, to wave back. Their faces, distorted, might have been plates in Jasper's plastic surgery texts.

'I don't get it,' Daniel said. 'Ever since I've been old enough to walk, all I can remember hearing about is Law and Order. Law and Order, Law and Order. Now suddenly we're all supposed to feel sorry for a gang of vicious killers because they can't hear or speak.'

As they rose into daylight, corrugations in the road alerted Carole to brake for the toll booth. The toll attendant, chewing gum, held out a cupped hand.

'Looks like she's begging,' Helen said.

'Luigi sends his best.' Carole accelerated. 'He wanted to come only he had a meeting with some West Coast producer. Apparently they're after him for the lead in a spy film.'

'There's only one thing holding up the deal' – Daniel kept a straight face – 'a shortage of one-legged stunt men.'

'Look, there. See.' Carole pointed out of the window at an old blind man with a white stick on a street corner. People were clearly going out of their way to avoid him.

Jasper leaned back and shut his eyes. His body might be back in New England, his soul had still to catch up with him. Kenya had been beautiful, vast beyond Jasper's remembering. The light, the trees, the sweep of it all – all those years had he been blind? Oh he recalled being impressed, writing letters about how impressed he was – but this was simply staggering. Plastic surgery in paradise? The very notion was incredible, and thankless.

They rented a car for several days, a yellow Volkswagen with cross-eyed headlights, and drove through game parks and bird reserves. They sipped Pimms and watched crocodiles lured from swampy pools at night by searchlights and a trainer's seductive chant. 'Come, Sabaki. Come, Otto, come.' Inch by inch the primal beasts left the safety of the oozing dark, cold eyes intent on chunks of raw meat and gore in the trainer's gloved hand and stacked in a tub at his feet. When at last their patience snapped, the crocs scuttled forward, seized the meat and with a flick of the tail were gone again. The last time Jasper was in Kenya, the future had still awaited him.

In Masai Mara Park Jasper and Helen sat in their car a few yards from elephants who scratched themselves against low trees, rubbing so hard that the trees fell down. Helen wanted to drive closer. Jasper refused, afraid the beasts would sit on the car. Later at roadside they came upon an old lioness left behind by the pride to die, skin dripping from her bones. With mangy dignity she lay licking the bleached rib cage of a buffalo, her last feast. Vultures hopped about in nearby shade making a rude display of their hopes. And as the Whitings turned the next bend in the road, the sun in their eyes, hundreds of zebra bolted across their path, running in zigzags, raising dust, their sleek striped hides pulsing with muscle. Helen shot roll after roll of film. Jasper loaded and unloaded the camera for her. And all the time everything made him think of Rhoda.

Without either's saying it, both Jasper and Helen knew that at the end of their journey they would make the trip to Western Province to see their hospital again. 'No, don't drive up. Wait,' Helen had said. 'It looks exactly the same, doesn't it? But exactly.' They sat in the car and stared up at the modest complex of white-washed cinderblock buildings connected by cement walkways roofed with peaked, corrugated zinc sheets. They had lived and worked there happily for almost three years. 'Rub your eyes. No, it's true.'

Two nurses came walking down the slope from the hospital towards them. One was a young girl, thin as a stick, glossy and feline. Her arms swung free. The other had tight gray curls and walked with folded arms. She was the one who recognized the Whitings from the office window.

'Dr Jasper,' she said and pulled at his red hair.

'Elizabeth.'

'This was the best doctor in the country,' the older nurse told the younger. 'He's the one the people still talk about. When he left us, we cried – we're still crying!'

Getting out of the car to greet her old friend, Helen ripped the pocket of her dress. 'Madame!' Elizabeth clapped her hands.

She danced for joy and almost hugged Helen to death. She rubbed the scar on Helen's cheek, scowled as she might at a child who had muddied herself playing, and, with that, seemed to forget it.

'Welcome, welcome, welcome. How are the children? That little girl, Berlita, you never saw anything like her.' Later in the hospital office the Whitings found early snapshots Helen had sent of Daniel and Carole, faded, pinned to a cork board. 'This is my grandchild,' Elizabeth said proudly, smoothing a pocket flap on Berlita's uniform that didn't need smoothing.

'Elizabeth,' Helen asked, 'do you have a needle and thread?'

'You know what it is, doctor,' – Elizabeth told them over the inevitable sticky cup of hot tea with evaporated milk, a treat they couldn't refuse – 'the people don't come. Or if they do, they come too late. Ignorance has a long life, but not ignorant people.

'Nothing changes here, doctor.' Elizabeth smiled, prodding one of the coals under the pan in which she boiled water to refresh their tea. 'The beliefs, the practices, nothing.' She followed Jasper's eyes. 'Not even this pan. Yes, it is the same one.' They laughed together.

Tea was interrupted by a high-pitched scream from the maternity wing. Jasper and the nurses hurried to the spot. No one was in attendance. A brown-skinned woman was in labour, squatting on the floor beside her bed, knees wide and shiny. Other women were sitting up in their beds and watching. A child was already on the way out. Its wrinkled head was emerging but the slimy umbilical cord had become entangled around neck and throat.

Elizabeth gave Jasper a slight push forward. He started to protest that his hands weren't clean.

'Hurry,' Helen said. 'Oh damn, the camera's in the car.'

Jasper stammered a few words to the woman in her language which were meant to be reassuring. He knelt down and took the baby in his grasp. The woman kept pressing, her scream a series of sharp pants now. She fixed Jasper with huge eyes as if with his red hair on end he were an apparition. The other women were clapping now, rhythmically, shrieking, enjoying themselves. Jasper turned the baby, twisted the pliable body confidently until the cord unraveled and the new life was no longer in danger. Birth proceeded easily. Jasper gave the infant the slap of life.

Outside Elizabeth brought a kettle of water and a basin. Jasper rinsed his hands over the earth. He had to pull his feet back so his sandals wouldn't be wet by trickles of bloody water.

'Doctor, please.' Berlita took Jasper by the arm and led him down a covered walkway to the ward reserved for serious cases. 'That child, what's wrong with him?'

Jasper looked down at the patient and his heart ached. Under the bed a woman lay on a coarse blanket. The boy's mother. She didn't move, except for her eyes. 'The doctor says it is a fever. The mother says it is witchcraft. Who is right?'

'Where is the doctor, Berlita?'

'Nairobi,' she said, 'bribing for a transfer.'

It hadn't taken Jasper long to diagnose cerebral malaria. The boy was dehydrated, stiff in the joints. Even at the gentlest touch, he cried out in pain. Jasper wrote out treatment instructions. The child, he thought, would live. With what neural damage he couldn't say. Yet there was no alternative to his acting to save the boy's life. The ward was totally still, except for the row of rotor fans overhead. Only a few beds were occupied. Patients with enough strength left to be interested in the world were grinning at him. It was phenomenal, the intensity of gratitude in their eyes. He hadn't seen that look in twenty years.

Witchcraft, Jasper thought, shivering slightly, Helen's knee next to his as Carole raced down the alleyway of trees that lined Memorial Drive. It struck him as honest and refreshing – to face up squarely to the fact that at some level people make other people sick, through acts of the will. With deformity, too. In Kenya a cripple was never a cripple by chance. The chap had entered into some contract with the devil to get rich, or his parents had. Or else he was a thief who stubbornly refused to confess until sorcery sorted out the truth for all to see. Nothing accidental about the body.

And the whole, the healthy – they drove the deformed out, didn't they? Out from their birthplaces, away from their home villages. They poisoned their food, or drinking wells. So the cripples headed for town. And there – years ago when Helen had first told him, Jasper listened as if to a distant fable – there they organized. The King of the Blind. The King of the Lame. They became a political force. Every new arrival with old tires lashed to his knees, or wooden blocks in his hands, with open sores, needed permission to stake out a territory. Everyone joined. There was absolute discipline.

'Honey,' – Helen pulled her hand free from Jasper's and put it on Carole's shoulder – 'is there enough milk in the house?'

On the flight back to Boston Helen had slept for some hours stretched across a number of empty seats with the arm rests lifted, head on Jasper's lap. Jasper wouldn't let the stewardess wake her for dinner. He ate awkwardly, with one hand. At sunrise, always eerie above the clouds, hot towels were distributed, lifted steaming with a pair of sanitary tongs from a tray. When Helen sat up, Jasper felt pangs of love. She was a child, features wrinkled, her sharp mind disoriented. Jasper watched her make faces as she sipped a cup of acid-tasting orange juice.

Over Back Bay Helen said to Jasper, 'Let's leave the mail until tomorrow, okay?' When they started their descent, as the wheels were lowered noisily from the belly of the plane, she leaned over and kissed Jasper on the cheek. 'What a good idea, to go back.' Jasper covered her hand with his own on the arm rest. He knew landings frightened her. 'We did the right thing, though, don't you think – bailing out when we did?'

'Fa,' Daniel spoke up as they entered Arlington, 'you haven't said anything about the trip.'

'Your mother amazed me – how quickly her Swahili came back.'

'Have things changed very much?' Carole asked.
'No,' Jasper said.
'Yes,' came Helen's reply at the same time.

2

Rhoda Massler visited the Charles Street Jail every day. It cost her no little effort. She was a born teacher. Obstacles seemed to bring out the best in her. She taught an expanding universe of fantasies to children afraid to peer out from behind their eyes. She taught skills and nonsense, argued, taunted, teased, caressed. With the paralyzed she danced, shared in the confidences, lurid and existential, of the dumb, walked emotional tightropes in high winds with the blind. And the disabled, what was in it for them? They fell, they collapsed, their conditions grew worse, turned critical, they disappeared, God knew where. They died, too, going out like candles, crumpling, toppling, wasting. Rhoda wasn't in the game just for the triumphs. But bars and locks, these were new.

The day the Whitings flew back to town, Rhoda, as usual, called in at the jail. She was signing the visitors' book when half-way through her name the ink in her pen gave out. She borrowed a pen from the desk sergeant, but handed it back when she saw it wrote red.

'Well,' the sergeant laughed, 'we know who you are.'

Inside the elaborate system of double gates, Rhoda hadn't taken more than a few steps when a trio of defense lawyers swooped down on her. They were volunteers, young and often brash. Their hearts, Rhoda was forever reminding herself, were at least in the right place.

'There you are.'
'He's been asking for you.'
'Me? Why?'
'He won't say.'
'He'll only talk to you.'
'Has anything happened?' Rhoda asked.
'They've been fighting . . .'
'. . . among themselves.'
'Guards had to drag Anselmo away . . .'
'. . . and put him in solitary.'
'What do the others say?'
'He was trying to make them change their story.'
'To say what?'

The lawyers looked at each other before one, eyes downcast, finally spoke.

'That they were just following orders.'

Right from the start the defense for the Deaf and Dumb Eleven had run into heavy going. Most of the accused appeared to appreciate their position. Death of police fanned the public temper. The accused were scared, as well they might be. When their lawyers had explained how they intended to argue that Patrolman Lyons's death was accidental, a shock to them all, they caught on quick, no problem. How were they to know about his bad heart? Besides, they were only sticking up for each other. It was self-defense. In the heat of the moment, things got out of hand. They were sorry, honest and truly. Most of them were waiting for their day in court to stand up, hang their heads and make the proper signs of contrition.

Not Anselmo. He wouldn't play along. He made no secret of the fact that he felt not a single shred of remorse. As far as he was concerned that bastard Lyons only got what he deserved. So free with his hands. Anselmo would do it again, without blinking. Accident? It was no accident. Whoever said so was a coward and would have to answer to him.

Rhoda Massler was the lawyers' only hope. She had to make it clear to Anselmo that his obstinacy – it was the kindest word they could think of – put the whole group in jeopardy. 'What does he think he is, for God's sake, some kind of damn revolutionary?' Rhoda was asked to use her influence. To bring him around. 'This case doesn't need a martyr.'

The problem was Anselmo refused to see her.

'First get us out, then we'll talk.'

On her visits to the others Rhoda did her best to be reassuring, but clearly Anselmo's influence ran deep. It was all too likely that during the trial others, inspired by his example, if not outright intimidated, might bolt and end up denying they felt any repentance.

The court set bail sky-high. It became increasingly clear, moreover, that someone behind the scenes was applying pressure to hurry the case to trial. Rhoda wasn't going to be able to reach Anselmo in time, she was afraid. Part of her was proud of him, however, and of his refusal to compromise. A pride that made her angry with herself, for surely Anselmo would detect her feelings and that would only confirm him on his self-destructive course.

Anselmo entered the visiting room between two guards. How shabby they looked next to him, almost subhuman. A prison haircut had reduced his mane to a burr, the white streak now a dividing line, no flame. Still, his bearing was princely. On her side of the wire mesh, Rhoda went weak in the knees. Anselmo hardly gave her a sign of recognition. He sat slowly. The guards backed up against the wall.

'Hello.' Rhoda's mouth opened but no voice came out. Anselmo put his hands up on the ledge in front of him and looked down at them. He was, it seemed to Rhoda, bewildered by his hands.

'You wanted to see me,' Rhoda enunciated as if juggling knives with her lips. 'I came right away.'

'Is it true?' his hands stuttered.

'Whatever's wrong, don't worry – we can fix it. If you . . .'

'Is it true?' Anselmo repeated, signing with more urgency.

'Is what true?' Now for the first time Rhoda accompanied her voice with her hands.

'Is he dead? Marcus?'

Rhoda's mouth fell open.

'Featherstone, is he dead? He is, isn't he? Why didn't you tell me? Today those idiots, the lawyers, started saying how it was too bad Marcus wouldn't be appearing for the defense. First I thought, Good, he understands.'

'No.' Rhoda shook her head. Poor Anselmo, some battery had broken inside, he was leaking acid.

'When did it happen?'

Rhoda counted out the days on her fingers. Anselmo slammed a fist down on the counter. The room seemed to jump. The guards made a face to each other. They were alert for trouble. If Anselmo became violent though, they would need help to control him.

'The rest of them, Angel, the others, they started cheering when they heard.'

'That was wrong of them.'

'How? How did he die?'

Rhoda signed a heart attack. There were tears in Anselmo's eyes.

'I've been waiting for him. Every day. I said things when he came . . .' Anselmo's hands fell in mid-phrase. With effort he lifted them and went on. 'Things I didn't mean.'

'Like what?'

'I don't know any more.' Rhoda's heart contracted like a fist. 'I was angry.'

'Angry?'

'He wanted me to pretend I was sorry. To save myself.'

'He meant well.'

'Shut up! You never gave him a chance! Marcus doesn't need you to defend him. Not now – not ever, but, please, God, not *now*.'

'You're right,' Rhoda said. 'Very right. I'm sorry.'

Here Anselmo stared at Rhoda. 'Don't start something you

can't finish. Remember who told me that, Rhoda?' He pointed. 'You. And I told him.'

'Is there anything I can do for you?'

'You always think you know everything, but you were wrong about him.' Rhoda looked down. Anselmo rattled the screen between them to make her lift her eyes again. 'He loved me.' The slang sign for love, only Anselmo's middle finger extended, flashing up. 'More than my father. More than anyone, ever.' It was, Rhoda reminded herself, no time to compete. All she could do now was nod, slowly. 'Nothing mattered, he said – as long as I saved myself.'

'What did you say then?'

'I told him to come back when he stopped sounding like an old woman.' Again Anselmo looked at Rhoda levelly and long. The moment was almost an embrace. God, she felt there was a crack in the earth between them, and slowly the sides were sliding apart. 'Do you want me to change my story, too, Rhoda? Well? Don't just sit there, damn it! You always have plenty to say. What about it then? Am I supposed to get down and crawl? Is that what you want?'

Rhoda took a deep breath.

'What's the matter, Rhoda? Suddenly you're not talking.'

'All I want is for you to be realistic. A little bit. Try.'

Before either guard realized the boy had moved, Anselmo gave a guttural cry and was out the door. Rhoda sat there paralyzed. Where the boy would lead, could she follow? 'Well?' The lawyers crowded around. 'Well? Well?'

'He was asking, not telling.'

'Time's running out, Mrs Massler.'

'You don't need us to tell you that.'

'No,' Rhoda agreed, 'no, I don't.'

She went in to the others. During the day they were kept in a large, modestly furnished lock-up. Most were still wearing their school sweatshirts. It took Rhoda only one look to see their nerves were raw and jagged as well. By one barred window the prison doctor, a short coarse man with hair growing out of his nose and ears, was dressing Angel's ribs. The doctor sighed a lot and grumbled as he taped bandages to the boy's body. Angel had needed thirteen stitches as well for a cut on the back of his skull where Anselmo had slammed his head against the wall.

'How did the fighting start?' Rhoda asked.

'He started it.'

'Just like that?'

Lightning glances flew back and forth without anyone's daring to meet her eyes.

'Someone made a joke about Featherstone.'

'A joke?'

'Featherstone and Anselmo.'

'He's crazy,' Angel said, holding the sign for emphasis. The others, by their quiet, showed they disagreed.

'We were a bunch of weaklings, he said.'

'He started threatening what he'd do to us if we let him down.'

At that point a guard hurried in to fetch the doctor. Down the hall, in solitary, Anselmo was dashing himself against the walls of his cell.

3

As Jasper emerged from the MTA at Haymarket Square, the streetlights flashed on. He headed into the North End, on his way to Charter Street. All day his first day back to work – in an office freshly painted during his vacation, a surprise arranged by Helen in conspiracy with Morrison – Jasper had gathered the courage to go in search of Rhoda. He thought he saw things clearly now. He had achieved distance. She had better wake up, and soon. He wanted to persuade her of that. In the grip of delusion, she was helping no one. Commitment was a different animal from fixation.

The closer Jasper came to Charter Street, however, the more he had to concede to himself he wasn't acting by choice either, but by compulsion. What reason could compare to his need to see Rhoda, to touch her? And once he acknowledged his longing, it only grew worse – to distraction. Half-way down Hanover Street, opposite Bulfinch Church, he cut back across the elongated shadow of Paul Revere's statue. On the mall the stunted trees were in leaf. Lamp-posts gave off a sickly sweet glow.

During the plane ride home from Nairobi, the one thing Jasper had decided he wouldn't do was let himself become involved again in the twisted, tangled undergrowth of Rhoda's convictions. Yet by now he was beginning to know himself well enough to feel uneasy about how very firmly he seemed to have made up his mind.

At Rhoda's door Jasper didn't knock. He still had his key and used it. On the unmade bed, wrapped in a towel, sat Murray. The tangle of hair on his chest, gray and white and black, was glistening and wet. His body was old but strong. Murray was staring down into an empty glass. He looked up as Jasper entered and his lips spread slowly, wider and wider, into a warm smile of welcome.

'Doctor.' Murray held out his hand, pulled Jasper to him for a hug. 'My friend.' There was no trace of embarrassment in his manner. Murray's clothes lay in a neat pile at the foot of the bed.

Rhoda appeared in the bathroom doorway, naked, and retreated, pushing the door half-closed behind her.

'Please, can I ask you a favor? The boy is sick, Sloan upstairs. The doctor came but' – Murray shook his head violently from side to side – 'a doctor afraid to touch the patient, what does he know?' Murray frowned. 'Please, before you go, please, see him.'

Rhoda came into the room swinging her hips, carrying a fizzy drink that sloshed about in her tall glass. She wore a short, loosely belted terrycloth robe, canary yellow. Jasper had never seen it before. Murray snatched up his clothes and disappeared into the bathroom.

'Their shower's shot,' Rhoda greeted Jasper. 'How's yours?' She appeared to look for someplace to put her drink down. The room was uncommonly tidy. Murray had straightened things up, that was Jasper's guess. 'Hey, guys, look who's here.' Rhoda addressed the plants. 'So, Jasper Whiting, what brings you to this neck of the woods? What's her name, that daughter of yours, didn't she tell me you and the wife were taking a little vacation?'

'You've been drinking?'

'Right.'

'Too much.'

'Right.'

'Why?'

'Right again.' Rhoda drained her glass, went to the window. 'Remember the doctor, guys. Sure you do. He used to give some of you a little extra water sometimes. And who knows, maybe he even talked to you.'

Murray appeared, now oddly blushing and awkward in his clothes. Rhoda kissed him hard on the mouth, her eyes wide open. He held his hands in the air during the kiss.

'I'll tell them you're coming,' Murray said to Jasper. 'Promise.' And he let himself out, shoes in hand.

'So,' Rhoda said and trailed her hand along the leaves that lined the window sills. 'What do you think, guys? What's it going to be this time? Is Jasper with us, or against us?'

She had to wait several long seconds for the answer.

'With you.'

'Hooray.' Rhoda's voice was without enthusiasm, almost bitter. Yet her eyes closed and her body relaxed, as if she had just put down an invisible weight. Jasper went to the kitchen and poured himself a drink from the bottle on the counter by the sink. To his surprise, when he came back Rhoda had not moved, nor opened her eyes.

'How was Africa, Jasper?' she asked. 'Bag a lot of game?'

'How're rehearsals?' he replied.

'It's off.'

'Off?'

'Off – ff – ff.'

'So.' Jasper weighed the news. 'Rhoda.' It was difficult for Jasper to speak the name. He said it down into his glass. 'What happened then?'

'No money, no theatre, no opera.'

'But . . .'

'But *shit*!' She held up her hand and folded down the fingers one by one. 'Scenery that goes bang in the night, a few broken bones among members of the chorus, half the musicians turned inside-out by food poisoning . . .'

'So you had a few problems.'

'Sure, there's no biz like, right?'

'I'd expect you to take such things in stride.'

'A lot of things I can handle. I'm a handler if there ever was one. Tell me, what am I supposed to do about threatening letters to the producer's wife?'

'You let them . . .'

'Me?' Rhoda laid a hand of theatrical protest over her heart. The abrupt gesture parted the folds of her robe. '*I* didn't *let them* anything, sugar.'

'What now?'

'I'm what you might call between engagements. No, don't touch me. No, I said, no.'

Jasper pushed Rhoda's hands aside, forced his arms under her robe, held her close, pressed her back, down onto the bed. Soothing sounds he never dreamed he could make rose naturally, effortlessly to his lips. She fought him with enough will and strength to excite them both. Her slackness when it came, her compliance, the whimpering, were sweeter than any remembered act of lovemaking. Yet, Jasper surprised himself. Sweetness wasn't enough.

He contained too much anger and too much fear to settle for sweetness. He earned forgiveness by inflicting punishment, revealed how deeply he was devoted to Rhoda by displaying a physical selfishness and arrogance past all previous performance. Whether Rhoda was beneath him or swinging in an arc above, black and silver hair slicing across her eyes, full breasts in collision, heaving, the nipples dark and enormous, her hands clasped into fists like ingrown buds, teeth gnashing, it was Jasper who controlled her breathing. He forced gasps from her, or moans. He denied pleasure when he felt she would most enjoy denial, offered her sweet liquid satisfaction, his full thrust and weight, when instinct told him she would find pleasure almost unbearable. He made love without pride, with more inventiveness than was decent, and a stamina that only occurs in puppet shows or pornographic marathons.

Rhoda and Jasper danced and shuddered on the flats and slopes of the lumpy mattress and twisted bedclothes. They became bright circles revolving within dark ones, all aching pulp and cramped muscles, a kaleidoscope of hearts, eyes and hair, high on the shock of finding themselves neck and neck riding the same breakaway screams. Or, to tell the candid truth of lovemaking so abandoned, they were alternately blind and deaf, broken and dying, paralyzed and manic with tics and spasms, flailing, maimed, speechless, desperately and forever alone, unable to breathe cleanly, shorn of memory, bereft of even as much as a child's coordination, joined to the world less by consciousness than by their inalienable weight, unable to shed or conciliate their accidental flesh.

Orgasm, when it came, was merely a whisper, hardly noticed, the way sirens in a big city turn the heads of strangers, not anyone who lives there.

'I want to help,' Jasper told Rhoda as peace wore off, but he was afraid the words came out inaudibly and he wouldn't be able to repeat them.

'No.' Rhoda uncannily understood, shaking her head, yes. 'You'll have to tell me how.'

Rhoda rolled onto one side. Jasper reached for the rest of his drink, moving so their bodies never separated. The sheet was wet where Murray had been sitting earlier in his towel.

'I *want* to help, but I don't see what I can do.'

'There's one thing.'

'What's that?'

'Alex.'

'An operation?' It didn't disconcert Jasper that he knew. He had known for some time that it would come to this in the end. Perhaps since Rhoda first read him Alex's letter about the strafing of innocent deaf and dumb children in Beirut? Or since Helen insisted she would 'keep' her scar? Or perhaps since Alex's own dolphin smile when Jasper refused to hide him.

'There's a contract out on Alex. You understand?'

'Nose? Jaw?'

'He has to become unrecognizable.'

'When?'

'As soon as possible.'

Jasper had never thought of his skills as conferring power before. At any rate not the power to do right or wrong.

'Getting him into hospital may prove tricky.'

'No, it won't. He'll check in to Mass Gen tomorrow.' Rhoda told Jasper Alex's assumed name and gave him the room number. E Wing. 'He'll be registered as a heart patient.'

'You're sure he's in danger?' Jasper didn't expect an answer. He was talking to hear himself think. 'I'll see what I can do.'

'No shower?' Rhoda watched Jasper climb back into his clothes. 'Jasper, they come from all over to use my shower. It's got a really nice spray.'

Jasper turned to look at Rhoda just as she brushed the hair back from her face with both hands. 'Every time I begin to believe maybe, maybe you're making sense, you take it one step further.'

'I don't, it does.'

4

The Gayle Glintz who opened the door was a mere shadow of the woman Jasper knew. All the starch had gone out of her bearing. The piercing gaze had been bleached into a weak, unfocused stare. She was thin, flat-chested, breakable. Her smile of genuine pleasure to see him lasted briefly. It only threw the drawn despair of her triangular face into sharper relief. Thousands of tiny lines of confusion and defeat tugged at the sides of her mouth, twisting her lips like a rag. She wore black, but the choice hardly conveyed anything of intention. She had lost interest in color, that was it. Spots and stains on her black smock could have been milk, or spittle perhaps, or dried sweat.

'You've come. Murray said you might.' Gayle Glintz's voice lagged behind the flutter of her lips, as if it had to struggle back from some remote and solitary place. 'He'll be so pleased.'

Sloan's condition came as a shock. Murray had simply said the boy was sick. Not even Gayle Glintz's wraith-like reception, however, prepared Jasper to find him so wasted. Jasper walked into the bedroom to find death personified, a corpse still entangled in life momentarily in spite of itself. For a split second he even fancied the whites of Sloan's eyes were dark, the pupils pale, marble, so completely did the brain-damaged boy give the impression he was anything but flesh and blood.

However unnatural and abstract Sloan's posture may have seemed before, however painful the jumble of his limbs at the best of times, the slump of his pinched shoulders, the loll of his outsized head, they had, it was now for the first time apparent, once been veined with life. All coherence, however, had been squeezed out of him. No vital connection remained unfrayed, unslashed. He had been the victim of thousands of tiny, invisible bites. This surely was the work of witchcraft. Sloan Glintz was not simply a glove from which the hand had been removed, he had been turned half inside-out during the removal.

'He suffers,' Gayle Glintz whispered, punching, fluffing the pillows under Sloan's body. 'He suffers, I know, only he doesn't want to let it show.'

'Sloan?' Jasper's voice came out so loud it startled them all. Today he had been calling out names as if names were sufficient in themselves to convey the weight of his meaning. It was, this time, enough. Sloan appeared to want to lift his head, to smile, features rippling minimally the way light, when the cords of hanging blinds are twitched, enters a room previously kept dark.

Jasper strained to hear what Sloan was saying. The boy's voice was soft as falling rose petals, losing scent on their way down. 'What?' Jasper couldn't understand. Sloan's attempt at speech seemed an act of divine ventriloquism, tongue tame at last, delicate, but garbled.

'He's asking,' Gayle said unflinchingly, 'how you've been.'

Jasper had not been back inside this apartment since the day he'd rushed up the steps as a recruit to pattern Sloan. He could count the number of times he'd seen the boy and Gayle Glintz on the fingers of one hand. Yet, they seemed to number among his oldest, closest friends. The cheer of Sloan's room, the childish bright hanging paper forms were now painful, even distasteful to look at.

When Jasper laid one hand against Sloan's cheek, the boy looked up at him with a devastating mixture of happiness and curiosity in his dying eyes.

'Medicine won't help, will it? It's not an infection of this or that, it's an infection of everything. But there was no saying no, doctor.'

Gayle Glintz sat in what must have been the cleanest, whitest kitchen on Charter Street. Squares of black and white lineoleum on the floor made her look like the sole survivor of the black pieces of a chess set, one chiseled with a sharp instrument held in shaking hands.

'I'll tell you what happened. Murray heard us talking, Rhoda and me, about Alex and what's been going on. She was complaining that maybe he wasn't helping things by calling for more beggars on the street. And I said did she know a better way? Deformed people have to stop being invisible. Murray sat and listened to everything. He – I guess it made a deep impression. More coffee, doctor?'

'Thank you.'

'Cookie then?'

'No, thank you.'

'So Murray took Sloan out to beg. First he told Sloan what they were going to do, and why. I was there. I always am when they make their plans. Sloan was all for it. They went out every day. Maybe I should have interfered, but each time when they came back Sloan was so alive! There was no saying no, doctor.

'Over the weekend, the last one, Murray took Sloan to Quincy Market. The place behind Faneuil Hall where they sell all those plants. You know where I mean?' Jasper nodded. 'They always had the most fun there because of the crowds. It started to rain. Sloan wouldn't come away.'

'What do you mean, wouldn't come away? All Murray had to do was push him.'

'It's not that easy, doctor. Murray tried. Sloan started screaming and slugging at him with his fists.'

'At least they could have come in out of the rain.'

'That's what you say, doctor. Sloan sometimes gets that way with me, too. The only thing to do is let it pass.'

'You just don't stand there, you try to do something.'

'Murray told Sloan he would leave him there if Sloan didn't stop it. That was the wrong thing to do. Murray couldn't know,

I'm not blaming him. Sloan just stuck his hands out, like this, like he was begging from Murray, too. So Murray went to a booth and called me at the shop. And I came running over. That didn't help things much either. We stood there, Murray and me, like two jerks with umbrellas.

'I can't tell you how people looked at us – like we were crazy, or criminals. They said some horrible things, too, very vulgar. Someone even threw something. Food or garbage. Anyway it was warm and sticky. Sloan didn't mind one bit. We stood there trying to keep him from getting wet and it rained harder and harder. Finally the place was deserted, except for the three of us. Sloan decided he'd made his point and was ready to go home.'

'Does Rhoda know?'

'No.' Gayle Glintz shook her head, biting her lip. 'I'm afraid to tell her.' She lowered her voice so Jasper had to lip-read to understand her. 'I'll take another one, so help me God.'

5

The morning of Sloan Glintz's funeral, on his own initiative, Daniel washed the Mazda. After he was through, it looked dungier than before. Veils of soap film criss-crossed each other, catching the sunlight. Carole turned up at Spy Pond Lane about ten and promptly secluded herself in her room. The others could hear her throughout the morning practicing the harpsichord. Lunch was a self-help affair. Helen began urging the others to get ready about one. She was staying home.

Instead of wearing a necktie, Jasper decided to carry one in his pocket. It promised to be a long day for him especially. After the funeral, he was to visit Alex for the first time in hospital. With Sloan's death displacing other pressing matters, Jasper had not, he felt, given enough thought to the coming meeting. Whenever he did try to think about it, moreover, his thoughts, like spilled peas, scattered in all directions.

'Did anyone take the flowers?' Carole eased herself in behind the steering wheel, leaned down and swung the lever enabling her to push the seat back. 'Or did we forget them?'

'Right here,' Jasper said. On the floor between his feet was a plastic bucket containing several inches of water and a large bouquet of white peonies.

'I thought they wanted contributions instead?'

'Yes, Daniel.' Jasper was abrupt. 'From us they're getting both.'

Jasper didn't plan to see Alex for long. A few minutes to complete a perfunctory examination would do. Indeed, he was still at a loss about whether to go ahead with the face change. Sloan's death seemed somehow to close off all avenues of retreat, to seal him into a bargain which otherwise, he protested to himself, he would never have consented to carry through. After he had found Sloan so gravely ill, on death's doorstep, he had climbed down to Rhoda's again, prepared to call off what he'd quickly come to regard as an unholy bargain. He'd gone home, however, without clarifying his position. The sight of the bed, the scent of their recent sex, Rhoda's bare flesh – he was at too much of a disadvantage.

What made things worse was that Jasper felt a deep antipathy towards Alex. This dislike, he knew, was irrational, unfair, unworthy of him – but that didn't make it any the less strong. Things had reached such a pitch with him in fact that Jasper was fearful should he proceed with the operation that the force of his emotions might well interfere with his precision.

'Watch out, Carole.'

'Sorry. How're we doing timewise?'

'What about lifewise? You won't get us there any faster by running down old ladies.'

'Oh shut up, Daniel.'

'Whaa,' Jasper gasped. Cold water from the flower bucket splashed over his feet, soaking his socks.

'Why the big deal?' Helen had said that morning, not without pique. 'That boy's death was a deliverance. You said so yourself, Jasper.'

'Did I?'

Daniel had asked to come along. 'Who all's going to be there?' His question hung in the air unanswered. 'You guys are a lot of fun. Practicing being solemn, is that it?' The car swerved again. 'Carole, what the. . . .'

'Look, when you're old enough to drive, you'll be old enough to criticize.'

'That's a date.'

A man who lived and died without sex, Jasper pondered, with arousal, of course, but without consummation – strength or weakness? Enviable, or – Jasper shied away from the alternative.

The doorman came forward as soon as Carole pulled up at the curb in front of the Ritz Carlton. 'Listen,' she said, eyes straight ahead, 'why don't the two of you hop out. I'm just going to park. There's still loads of time.'

'Why bother, Carole. Put it in the hotel lot.'

'You must be kidding, Fa. You know what that'll cost? This time of day there'll be plenty of spots over by the river.'

'Do you want me to come with you?' Jasper asked.

'You're sweet, but I can manage. Watch the flowers, they're dripping.'

'Don't be late,' Daniel ordered gratuitously. 'That would be very disrespectful.'

Without thinking, Jasper stepped into the revolving door. His hands rose to touch the brass bar. Contact gave him chills.

In the splendid lobby the Whitings took no more than a step or two towards the gleaming Art Deco elevators before a nervous, well-dressed gentleman with a white carnation pinned to his lapel came bearing down on them.

'The Glintz party? Names, please – yes, yes, thank you.' Huffing and puffing on behalf of the management, slightly larger than life, stiff, deferential, he went on to explain the special security measures put into effect. Upstairs, before entering the penthouse, they would be asked to submit to a brief body search.

'Unless, of course, you have any objections. . . .'

'As a matter of fact, I. . . .'

'Daniel!' Jasper twisted his son's earlobe.

The elevator controls were set to make intermediate stops impossible. There was no background music, only the slight creak of the cage palpitating in its ascent.

There was more of a crowd in Luigi's suite than either Jasper or Daniel had expected. A hotel maid came to relieve Jasper of the peonies.

'Did I *mind*? Are you mad?' The first recognizable sound to reach Jasper's ears was Matasapi's high-pitched giggle. 'The question now is how to get him to search me again.'

'It's perfectly hideous,' Daniel said, taking in the surroundings, 'melted marshmallow. But once that's said, I kind of like it.'

Indeed beige and broken white were dominant: fibrous wallpaper, a shaggy carpet, plush curtains, deep armchairs upholstered in distressed velvet, and a vast multi-sectional L-shaped sofa. Cut flowers in profusion were everywhere, fistfuls of color, naked in their brightness, rising out of fluted crystal vases like strangulated screams.

'Dr Whiting, Jasper, from the looks of him, this one *must* be yours.' Matasapi wore glitter even in mourning, black sequins. 'How sweet of you to bring the family. The likeness is' – he seemed to chew on his tongue as he spoke – 'eloquent.' Still and all there was such deep penetration to the man's eyes that Daniel stood for it when Matasapi caressed his cheeks with the back of a small, plump hand. 'Ah, doctor, young flesh. There's nothing like it, is there?

'Sloan must've been about your age, —?'

'Daniel.'

'You're lucky to have such a fine, outstanding man for your father, do you know that?'

'Yes, sir.'

'No, no, Daniel, you don't. How could you? Cheeks like a baby. You may realize it some day though, when it's too late. Oh, listen to me. Listen to the utter drivel. Sorrow may bring out the best in some people. Alas, I am obviously not one of them.

'Death – why not admit it, isn't that what we're here for? – death *depresses* the hell out of me.' Matasapi clasped his hands under his chin and sighed. 'He was a dear, dear child. We shall miss him.'

'Fa, I'll be outside.' Chin down, Daniel drifted through the room, passing people who stood in uneasy little groups. Jasper watched him slide back the glass door to the roof terrace and step out onto the fine white gravel.

'Notice anything different about me, doctor?' Matasapi drew Jasper aside. 'Doctor, doctor, you're not even trying.' Jasper sniffed. More Moon Madness? He wasn't sure. '*Look at me*. There, that's better. You see, I'm clean.' Giggle. 'Not a single spot.' Matasapi closed his bottle-glass eyes and raised his chin in the best manner of a sun worshipper. In an instant his eyes flashed open again. His lips practically brushed the whorls of Jasper's ear. 'And all thanks to that boy, that dear, sweet child. Since Sloan blew out the candles on his cake, I haven't had a minute's worry.'

The many faces buzzing through the room, who were they? Where were the people who loved Sloan? Rhoda. Luigi. The occasion felt wrong. Chill, impersonal, repressed. Wet socks didn't help things either.

'You remember the look on Sloan's face, don't you? Those eyes, doctor, those eyes he made when he saw that wonderful cake coming closer and closer.'

'Oh, doctor, Jasper, God bless you.' Gayle Glintz, dressed in scratchy black, buried herself in Jasper's embrace. Her long frail arms cut into his back, the point of her chin grated on his collarbone. Grief had exaggerated all her angles. She collapsed against him and hung there, weightless, sobbing.

'Shh, shh, shh, shh.'

At that moment Rhoda and Daniel walked in from the terrace, arm in arm, neither smiling, the two of them sculpted by the bright daylight outside into dark statuary.

'Come see.' Gayle Glintz led Jasper by one hand to an alcove off the entrance hall. Sloan's wheelchair, the straps and grips worn, the familiar frayed treads of the four small wheels, stood there, surrounded by candles, with the origami birds and stars which had hung suspended above his barred cot dangling, dancing in the warm air set in motion by the candle flames. A large sunburst mirror in baroque gilt frame behind added depth and multiplied the points of light. On the seat of the wheelchair, the faded square cushion, the beautiful quilt lay folded that Luigi had stitched together. And snuggled into the quilt was a graceful silver urn.

'Oh yes, it's easier,' Gayle Glintz admitted to Jasper, 'since Sloan's gone. It is. Much. But I miss him every minute of the day.'

Madge joined them, pressing Jasper's elbow with unexpected clannish familiarity. Gayle Glintz let her head fall onto the sturdy woman's shoulder. Madge's black blouse, open at the throat, frilly collar and cuffs, was becoming. Since Sloan's sudden final illness, Madge looked younger. Everyone agreed. Less severe, brighter of eye.

Of the people Jasper couldn't place, some he assumed must at one time or another have been members of a patterning squad. Others – colleagues from Rhoda's school, perhaps? Gayle Glintz's clients? As far as he could make out, only one handicapped guest was present. This girl, whether by choice or chance, sat half-concealed in a corner of the room, screened by an exploding bouquet of wildflowers and ferns. And there by her side was Rhoda. Jasper smiled inwardly at how inevitable the vignette struck him. Rhoda was crouched, stroking the child's hand, looking up into her eyes.

A fashionable woman stood close by. No doubt 'the poor mother', she looked on as if from a distance.

By tracking Madge Cutler's movements, at a certain moment Jasper located Murray. Jasper himself felt unable to move. He lingered in the alcove, his back to the memorial altar, highly conscious of the flickering candles and their reflection behind him. Madge circulated, discharging an eerie vitality. It wasn't that she led Jasper's gaze to her husband. Rather from her circlings a distinct pattern emerged. She appeared repelled from one area of the room, returning to it again and again only at the last moment to shy away and veer off in some other direction.

Since running into Murray naked, wet, in Rhoda's room, Jasper hadn't given him a second thought. Here death had left a mark, deep and consequential. The suit Murray wore once had been stretched taut by his broad frame. Now it hung loose. He stood looking down, hands writhing in each other. At their ends Murray's lips turned up ever so slightly, but not in any amusement, not unless despair is some final form of comic appreciation. No, Murray was talking to himself, or – Jasper felt a stitch in his side – to Sloan, rapidly.

The man, Jasper couldn't shake the thought, was passing sentence on himself, too stunned by grief even to enter a plea for clemency.

'. . . to bear with me.'

Luigi was off and in mid-sentence before Jasper was aware the funeral service, as such, had begun. The model, steadying himself against the back of an armchair, had never looked more glamorous. He wore gray silk, free-flowing, his chest studded with ornaments of jet and obsidian. Luigi's face was so pale it appeared the blood mounted no higher than the root of his neck. He had ringed his eyes with kohl and tied back his soft hair with a braided black filet. Anyone else would have looked theatrical, striving for effect.

Jasper edged closer. Luigi was not speaking loudly. His voice had little of its customary confidence or finesse. It sounded distilled.

'One thing, however, I do know. Whatever a cripple does, whatever he says, however he squirms or doesn't squirm, whether he cares to notice or not – every minute of his life he lives under total suspicion. Nothing he, nothing we do, is taken at face value.'

Tension in the room crackled. Luigi, up to now neutral, swinging on a star high above No Man's Land, was taking sides.

'Even for someone who is strong, and most of us, let's face it, are not, not even as strong as we think – not that we can fool ourselves for long, not really – even for the unusual strongman then, total suspicion soon becomes intolerable. Today or tomorrow it warps us, distorts us, ties us into knots that never come out. We begin questioning our own motives for every simple little thing we think or do. We end up believing we are capable of unlimited treachery, believing it with all our hearts, accepting as gospel a terrible truth about ourselves which we would never have dreamt of in the first place, not if others hadn't so obviously suspected it. That is the tragedy of total suspicion, how expectation creates behavior. Few rise above it, precious few. Few, too, are strong enough, whole enough, to reject the offer of pity for what it really is, counterfeit fear – and, free from *self*-pity, reject it. I'm speaking from experience now when I say that to accept pity is to justify suspicion.

'Sloan,' – here Luigi looked slowly around the room – 'may the Lord God lift up the light of His countenance upon you and grant you peace, His most precious gift. Amen.'

'Amen.'

Four security men with white carnations entered from the bedroom carrying a harpsichord, pink and gold. A flurry of questions and consternation followed. Where, people were asking, was Carole Whiting?

'He should know better.' Matasapi materialized again at Jasper's elbow. 'He's pretty, very pretty. But he's asking for trouble, stepping out of line. Helen Keller, doctor. Do you know what her last words were? A closely guarded secret.' Jasper gave him no encouragement. 'No? I'll tell you then. Food for thought. Just before she died, she said, "I hated every minute of it." '

'Oh, if I have to,' Rhoda was saying, 'I can.'

'Or do you think we should wait?' Luigi asked. 'Would you rather wait, or go ahead?'

'I don't understand it.' Jasper tugged nervously at his belt. 'She was just going to park and come right up. That's what she said.'

Jasper had no inkling of Carole's having consented to perform.

'In that case maybe we should give her, what,' – Rhoda shrugged – 'five more minutes? Ten?'

'No,' Luigi decided. 'Now that we've started, a break would be wrong. Let's go on. Carole will understand, I'm sure. Rhoda?'

'Susan? Susan, honey, we're on.'

Mrs Benedict-Vincent proceeded to maneuver Susan in her wheelchair across the shaggy carpet to the curved side of the pink and gold harpsichord. She locked the brakes, patted her daughter's arm and stepped back. In full view the girl's body, tilted back in a simple long dress, was revealed as twisted, the parts out of proportion. She had beautiful hair though, undulant, burnished with brushing until it flashed red-gold. Rhoda, in casual sweater and slacks, black, sat at the keyboard, smiling with gratitude when Matasapi dashed forward to prop a pillow under her.

Rhoda struck a preliminary chord, paused and then began to play. Susan's face, until then fishlike, impersonal, assumed an expression of almost painful concentration. The room hushed. Rhoda and Susan performed the aria 'Nobody's Perfect' from *Love Comes to Its Senses*:

Nobody's perfect, Nobody.
The world completes itself
with love.
Come, let us celebrate
our imperfection,
Together, together.

Nobody's perfect, Nobody.
Now through sweet kissing
Fulfill what is missing.
The end of desire makes
Lovers entire, expiring
Together, together.

Susan's singing voice wasn't strong or clear, but hesitant and fearful. Rhoda's playing was certainly not polished. No one who heard the performance, however, would ever forget it. There was nothing flimsy or precious about the lyrics; utter sincerity gave them a tensile strength. The simple, assertive music was haunting.

After the last note died, with the merest suggestion of a smile, defiant, Susan slumped back in her chair. Her mother, crying, wiped Susan's forehead and kissed her. Susan crossed her legs at the ankle. Rhoda sat staring at her hands, open, palm up, on her lap. No one spoke or moved.

It was Daniel Whiting who broke the spell, seizing flowers from a table that had been shoved to one side to make room for the harpsichord and laying them shyly across Susan's lap.

'Not bad?' Susan asked Rhoda.

'Not bad.'

'All right, how much?' Matasapi asked Rhoda. 'And for once in your life be honest.'

'You liked it?'

'I liked it.' He had both hands in his pockets, rocking back and forth on his heels, squinting in thought. 'A butterfly doesn't make a summer, I don't need to tell *you* that, of all people, but yes, I liked it.' He rubbed the side of his neck. 'Of course the circumstances, shall we say, were highly favorable. But, yes, it has something, I admit.'

'As long as we can open,' Luigi said, a hand on Matasapi's elbow, 'from that point on money won't be a problem.'

'All right.' Matasapi took a checkbook out of the bag that hung from a strap around his wrist. On cue, without a word spoken, the slim young man at his side bent his back into a writing table. 'But,' he wagged a cautionary finger, 'the name of your angel remains our little secret.'

'Fa, what's the story?' Daniel had returned to Jasper's side, the knot of his tie pulled down, shirt collar open, stiff spikes of hair erect in a cowlick. 'How could Carole cop out like that?' Jasper didn't say anything. 'That girl, the one who sang – Susan – she gave me chills.'

Jasper looked his son in the eyes. 'Me, too.'

'I was just talking to her mother. She's done a book about what living with Susan is like for the rest of the family.'

'So.'

'She said some really amazing things.' Daniel, embarrassed by his own candor, so determined not to run away from unexpected emotions, reminded Jasper of Helen when they'd met. 'Of course, when you can't help something you have to try to look at it positively. She's no phoney though, I'll say that much for her. She isn't trying to beat any tamborine. Good-looking woman, Fa, don't you think?'

Gayle Glintz stood at the door clasping the hands of departing guests, hugging some – pulling her own long hairs out of her mouth, shivering slightly, forlorn. 'Thank you so much for coming. I don't know yet. I'll have to see. Business as usual, I suppose. Of course, of course. Yes, no, exactly.'

'Fa.' Daniel was talking with the need of someone terrified that silence might smother him. 'I want to ask you something, can I? I'd like to watch you work. It's crazy, really, when you stop to think about it. I've never seen you do an operation.'

Daniel's request jolted Jasper into thinking about the awaiting interview with Alex.

'What happened to Carole?' The make-up around Luigi's eyes had run. He seemed drugged.

'The sad thing about my sister,' Daniel started to say, but he was interrupted by a commotion at the door. There was a flurry of bodies and voices and then Carole herself burst in, frenzied, muttering out loud, her gangly long limbs uncoordinated.

'Oh, I am so sorry,' Carole wailed. She kissed Gayle Glintz, hugged her father, kissed Luigi on the cheek and blushed. Then for the first time in her life she bent and kissed Daniel, too. 'I'm *so* sorry. Oh, this is just terrible. Everyone's gone. What happened? Somebody tell me. Didn't she sing?'

Luigi's smile was boyish and sweet. He made Carole sit down. He took off her shoulder bag. He held her hands in his and described Rhoda and Susan's triumph.

'We have the backing to go ahead,' he told her.

'Where were you?' Daniel demanded.

'Don't you people know what's going on out there?'

Everyone still in the suite turned to listen.

'Hundreds – what am I saying, hundreds – thousands, the place is crawling with them, they're like ants around a drop of honey.'

'Slow down, Carole,' Jasper said. 'What're you trying to say?'

'The hotel is surrounded, that's what I'm trying to say. They're all down there in the street with candles.'

'Who?'

'Sloans,' Carole exclaimed. 'I had to claw my way through, literally. So many dirty looks I can't tell you. Excuse me, pardon me, Jesus. At a certain point I just got stuck. It would all be very impressive, I suppose,' Carole spoke feelingly, 'if only – if only it was a little bit less macabre.'

'What is it?' Matasapi came out of the bedroom.

'The rejects – they've turned out to hold a vigil.'

'For Sloan?' Jasper tried to explain to himself out loud.

'There's this, too.' Carole pulled a newspaper out of her shoulder bag. In large letters the headline read: POLICE PROBE DEATH OF POSTER CHILD. 'There are eyewitnesses who swear they saw Sloan dragged out of his chair and beaten.'

'That's not true,' Jasper blurted out angrily.

'Read it yourself.'

'There was no trace of violence. None. I saw him with my own eyes.'

'He hit me a few times,' Murray said. 'Later he was sorry.'

'Poster child?' Daniel asked. 'What's that about?'

'Me.' Matasapi's voice, almost a whisper. 'For fund-raising. I, I photographed him – extraordinary, believe me. Simply extraordinary. Still, I wasn't happy. I wanted – never mind.'

'Oh, Rhoda, how can I ever thank you.' Carole embraced Rhoda whom she had just noticed reading the paper over her shoulder. Jasper could not remember ever seeing Rhoda look so tired. But then, he'd often had that impression. Rhoda hadn't said two words to him all day. More to the point, they hadn't exchanged a single meaningful look. Nothing showed more, Jasper consoled himself, how much she was relying on him.

'What the hell kept you?'

'A mob,' Daniel defended his sister. 'They've taken over the streets.'

'They?'

'You know, those who live under total suspicion.'

Carole led the rest out to the roof terrace. Before anyone else passed through the sliding doors, she screamed. It is probable she had no clear idea what Luigi was doing so close to the railing.

Luigi did not seem to hear the scream all at once. When the sound had almost died away, slowly he turned to look. He didn't seem to realize either how crowded the terrace had become. He glanced at the astonished, worried faces, nodded, and then, ever so calmly, returned to his business. He carried on as if still alone, so intense was the privacy of his need.

In his left hand Luigi held Sloan's funeral urn by its silver throat. In his right, cupped, there was a small mound of pale, pulverized bone, Sloan's irreducible remains. Luigi's dove-gray shirt, sticking out from his trousers, half in front, half in back, was sweated through down the spine. His lips were moving, but a faint, high-level breeze seized the sounds he mumbled and carried them out over the city. No one could catch more than a sorrowful sing-song. When the chant ended, Luigi stood a moment with his mouth open, then crouched and with a tremendous effort flung the contents of his hand up and out over the rail, eyes trained high as if he expected to see the cinders take flight.

'Let him,' Gayle Glintz said, 'oh, yes.'

Slowly, carefully, Luigi poured another handful from the urn, to all appearances the last. After the flow ceased, he turned the urn quite upside down and shook it hard but this dislodged only a few small bits of flake further.

Now Luigi shuffled across the terrace to the south wall, where he appeared to repeat his previous devotions. When the time came to draw back his arm, however, something stayed him. He faced about, troubled. He hobbled back to the others, very close to them. First he seized one of Gayle Glintz's hands. Her fingers were closed on a handkerchief. He prised them open, threw the handkerchief to the gravel, and with extreme care poured a sprinkling of pale particles from his hand into her palm. Next he sought Rhoda. She held out her two hands promptly, cupped together. Then in turn Luigi went to Murray, to Jasper and to Matasapi, to the latter's manifest discomfort and delight. Somehow the single last handful of Sloan stretched. Jasper clenched his fingers in a fist, aware of his responsibility to commit the boy's body entire to the air.

Step by step the others advanced behind Luigi up to the rail, the polished copper now on fire with late sunlight. When Luigi with a supressed cry flung his arm up and out, they flung theirs, too. Although no one spoke, no one, as each turned back from the rail at his own speed and one by one they faced each other again, it was clear to all how much better they felt.

'Now that,' Matasapi said with no flicker of sarcasm in his voice, 'is what I call a real goodbye.'

'Look, it's amazing!' Daniel was leaning far out over the rail, peering down. Below indeed spread a host of persons, out over whose assembled heads they had just sprinkled Sloan Glintz's earthly remains. There were thousands of tiny candle flames, eyes of fire, not romantic by day, but frightening. The crowd filled the street, overflowing into the Public Gardens. It seemed to grow while they watched. Passengers in the swan pedal boats held candles, too.

'From up here,' Daniel said and Jasper hooked a finger through a loop in his son's trousers, 'you can't see there's anything wrong with them.'

6

Matasapi had kept a car and chauffeur waiting in the underground Ritz Carlton garage to take the Charter Street contingent home. Madge needed to talk. The others could have done with silence. Rhoda, at the driver's elbow, had a splitting headache. Madge rattled off sure-fire remedies. She knew no less than half a dozen. In the back Murray slumped against the door, the flowers which Luigi had pressed on him in a jumble on his lap. Under the glowing heads of the peonies nestled black clots of lice.

At the bottom of the steep exit ramp up to the street they were obliged to wait. Police had to struggle to clear a path. Madge delivered a monologue about carbon monoxide poisoning. Matasapi, enthroned in the middle of the spacious back seat, spent the time primping. He powdered his face, using a small tortoise-shell compact which lit up when snapped open. Gayle Glintz, to Matasapi's right, admired it silently. He saw, and gave the compact to her.

Even once the car could nose up and out into the dying daylight, it had to inch its way through the throng of demonstrators' bodies tightly packed on both sides.

'*So many* need help, that's what I can't get over.' Madge tilted her head back so those in the rear could hear better. 'Murray doesn't see it. The pighead won't listen. I mean one less is hardly here or there, is it, given the size of the problem? Like a pebble on the beach.' Rhoda leaned back, closed her eyes and put one hand on Madge's knee, hoping it might quiet her.

'What do you think about starting a club? A nice friendly old-fashioned kind of arrangement. Take them places, do things. Murray would be the perfect person for it. That way he could be doing something he likes and at the same time help people who need it. He wouldn't have to earn much.'

'Shh.' Rhoda squeezed Madge's knee gently.

'Maybe it's too soon. Maybe he just needs a little time.'

Matasapi leaned across Gayle Glintz and pushed a button to lower the back window. He began to photograph the crowd.

'At your own risk,' Rhoda cautioned.

'But, darling, they *know* me,' Matasapi practically squealed. 'They know a true friend when they see one.'

'You know what he did, Murray,' Madge went on, 'you're not going to believe this. When he found out about Sloan, he went and took all the things he'd gone out to buy for the boy's birthday and dumped them down the incinerator. A lot of things he'd made himself, too. That kite, for instance, a real beauty – gone. I didn't tell you this already, did I? For Pete's sake if I start repeating myself, stop me. My mother used to do that and it drove me crazy. Where was I?'

No one helped.

'The kite,' Murray said.

'Oh, yes. How long did you work on it? A week? Right down the chute. What a waste. A lot of people could've gotten use out of those things, I told him. Why destroy them? All right, Sloan's gone and nothing anybody can do will bring him back, but what about the rest? Look at them.' Murray reached across the car and patted Madge's shoulder.

'Where do they all come from?' Matasapi hummed. 'In its own way it's rather a lovely sight, isn't it? Certainly impressive, God, yes. Hello, something I fear is wrong with my camera.'

'Wrong?' Gayle Glintz asked.

'It's jammed.'

'What's tipped the balance, for me,' Madge began again, 'is the kind of things people at work have started saying about cripples. Really gross.' The limousine glided through a crossing where on all sides store fronts and electric signs had been shattered. The seething crowd had gradually become a blend of demonstrators, looters, curious hangers-on and young street toughs. 'I guess they just take it for granted that we all think the same way.

'I've considered saying something, you know, speaking up, but that would only make it worse. The stories would get nastier. They'd laugh that much harder. I know them.'

'He would have loved this,' Gayle Glintz said and snapped her new compact open. 'Would've broken it, too, in five minutes flat.'

'I mean, take Sloan. Once you made your mind up, there was nothing to be disgusted about physically, not really. Who of us hasn't got our faults?' Madge looked over her shoulder. 'I have a lot to make up for, I know, but better late than never, right? Now what happens – Murray turns around and tells me he never wants anything to do with them again.'

'Them?' Rhoda exhaled the word, shook her head.

'All of a sudden Mr Big Heart's the one with an aversion. If I didn't know better, I'd think he was out to spite me.'

At last the limousine reached the far edge of the crowd, fewer and fewer demonstrators with candles. A minute later it veered onto a spiral ramp to the John Fitzgerald Highway and gathered speed.

'Free at last,' Matasapi said.

'Tomorrow,' Madge went on, 'I'm going to the agency and buying two tickets to Lauderdale. Two. I've still got two weeks coming to me. He can come if he wants, or stay. Either way, it's up to him. But this silence,' – Madge fell still, turned to stare out the window – 'I can't take it any more.'

The chauffeur began to chuckle softly to himself. Murray scowled.

'You stay with me tonight,' Rhoda told Gayle Glintz.

'No, thank you.'

'For tonight, just tonight.'

'I have to face it sometime. I'll be all right.'

'You're sure?'

'No.' Gayle Glintz smiled. 'But I have some cleaning to do and that usually helps. What about you?'

'Rehearsals.'

'When do you start?'

'Day after tomorrow, I expect – at the earliest. I don't suppose we can get in touch with everyone before then.'

'Can I help? You know, sewing or anything? Hairstyles?'

'Of course.'

Madge twisted in her seat to face Rhoda. She was biting her lip. Tears made her eyes enormous.

'Time's so short we can use all the help we can get.' Rhoda stroked Madge's hair. 'Everyone's welcome.'

At Charter Street the friends parted rapidly. Murray and Rhoda helped support Gayle Glintz whose strength failed at the last moment. Madge entered the building behind them, carrying all the flowers. Matasapi sat for a while alone in the sleek rented car, caressing his camera. He opened it slowly and, inch by inch, pulled out the film. Then he climbed out and paced to a vantage point across from the gates of Copps Hill Cemetery. His idea was to bury the roll of film, but the ground was too hard to dig up with his bare fingers. Below, triangles of light strung along the mast and sails of the USS *Constitution* gave him a moment of mercurial pleasure. He looked up through the dim air tinged with the stench of charred rubbish at the brick façade of No. 39. He'd never been inside. Never been asked. Staggered windows glowed soothingly. Still, ordinary lives, they, too, he supposed, were an illusion.

It had been a long day, one of extraordinary pain for him, pain for which he had failed to find release. He had behaved, as usual, dismally. Whenever he opened his silly mouth some abomination tumbled out, glib, cheeky. He felt deeply ashamed, utterly alone. He could only hope and pray that some of the good people with whom he'd stood on the terrace outside Luigi's suite understood, and did not condemn him too harshly for his pathetic weakness. Matasapi rubbed his fingertips across his smooth complexion and smiled ruefully at the glitter of his black sequins. His emptiness ached.

Matasapi let his no-colour eyes drift out gradually across the dark surface of the straits. So few details demanded attention, his mind could rest. Blunt sluggish tugs, an early star or two, wispy clouds shredded by an inconstant ocean breeze. Yes, at last Matasapi conceded to himself, the photographs of Sloan Glintz were the most remarkable he'd ever taken. By far. As the prints emerged from their clear chemical bath, he had blinked. Sloan, of course, had been, as always in one of Matasapi's exploratory sequences, buff naked. In these photographs, however, the photographer and not his subject had been the more unguarded. As a result, part of Sloan's self that by rights should never have been accessible to the lens had risen to visibility. A secret vanity had emerged, unmistakable, innocent and fierce. No one could look at the photographs and turn away unmoved. They were radiant with life, persistent and, yes, triumphant.

Matasapi had showed them to no one.

Jealous of these rare photographs, he was unable to share them. He pretended to be unhappy with the results of the sitting. He found unpardonable flaws with the pictures and blamed himself for being so careless, losing his touch. He arranged another date for Murray to bring Sloan to the studio, promising himself he would go about making a pedestrian series of photographs suitable for a mass distribution charity poster. Sloan with Alex, if things had gone differently, that had been his ambition.

Outside the Ritz Carlton this afternoon, the sight of so many deformed people, the pretty ones and the dull ones, a jumble, indiscriminate, had led Matasapi into a new lie. His camera jammed? Never! That no one had challenged him! He simply lost nerve. He realized he had done his best work already: the Sloan photographs. He would never surpass them.

When he had lowered his camera, he was letting the people in the streets go. And, in opening their cage, as it were, he was freeing himself as well.

7

'Are you all right, doctor?'

After the third patient in a row expressed concern, Jasper decided to skip the rest of his scheduled round of visits. Better to go at once to Alex Thane in E Wing. He went to leave word at the nursing station opposite the elevators.

A young nurse was on desk duty. Her eyes were glued to coverage of the Ritz Carlton vigil on a small portable television. She sat shoveling bon-bons from a heart-shaped box into her mouth. A mound of foil wrappers, silver and gold, lay crinkled at her elbows on the desk blotter. The nurse was concentrating so hard on the screen that Jasper's shadow gave her a start.

'Oh, Dr Whiting, you scared me.' Her white cap landed at Jasper's feet. Wary of vascular insufficiency – from which he knew he didn't suffer – he bent slowly at the knee to pick it up.

'Thank you.' From the way the nurse was talking, Jasper thought he should recognize her. 'It's me,' she said, 'Merriweather, remember?'

'Merriweather?'

'I was on the left arm. Sloan's.'

'Oh, yes.'

'Sorry, I'm not exactly the world's most tactful person.'

'Yes, of course, Merriweather.'

'Please, help yourself.' Merriweather held out the box of chocolates. 'Courtesy of Mrs Jewkes. She's getting a pacemaker tomorrow, and this is what her daughter brings. Sarah says they just want a cheap and easy way to get rid of her. She has no willpower.' By now Merriweather had four pieces of chocolate in her mouth at the same time, liquid fillings, nougats and creams. 'You know,' – Merriweather gulped, breathed deeply – 'I can't believe he's dead. Who would want to hurt Sloan?'

Jasper stared at the image of crowded downtown streets as if he were watching agitation in some foreign country. 'Nobody,' he said vaguely. 'I just came from there.' Jasper nodded towards the television screen. Deformed demonstrators were hurling flaming bottles at lines of police in masks. Few could throw well.

'Student groups have been coming out, you know, in sympathy with the – well, they call them the handicapped but they make a point out of saying the term is not acceptable.'

'Did you know Sloan very well?'

Merriweather hesitated. 'I used to sit with him sometimes and tell him my problems. Oh, please, take these away.'

National attention was inevitable now, Jasper feared. Talk of infiltration and payment from outside sources. A curfew?

'They've been interviewing people. Some of the handicapped are very well-spoken, really. What I think is that when they see all the damage, a lot of people who didn't used to care one way or another are going to get angry. Who's going to pay for it – that's what they're going to want to know. Are you all right, doctor?'

Jasper nodded.

'Those were good times though, at Charter Street, weren't they? And Sloan was so much better. Seems ages and ages ago.' Merriweather suddenly forced the red heart-shaped top back onto the half-empty box of candy. She looked up and down the corridors to make sure they were alone.

'Dr Whiting, if I ever had a kid like that, I'd kill him. I swear to God I would.' She crossed herself quickly. 'Kill him and get it over with. I'm not saying that's what everyone should do. Maybe I'm just extra selfish. I wouldn't love it. I couldn't, not my own. Somebody else's, well that's different. Like Sloan, for instance. But if it was my own, it would be him or me. That's the way it would be, why pretend any different?'

To enter Alex's room without knocking felt wrong. Still, to hesitate might attract unwanted attention. Jasper drew a breath, smoothed down his hair and went in. He closed the door behind him harder than necessary.

The far windows overlooked the parking lot and rooftop of the Holiday Inn where large, garish green neon letters blinked with a defect in their circulation. A corner window was raised slightly. The wind stuck its tongue into the room, and fluttered it.

From where Jasper stood in the entrance hallway a pleated white cloth screen in accordion sections shielded the bed. In direct view, head high and tilted forward, a television perched on a wall bracket. More Ritz Carlton live.

'Quite a show.' Jasper cringed inwardly at his own false first note. 'Wonder what the ratings will be.' He advanced to the panel screen, turned the edge and found himself smiling face to face with an empty bed.

'Over here, doctor, behind you.'

Jasper blushed and turned. Alex was seated sideways in a chair shoved into a blind corner of the room beside the clothes closet. Jasper had walked right past him.

'Safety?' Jasper launched onto the very subject he had decided to avoid.

'My sitting here? Nothing so intentional, no.'

Alex was altogether smaller than Jasper remembered him, everything about his person somehow finer, more fragile – his facial features, hands, gestures, voice. He was wearing wrinkled, peppermint-stripe pajamas.

'When I grow tired of staring at one wall, I pick another, that's all.'

Alex stood and took a few steps forward. He limped. Jasper couldn't conceal his shock.

'Ow.' Alex leaned over, holding onto the bed and rubbing his thigh. 'It's gone to sleep. Ah, ah, ah.' Jasper retreated, almost knocking over the screen. 'If only we could put the parts of our bodies to sleep one at a time, doctor, eh, in rotation. Think of all the time we could save for more useful things.'

'Yes, no.' Why should Jasper like Alex, or even expect them to share mutual respect? His thoughts crashed into each other like empty barrels.

'You've been half-way around the world, doctor, since last we saw each other. Imagine that.'

'And come back.'

Alex burrowed about in the top drawer of the night stand beside the bed. There were baskets of fruit and flowers, several about the room, all looking untouched, gaudy. 'Freedom of movement, doctor, is a wonderful thing.' At last Alex came up with a pair of shoemaker eyeglasses. 'That's better.' He put them on and peered at Jasper. 'Welcome. You still have your tan, I see.'

'Fading fast.'

Alex laughed. Jasper laughed. Silence.

'*Ach*, I've forgotten my manners. A drink?' From the closet Alex produced a chrome thermos and conical paper cups. What he poured was scotch. 'Health, doctor.' The two men raised their cups.

Alex, Jasper observed professionally, had a face that had matured in time to a degree of expressive perfection which he had seldom encountered, certainly never in anyone seeking his special services. It was precisely the kind of face he had always worked towards, knowing he could never achieve it. This, then, was the face he was being asked to destroy.

'How did it go?' Alex smacked his lips like a vaudeville clown. He kicked off his slippers and sat up on the bed. Jasper eased his weight onto the window sill. His back was cold, his legs, dangling over the radiator, warm.

'Go?'

'This afternoon.' Alex's bare feet revealed toes long as fingers.

'This afternoon?'

Alex betrayed no trace of annoyance at Jasper's silly parroting. He nodded. 'Yes, how did it go this afternoon, the memorial service.' He spoke rapidly, every syllable distinct.

'It went well.'

'Good, I'm glad.' Alex saw Jasper's eyes on his feet. 'Me and the peacock,' Alex said and wriggled his toes. Jasper looked up. The next words left his lips before he chose them, proof and a warning that Alex had already somehow penetrated his defenses.

'And how did *you* find the street vigil? Was it to your liking?'

'Powerful, I would say.' Alex hadn't once glanced over at the television. 'Very well organized, despite appearances.'

'Who's behind it?'

'Would you believe me if I told you I don't know?'

Alex left the bed and turned the set off abruptly. Jasper drained his cup and crushed it. A few drops spilled onto the back of his hand. He licked them up, the way he might if he had scratched himself.

'You know why I'm here?' Jasper asked.

Alex couldn't resist a smile. 'I do.' He fought against his amusement. 'I've been led to believe you've been having quite a little bout with your conscience.'

'I still have a number of calls to make, so please, come over here by the lamp, I'd like to examine you.'

With one hand, fingers spread, on the crown of Alex's head

and the other clenched under Alex's chin, Jasper rotated Alex's face slowly. He was aware the whole time how, at short range, Alex was following his eyes with his own. A nose may be stationary, the rest of the face is not. Eyes, nose, mouth, all work together as closely as the fingers of a hand. There was no detail that was not part of a living whole.

By force of professional habit, after releasing Alex, Jasper went to wash his hands.

'The worst of it is' – Alex clicked the eyeglasses in his hands – 'with those face lifts, I'll never know what I should've looked like by now.'

Alex allowed Jasper a period of silence. He sat watching Jasper dry his hands longer than necessary. Both men were aware how fast Jasper's heart was beating.

'That boy, Sloan. . . .'

'Yes?' Alex said encouragingly.

'Did you ever stop to think a good case could be made that you killed him?'

'Me?'

'Who else?'

Alex considered the accusation. 'You see it that way, do you?'

'Yes.' Jasper couldn't leave it there. 'And if you were honest with yourself, you would, too.'

'Tell me then, doctor, is it such a terrible thing, to die?'

'He had no choice though, did he?' To Jasper's annoyance, Alex didn't visibly react. 'Murray, who loved Sloan so much, the one who took him out begging, he' – here Jasper's gaze wavered – 'was in your power.'

'You have a way of putting things, doctor, so they stay put.'

'Well, am I wrong?'

'Rhoda told me you felt entitled to answers – even when there weren't any.'

They had talked about him then – probably not, Jasper winced, without laughing.

'All right, suppose you tell me how you wanted Sloan to die, doctor. When? Would it have been better for him to be hit by a car or choke on a fishbone? Or maybe what you had in mind was years and years of wasting away, years of silent suffering, years of hopeless deterioration?'

'I didn't want Sloan to die at all. I wanted Sloan to live.'

'Am I really expected to take such sentimental claptrap seriously, doctor? Come now. If I hadn't heard you myself, I would've thought someone was making it up – someone with a not very high opinion of your intelligence.'

Alex started to pace. Down one side of the bed, across the bottom, up the other side. Then back. He stopped several times, about to speak but sucking on one earpiece of his glasses and tilting his head not unlike a parakeet, he apparently thought better of it and went back to pacing again.

When finally he did speak, he did so quietly, which gave his words all the more force. 'When you stood over that boy's *body* the first time, doctor, slapping his legs down against the table, fighting your disgust the whole time, fighting the cramps in your muscles, tell me, did you ever in your wildest dreams imagine that Sloan Glintz might one day assume heroic dignity in the eyes of the world? Or more important, much, in his own?'

'While you, you hide.' Jasper felt if he wasn't careful he was going to start shouting. He rubbed his eyes – the gesture was Rhoda's. 'Sloan dies for the cause while you, you disappear and choose a new face.'

Outside as daylight faded the green letters in view of the window seemed to grow.

'Why don't you just come forward?' Jasper tried to take the initiative. 'The police say they're looking for you, but from what I can make out, they're a lot happier with you missing. The way things are now they have someone to blame for everything.'

'So acting on the axiom that what the enemy doesn't want can't be good for him, I should turn myself in? You're forgetting one small thing, doctor. The police are not the only ones looking for me.'

'Who else is?'

'Fanatics.' Alex closed his eyes and smiled faintly. 'No,

doctor, all things considered, I think I'd better have that new face.'

'As you wish.'

'No, not as *I* wish.' Alex's voice acquired an edge. 'Haven't I managed to make even that much clear to you? *I* have very little say in the matter, believe me. My life stopped belonging to me a long time ago.' Alex paused, then added harshly, 'I follow orders.'

'This new face of yours,' Jasper carried on, 'I don't see the point. The first time you open your mouth in public everyone will know.'

'And if I keep out of things?'

'Not very likely, is it? You're soon going to be in more demand than ever.'

Alex lay back on the bed, face, hands white as his pillow case. A rumpled little man.

'There are others to replace me, doctor,' Alex said, lacking his customary conviction. 'Don't object, there are. And if there aren't, there will be. I am in the way, doctor. I belong to the past. After all, I'm not one of them. You understand how that compromises me, if not in their eyes, not yet, then in my own?

'You know what I would ask of you, doctor, if I were a brave man, or even, as you say, an honest one?' Alex's eyes shone playfully, but his voice was suddenly the one Rhoda had warned could change lives. 'I would ask you' – Alex paused for dramatic effect – 'to make me *hideous*.'

'Those, I take it, are *not* your orders?'

'No.' Alex appeared relieved to see Jasper smile. What he didn't appreciate was how often Jasper's smile expressed confusion. 'My orders, no, but there's always room for – self-expression.'

'To be ugly – that's what you want?'

'If you would do me that favor, yes.' Jasper shuddered. For a stunned heartbeat Alex seemed to contemplate an image of himself, the monstrous alter ego that had haunted him so much of his life. 'If only you would let yourself go, doctor, for once.

'Can you imagine having hands that are useless, doctor? *Useless!* A body that can't pass its own waste, can't lift its own weight? A face, incomplete. I can't, and I have spent the better part of a lifetime trying.

'Maybe it's not as perverse as it sounds. When children make fun, they're doing the same thing really. Didn't you ever play hunchback or harelip – behind some poor creature's back? And when a parent catches his child in the act, what does he do? He gets angry, and he warns him to watch out or his face or body will get stuck.

'Inside me, doctor, down inside,' – Alex pressed his hands against his chest – 'something is stuck.

'Yet' – Alex exhaled through pursed lips – 'these last few years I think I've hit upon a funny truth about people who are "that way". *Imprisoned* in their bodies is the last thing they feel. That's what we think. We're only deceiving ourselves. For them imperfection, their imperfection, is the most natural thing in the world. It's theirs, a part of them. They wake up with it in the morning and take it to sleep with them at night. They know nothing else.

'We accommodate so easily, doctor. Most of us do. Give us time and we get used to just about anything – that's the bottom line. It is our strength as a species, and our weakness. We cry a lot about those few who don't, who can't accommodate. We make movies about them and television programs – some are inspirational, most are bad – but they're the exceptions, really, the odd ones out. The rest of us, we're all true-blue dyed-in-the-wool chameleons.

'Health, vitality – *these*, if we have the courage to admit it, are strange, *these*, doctor, are exceptional. Enviable? Not always. How often have friends told me that healthy people seem so frantic to them, so excitable?

'But I mustn't keep you from your other calls. You've been more than generous with your time, doctor. I just wanted to say that despite popular opinion to the contrary, few cripples hate their bodies. Life is a matter of limits after all – recognizing them, accepting them. As long as they can dream their

Saturday night dreams, too. New curlers, murder mysteries, chocolate, masturbation, the crossword puzzle, the state lottery.

'What a radical sickness has gripped us, doctor, our world, that we become so easily drunk on the parabeauty of normal function – the aesthetics of tape measure and stopwatch. After all, under the skin, we're all cripples, aren't we?'

In answer Jasper took out his pocket agenda. 'The first chance to operate will be Friday a week.'

'What's today? But that's two weeks.'

Neither man heard Daniel enter. Jasper simply saw Alex's face darken. When he turned, there stood his son.

'What are you doing here?'

'I knocked, Fa, honest. At the desk in C Wing they told me you had one quick call down here and when so much time passed without your coming back, I began to get worried. I thought maybe something was wrong or you'd gone home without coming back to collect your stuff. I'm sorry. I'll just wait. . . . '

'Is this your son, doctor?' Alex's eyes had gone hard. His age was most apparent, Jasper noted, from his teeth: they were yellowish, nearly transparent near their biting edge.

'Yes, this is Daniel. And he should know better. I'll be out in a minute, Daniel.'

'Sorry, Fa. I. . . .' Daniel looked back and forth from his father to the patient who sat now with his knees drawn up, peering at him through rimless spectacles. There was not a shred of doubt in Jasper's mind that Daniel recognized Alex, and had recognized him instantly.

Daniel completed a highly awkward exit, clumsy, bowing and apologizing non-stop as he backed into the hospital corridor. Jasper poked around in his agenda some more, crossing out some entries with his pen. His legs were shaking. He hoped Alex didn't notice.

'I'm afraid the ninth's absolutely the earliest I can do. The afternoon, three o'clock.'

Alex stroked the basket of fruit at his bedside. He removed a green apple and buffed it against his pajama top. 'I used to be better at waiting, doctor.'

'No doubt that had something to do with the things you used to wait for.'

When Alex bit into his apple, the crunch made Jasper reach up and press his hearing aid.

'They're building again, incidentally, in Beirut.'

'So.'

'Yes, bigger and better. Bigger certainly. And classes are under way. The United Nations has taken charge. Destruction was a blessing in disguise.'

'Your people will be supplying a surgical assistant. At least that is my understanding. And the anesthetist.'

'Yes.'

'Are they people you can trust?'

Alex looked at the bite he had taken out of the apple. The flesh of the fruit was stained with a bit of bright blood. A bubble. 'That goes without saying.'

'Professionals?'

Alex laughed. 'Are you trying to frighten me, doctor?' Jasper blushed. 'That boy of yours – he must be a familiar figure around here?'

'I suppose so, yes.'

'He should be able to pass in and out without anybody's thinking much about it.' Alex put the apple down and sucked on his teeth. 'If you don't mind, maybe you could ask Daniel to pay me a visit, sometime in the next couple of days.'

'For Chrissake, Fa, gimme a break. What was I supposed to do?'

'Go with Carole.'

'She's still back there with lover boy. When I came in from the terrace, nobody was left, really. Me and the cleaning lady. Carole was banging away on the harpsithing with her eyes shut. You know how she gets. Luigi was just lying there with that patchwork blanket over his face and his stump hanging out.'

'Daniel!'

'I don't know why you were in such a hurry to get out of there. I didn't ask to get left behind.'

'You should have gone straight home.'

'With what? Fine, next time I go to a funeral I'll remember to take carfare.' Daniel grabbed his father's arm.

'What's he got, Fa?' Jasper just kept walking. 'What's he in for?'

8

Back at his gigantic loft, the first thing Matasapi did was shed his mourning. He tried to sleep, but kept turning over and over, 'Nobody's Perfect' repeating relentlessly in his brain. He put the *Actus Tragicus* on his tape deck and wept like a baby.

Some hours later he woke in the pitch dark. He took a bubble bath. The cats all came to see, even stalking along the edge of the double tub. Out in the free core kitchen he used an electric carving knife to slice a banana. He drowned the banana in Bulgarian yoghurt, added maple syrup and sat to eat, naked. He had never been naked in the company of another human being. The cats twined around and around his ankles, better than slippers.

Humming 'Nobody's Perfect', Matasapi threw open his vast clothes closet. This was always a moment he enjoyed, the sense of limitless alternatives. He laid out half a dozen snappy combinations on his queen-size bed. 'Off,' he chased the cats with a pair of red elastic suspenders. Finally he climbed back into his black sequins. He stood in front of a full length mirror. 'I'm tough as nails,' he said. 'I can do anything.'

For the early hour, the Fallout Shelter was doing a brisk business. Matasapi was soothed by the fuss people made on his arrival, the flurry of fawning attention. He liked being the boss. At all the tables he passed, calling or responding to a greeting, the conversation was about one thing only. The candlelight vigil for Sloan Glintz. A few present had been there. Six blind punks, for example, with needles through their noses and half their scalps shaved bare. They were the loudest of all, mocking and jeering.

Soon Matasapi fled from the throb of the music into his private back office. It took him a moment to adjust to the silence. He was again on the point of tears. 'Sissy,' he hissed at himself. Behind his desk he bent and unlocked a lower drawer, tossing a number of small plastic sacks filled with white powder onto his green blotter.

He considered various ways to stage the evening's business – and pleasure. Finally he placed the sacks of powder on the low white Italian table, round, with the signs of the zodiac inlaid in boulle. It would not be long, he knew, before crippled friends and clients would begin to seek him out. He reclined on the couch next to the table, striking a pose of grief.

'Come in.'

Some of Matasapi's callers were so far out on the edge they already had their money bunched in one fist. But tonight Matasapi was giving hits for free.

'What're we celebrating?' they asked.

'Whatever you like,' he replied.

When it came right down to it, Matasapi believed that only he knew how to help. Work? Touch? When the rest of the world was at long last learning to see through these illusions, why dangle them in front of the disabled? Carrots with worms.

Matasapi, breaking precedent, rubbed a bit of coke into his gums. Aladdin couldn't have done better: when he looked up, Luigi was there.

'Why, if it isn't the Lost Explorer.'

'Don't call me that.' Luigi pushed Matasapi's legs aside, leaned his cane against the Italian table, and sat down.

'And here I thought you liked the name? Just goes to show you. Oh, lost your tongue, have you? Well then, a lot *has* happened since this afternoon. Where's Dulcinea? Has she come to entertain the troops?'

'Carole's sleeping.'

'Tuckered out, is she, poor thing. Tell me, is this time off for good behavior, or did you merely' – Matasapi's plump hand shimmied through the air – 'slip away?'

'If I was an acrobat,' Luigi said, rubbing the muscles of his good thigh, 'I would never walk down the street. Never. I'd turn somersaults and cartwheels all day. I'd walk on my hands. Anything – but walk? Never.'

'You're not an acrobat though, are you?'

Luigi closed his eyes. 'And I never will be.'

'What's got into you?'

Luigi looked around the office. It was furnished with a taste beyond reproach and he had helped. 'I owe you a lot.'

'True,' Matasapi said, 'but that doesn't mean I'm going to give you any more.'

'Tonight's the last time I'll ask.'

'You may be right.'

Matasapi rose, scooped up the remaining sacks of powder and locked them back in his desk. Luigi was sweating in a bad way.

'There's something I keep meaning to tell you,' Matasapi spoke rapidly now, recklessly, 'but you're such an exquisite little tramp every time I lay eyes on you it slips my mind.' Luigi crossed his arms and started to rock back and forth. 'Aren't you going to ask me? Dear me, what ever has happened to your curiosity? It was always one of your most endearing traits. The hunger to know. Well, I'll tell you anyhow.'

'Don't,' Luigi said.

'The best whorehouses in Europe have the same special drawing card. All of them. Guess what?' Luigi looked up. 'A woman who's missing part of a leg.' Matasapi grinned at him. 'And believe it or not – even when business is slow for the rest of the girls, she never has to complain.'

'Please,' Luigi whispered.

'Please?'

'I'm scared.' Matasapi spun away. 'What's wrong? If I can't tell you, who can I tell? You told me not to meddle, but. . . .'

'No buts.' Matasapi sighed. 'I don't like to think of you as afraid – of anything.'

'You wouldn't want me to hide it?'

'I wouldn't want you to make a habit out of showing it, either.'

'Those freaks on the street today, half of them didn't have any idea what they were doing out there. And the other half were just looking for trouble. Trash.'

'What have I been telling you all along?' Matasapi spoke slowly, deliberately. 'Most of the time when we think we're making choices, we're only choosing between what other people have to offer.'

'Sapi, listen. You don't know what it's like to be surrounded suddenly by people who take your decency for granted.'

'No,' Matasapi said. 'No, I don't.' Luigi was too caught up in his own confusion to realize how much pain his words inflicted.

'Sapi, the hell of it is I want to be who they think I am.'

'Correct me if I'm wrong, but didn't that lovely girl give you a sweatshirt, blood red let us call it, bearing the remarkable text, in puce, Choose Life?'

'Listen to me, Sapi, and don't attack, please.'

'All right, I'm listening.'

'Keeping it up is driving me crazy. Anything they don't want to see, anything they don't want to know about they ignore, they just pretend it isn't there. But it's only a question of time until they find me out. I don't want them to, but Jesus no one can be *that* blind!'

'Mr Total Suspicion' – but Matasapi wasn't mocking any longer. 'So many doubts about yourself so long you think they must be catching. You can't say I didn't warn you. The game is easy really until you have something to lose.'

'She wanted to be a stewardess. Carole. Set her heart on it. The Whitings are one of those families where Dad scratches the height of the kids on the doorpost. The day she grew too tall she cried her heart out. She tells the story like it was world tragedy number one. I've heard it four times. She expects me to feel sorry for her, and I do. Son-of-a-bitch! That's bad, isn't it, a bad sign? Luigi Sasakawa soft on other people's broken dreams.'

Matasapi crossed to Luigi on the couch. He sat and put his arm around Luigi's waist. It was the first time, both knew, their bodies had ever touched.

'Baby,' Matasapi said, 'stop now. Make an old queen happy. If you're going to do it, do it right. Clean up your act.

'After all, it wouldn't hurt me' – Matasapi turned Luigi's face up to his and he fixed the model with his bottomless, clear eyes – 'to have something to be proud of.'

9

Shortly after the oldest church bells in New England chimed nine, Luigi, cane-propelled, turned up at the Fallout Shelter with the keys. From the portico of the Old South Meeting House, Murray and Madge came down the alley to meet him.

'Been waiting long?'

'Couple of hours,' Murray said.

'No' – Madge jabbed Murray playfully in the ribs – 'we only just got here.'

'Got your work clothes on?' Luigi asked. Murray was wearing a red sweatshirt with a hood and baggy checked trousers. Madge had on a hand-knitted cardigan, pink, that hung down to her knees. Luigi himself was in a gray and green satin jogging outfit. On his body it looked like gift wrapping. 'Down we go.'

'What a zoo, bah!' Madge exclaimed at the foot of the stairs. The air was stale and rancid. Thonet stools lay where they had fallen, their curves upended in the early hours of the morning. Puddles of beer, trails of cheap wine, deposits of broken glass lay littered about. Feathers trampled upon, and flowers. A shoe even, on its side, patent leather. The room still seemed to shake with too much laughter, agitated whispers, sobs and pulsing, relentless music.

'I'll open a window.'

'Can't, I'm afraid.'

The row of small windows at street level had been blacked and screwed shut. The distant front door, once Luigi hooked it back, was the only source of natural light. A narrow tapering shaft of daylight, an obelisk, was exhausted by the time it reached the bottom of the entrance stairway. The mouth of the tunnel to the club proper was dark. Sunken neon fixtures in the ceiling didn't do much to brighten things, neither did squat table lamps with lizard-skin shades and black tassels.

'You need a new broom,' Murray said, but set to work with the old, ragged one. Behind the bar Madge ran water into an aluminum pail. It made a dreadful clatter, good for chasing ghosts. She took a fistful of rags which she hunted up in a supply closet. The sleeves of her sweater were too long. She rolled them up but still every time she dipped a rag in water the ends got soaked.

'Hi there,' Carole greeted Murray and Madge. 'Grub,' she nodded with her chin at the bags full of rolls and pastry in her arms. 'Lot to do, huh.'

'Keep us out of trouble.' Murray grinned.

'Out here,' Luigi called from the kitchen. Carole found him

searching for a clean pot in which to boil water for coffee. They kissed.

'It's fun, isn't it,' she said, 'starting something new.'

Carole pushed and pulled the upright piano out onto the dance floor, free from the shadows of the nook where it stood during club hours. She sat, hands poised on the keys. It was as if she expected the keys and pedals to start to move on their own accord. Any moment now it could happen and she wanted to be there when it did. Luigi stared from the kitchen doorway. He knew what she was living through. Opening night, the agonies of stage fright.

'Look,' he had reasoned with her, 'public performance is not a death sentence.'

'Go on,' she replied, 'now tell me it's the kiss of life.'

'Hmm. Not exactly La Scala or the Met,' Luigi chirped as he swiveled through the premises, capturing Carole's smile. 'No matter, we'll make a theater out of her, wait and see. A few changes will work miracles – maybe. The pillars don't help, of course. And then there's the ceiling. Any lower and we'd have to crawl. But you know what they say, Where there's a will. . . .'

Carole ran the back of her hands down the length of the keyboard.

'We're going to have to blind the mirrors, too, every last pretty inch of them, or we'll go stark raving mad, ahead of schedule. It could be a lot worse, I suppose, only don't ask me how.'

'Oh stop,' Carole said. 'There are possibilities, definitely.'

'Jesus, is this going to be a bitch,' was Luigi's answer. With Madge down on hands and knees, scrubbing, embroidered butterflies flitted into view on the hind pockets of her jeans. Luigi put a finger to his lips and stalked them, finally swooping with both hands to capture one.

'Never cared much for big sets anyway,' Luigi rattled on, 'which is a damn lie if I ever heard one.'

When Carole laughed, the others turned to see why it

sounded so odd. She had half-disappeared into the top of the piano, groping for snapped strings and crooked hammers.

'I think we'll have to go with footlights,' Luigi announced from a crouch. 'All those broken shadows shifting behind, might be kind of nice. Don't laugh, you,' he shook a finger at his reflection in a pillar, 'this happens to be one thing I know something about.'

'Morning, kids,' Rhoda greeted them. She had a purple scarf knotted around her head, large sunglasses, purple corduroy trousers, wide-wale. 'Place looks great. Jesus.' She carried a bulging shopping bag full of scripts and music and designs. She, too, had brought food. Glazed doughnuts. 'I start auditioning this afternoon. No lack of talent. And all the orchestra we need is with us, at least until they lay eyes on this hole.'

'I wonder, do you think,' Luigi asked, 'is there anything in Equity that forbids musicians to play sitting on each other's laps?'

'No problem,' Rhoda pulled off her scarf. 'We may have to trim some of their instruments down to size, that's all.'

'It's a sweet piano,' Carole said. 'Listen.' She began 'From Darkness to Darkness I Stumble', Fidel's aria at the height of the storm while he gropes in the mouth of the forest cave. Its wit was infectious.

Luigi and Rhoda pushed two tables together. She spread out various designs left over from the stillborn Boston Opera production. 'Ambitious, huh.'

Matasapi turned up in pants and shoes so tight he wasn't able to move forward in a straight line. Just then Madge and one of the Fallout Shelter waiters she'd found curled asleep in the coatroom emerged from the kitchen with steaming coffee and fresh-baked goods.'

'Ah, the delectables,' crowed Matasapi, his eyes never leaving the boy. 'How are you all this morning? Imagine, last night I was too tired to make love to myself. I can't tell you how insulted I was.' Licking thumb and forefinger, he picked up a piece of crumb cake. 'Look who's here,' Matasapi said, pretending to notice Luigi for the first time. 'The Lost. . . .'

'Good morning.'

'You look awful. Where's the Olympics?'

'I feel fine' – Luigi smiled.

'Did I ever tell you about the time I photographed the famous one-legged high jumper whose name now escapes me? Extraordinary. Like a praying mantis doing the backstroke. Oh, look at those things.' Matasapi sat to inspect the designs Rhoda and Luigi had been discussing, and to look at some of their hasty sketches. He glanced at them all and then, half-standing, laid his hands, fingers spread on top of them. 'Very imaginative, completely wrong. Costumes, my dear friends, are not clothes. They exist in a different world. You understand? We want magic, illusion, nothing else will do. I will show you, don't worry.'

That first day jokes tinged with despair flew fast and furious. Rhoda kept people as short a time as possible. She had emptied out her memory to bring them together, each missing something, all with special gifts.

'No, we don't have enough time,' Rhoda said, 'so, please, nobody ask. And no, this show is not worth doing if we don't do it right.'

The first performers to arrive were so jittery they made the room seem to vibrate. They kept trying to avoid looking at themselves, broken into partial images in the many mirrors.

'None of you were followed, don't fret,' Luigi reassured them.

'How do you know?'

'I was right behind you, all the way.'

From the very start Rhoda struck the note which she held throughout rehearsals, polite but reserved, almost distracted – as if she carried the entire production in her head. Too sudden a move, too impulsive a response and she might spill it irretrievably.

Gayle Glintz stayed at home.

10

'What is it, Fa?' Jasper put down the phone and just stood there. Carole touched his arm. 'Trouble?'

Helen was out marketing. Any minute Daniel would be home from school. Jasper scribbled a note on a napkin, the pencil shredding the paper. He propped the note against the fruit bowl on the kitchen table. 'Gone Mass Gen,' it read, 'back soon as possible.'

Most traffic at that hour was heading away from downtown. Carole made good time. They left the Mazda in a tow away zone. In front of the entrance gardeners were on their knees trimming the edges of the hospital flower beds. Jasper, cutting across a round patch of lawn, nearly tripped on discarded tools. Carole, with her long strides, stuck to the pavement.

'Wait here, honey.' In the lobby Jasper pushed Carole into a faded armchair. 'I won't be long, promise.' With the barest hint of petulance, Carole pulled her bright plastic raincoat around her tights. Jasper bent to kiss her forehead. He was trembling.

'I'll come with you.'

'Don't make things difficult.'

'What is it? What's happened?'

'Wait here.'

Jasper rode the elevator in E Wing to Alex's floor. He made no attempt to disguise his movements. He was conscious of being careless, but his errand had haste and his anger left no room for caution.

The door was ajar, an inch, no more. Above the pounding of his own heart, Jasper heard voices inside. Two men, talking amiably. Laughing.

'Afternoon, doctor. What an unexpected pleasure.'

'Fa!' Daniel turned and grinned at Jasper. 'Fa' – the boy had never looked so likeable, so distant – 'ever stop to think how many great men have been grotesque?'

'We've been discussing Dan here's homework.'

'So.'

'Once you start counting, it's incredible. Take a look.' Daniel held out a thick book, his history text.

'I'm afraid there's been some bad news.' Jasper brushed the book aside. 'Terrible news.'

Alex smiled so slowly it was as if an unseen hand was ripping tape from his lips, bit by bit. Daniel circled to the far side of the bed.

'Daniel, Carole's down in the lobby. I want you to go wait with her. Now.'

'No!'

'It's all right, doctor.' Alex reached out and patted one of Daniel's hands. 'We've done a lot of talking these past days, Dan, haven't we?'

'Fa,' Daniel looked across at his father, eyes pleading, 'I want to help.'

'And, no, he's not in my power, if that's what you're thinking.' Alex looked at Daniel, then straight at Jasper. 'If anyone's under a spell, it's me.'

'Rhoda just called.' It was easier for Jasper to talk with his eyes shut. Images clotted his brain, their outlines intermingled, swarms of them, revolving. 'She couldn't put two words together. Anselmo, the one they called St Anselmo, he's dead. He hanged himself in solitary.'

'Christ.'

'Electric wire. Nobody knows how he got hold of it.'

Alex went to stand by the window, staring out at workmen on ladders trying to repair the lights of the Holiday Inn. 'Is that all?'

'No.' Alex turned into the room. 'The others want you. They're *afraid*.'

'Are they?' Alex put a hand lightly on Daniel's shoulder. 'We were just talking about fear, Daniel and me, weren't we? How much it's like alcohol. After a while, fear becomes a habit, too. If you want to feel it, you keep needing more.'

'Don't go,' Daniel said. 'Fa, tell him to stay here.'

Jasper and Alex looked at each other without either's speaking a word. Alex wet his lips with his tongue, and nodded to himself. 'There've been many times,' he began, 'many, many times I've wished I could be afraid, afraid *here*, afraid *now*, but by then my threshold, my need, was already too great. Any sensible person in my position would've felt fear, that much I knew. I could even remember a time in the past, recently, when under the same circumstances I myself might even have been afraid. Quite possibly. But not any more.' Daniel was gripping his father's arm hard. 'My skin was simply too thick. Fear had lost its kick.'

'If you ask me,' Alex finally broke the silence that oppressed them, 'the justice people have been a trifle careless.'

'Very,' Daniel agreed.

'Or not?' Alex raised his eyebrows. Deep lines marked his face.

'Don't go, Alex. They'll get over it.'

'Thank you, doctor, for coming here, and for your concern. Maybe you'll be kind enough to leave me alone now, for a little while. I. . . .' Alex waved a hand through the air in a gesture of sheer loss.

'You won't take any chances,' Daniel insisted, about to follow his father to the door. 'Promise!'

'I don't have children of my own, doctor. How can you ever refuse them anything? Hey, don't leave me with this.' Alex handed Dan his history book from the bed. 'I'm not the one with a paper to write.

'Wait, I'll see you out.' Alex slipped on a wool robe and a pair of worn leather slippers with crushed heels. Daniel almost forgot to take his track gear which he'd tossed into a corner on his arrival. Alex handed him the nylon duffel bag, running spikes knotted through the handles.

'From what Dan tells me, his track coach understands the uses of fear.'

'How's that?'

'Every time I put my foot down, Coach says I should think the earth's on fire.'

Alex accompanied the Whitings to the elevator. He hugged them on parting. He had such a tiny, insubstantial body. His face struck Jasper as a skull.

'No, I think I'll come down with you. I'd like to meet Carole.' Later it puzzled Jasper that no one even thought of objecting. They had the elevator to themselves, a cell of diffuse light. They rode in silence, highly aware of the charged space between their bodies. Once, at a lower floor, they stopped. The doors opened with a *ping* but there was no one waiting to board.

As the doors closed again, swallowing them, Jasper felt Daniel move a step closer to him.

'Poor Rhoda,' Alex said.

In the lobby there were stirrings of life. The change of scene seemed to cheer Alex. 'Wouldn't it be lovely to walk to the river.'

Carole spotted them at once. She rose from her chair and was coming towards them, sober and vital, when half-way she bumped into an elderly woman with a German shepherd on a leash. The woman lost her footing. Carole steadied her. In clinging to Carole, however, the woman let go of the leash.

Alex screamed, his face lacerated with fear, eyes fixed on the dog, a blur of black and gray and pale gold, muscles rippling as it came running, mouth wide, charging at him. Daniel's reflexes were instantaneous. He hurled his bag and the shoes with the flashing spikes at the dog's head, kicked out with his foot, shouted. But with a whine, the beast ducked its massive head. At the last instant Alex threw his arms up and Jasper tried to shield him with his body, but the dog veered past, running still.

In the depths of the lobby, the German shepherd skidded to a standstill, claws scratching against the polished floor, and began to bark, tail wagging madly. A young boy stood backed up against the plate glass window of the brightly lit hospital gift shop. A miniature poodle, white with a bow around its neck, quivered and whimpered and yapped in his sheltering arms.

11

At Spy Pond Lane Jasper's note was still leaning against the fruit bowl. He crumpled it up and threw it into the garbage under the sink.

Carole went right upstairs. She was working on the aria Vera sings before she enters the dark forest cave. The sky shivers and flashes with lightning, trees sway, branches crack and crash to earth but the deaf princess hears nothing. 'Even sounds of danger would be sweet,' she sings, and takes the plunge.

Rhoda was right: Carole's playing was lacking in suspense. She needed to put herself in Vera's shoes. She – *click* – Anselmo! Carole made a connection between Anselmo's lonely, violent death and Vera's wry lament. Her fingers twitched, she half-stood, Luigi's name on her lips. Then she forced herself back down onto the piano stool again and, set on getting it right, began to play, this time for real.

To live and die in a world without music, days and nights of uninterrupted silence – just thinking about it was almost unbearable.

'How often?' Daniel and Jasper sat out on the screen porch in the gathering dark. 'Every day. Is something wrong? You're the one who told me to go.'

'True.'

'Shit, I give up. I can't win.' Daniel yanked off his shoes and socks as if that way he could breathe more easily. 'You wanted to know what I thought of him, right?'

'Yes.'

'How was I to find out, remote control?'

Jasper tilted his head back, listening to the penetrating ripple of the harpsichord through the ceiling.

'Well, do you want to hear it, or not?'

Alex had been the first to recover and laugh at himself after the charge of the German shepherd in the hospital lobby. Carole had trapped the writhing leash with one foot and led the dog, whining, back to the shaken but grateful old woman. 'Well, what do you know,' said Alex. 'I believe I was *afraid*.'

'All right, Daniel, tell me' – Jasper looked at his son – 'but in a normal tone of voice.'

To think better, Daniel got down cross-legged on the floor, fingers poking between his toes. 'When I first went to see him, all Alex wanted to talk about was you. He seemed disappointed how little I could tell him.' Daniel shrugged. 'Then we started getting off on to other things. Little things, unimportant.'

'What's your opinion then?'

'Of Alex?' Daniel hesitated briefly. 'I'd say he's spent too much time alone.'

'And?'

'And' – Daniel's eyes narrowed with concentration – 'if there was some other word for *lonely*, only ten times worse, that would fit him. With most people who are lonely, company helps. Somebody, one special person, one friend would be enough to make them not be lonely any more. There's a cure. But with

Alex it's a different story. He's been so lonely, so long, and there's never going to be an end to it.' Jasper could see a chill run down Daniel's spine. The boy shook his head and shoulders. 'Fa, it makes *me* lonely just to think about it!'

At that the light flashed on overhead. Helen was home. 'What are you two sitting in the dark for?' she said. 'I picked up the Kenya photos.' She put down a paper wallet full of color photographs on the glass table at Jasper's elbow. 'They're better than I thought. Dinner in half an hour.' When she left, Daniel stood to go, too. At the door, however, he turned. There was something more on his mind.

'The funny thing is how you can meet somebody who's lived through so much shit that you think what he has to say will be a revelation – like Alex. I mean his life hasn't exactly been humdrum, has it? But it isn't. What he says. It's all so ordinary. And he's not kidding. You come expecting a revelation, and what do you get? Questions about the quarter-mile and homework. The most trivial things in the world.'

No, Jasper thought after Daniel had gone, he had no quarrel with the man. Rather, he suspected shamefacedly, he should feel some kind of twisted gratitude. What was Alex Thane, really, but living proof, more than any doubter could require, that a life truly consecrated to easing human suffering might in the end bring bitter little comfort.

Jasper told Helen what had happened while she finished chopping and slicing for the salad. 'I'm sorry,' she said, 'it must be very upsetting for you.' Dinner was over quickly and the family trickled away afterwards into separate rooms.

'News, guys,' Daniel called later. He always sat so close to the television that light from the screen flooded his face.

'Thomas J. Schelling Jr, by all accounts the leader of those accused of beating Patrolman Michael Lyons to death on the Boston Common last month, hanged himself in his cell in Charles Street Jail early this afternoon.'

For anyone who knew Anselmo, that other name, formal, legal, was a shock, the final confirmation of his death. His photo as a child filled the screen, a stunned chipmunk, the mischievousness already ingrown.

'Who's that?'

'The State Prosecutor. Shh.'

During his interview, the State Prosecutor conceded under pressure that he was seriously considering dropping the charges against the remaining defendants in the Lyons case. 'Recent events, ending with today's tragedy, have shown us beyond a doubt, I would have thought, that despite what some more extreme analysts choose to argue, we are *not* dealing here with a politically conscious band of trained assassins, no hard core of deaf and dumb terrorists. Hardly.' At this point the State Prosecutor's face fell forward and he closed his eyes, then abruptly his head jerked back and both eyes seemed to pop open. 'One bad egg is more like it.'

'Ex-bad egg,' Daniel said.

'Of all the accused, defense lawyers revealed late today,' the newscaster hurried on, 'only Schelling never expressed remorse over the policeman's death. Instead, he insisted that if the circumstances justified it, he would not hesitate to kill again.'

'It's so convenient' – Daniel bristled – 'it stinks.'

'The question is, sir,' – the interviewer was in the office of the director of the State Penitentiary system – 'how can something like this happen *in prison?*'

'Took the words right out of my mouth.'

'Oh Daniel, now we missed it.' Carole was biting her nails. 'What'd he say?'

'He's ordering an investigation, or couldn't you guess.'

'Daniel, what are you drinking? I thought you were supposed to be in training.'

'It's only a sip for Chrissake.' Daniel held his glass up so the light from the television shone through it.

'Jasper, did you give him that?'

Daniel tilted his head back and drank off the rest of his brandy in a single swallow. Helen, Jasper felt, was about to snap. She had the Kenya photos on her lap. When the late news came on, she and Carole had been sorting through them, choosing the best for a vacation scrapbook. Jasper reached out for her hand, and pushed his leg against hers.

How was Rhoda? Who was with her? Was he being honest with himself when he said he wanted to comfort her for the loss of Anselmo? Or did he want to think he could comfort her? 'I cease to matter, to exist,' – Rhoda had once explained to him why she gave herself, so completely, to the disabled – 'and as such I escape from longings. The indefensible ones, the undefinable ones. If people bring me to life, who am I to worry why?'

'Schelling's death,' the newscaster continued, 'is merely the latest in a chain of increasingly disturbing events in the Boston area.'

Images, many familiar, passed in review. First there were scenes from the mammoth Common rally. Alex Thane – 'whose whereabouts are still unknown' – hands reaching out in a gesture of benediction, spoke into a microphone. 'Hate may be a very human emotion, but it can also be a very wasteful one.'

Then there was Anselmo discarding his cape, lifting his baton, back twitching in manic contortions, conductor of the deaf and dumb orchestra.

'Remember, Fa.'

Lyons' public funeral followed. Hundreds of police in uniform, four abreast, following the coffin. Widow in a veil and dazed children walking in front.

'Isn't that Madge?' Carole pointed at the screen just as the picture changed.

Beggars about town came next, rapid cuts. Their hands out, eyes mocking. A spree of crippled women in the lingerie department of Bonwits downtown, raking through plastic trays of lace-trimmed nightgowns, cavorting in the changing rooms until store detectives intervened.

'The Marx Sisters,' Daniel said.

Jasper's eyes clung to the screen. Would they show the dog attack on Ricardo in front of the Ritz Carlton? No, that incident, it seemed, had never been linked to the others. Was it the only one?

'Sloan,' Jasper said. 'See, Helen, that's what he looked like.' Brief footage of Sloan Glintz sunning on the Common in leopard skin briefs. An attractive girl in a bikini was bending over him, rubbing sun cream into his body. 'She's a nurse,' Jasper said. 'I know her.'

Flurries of violence during Sloan's funeral vigil ended the special report.

'Scary,' Carole said, 'when you put it all together like that.'

'Fast work,' was Daniel's comment.

'I think' – Helen seemed more collected now – 'what we all need is a little time to let our imaginations cool down.'

'Panic, Mom,' Daniel turned off the television, 'that's what it's called.'

'What if I send these three? That one's really quite good of you, don't you think?' The rolls of film Helen took at the hospital near Mumias had come out sharp. There was one shot of Jasper with the cerebral malaria patient. He hadn't even known Helen had been there.

'I'll get it.' When the telephone rang Carole came flying down the stairs. 'For you, Fa.'

On Jasper's end the conversation, which lasted some minutes, consisted mainly of 'so' and 'I see' until finally he said, 'Yes, certainly. Yes, thank you. I do. I will.'

By the time he hung up, he was surrounded by his family.

'The Governor's forming a blue ribbon panel' – he walked into the living room and they followed – 'to protect – no, let me get it right, to promote *and* protect the rights of handicapped citizens. My name's on the list.'

What he didn't add was, 'So is Alex's.'

12

The morning's rehearsal of *Love Comes to Its Senses* went from bad to worse. Some of the cast weren't trying. Others were trying too hard. The production had quickly reached a stage where the performers had exhausted their generosity toward each other.

That Rhoda was looking worn the others attributed to how fully she gave herself to them and her work. They were accustomed to a degree of emotional eclipse in her behavior; it seemed to allow her to penetrate all the more accurately to essentials. No one in the cast knew of the loss she had suffered. She didn't want or expect them to. Rhoda had loved Anselmo with the passion of a teacher for the rare pupil who responds. The one who is compensation for all the rest. She found exonerating herself for her failure to save him, whatever rational arguments she could bring to bear against her guilt, next to impossible. Gone was gone.

'There's a chair there, Gino. All right then, is that everybody? Claire, sit, please.' Before the afternoon rehearsal, Rhoda called everyone out front. 'You know something, if all of you have mothers and fathers, we may fill this place yet.' Rhoda sat up on the bar. She stuck her tongue in her cheek and raised an eyebrow, then, with a downbeat of her head, she began to speak. 'While there's still time, there's one little question I thought I'd better ask you all. What I want to know is quite simple really. What do you think you're doing? What is this opera all about?'

Rhoda carried right on. 'First of all, it is *playful*. Comic. And we're losing sight of that. Oh, yes, we are. Maybe that's natural, working against the clock and with so much that is anything but playful going on *out there*.' Rhoda gestured as if she were referring to some lost galaxy light years away. 'If the world should happen to blow up tomorrow, that would be a great pity, I grant you, but *Love Comes to Its Senses* would still be funny.

'This afternoon, while we work, listen to the music, if that isn't asking too much of you. It's a spoof. You know what a spoof is? Of course, of course, like any comedy worth its salt, there are moments of painful honesty. After all, there's no law that says comedy can't have a point to make. But, look, we're not caught in some siege down here. Relax, smile.'

Matasapi applauded, alone, flat palms detonating in the silence. Rhoda was making her speech because she worried that too much was being made of the opera as occasion. Under the weight of political expectations the whole production would be bound to buckle and collapse.

'Synopsis: a deaf princess and a blind prince fall in love in the bowels of a forest cave. A few hundred years ago people apparently felt free to enjoy such nonsense. Half the audience probably couldn't see all that well, the other half could hardly hear, but at least they could afford a good laugh at themselves. And as for the sealed instructions, come now – it was part of their lives, like the CIA is part of ours.' Rhoda's listeners caught each other's eyes uneasily. 'A royal house without a pedigree of murder wasn't for real. Listen, guys, we have a nice clean funny show on our hands. None of your nineteenth-century muck – consumption, burial alive, poison, firing squads. No, what we have is a set of theatrical conventions stood on their head until they stick out their tongue at the audience.'

Luigi laughed, pushed his chair back so the legs stuttered against the floor.

'Of course we want to drive our point home – but the best way to do it, the only way, is with a lively production. If the people out there don't think, don't *feel* how much we're enjoying ourselves, then we might as well forget it.'

Here Rhoda wrestled off her sweater over her head, practically falling off the bar.

'We don't need to feel pity for the prince and princess, no. You've grasped that much, most of you have, I think. But we don't have to build them into heroes, either. Most important, however,' – Rhoda mastered the trick of looking everybody in the eye at once – 'we shouldn't try to build ourselves into heroes.'

Rehearsal was in full swing when Jasper stopped off at the Fallout Shelter. He came as often as he could. He didn't try to speak to Rhoda, but somehow watching her at work helped him.

The cast, it seemed, was always running through the same few scenes whenever Jasper was there. However amusical Jasper was, even he by now could hum 'Love Will Find a Way', the glad aria in which the two couples, tutor and nurse, prince and princess, decide to thwart the prideful king-fathers and run off to start a new life. Today, in the shadows of the club, Jasper learned more. He saw the kings' armed soldiers emerge from behind rocks and trees in the storm-scoured forest to seize and bind the rejoicing couples. Harsh, mocking military cadences dispelled visions of any idyll to come.

A quintet of soldiers sang about obedience, the guiding principle of the cosmos. They harmonized about their orders to put prince and princess to death. And since tutor and nurse had faltered in fulfillment of their royal trust, their old lives were to be forfeit as well. The soil would run with blood. Music simulated the sharpening of swords against stone.

'Good, kids. Good.' At this point Rhoda called a break. Instantly she was swallowed up by singers and musicians who had questions or needed attention. Carole let her head sink onto her arms on top of the harpsichord.

'Coffee, doctor?' Madge asked. She and Murray made themselves useful in half a hundred ways every day.

'Like to, but I have to go.'

'She told them off, pity you missed it.' Madge lowered her voice. 'Told them not to think they were such heroes.'

'Who? Rhoda?'

'She knows what she's doing.'

Jasper ducked his head to pass through the entrance tunnel, mounted the stairs quickly. At the head of the alley, in front of the Boston Five Cent Savings Bank, vigilante guards in wheelchairs saluted Jasper. He smiled back, more cheerfully than he felt. They struck him as absurd. Some, Carole had told him, were armed.

Emerging from the Fallout Shelter, a person would have to be without senses altogether not to be stunned by the hazy afternoon light, soft and radiant. What Jasper had just seen and heard underground, the twist of the opera plot, depressed him. But then why had he always assumed *Love Comes To Its Senses* would have a happy ending?

There were, why not admit it, too many pieces to life, a jumble. Maybe all of them didn't belong to the same puzzle! He at least couldn't sort them out. It wasn't his fingers, his talented hands, but his mind and heart that were clumsy. Forcing joins that didn't fit, rushing towards a complete picture that even under pressure wouldn't lay flat. As kids Daniel and Carole had always started their puzzle-solving with patches of sky. It didn't matter how often Helen patiently explained to them that they were only making things difficult for themselves that way, they always went first for blue.

The walk to Pinckney Street took a good twenty minutes. The gold dome of the State House shimmered. Sun worked on Jasper's face like an anesthetic. He seemed to lose weight as he went along. Why spend so much time shut up inside rooms? He would revolutionize surgery, hold operations out of doors, chase germs with sunbeams. In the operating theater he was alone, isolated in a circle of light, the kind of defined zone cast by special suspension lamps behind laminated glass. A performer, he was surrounded by darkness, an inhabited darkness where when he stepped back to catch his breath, to let his assistant wipe his face dry, he heard soft breathing and indistinct whispers.

13

Jasper Whiting arrived at Alex Thane's room in E Wing to find it unoccupied. His heart was still crashing against his ribs when Alex strolled in. He was wearing robe, slippers and sunglasses. Rhoda was on his arm.

'We stepped out,' Alex said, 'to watch the babies wriggle. I hope you haven't been waiting long. We were predicting their future, a fascinating business.' Alex's scare in the lobby hadn't put an end to risk-taking. Anything but.

'Better?' Alex pulled up the blinds. 'The way they move, the babies in those white cribs, its like something, or someone, was chewing them.' Rhoda was sullen, uncommunicative. Oh, she smiled, but from a distance. Alex was expansive, theatrical, taking up her slack. It was the first time Jasper had ever seen them together. How they belonged to one another, the perfect couple!

Jasper looked for a place to sit. There were newspapers everywhere. 'I see,' he said, 'that they're dropping the charges against the rest.'

Rhoda snorted, ran a hand through her hair. 'That remains to be seen.'

'The prosecutor. . . .'

'. . . has a little surprise in store for him. Now Angel and some of the others, Carla, Mickey, want to change their plea.'

'To what?'

'To guilty. They want to say they're proud of what they did.'

'But that's crazy,' Jasper protested.

'They feel they owe it to Anselmo.'

'They'll listen to you, won't they?' he asked Rhoda. She turned to Alex.

'They would listen to Alex. They would do anything *he* tells them.' Alex was looking down at a newspaper, smiling. He didn't seem to be listening to them.

'Hold still,' Rhoda said to Jasper. She came to him and lifted her hand to his nose. He felt a slight pain and took an instinctive half-step backwards. 'There,' Rhoda said. She held up a thin strip of skin between thumb and forefinger. 'You were peeling.'

She put on a hat, and dark glasses. And without a further word to Alex, or to Jasper, she left.

'You said' – Alex was fretful – 'you'd be in first thing this morning.'

'I said probably.'

'The whole morning I expected you.'

'You do realize' – Jasper tried not to sound testy – 'I have other things to do as well.'

A notepad lay open on the night table, charred bits of paper and ash, fragrant still, were in the ashtray.

'My world has shrunk, doctor, forgive me.' Alex paused to search his reflection. After a moment he closed his eyes and turned away. 'It has become *very* small. About the size of this bed, in fact.'

'It must be difficult for you, being here, I can see that.'

Alex laughed. 'Good for Daniel!'

'What are you talking about?'

'What?' The fruit and flowers in Alex's room were wilting. 'You care deeply about people, doctor, that's what. That is your son's conviction. Me he dismisses rather as someone who cares instead for an idea, and as such he has not hesitated to let me know that he considers me incomplete, and dangerous.'

'Daniel said that?'

'Primarily dangerous to myself, true, but not only myself.' Alex collected the newspapers and tossed them into the armchair. '*Rabid*, that was the word he actually used. That's the way he describes how people act who, by dedicating themselves blindly to one cause or another, try to fill the personal vacuum of their lives. *Dry fucking* – his words, too.'

'And those who care deeply about people?'

'Dan's better on the bad guys, but then who isn't?'

'You've heard about the Governor's panel?' Jasper asked.

'What Rhoda calls the Quibble Commission – yes.'

'And that you're being asked to sit on it?'

'Oh yes. This room' – Alex stood – 'needs airing, doesn't it?'

'You see of course how this changes everything?'

'How?'

'To serve on the panel you're going to have to hang onto your old face, for at least a little while yet. It is after all the one other people identify you with.'

Alex opened one window wider, shrugging it up inch by inch. 'Doctor, there is simply no way' – Alex turned to Jasper – 'that will ever happen.'

'Your orders. . . .'

'. . . are explicit on that point.'

What visitors had Alex received? Jasper was tempted to check downstairs, or to ask the floor nurses if they'd seen anyone going in or out of the heart patient's room. Was a record kept of telephone calls? He had forgotten entirely that ten minutes ago Rhoda had been standing in the room.

'What the Governor has done, doctor, is toss us a bone. Fair enough, we'll gnaw at it and make the appropriate noises. But once the surviving defendants in the Lyons case *are* released, beggars will be back on the streets – more of them, I can assure you, than ever before. And my empty place at the peace table will help people remember, will keep them inquisitive until enough pressure builds up again for us to push through something real.'

'I've accepted.'

'You will, no doubt, be a credit to the commission.' Alex sounded sincere. 'You did notice, however, that there isn't even a token cripple on the panel? An oversight, I'm sure.' Alex shook his head. 'Not one. What's wrong, doctor? You look like something's preying on your mind.'

'I don't want you to have any disillusions about what I'm prepared to do for you, that's all.'

'Illusions, I believe, is what you mean.' Alex fell silent, and pulled thoughtfully at the flesh of his neck, the neck of an old man. Facing the mirror above the dresser next to the window, Alex parted twin brushes and stroked his hair back from both temples. Then he began making faces at himself, distortions of his appearance, minor ones at first, but little by little more and more grotesque. Jasper, who couldn't bear to watch, looked out the window where sunlight shattered into a thousand points on the windshields and hood ornaments of cars in the parking lot below. Even so he couldn't block out the steady rhythm with which Alex plied his brushes.

'There is one torture,' Alex said, 'the mere thought of which has always alarmed me more than I can tell you. And it's very simple really. All you do is take a man and hold him so he is forced to look at his face in a mirror. After only five minutes, the effects of this sadistic enterprise have been known to be quite horrific. Irreparably so.' Alex fitted the bristles of his brushes together and put them down. He waited for Jasper to turn towards him before he spoke again.

'I have seen quite enough of my face, this face, doctor. It isn't me. If that sounds strange to you, unbalanced even, I can't help that. Of course – of course my personal feelings are here, once again, of little account. We have, I take it, agreed to disagree about the fact that I have chosen to accept the consequences of my politics by renouncing freedom of choice, *all* – but I can't help thinking that it might help you to know how I feel. It might make *your* task easier.' Alex stood close to Jasper. 'Believe me when I say I doubt there is anyone who could possibly appreciate what it is we are asking of you, more than I do. That is the very reason why I have the fullest confidence you will, in the end, give us no reason to be disappointed.'

While Alex was speaking to him, Jasper had to fight off highly plastic fears about what in fact might happen with Alex unconscious on the operating table in front of him. These fears began in his fingers, his hands, then shot up through his arms into his brain and lodged there, shrill and insistent. What had Rhoda asked him oh so long ago? Was there never a time he had looked down at a patient and felt the uncontrollable urge to smash the face that lay there beyond recognition?

'Would it surprise you to learn, doctor, that the thing most people ask me, I'm talking about the handicapped now, the thing they want to know most is whether or not I believe in miracles?'

'And?'

'I do. Miracles as the work of the devil. And when they start to make faces – like you're doing now – then I preach the gospel the way I imagine it. God with his harelip, his club foot, his spasms, the gabble of his speech, his fears of sexual inadequacy, his moles, his beauty marks, his imperfect sense of balance.

'You see, doctor, contrary to your son's opinion, I am perfectly willing to do some serious thinking – on certain subjects.'

'God just doesn't happen to be one of them?'

Tossing God back and forth, afraid to be caught holding the beanbag when the music stopped. Matching wits, interrupting each other like schoolchildren. Would it be any easier now to inflict deformity on this man?

'Night, doctor,' volunteers called to Jasper from the admissions desk as he passed through the lobby. 'How's Mrs Whiting?'

'Fine, thank you.' He was feeling much better after his visit with Alex. 'See you tomorrow.' He felt so good he was on the verge of giggling. Except for the nagging question: why?

Jasper tracked the Mazda down where he'd left it beyond Charlesbank Playground. Next door construction was under way for an annex to the hospital. At intervals along the protective palisade of two-by-fours there were viewing slits. Mammoth jackhammers were excavating a deep cellar, the din of their metal teeth forcing workmen in bright helmets to communicate with sweeping gestures of their arms. A massive iron ball at the end of a braided cable swung through the air in a graceful arc and smashed into a low brick wall far below street level, the remains of some ancient foundation. There was a thud, and an explosion of dust. High above, in the cabin of a crane, the driver pulled back on a lever and the iron ball was hauled aloft, jiggling now as if groggy. Jasper, playing sidewalk superintendant, took it all in.

'People always say that wanting to learn, motivation, makes it so much easier. Bullshit,' Rhoda had told him. 'I should know. After all, I'm a teacher. Those kids, they're dying to learn. All that desire just gets in their way. How can you learn anything with your teeth clenched the whole time? Like you, Jasper.'

This time when the iron ball struck, a shout went up from the men. The squat brick wall shivered, a few bricks were dislodged, others shifted, turned in place. The moment of demolition would not be long now. Jasper turned away and climbed into the Mazda. He had to work hard to ease it out of its spot.

What people didn't realize – Jasper decided to cross the river and follow Memorial Drive home – was that changing a nose was a tricky, tricky business. Even the slightest variation in slope, flare, thickness, length, the merest dislocation of symmetry or minuscule variation in curvature of tip or bridge would be sufficient to mean that the person who went with this nose would end up wearing a different-style wristwatch, would run with longer strides, eat more, laugh a different laugh. At heart the idea of detail was false. Change one thing, the whole changes: ecology of physiology.

And at the sound of the last trumpet – Jasper honked at the

van that cut suddenly in front of him – Jasper was convinced that the noses of his patients would be restored and finally, together with moles, coughs, genitals too short or too long, with bleeding gums, knock-knees, sixth fingers even or toes, with eyes blue longing a lifetime for black, breasts despised through the years as too pointed, too heavy, or flat to a fault – all would be disclosed as perfect and inevitable, just as single sperm and egg, accidental in conjunction, produced an absolute, intransigent fruit.

'Odd, isn't it,' – Alex had been back at the mirror again, brushes in hand – 'ever since the dawn of time, A will love B who loves C who loves A. Where the heart's involved, no one expects a happy ending. But the same is true for people who love the world, isn't it, or ideas? They suffer for it too, doctor, unrequited.'

Jasper Whiting gave people new noses but through the years he had come to suspect that any change in their lives was superficial, brief, deceptive. What was Alex's technique then? Did he go deeper? It was as if back there in the hospital room today Alex had stroked Jasper's heart, slowly at first and then with increasing speed until, choosing his moment, he had snapped his fingers.

'It's no shame, doctor, if you can't believe in a cause, to adopt it because someone in whom you do believe, deeply, does.'

Parallel to Jasper, on the gleaming surface of the river, sculls glided by. Tree trunks broke his view into segments like the frames of a film. The blades of the crew's oars swept back, dipping, rising again in unison. A soloist, Jasper had a weakness for teamwork. Rhoda, how she had worked magic with the children in Spinedale Pool, her eyes brighter than the light that veined the water. Jasper shifted uneasily in his seat as he grew hard with desire.

'They can hear in their dreams, deaf children – there are some, I swear,' – Rhoda's excitement was catching – 'when they wake up, they're so alert at first, straining every muscle to listen, only slowly that look of disappointment comes over them.'

By Fresh Pond, in front of the International House of Pancakes, Jasper got caught at the light. Eyes rolled up to catch when it would turn green, high above Jasper saw a white fluffy curve, some half-executed letter afloat in the sky. The beginning of skywriting. Since taking leave of Alex in the hospital – the sunken wall would be lying in smithereens by now – Jasper's sense of well-being had ebbed steadily. The more he thought, the harder he tried, the more inert he felt, the less capable of coping. Yet now, at the sight of a single lazy loop of white exhaust, attenuated, feathery overhead – what could be more ephemeral? – confidence flowed back through him. He stepped down on the accelerator too hard and nearly stalled.

If only there might be some button for Jasper to push and lo, as easy as changing stations on the car radio, the truth would flash across the sky. He didn't mind so much his not knowing the truth. What he minded was not knowing, in a world of accusation and countercharge, if such an animal actually existed or not. For people to pretend and lie like crazy was one thing, as long as there was a standard against which to measure their deviation. Let the absolute exist, never mind whether he himself ever learned the secret – the reason why Luigi lost his leg, for example, or whether Alex was justified in beating or starving autistic children to make them speak. Like playing a slot machine: Jasper could be a perfectly good loser coin after coin as long as someone guaranteed him that the next player, or the next, would hit the jackpot, that sooner or later the machine would be shaken to its roots and cough up a treasure of coins. But suppose Jasper made the heroic effort to push down the truth button only to see a bright series of question marks, asterisks, exclamation points light up the sky?

'Make me ugly' – the skywriting trailed behind Jasper where he couldn't see it – 'only you can.'

Years ago fundamentalists stamped and screamed that plastic surgery was tampering with God's will. Since the emergence of genetic engineering, however, these critics had redirected their attack. The workaday plastic surgeon was off the ethical hook. After all, by comparison to those who dabbled in the unravelling and reknitting of chromosomes, he was a plumber. A harmless door-to-door salesman of cheap cosmetics.

'Why make so much out of so little then,' Jasper fumed at himself. 'Do it, and get it over with.'

'You're looking pleased with yourself,' Carole said as Jasper let the front door slam behind him. 'Glad someone around here is. Poor Rhoda, that rehearsal was godawful. You've got to hand it to her, though. She doesn't give up.'

Jasper shut himself in his study. On his desk Daniel's history text lay open. The beginning of his essay curled up out of the typewriter. 'Those who make war are beautiful, those who restore peace grotesque. This is not a moral statement, anything but. It is an empirical observation. Can we conclude that beauty is aggressive – requiring, as it were, expanding markets?' Here the essay broke off. Daniel had skipped several spaces and typed underneath: 'Marx? – ask Alex.' A half-eaten candy bar lay next to the typewriter. Jasper finished it. In all his years as a surgeon, he had never spoken as personally with any of his patients as with Alex. He hadn't taken the trouble to know any of them.

'Stop thinking,' Jasper scolded himself. 'If you never operate again, so what?'

Face after face followed each other across the pages of Jasper's sketch pad. A parade of alternative Alexes. At some of them, maliciously feminine, Jasper smiled. At others he quailed. With a few strokes of his pencil he recreated the faces of the killers he would soon be rehabilitating. It was the Spitz Experiment, the wrong way around. Jasper jabbed his pencil against the pad to break its point. It was no good. There was Alex's voice, a man with a history – no other face would fit.

What would Alex and Rhoda's children have looked like? And the boy, the one with cerebral malaria whose life Jasper had saved in Kenya – was he crouching somewhere in the dust, now, slavering? Did people kick at him, spit at him? With both hands Jasper pulled Daniel's essay out of the typewriter and crumpled it into a ball. Then with both hands, slowly, he smoothed back his hair, holding it tight against his skull so it couldn't rise up again.

Sweet heavens, hadn't Alex and Rhoda already performed an operation on him? One of far more consequence than any mere rearrangement of flesh and bone.

14

'Sorry.'

The full dress of *Love Comes to Its Senses* was supposed to run without interruption, no matter what. Yet so much went haywire already in the first few minutes that Rhoda broke in.

'Wake up' – she had stamped – '*we* are not the sleepwalkers.'

It was as if they had all slid down a chute into the same open wound. Flail about for all they were worth, they only sank in deeper.

In the kitchen Murray had been waiting the whole morning for Madge to let him out of her sight. About one she left the Fallout Shelter to pick up pizzas for the orchestra. Even as he watched her back disappear, Murray edged into the club and along the bar. He held a hammer and chisel low in his hands. Not that anyone would think anything was strange about his carrying tools. A few steps took him to the door of Matasapi's private office. Matasapi was off near the coatroom, shrieking at actors to hold still while he made last-minute adjustments on their costumes.

The door wasn't locked and Murray slipped in. The silence closed around him. Elegant lamps shed soft, rich light. Yet the disorder of the last minute had even reached Matasapi's sanctum. Designs were scattered everywhere, bolts and scraps of material, too. Spools of ribbon and lace. An old black iron Singer sewing machine stood on the round white table like some new sign in the zodiac. Under the needle, a length of shiny blue cloth shimmered.

Any moment someone could come bursting in. Murray stepped forward. He wouldn't need much time. The pressure had been building intolerably, day by day, until now it had reached a point where he was no longer acting by choice. He crossed to Matasapi's desk, nearly toppling an ironing board with one hip. Of course he was ashamed, but it hardly seemed to matter.

When Murray sat heavily in Matasapi's desk chair, it swiveled and almost threw him. He licked his moustache, laid his tools on the desktop and set to work. One by one he tugged the desk drawers open and rifled them. When he didn't find what he was looking for, he moved on without troubling to tidy up. The bottom righthand drawer was locked. Murray made no effort to work silently with his hammer and chisel. For one thing the office was soundproof. Besides, there was still a storm of hammering backstage.

The splintering of the fine wood cost Murray some qualms, but he kept at it – tap, tap, twist – until the lock was sprung and he could slide the deep drawer towards his knees. He dropped the tools in his lap and dragged the desk lamp closer so he could see better into the drawer.

Inside the first thing to catch his eye was the petty cash box, open. He lifted it out and put it on the floor. Then he picked up a cloth sack with a drawstring. It turned out to be filled with a jumble of make-up and medicines, pots and tubes and vials. Murray tossed the sack across the room. Fear of failure made him start to tremble. Two small cameras Murray merely tumbled to one side. Then near the back of the drawer he came to a cache of small plastic envelopes containing white powder.

He used both broad hands to scoop the envelopes out of the drawer and onto the desk top. They made a slippery pile. Thick fingers at one corner, Murray held an envelope up to the desk light and shook it. How the crystals dazzled.

When the door opened, Murray was off guard. Matasapi entered. Hips churning, he was half-way across the room before he realized he wasn't alone. In one hand he held a pair of pinking shears that he kept clicking open and shut. And he was talking to himself.

'Oh my God!'

Instinctively Murray had stood and raised the hammer over his head.

'No,' Matasapi said, recoiling, 'no violence.'

Murray smiled a bit distractedly.

'Oh, it's you.' Matasapi cocked his head to one side. 'Look,' Matasapi's colorless eyes flashed at the sight of the pyramid of dope stacked on his desk. 'What is this? Another quaint family custom? If so, couldn't it wait?'

Without thinking, Murray brought his arm down so the hammer pounded against the desk. The blow sounded like a gunshot. Arms crossed over his chest, Matasapi backed behind the sewing machine. Murray went on with his search of the desk. He reached into the bottom drawer and drew out a stack of papers and documents. He riffed through them, let them fall. He was crying.

'Murray,' Matasapi said softly, drawing near, 'Murray, what is it?'

'I must have one. Please.'

All concentration now, Matasapi could still not solve the puzzle. 'One what?'

'A photograph.'

'Oh,' Matasapi gasped. 'Look, right there in front of you.'

On the desk, in a silver frame, oval, was Sloan Glintz. Sloan on the edge of a chair, thin arms crossed over his naked thighs, chin tilted up, eyes laughing, his lips pulled back in just the suggestion of a seductive smile.

Murray reached out and seized the frame. 'I couldn't remember,' he told Matasapi. 'I. . . . ' He touched his head.

'You take it.' Matasapi fell back on the couch, placed the cold tip of the pinking shears in his mouth. 'It's yours.'

'You know,' – Murray never removed his eyes from Sloan's face – 'I can't see' – he curled the fingers of one powerful hand and laid them against his chest – 'with my heart.'

'No, no, the frame, everything, it's yours, keep it.' There were more photos, Matasapi was thinking, at home. Many.

'Thank you.'

'My pleasure.'

'Thank you.'

'But now if you'll excuse me, I have to find the prince's other glove – or else we'll have to cut his hand off.' At the door Matasapi looked back. Murray had lowered the photograph, flat, under the desk lamp. What, Matasapi thought, what would have happened to his face, what hideous, unspeakable things, what leprosy, if he had refused Murray the gift he asked for?

15

As arranged, Jasper found his assistant surgeon and anesthetist waiting in the operating theater. Women, both of them. They wore green gauze masks and caps. He was favorably impressed by their eyes. The instrument table was in place. Everything gleamed. The knives sang as usual. Routine protected him from any late trill of nerves.

When Alex was brought in, the wheels of the bed caught at the threshold. 'Glad I'm not a superstitious man,' Alex said.

The assistant and anesthetist laughed. Then Jasper realized Alex had been joking and laughed, too. Alex was making obvious efforts at self-control. He was more addled than Jasper had anticipated. While the anesthetist prepared a needle to slip into Alex's arm, Alex winced.

'What? No rubber mask with big, happy lips? I don't go under slowly counting to ten? Not fair, I practiced that.' Alex overdid the light humor. The quick stretch of his lips told less than the condensed, throbbing fear in his eyes. Jasper approved of that fear. It was healthy. 'I trust you'll do your worst, doctor.' Alex's last words came out more of a plea than a joke: 'Stop,' he said, winking at Jasper, 'stop, or I'll shoot.'

Until tests confirmed he might get to work, Jasper had a few uneasy moments waiting. To quiet himself he pressed close to his patient's profile. Beneath the diffuse glare of the suspension lamp, Alex's face seemed to fall apart, the several features isolated, discrete, mere terrain, landmarks. The doctor flexed his fingers and gradually a look of pain possessed his own face, and a look of absolute absorption. This was the instant that cost Jasper Whiting the most misgivings. No matter how often he had stood here before, each time it felt new. Jasper Whiting, the Nose King.

He crouched over the unconscious, helpless man and began to stroke his nose gently with three fingers. From the bridge down to the tip, feathering slightly, then back through the air again, touching down lightly and launching on another stroke. Just as he had done with so many patients on their last visit to his office. They had been able to giggle, to turn away for an instant. He had talked to them, teased, offered comfort.

'Go,' the anesthetist whispered at last.

Jasper felt the cartilage under the skin shift. His fingertips had the sensitivity of a safe-cracker's. He stroked and stroked, each time exerting slightly more pressure, stroking with ever so slightly more speed. And suddenly, with a snap of the fingers really, he broke what God had given whole. *Gnnak*. The sound was audible only because of the silence. And with that *gnnak* the mystery was over. The work began.

With the exception of essential commands – pack, bind, pump, cut – the operation proceeded without sound. Jasper found himself fascinated by the action of his hands. His fingers, deeply sure and convinced of their own generosity, were totally independent of the fears of his conscience. On the operating table, slack, bathed in cold light, Alex seemed to have shrunk. Sometimes, like today, there was more blood than usual. It didn't flow so much as bubble up. Jasper took it for a sign of luck, a blessing. The going became slippery. Not tiresome though. The ease with which Alex's nose broke, his jaw as well, on one side high, the other low, the speed of the hooked needle dragging silk thread through layers of tissue and skin, was reassuring because familiar. Saw and chisel did service. How carefully Alex had brushed the hair back from both temples.

Part of Jasper's mind as he bent to work was, it is true, rigid. He indulged in none of his usual speculation about how the patient on recovering consciousness would respond to his new identity. In point of fact Jasper had not yet acknowledged his taking a decision at the deepest layer of his being never to lay eyes on Alex Thane again. With surgery he would acquit himself of every last shred of obligation. How the face might heal, the final visage did not concern him. Alex could better safeguard his desired anonymity if Jasper remained ignorant of his appearance, couldn't he?

'Doctor?'

'Oh, yes, thank you. That's fine.'

As a rule during an operation Jasper perspired profusely. He had to keep stopping for his assistant to mop his eyes. On the present occasion he failed to notice until at last he tasted salt. So much worry over what? The deed was an anticlimax. The whole thing seemed to be over almost before it began. Perhaps they would meet again some day. Life was long, after all. It would be up to Alex then to recognize him, or to walk past without a sign. And in his new life, Alex would have to keep away from Rhoda.

It was only once Jasper was washing up, gloves peeled and discarded, that his hands began to shake. This had never happened before. He stared down at them in disbelief. They felt like wet stacks of stones, very cold. He leaned for support against the sink where water at high force plashed merrily, masking his sobs. Alex's people had slipped out, and he was alone. Was it regret he felt? Not entirely: Jasper overheard himself praying in his heart for Alex's safe future.

Daniel was waiting in the lobby, face drawn, eyes feverish with excitement.

'Everything okay, Fa?'

'Sure.'

Outside the wind had hardly abated since morning. Gusts bent the tops of trees, filled the air with pods and seeds. The Charles River was choppy.

'You just made history, Fa.'

'So.'

'But God, you took your time about it.'

'Not really.'

The worst, Jasper sighed, was over. His hands tingled. They walked together to the car, stepping over stray bits of paper that came scudding along the ground. Daniel's hair had been cut short since Jasper last noticed. Jasper was stunned by the smoothness of his son's face, the harmony of its animation.

'And how'd this morning go?'

They climbed into the car.

'What?' Jasper asked.

'The Panel Show?'

'Not bad.'

'The *Globe*'s making you guys sound like shoe-ins for the Nobel Prize.'

Jasper had attended the opening session of the Massachussetts State Panel for the Advancement of the Rights of Disabled Citizens in the conference room on the top floor of Boston's prize-winning City Hall. Somehow the morning meeting had already shrunk in Jasper's mind. Round and around the table they'd gone, declaring their good intentions, confessing grave feelings of inadequacy to discharge the heavy responsibility with which they'd been entrusted. At Jasper's turn to speak he led off by commending their mutual commitment to an uphill task. But what about Alex Thane? Had he been heard from? Did anyone perhaps know?

Leaning forward over the conference table, Jasper had been nearly breathless at his own duplicity. How many in that room knew Alex, had met him personally? How many knew he was little more than shouting distance away, on the other side of the Holiday Inn parking lot? And in a few hours he would be yielding up the face God had given him for another of his own choosing? Who was trying now, like he was, to scrutinize other faces without being caught? Were there many puppets present? Could he himself lift a finger that wasn't knotted to a string?

'Dr Whiting, you were saying?' the chairman urged him to continue.

Regardless of whether one personally admired or despised Alex Thane, Jasper went on to say, the man's participation had to be regarded as of the utmost importance to any likelihood the panel might have of designing measures adequate to defuse the present explosive situation. 'We cannot, of course, conjure him out of thin air. We might, however,' – here Jasper had looked over one shoulder at chairs set against the wall under historic paintings – 'consider some suitable symbolic act.'

Then Jasper rose and brought a chair from the wall and placed it next to his own. Give it a little time – Jasper smiled a bit smugly – and he might develop a taste for this kind of thing.

'Guess what?'

'What?' Jasper started the car.

'Ran my fastest quarter ever today. The coach couldn't believe his watch.' While Jasper adjusted the rearview mirror, Daniel stole a look at his father out of the side of his eyes. 'And the whole time I was thinking of you.'

'Me and the earth on fire. I hope you don't expect me to do this kind of thing every time you have a race to run?'

'You look done in, Fa.'

Jasper closed his eyes. 'It'll hit me later, I suppose.'

'Seat belt, Fa. And I'm afraid we have to hurry. Mom's asked me to pick up some things on the way home.'

'Anyone seen Carole?'

'She's in a state, but she won't take anything for it. She's afraid it would put her to sleep. Is there anyone who can do it if she funks?'

'She'll be fine.' Jasper knocked on the dashboard.

'Any bets?'

Their last errand took them to the dry cleaner's. Daniel came dashing back through traffic with Jasper's tuxedo and one of Helen's best dresses draped in sheer plastic over one arm.

'They were all talking about the opening.'

'But there's been no publicity.'

'Fa, don't tell me you missed all the skywriting?' Jasper craned forward and looked up. There was nothing above now but a few stringy wisps of cloud streaming along at a fast clip. 'It's one of the worst kept secrets of all time.'

'I hope they know what they're doing.'

'Want to know something funny, Fa?' Daniel's voice was suddenly low and urgent. 'I didn't think you would go through with it. Either of you.'

Jasper twisted back and leaned over the seat to straighten the clothes Daniel had tossed haphazardly in back.

'I thought you were just playing chicken.'

'Just goes to show how wrong you can be,' Jasper said, 'doesn't it?'

16

Minutes before *Love Comes to Its Senses* was to start, Rhoda Massler brushed Jasper Whiting's cheek with her fingers. 'Thank you,' she said, 'for all you've done.'

She seemed carefree and happy. Jasper felt self-conscious, his tuxedo reeked so of chemicals.

'Everything ready?' he asked.

'I'm glad I didn't have to pay for a seat.'

The Whitings had places in the third row, toward one side. Half-way down the makeshift center aisle Helen was greeting people she hadn't seen in a long time. It was her first appearance in public since her accident.

'When can I see you?' Jasper asked under his breath, his body pressing Rhoda's lightly but insistently.

'Do me a favor,' Rhoda smiled, pressing back, 'one more of your inimitable favors.' She looked in his eyes briefly. 'Every chance you get, clap like crazy. Who knows, you may just take some of the house with you.'

The small orchestra tuned frantically. Jasper thought Rhoda, in her turtleneck jersey and slacks, unchanged in days, had never looked lovelier. Her hair reached practically to her shoulders again. Only a slight twitch of the cheek near one eye betrayed the pitch of her excitement.

'You know something,' Rhoda said. 'You look cute.'

'Pssst, how does it end?' Jasper asked as Rhoda turned away.

In answer she turned back and kissed him. Her tongue made him dizzy. 'Stick around and find out.'

'Good evening, Dr Whiting' – a woman with a violin squeezed past Jasper. She had one hand wrapped around the instrument's throat. In her other she held a bow which she raised slowly and tapped against the side of her nose. Helen's nose. 'I hope you enjoy the performance.'

'Jasper, honey, just look!' Carole sat at the harpsichord, every inch a picture of self-possession. Resplendent in loose flowing black and gold, for once in her life unruly hair in place. 'I'm jealous,' Helen whispered confessionally, 'oh Jasper, isn't she beautiful.'

'You're beautiful,' Jasper said and meant it.

'Who are you looking for?'

'Luigi.'

'He's with Murray and Madge in the kitchen. He's helping with the props.'

'Luigi?'

Helen giggled. 'Carole said if he sat out front, she couldn't play.'

'So' – Jasper squeezed his wife's hand – 'I wondered why I wasn't invited to miss the opening.'

The Fallout Shelter was packed beyond capacity. People grudged their neighbors every inch of space. Yet, once the overture began, with the dimming of the house lights and the first few bars of music, the congestion dissolved.

Jasper sat through the opening scenes with absent-minded detachment. He played back Alex's operation, every flap and splinter of it. He couldn't help himself. Gradually, however, he was drawn into the action on stage.

Things moved right along. That is not to deny a few rough spots, however. At one point Vera, the princess, slipped and fell, almost bringing down half the pre-storm paper and rag forest with her. Only those with inside knowledge gasped though, for the plot made such a mishap plausible and the singer covered like a pro. When Fidel, distracted and distraught, staggered on stage at the height of the storm, his ornate jacket was on inside-out. What saved Matasapi from instant suicide was how the audience lapped up the *bêtise* as a cunning touch of realism.

From time to time Helen nudged Jasper so he would notice how the elbows of the string players nearly collided. Carole, when not playing herself, kept sticking her tongue out and curling it back to touch the tip of her nose. At times she hummed along with the other instruments, a shade too audibly. A couple of late lighting cues also added to the performers' difficulties, and increased audience sympathy. On the whole, happily, the magic exuded by art produced through teamwork settled over the tense house soothingly like fine stardust.

During the interval the audience superstitiously talked about anything and everything except how they were enjoying the opera. Their avoidance of the subject was a reliable barometer of its gathering power. With drinks in hand, the crowd spilled over into the steep alleyway outside. The wind had fallen at last, the Milky Way was unusually close overhead. Police in unmarked cars had staked out the area. The patrol of disabled was also on duty.

People drifted back to their seats early, not waiting to be called. Helen was one of the last to take her place.

'It's definite,' she whispered to Jasper, 'they'll be free in the morning.'

'Who?'

'The rest of the defendants.'

'So.' Jasper nodded. 'How do you know?'

'People were talking.'

'Rumor.'

'By people' – Helen pointed to a figure seated against a pillar not far behind them – 'I mean the State Prosecutor.'

Jasper felt very much in love with life. He felt safe, righteous, hopeful – as only the survivor of an ordeal can.

'Pity Alex isn't here,' Jasper leaned over to whisper to Daniel.

'No!' Daniel replied, turning his face with a broad grin. 'He *hates* opera!'

'Love Will Find a Way' hardly had ended on its note of giddy affirmation, prince and princess, tutor and nurse beside themselves with happiness, when soldiers with drawn swords sprang out from behind rocks and trees. Soldiers – Jasper flinched – not unlike those who had invaded Alex's school in Beirut, faces panic-stricken and bewildered. In the dark Jasper sought Helen's hand, interlaced his fingers with hers. She dropped her head onto his shoulder.

Tension in the music increased painfully, ambiguity heightened by bold modulations, dynamic excursions from the tonic. The soldiers announced their orders to kill the two pairs of lovers. It seemed to Jasper he had been waiting much of his life to learn what would happen next.

The captain of the guard moved downstage and a theme of exquisite sweetness filled the hall. The captain was short and stout and gruff. He removed his helmet with both hands and set it on a rock. His lower lip looked like he'd been pulling on it since birth. The rest of his face was firm. The man had an easy, self-assured manner of standing, one foot slightly in front of the other, his weight thrown back. Commanding the attention of everyone in the forest, and the audience as well, the captain now held up his hands and removed one spangled Matasapi glove. A gleaming metal hook emerged.

'What soldier can know,' he sang, 'by how much the price of his glory will exceed another's? The journey of life is wonderfully strange, and full of hazard. Brothers, take heart, kneel to these lovers, that they may bless us.' Then the captain sang 'Nobody's Perfect':

Nobody's perfect, Nobody.
The world completes itself
with love.
Come, let us celebrate
our imperfection,
Together, together

The captain sang simply and distinctly. Then Vera and Fidel joined him:

Nobody's perfect, Nobody.
  Now through sweet kissing
  Fulfill what is missing.
The end of desire makes
  lovers entire, expiring
Together, together.

The aria ended before Jasper fathomed he had heard it before. Tonight it sounded so different from Susan's rendition at Sloan Glintz's funeral. Not better, different. Jasper instinctively turned his eyes to the wings, as if he heard Rhoda calling him faintly. There in the kitchen doorway, open on its hinges, half an inch, no more, he saw a pale sliver of Rhoda's face. She was biting a fingernail, her one visible eye gleaming like a dark candle. After the last note, Carole's hands hung over the keyboard. A wave of silence washed over the spectators who didn't struggle but yielded to it gratefully, carried on its crest, safe from the depths.

Execution of the final scene, new to Jasper, was marred by the cast's overexcitement. Yet the achievement of the evening was safe. Delight spread first among the performers and then out over the hooded footlights, like a slow, leaking gas. The action shifted back from the forest to the palace of the prince's father. To all appearances the princess's parents had come for the marriage rites. Their daughter, they related somewhat nervously, was expected presently.

Enter a nearly incoherent messenger with news of double disaster. Prince and princess, both were lost during the storm. When their guardian soldiers found them again, and found their nurse and tutor, death had laid them low, miraculously leaving no mark. The couples were discovered in the mouth of a cave the lining of which shone like pearl in the after-storm light. Even now the soldiers were approaching with their sad burden.

After a few strident notes, a reprise from 'Murder, Murder

Most Dire and Foul', a hollow exchange of condolences between equally culpable royal parents followed.

'Whoever thought our dreams, our hopes and prayers, the effort of so many years, would end like this?'

'Yesterday they were born, mirrors of perfection.'

'God's will be done.'

'It is for us, united in grief, as once we thought to be in joy. . . .'

'. . . to accept, not to question.'

'May they be remembered always, our matchless children. . . .'

'. . . as long as the eyes of lovers shine to see each other, and the ears of lovers ring with mutual praise.'

Harshly, solemnly, the little orchestra signaled the return of the pall bearers. Helen wiped tears away with the back of her free hand. Jasper kissed her hair. Upon command everything in sight was draped in black. Kings, queens, thrones, the very pillars of the court. Majestically, in procession, the soldiers, bare-headed, bowed with modest solemnity, bore two sets of matching coffins onto the stage – crowding it worse than the MTA at rush hour.

In the foreground, while the coffins, garlanded with flowers, white and purple, were propped at a steep angle, royalty bent its knee and mourned, wailing in a quartet of hypocrisy. Their harmonies evoked bitterness in every listener. Yet here the music was subtle indeed with a suggestion of self-incrimination under the surface, a smoldering contrition which, at the first full sight of prince and princess side by side in eternal composure, sublimely inanimate, burst into remorse and a flood of self-pity. (It was Matasapi's moment of triumph. He had worked with feathers and lace, all white, and transformed the young lovers into songbirds whose matchless plumage, snow and silver, deepened the dark night of grief surrounding them.)

The first hint of the opera's final reversal dripped teasingly from Carole's fingers. Chords of 'Nobody's Perfect', distant, fragile, persistent. While the audience drew a collective breath of pleasure, Vera and Fidel rose by slow gradations from the dead, singing, rejoicing. He could see: a happy future. She could hear: the laughter of their children and their children's children.

Both sets of parents collapsed with shock and wonder, relief and fear, staggering in each other's arms, confessing their base unworthiness, announcing a desire to withdraw from the world.

'As long as the eyes of lovers shine to see each other. . . .' sang the blind prince in a burst of tenor glory.

'. . . and the ears of lovers ring with mutual praise,' – the deaf princess took flight in pure soprano pursuit.

'. . . we will be remembered.'

The resurrection of nurse and tutor, accompanied by the theme of their infatuation, was adept buffoonery. For them Matasapi had chosen youthful greens and blues and highlights of gold. The doddering tutor was so overcome by the intensity of his feelings that instead of helping his love out of her coffin, he tried to climb in on top of her.

And, after the finale of reconciliation, forgiveness and renewed plans for celebration, all in rollicking tempo, singers practically lifting the roof, *Love Comes to Its Senses* ended on a quiet note. The two kings at the far sides of the stage sang *a cappella* to their queens. The prince's old father asked his wife, 'Say, what does she look like, that daughter of theirs? My eyes are not what they were.' And the princess's father, tugging at his consort's sleeve, wheedled her, 'Tell me, what nonsense are they talking now, the children? Unfeeling age has stolen my ears.'

17

Pandemonium broke out instantly. Shouts, whistles, applause and stamping. Flowers rained over the footlights. It had been agreed beforehand there would be no curtain calls. Out in the kitchen, the cast hugged and cheered each other as well. Four empty caskets occupied the stage, lined with white satin and draped with yards and yards of black cloth.

Where was Rhoda? Many joined the search for her in vain. Only after most of the audience had filed out – and, empty, the Fallout Shelter looked small again, as if it could never possibly have contained so many people – did Rhoda finally come creeping out of the utility closet behind the bar.

'Rhoda.' Carole rushed to kiss her.

'I made a point of checking the emergency exits,' Rhoda laughed, picking mop lint from her trousers, 'but *you*,' – she pointed accusingly at Matasapi – 'had to park your fat ass right in my way. Hey guys, what do you know, it's over and we're still alive.'

A large part of the audience, ranks fattened by well-wishers, would meet soon again at the Ritz Carlton whose management (cerebral palsy in the family) had agreed to donate the use of the downstairs ballroom, the one with the three-ton chandelier, for a cast party. Jasper was dead on his feet. He'd had his happy ending though, that was something.

Madge started arranging carloads to transfer guests to the hotel. No one knew where Daniel was.

'Your boy? He left as soon as it was over,' Matasapi said. The man sparkled with elation. 'Not to worry. He knows about the party, doesn't he?' Then he lowered his voice and moved closer to Jasper. 'If it would make you feel any better, I could check the closets.'

'Honest to God, I could fly!'

'Driving will do, dear,' Helen teased Carole.

Rhoda was lavish with praise for Carole's performance. By rights Jasper, too, should feel high. He didn't. He, they all, actually, had been living and working towards the events of this day. Well, the day was over.

By the time the Whitings minus Daniel entered the ballroom a fair-sized crowd, one that was growing rapidly, had convened at the Ritz Carlton. Luigi, dazzling in a version of the operatic prince's all-white finery, came to welcome them. He was wearing his artificial leg.

'Luigi has a little lamb,' he said and introduced them to a man mountain who followed him everywhere. 'My producer made me an offer I couldn't refuse. Carole likes him. She's the one who's christened him Lambie. I dunno, maybe it was his curls' – the man blushed. 'We still have to work out a satisfactory sleeping arrangement, don't we, Lambie? So, how'd you folks like the show?'

Drink in hand, revived by Luigi's contagious elation, Jasper began to enjoy himself. The cast, in twos and threes, were rehashing a thousand and one torments from the production. It was, Jasper smiled to himself, an integrated crowd. There were cripples mingling, a man with a growth on his skull, a dwarf with a beard, patrons of the Fallout Shelter who'd donated their time, who had become drinking companions of members of the cast. A blind man was telling the group that had gathered around him how he imagined various scenes of the opera, from storm to resurrection. Matasapi was listening, eyes straining in their sockets, nodding eagerly. The man's fantasy shamed even his wildest conceits.

'If I ever have the money' – Matasapi wrung his hands – 'that's the way it should be done!'

Jasper spotted Rhoda near the punch bowl, trapped, it seemed, by Mrs Benedict-Vincent. He headed towards them, trying not to make his intention too obvious. He drew up at their elbow just as Mrs Benedict-Vincent was explaining that 'Susan's book', *Nobody's Perfect*, had been selected as a Book-of-the-Month Club alternate.

'Pity my membership is up,' Rhoda said.

'And it's dedicated to Marcus Featherstone – that's what Susan wanted.' Here Mrs Benedict-Vincent took a sip of punch. 'I'm sorry about the school.'

'You're sorry about the school what?'

'Don't tell me you don't know?'

'I don't know.'

'Rhoda,' Mrs Benedict-Vincent spoke with her eyes lowered, 'the school is closing down.'

'Why?' Jasper asked.

'Oh hello, doctor.'

'You two know each other?'

'After what the doctor and I went through together at City Hall this morning, I feel like we're old friends.'

'Why is the school closing down?' Jasper persisted.

'Too much unfavorable publicity. First there was. . . .'

'Couldn't this wait until tomorrow?' Rhoda glared.

'You're right. I'm sorry.'

'Tonight's supposed to be a celebration.'

Mrs Benedict-Vincent tossed back her head. 'We'll fight it.'

'You do that.'

'How's Alex?' This time Mrs Benedict-Vincent caught Rhoda off balance. 'We go back a long way, Alex and me,' she was saying. 'Our brothers went through school together. Even back then we thought Alex would change the world.'

'Did Susan like the opera?' Jasper cut in. He lifted a hand to shield his eyes from the glare of the chandelier.

'She loved it. I was telling Rhoda – I've never seen Susan so enthralled in her whole life. I don't honestly think she breathed twice during the entire performance.'

'All right,' Rhoda said, letting her hand fall on Mrs Benedict-Vincent's arm, relenting, 'peace.'

'Any time you're ready,' Helen said to Jasper, yawning. She found him with Murray at one end of the long table covered with whips and dips and mounds of cold meats and salad.

'I haven't seen Carole yet,' Jasper stalled. His speech felt comfortably slurred. He made no effort to hide it. 'I want to tell her how much I enjoyed her playing.'

'Don't you worry, Carole's in good hands. Besides which you've told her several times already.' Helen looped her arm through Jasper's. 'Night-night' – she nodded at Murray.

'We just got here.' Jasper wriggled his arm free. He didn't want to leave Rhoda. He was happy watching her receive so much admiring attention. 'Can't go yet anyhow. Have to wait for Daniel. Has anyone seen Daniel?'

'There he is – your son,' Murray said, pointing with a half-gnawed stalk of celery.

Jasper turned. When he saw Daniel, he started to wave and smile but he knew instantly that something was very wrong. Nothing had ever been so wrong in his life. Daniel's expression was guarded. He conveyed no panic in the way he moved through the crowd. He even smiled and nodded a few times when people greeted him. Jasper also understood tomorrow wasn't an unknown, not any more. Daniel's eyes found his father's and clung. What an impossible combination, the boy's youth and strength and whatever it was he carried inside him now, some discovery which spread like a crippling disease through his body, but not slowly, no, rather instantly, like light through water. Jasper's mind went blank, a smooth surface, one he could not climb. He locked eyes with Daniel to keep them both from falling.

'No, we will *not* incorporate the backwards jacket into the performance.' Matasapi was holding forth to loud laughter. 'Gino is lucky I have a forgiving nature.'

Daniel simply grabbed Jasper's arm and pulled him out into the lobby. It was like being an icicle torn free from the eaves, the boy's hand was that cold. Jasper spilled his punch trying to put his glass down. He saw Helen begin to move through the crowd after them, too – and it was a comfort to know she had read the same message on Daniel's face. The roomful of people was like a colored wind blowing against them, the chandeliers like bursting stars. Unable to speak, Daniel buried his face against Jasper's chest and began to cry without holding back.

Luigi came from nowhere, his whiteness impersonal now and blinding. Lambie stood at a respectful distance. 'Take him up to my room. What is it?'

'Daniel?' Helen asked, and like a trapeze artist leaving one bar in mid-air for another, Daniel released his hold on Jasper and flung himself around his mother's neck.

'Here.' Luigi pressed his keys on Jasper and saw the family into the elevator. 'I'll try to get away and come up soon.'

In the elevator, in a few seconds, Daniel said it all. Alex was dead. He never came to after the operation. Every effort to revive him had failed. Heart failure. As soon as the opera had ended, Daniel tore off to find out how Alex was. Alex had told him not to. There were two women in Alex's room, watching the body.

'What operation?' Helen asked.

'Later,' Jasper said. When the elevator reached the top floor, they stood there talking. Jasper held the doors open with one hand and one foot. 'Give him something, Helen, and stay with him. Try to. . . .'

'But all those people downstairs. . . .'

'You're right. Dan? Dan, listen to me. Can you come with me? I'm going to the hospital. If you can face it, I'd like you to come, too. Your mother's got to go back to the party, at least for a little while, otherwise people will start looking for us and want to know what's wrong.'

'He's dead,' Dan said quietly, 'that's what's wrong.'

18

Jasper and Daniel left the Ritz Carlton by the revolving door. The outside world rose up like a cold slap in the face. Finding a cab took longer than the ride to the hospital.

'I wanted to say goodbye,' Dan told his father in the taxi. 'I wanted to tell him if he needed me, for any reason, he could count on my help. He was going to be more lonely than ever, I saw that. I wanted to wish him luck.

'The door was locked. I didn't knock but went back down the hall a little way near the ice-maker. And I waited. Someone came out, a man. I didn't get a look at his face but he limped. Two women in white uniforms walked along with him, all the way to the elevators. When they came out they didn't close the door, so I took my chance and slipped in.' Here Dan fell silent.

'And?' Jasper asked.

'Didn't you bandage his face?'

'Of course.'

'I thought so. They must have taken the bandages off. It was all. . . .'

'Yes, I know what it would look like.' Jasper hugged Daniel. As the taxi sped through the nearly empty streets, shop windows, electric signs, street lamps blurred. 'Go on.'

'I came in talking, telling him about the opera, what a hit it was. I was afraid Alex might be angry about my coming to see him, but I was hoping he'd be pleased, also. I'd expected a face full of bandages, just little holes for the eyes and nostrils and mouth. I was going to slip in and slip out – just so he would know he could count on me. But when he didn't answer, when he just lay there – I thought something was funny. I didn't go closer, no. I couldn't. I just stood where I was, a little ways from the bed, and went on talking. If I stopped, that would be admitting he was dead, but if I kept on – I know it sounds crazy – maybe if I said the right things I could bring him back. Like all of a sudden he'd hear me and wake up.

'Then they walked in, the two in white. As it was I guess their day hadn't been anything to write home about. I must've made it perfect. One recognized me. At least she knew my name. When I asked what had happened, first they looked at each other, then one shrugged and the other one said, "Heart failure. Never came to." Then I said I'd better be going. What I should have said was that you were waiting for me downstairs or at the desk in the hall, but I didn't. I have an idea that they weren't all that sure they should just let me go.'

The taxi pulled up in front of Mass Gen, all was ghostly still. 'I – I said I wouldn't say anything to anybody. As far as I was concerned, I'd never been there. The smaller one said something to the other about orders. Orders being orders. They weren't from the hospital, Fa – at least I'd never seen them before, either of them. To get out I had to walk between them, but they didn't try to stop me.'

Jasper and Daniel rode the service elevator to the floor above Alex's room and then doubled back down the emergency stairs, the echo of their footsteps like thunder. The door was closed, but not locked. They went in. Jasper fancied he smelled death in the air. All his nerves had turned to fists. No one was there. Dan threw open the closet. It was full of clothes. There was also a fruit basket on the nightstand beside the bed, a new one.

'That wasn't there before.' Daniel pointed to the core of a pear nibbled wastefully and discarded in a hospital ashtray on the dresser.

'The patient in Room 811-E?' Jasper asked at the duty desk.

It wasn't a proper hour for nonchalance, nor was he dressed for it, but he gave it a try.

'Much better, doctor.'

'He's not there.'

'No? Then my guess is he's gone to obstetrics again, to look at the babies.'

Jasper went back to the room. What was Christianson going to make of this visit in the early morning hours? It would, no doubt, be reported. Daniel sat curled up in the armchair, head between his knees. Jasper moved to comfort him when a voice behind his back made both of them turn.

'Hello, Dr Whiting.'

In walked the missing patient.

'My, rather formal, aren't we?' The man looked, if you didn't press the point, something like Alex Thane. The same height and build roughly, the same facial coloring. This was a younger man, though, his fine features weaker than Alex's, his manner more extravagantly friendly.

'Should be asleep, I know,' – he was wearing the same peppermint pajamas and wool robe that Alex wore in hospital – 'but they're sending me home tomorrow.'

'Fa,' – Daniel sprang forward and seized a patchwork quilt that had fallen between the foot end of the mattress and the metal bedframe. He tugged it loose and shook it out. Jasper stepped back as the bright colors flashed.

'Nice, isn't it.' The patient smiled. 'A friend of mine made it. I expect it took him years.'

Back at Spy Pond Lane Jasper gave Helen an explanation. The words started like stones in his stomach. It took intense effort to make them rise and spit them out. She was sympathetic and strong. He did not elaborate about Alex's operation. It was to alter Alex's appearance. He left it at that.

'Has anybody seen them take him out?' she asked.

'We couldn't go around asking, could we?' Daniel snapped. 'For all we know, the body's still there, Fa, isn't it? It could have been under the damn bed.'

'Why don't you take something, honey?' Helen suggested.

'He couldn't have died of heart failure. The tests were positive.'

'It *can* happen.'

'The chances are *so* small.'

'But it can happen?'

'It was murder.'

'Jasper.' Helen shook her head. Her earrings danced and caught the light. 'You're overreacting.'

What Jasper had begun to think was that if there was a God, He would never have breathed life back into Alex Thane with the face Jasper had given him. The operation had been unnatural. This then was the result. His single hope was that someone had planned for this to happen, that there was a killer to blame.

'You actually saw him?' Helen asked Dan.

'I saw something,' he answered, 'someone. It could have been anyone, I guess. The whole face was bruised and covered with blood.'

'Always,' Jasper said defensively.

'And he was dead, you're sure?' Helen was relentless.

'Yes,' Dan answered, not shrinking, 'yes, yes, yes, yes.'

'And I'm in for it.' Jasper rubbed his eyes. 'Maybe that was their idea right from the beginning?'

'You could have told me,' Helen complained.

'Right,' Jasper said, 'next time I will.'

'Where are you going?' she called. Jasper was moving rapidly out the door.

'Rhoda will know what's going on. She'd better.'

'I'll come with you.'

'No,' Jasper said and was out of the house, running.

'Take me with you,' Helen shouted at his back. 'TAKE ME WITH YOU!'

19

Jasper tried the Ritz Carlton first. The party had reached its terminal phase: bumbling seductions, swerving dancers, ice melting in the punch bowl, conversations too serious by half. Luigi, Carole and Matasapi were singing around an upright piano, Madge at the keyboard in stocking feet. Murray was feeding Susan, and Susan was feeding Murray. Luigi waved Jasper over to join them.

'Hey, Jasper, you should hear the voice this girl has got.'

Madge blushed.

'Where's Rhoda?'

'Ah, the heart,' was Matasapi's comment.

'Home, I guess.'

'When did she leave?'

'What is it?'

'Answer my question.'

'She left right after you did.'

'Alone?'

'There were a lot of people, Jasper, I don't know.'

'If you're hiding any. . . .'

'Some woman came for her,' Lambie stepped forward and said. 'Didn't stay for a drink. Didn't even take her coat off.'

'Fa,' Carole said, drunk and happy, 'you'll never guess who laughed during the opera. Nurse Morrison. And you know when? When the soldiers came out from behind the trees!'

'How's Dan?' Luigi had sobered. He'd pulled on Rhoda's reindeer sweater over the glitter of the prince's outfit. A section of artificial leg lay on top of the piano with a white boot. 'When she came down, Helen didn't say much.' Luigi's eyes narrowed. 'Just that Dan was overtired and you were driving him home.'

'Fa, listen to this.' Carole tugged at Jasper's sleeve. She had taken off her shoes and looped the straps through her belt. 'It's from the *Monitor*.' She held the paper open to the review page. ' "*Love Comes to Its Senses* is a delicious and healthy bit of nonsense at a time when a great deal of sickness masquerades as serious thought or Art. The opera – performed for the first time tonight in over two hundred years by an engaging cast under difficult conditions – is a highly delightful entertainment. A great deal of ingenuity and devotion have gone into the production with laudable results. Worth a see at a time when the world can't put too high a price on humor and decency." '

Jasper left the Mazda near a hydrant across from the Old North Church. Everything on Charter Street looked different tonight, as if he'd never set foot here before. Under a faint, anemic cusp of a moon, the side-wall mural was a bleeding confusion of purples and dark murky blue, lines and forms writhing and aggressive, something between a bruise and a tattoo. No, Jasper blinked: it was Alex, his face.

There was a man slouched against the front door-post draining a pint of something with a long, noisy pull. As Jasper hurried past, the man lobbed the bottle upwards and backwards. As he wiped foam from his lips with a torn sleeve, the drunk stumbled forward as if to embrace Jasper, but Jasper was already inside. He never did get to hear the bottle crash. Neat rows of new metal mailboxes gleamed in the narrow foyer reminding Jasper of Carole with her braces asleep as a child. He hit out at them with a fist in passing.

The hallway, the staircase, each landing on the way up – Jasper found it all alien. Bulbs in hallway fixtures burned with an erratic display of extra brilliance, pulsing as if they would soon sizzle out. He heard echoes of bitter quarrels, throats raw with insult. A rat scampered down the banister, or was it the oblique shadow of a person climbing somewhere higher up? Tonight the mad slasher's sofa was back at the head of the stairs with its chorus of open mouths, its intricate arteries of tape. Jasper's footsteps seemed to precede him down the corridor. His breath lagged so far behind it would never catch up.

At Rhoda's door, pressing brass key to brass lock, bending close with his eyes, Jasper fumbled like a beginner at sex. It took forever to guide the point of his key in with his surgically gifted fingers. Dimly, before the door swung open, he suspected the chaos he would find. Plants thrown down, torn, uprooted, broken glass and porcelain, mattress half on the floor, sheets tangled. Water was flooding over the side of the tub, out across the bathroom tiles, seeping into the sitting room carpet. There was a mixed smell of rotting food, cigarette smoke, vinegary wine.

'Rhoda?' Jasper sloshed over to the tub. It was impossible not to step on leaves, crushing them, kicking clumps of earth that exploded against the wall. He plunged his right arm into the tub to unclog the drain, drenching his sleeve up to the shoulder. It took all his strength to turn off the water. The tap was freezing cold. 'Rhoda?'

Jasper began talking to himself out loud, asking God what he should do next. Where to go, who to call, where to look? Scattered all over the room were loose sheets from the opera score elaborately marked and coded in colored pen. The glass in one front window was shattered in the form of a spider's web.

'Rhoda?'

From the bathtub where the water now drained, swirling down the pipes, a fearful gurgling sounded through the drawn plug, an inhuman belch.

'Christ!'

'Rhoda?' Jasper whirled, arms extended for an embrace, one arm dripping, the other dry.

'It's you.'

Gayle Glintz stood leaning in the doorway, legs crossed. She looked like some twisted piece of wire, hair snaky and wild. Jasper had not seen her since Sloan's funeral.

'Where is she?' Gayle Glintz asked. She fixed him with her eyes. 'It's past time.'

'Time?'

'For the first shift. She knows that. Where is she?'

Jasper went to hoist the mattress back onto the bed. Night was ebbing and the sky was a toneless, lifeless gray.

'Leave that now. Murray and Madge are upstairs, waiting.'

Rapid footsteps raced down the hallway. Jasper saw a winged blur, shadow and self merging as Rhoda appeared. She wore a long white coat over her slacks.

'Sorry,' Rhoda said to Gayle. Then the two women were gone. As soon as Jasper could wrench himself from the spot, he followed, hurting inside like the victim of a beating performed expertly to leave no mark. Upstairs, guided by sounds to an apartment more to the harbor-side of the building than where Gayle had lived with Sloan, he found a team huddled around a ping-pong table in the entrance hallway, patterning a child with determination and strain. It was Susan, a steady trickle of sound humming away inside her sealed lips, eyelids fluttering while back and forth, up and down, her slack arms and legs were forced through the motions of running.

Jasper pushed forward. 'Let me help, I'm a doctor.' He tried to grasp Susan's head between his hands, but it was too slippery to hold. People were shouting at him, pushing him. He tried to beat them off with one arm, the heavy wet one, speaking reassuringly to Susan the whole time. He was a doctor and knew what was best for her. As a doctor your life didn't belong to you any more, not really. Duty, not freedom. (The metronome was conducting!) And he told Susan how much he enjoyed her singing in the opera. Under his fingers he felt her features turning, twisting.

Then Rhoda was hugging him from behind, her tongue in his neck, her teeth, pulling him backwards, the sweetness of her scent explosive as he sank heavily, smiling, to the floor.

20

Jasper revived in Rhoda's apartment, on the bed. She was tidying.

'Rhoda.'

She snapped up the shades. Jasper put one hand up to shield his eyes.

'What happened to the plants?' he asked. His throat was dry.

'We had an argument. I won.'

'Rhoda. . . .'

She wouldn't let him talk until he'd had some strong coffee.

'Well, they've decided that for some children it may be helpful. Susan's mother asked Gayle to keep Susan. . . .'

'Rhoda, for God's sake.'

But she wanted to finish what was on her mind.

'You don't look cute any more.' Rhoda smiled. Jasper still wore his tuxedo, but Rhoda had released the cumberbund, and opened his collar and tie. 'Don't worry, Alex won't be found in the hospital. Not in Boston, either. In a car, one that explodes.' Rhoda gave a bitter little laugh. 'Outside the Lincoln Memorial. They will identify him by his teeth. Tomorrow, I think. Or the day after. It depends on a certain flight connection. Don't worry.'

'Where's the body?'

'You went through it all for nothing, is that what's bothering you?' Rhoda's voice was kind, but strangely without affect.

'Someone tampered with the anesthesia.'

'No.'

'Yes, damn it!'

Rhoda stood between Jasper and the windows. She was dark and monumental. He had to move his head from side to side to make sense of her face.

'You checked it all yourself, didn't you?'

'Yes.'

'How could anyone have tampered?'

'They couldn't have – but there's no other explanation.'

'Accident.'

'No.'

'What's wrong – accidents happen.'

'Alex Thane was murdered.'

'Why?'

'Why? War. He was a great man.'

'Alex? It doesn't fit – especially not now.'

'He's irreplaceable.'

'That's true – to me. But only as Alex, the person.'

'Rhoda, what's come over you? What's wrong? What's going on?'

'I'm tired, Jasper, that's all. And it's over. I was wrong. We were.' Rhoda closed her eyes and rubbed them. 'Accidents happen. He was a good man, Alex, but good men also make mistakes. You convinced me, Jasper. Hate breeds hate. This war. It's a fantasy, really, wild, irresponsible, destructive. Childish. Wait, let me finish. They're your words, Jasper, all your very own. You were right, I'm telling you, everything you ever said. Doesn't it make you feel good, to be so right? Alex, God love him, he was busy with a pet obsession.'

'No. Oh no.'

'I'm tired, it's been going on too long.'

'We're just getting started, you know that. Just. . . .'

'Without me, then, okay? Count Rhoda out. Funny, causes are really so expendable. It's only people who aren't.'

'Rhoda. . . .'

'Maybe it would be better all the way around if you got out of here.'

'You're *afraid*, is that it?'

'Me, afraid? Of what?'

'Threats.'

'Who's going to bother with me? What on earth for?' Rhoda shook her head, shrugged her shoulders. 'You know what I think, Jasper? Want to know? I think the truth is maybe Alex killed himself.'

'What? Why?'

'Various reasons, not the least of which was that he was jealous of you.'

'Jealous of me?'

'Plus he might have thought he would be more useful to the movement dead, more valuable.'

'He didn't kill himself.' But Jasper wasn't sure.

'He had us fooled, Alex, didn't he? He was a wonder. Believe hard enough in something and it comes true. Even hate. What's the matter, Jasper? Chin up. Come on, doctor, I'm only giving you a taste of your own medicine. It just took this – his death – to show me.'

'Fa. . . .' Daniel and Luigi broke in. It looked like Daniel was half-carrying Luigi. Luigi had shed his white plumage. There wasn't a trace of costume to what he was wearing. Pain enlarged his eyes.

'Say, Jasper, how'd you like the ending?' Rhoda leaned against Luigi who smoothed the hair back from her eyes, kissed her forehead.

'Fa, this morning, real early, they arrested a group of cripples outside police kennels. They were carrying milk bottles full of gas.' It was clear Daniel had more to say.

'And?'

'The police are looking for Alex.'

'He left a letter,' Rhoda said quietly, 'in the event anything should happen to him.' She pulled an envelope out from under the base of the lamp on the night table next to the bed. Luigi took the razor out of the pouch around his neck and handed it to Rhoda. She slit the envelope open and let the razor clatter to the floor. She removed a sheet of pink paper and unfolded it. For Jasper the jagged ups and downs of the thin script were familiar.

'Look when it's dated,' Daniel called out, pointing to the upper righthand corner. 'Years ago.' Daniel's face reminded Jasper so much of his own at that age that he gasped as the boy snuggled close to him. Daniel's hair stood out from his scalp, unmanageable.

'You read it.' Rhoda handed the letter to Luigi. 'I don't have my glasses' – she smiled.

Luigi turned on the lamp, ducked his head close to the circle of light that fell on the page. He began, ' "People think worse of themselves than we imagine." '

'Again, please,' Jasper said. 'I – I wasn't listening.' Rhoda's eyes were red with tears. She sat with one hand on Daniel's ankle, head bowed.

' "People think worse of themselves than we imagine. Therein lies our hope. People are afraid they will be discovered. We will succeed if we can turn that fear to positive ends. Ask less of a man. . . ." '

Rhoda's voice rose under Luigi's. He grew silent and allowed her to continue. She was reciting from memory: ' ". . . than he asks of himself, he will despise you. Ask more – he will be your enemy. Ask as much as a man can give? The result will be mutual embarrassment at such unquestionable proof of love." ' Rhoda stopped.

'Go on,' Luigi urged. Rhoda shook her head.

'Ask nothing?' Luigi whispered.

When Rhoda spoke Jasper could not tell whether she was still following Alex's text. 'Even the thought of asking nothing is impossible.' Rhoda turned to look at Jasper, a mixture of forgiveness and longing in her eyes. 'Begging is as natural to us as breathing.'

Manado 1981 – Amsterdam 1986